FRIENDS AND LOVERS

"Do you ever wish we could go back?" Ryan asked.

Chelsea found herself nodding. "There's so much I would do differently."

"Me, too." Ryan's voice was husky, and his eyes were darkening with unexpressed emotion. "So very much."

Chelsea was afraid to ask him to explain. "I should go."

"Don't. Not yet."

A pulse raced to life inside her. Did he mean his words to sound so caressing?

Slowly Ryan lifted his hand and put it on her neck so that his thumb stroked the line of her chin and his fingers were hidden in her hair. Chelsea couldn't have moved if she had wanted to. And she didn't want to at all.

He leaned toward her, and she met him halfway. At first his lips were gentle on hers, as sweet as a memory. Then the kiss deepened into something that held more than mere passion . . .

* * *

BEST FRIENDS

LYNDA TRENT

ZEBRA BOOKS
KENSINGTON PUBLISHING CORP.

ZEBRA BOOKS are published by

Kensington Publishing Corp.
850 Third Avenue
New York, NY 10022

First Printing: January, 1995

Printed in the United States of America

To Krista Renee Trent, the second half of our delightful duo and a princess in her own right

Prologue

Chelsea shut the door behind her and slumped against it, her eyes closed. She was shivering from more than the cold.

A single tear formed, stinging her eye before making a pathway down her cheek. She brushed at it in frustration that bordered on anger. She hated to cry. Particularly when she was alone.

Her apartment, usually her refuge, a place of complete safety, now was only a cavernous, empty room, an undivided space over a mechanic's garage. With Ryan gone it was no longer a sanctuary. The TV was still on. She turned it off.

With leaden feet, she made her way to the other end of the room that served as her bedroom. As she undressed she stared at the bed. Ryan had slept there only the night before. They had made love for hours in the velvety darkness, and she had believed herself completely safe from heartache. Now he was gone, and she had no idea if he would ever return.

Chelsea tossed her clothes into the laundry hamper and enfolded herself in Ryan's robe. At once scents that were uniquely his filled her nostrils, the soap he bathed with, a hint of his musky aftershave, and the heady, masculine aroma she always associated with him during their passionate lovemaking. The reminders tortured her, but she couldn't bear to let them go for they were all that remained of him. She wrapped her arms around herself to ward off the chill permeating her body and moved closer to the glowing embers in the fireplace.

It had been risky leaving the fire burning, but there had been no time to extinguish it. She added a log to the fire, then knelt and jabbed at the banked coals with a poker until flames erupted once more and the radiating heat began chasing the chill from her. Staring into the flames, she noticed a dampness on her cheeks and realized she was still crying. This time she made no attempt to check the flow of tears. The anger was gone.

A numbness pervaded her, protecting her from the pain she knew she would feel later. He wouldn't be coming back to her, and if he did, she would have to send him away. Chelsea wondered if she would ever be strong enough to do that. She had loved Ryan for so many years.

She tried to tell herself it was enough that they had had the last few weeks of happiness; it was more than she had expected they would ever have. She should have known nothing so wonderful could last. She had reason to know that better than anyone. But for the past few weeks she had let herself hope, and finally had come to believe, they would be together always. Now it was over. Not because either of them wanted it that way, but because this was the way it had to be.

As the flames danced and crackled in the fireplace Chelsea thought back to the beginning of their relationship. Falling in love with Ryan had been so easy. It happened the first time she saw him and quickly grew in intensity. Her best friend Karen had never believed in love at first sight and was so headstrong that Chelsea hadn't tried to convince her it existed. At that time they had all been so young, so confident that their lives would go on forever and that they would have complete control over all of life's circumstances.

Chelsea almost smiled. Had she ever really been that naive? It seemed impossible. Happiness wasn't something that dropped into your lap and stayed forever. There was no such thing as "happily ever after."

Looking back she could see so many times when she had made wrong decisions, as if she had been her own worst enemy. In retrospect it was evident that in respect to men, her judgment was flawed.

Except for Ryan.

Her love for him had been the only thing in her life that was pure and untarnished and perfect. And he had loved her in return. But life wasn't that simple.

Chelsea's mind drifted back to the day that had changed her life forever, a day that had begun like any other.

Chapter One

Early Spring, 1977
Southern Methodist University, Dallas, Texas

"I wish you'd change your mind and come with us," Chelsea pleaded as she stopped brushing her long auburn hair and looked back at her roommate.

"I have to study for that English test. You know what my grades are like in that class." Karen stared dismally at the open book before her. "I hate literature!"

"So what if you make a *B* instead of an *A?* It's no big deal. It's not as if this is a final exam. The semester has barely started."

"That's easy for you to say, but it upsets my mother if my grades drop. She's still against me living in the dorm."

Chelsea laughed as she turned back to the mirror. "Karen, that's silly. We're seniors. You've lived in the dorm for almost four years."

"I know, but Mother still doesn't like it. If Daddy hadn't stepped in, I'd be commuting. She says it's silly for me to live on campus when they're only a few miles away. Daddy says everyone in his family has gone to SMU and has lived on campus—and it's good for me. If my grades drop, though, I'll never hear the end of it!"

"Okay. Stay here and study. But you'll wish you'd gone. We're driving out to the lake. We may not have such mild

weather over the next six weeks, and it's a shame to waste
it."

"Who else is going?" Karen sounded wistful.

"Just Ryan. It's not a party or anything."

Karen shook her head. "I can't. I must be crazy for even
considering it."

Chelsea glanced at the clock. "I have to run. I told him
I'd meet him out front. You're sure I can't change your
mind?"

"Have fun. And feel guilty that I'm stuck here with
English Lit. while you're out having fun."

"I promise to have a miserable time, just for you."

Karen finally smiled. "No, I'd rather you have fun. Hug
Ryan for me."

"I'll do it." Chelsea grabbed a paisley shawl as she
headed out the door. She jogged down the hall and stairs.
Although she saw Ryan every day, she was always eager to
be with him.

She and Karen had met Ryan Morgan at a college dance
in their sophomore year. Since that time, they had become
a threesome. Each loved him in her own way, and he
seemed to love them both equally. Chelsea had often
teased him about wanting to marry them both. He had
agreed that it was true.

Ryan was already downstairs, waiting, and soon they
were in his car and heading toward the lake.

"Karen studies too much," he said. "You just watch
and see. She'll be the successful one, and we'll end up living
off her fortune in our old age."

"A trio to the end." Chelsea smiled at him. She was
seldom alone with Ryan and was secretly glad that Karen
had declined the invitation to come.

"We only have a few months of school left, and then
we'll be on our own. Do you ever think about that?" Ryan
reached out and took Chelsea's hand.

She studied his profile. He was handsome, tall, and, best
of all, intelligent. In Chelsea's opinion, intelligence was

sexy. She could never fall in love with a man who didn't possess it. That Ryan had chestnut brown hair and hazel eyes the color of pine trees was an added bonus. He was well built, muscular without being beefy, and he made Chelsea feel protected. "I think about graduation a lot. It's a little scary, isn't it? The prospect of being on our own?"

"A little. I've been typing résumés to send out to companies that might be hiring computer programmers. I want to stay in Dallas if it's possible."

Chelsea sobered. "I hadn't considered that you might move away—I'm so used to seeing you. You and Karen are my best friends."

He squeezed her hand reassuringly. "I'm sure there must be someone in all of Dallas who'll hire me. I don't want to be away from the two of you, either."

Chelsea watched the Dallas skyline as they pulled onto the Stemmons Freeway. "It's funny, isn't it? I've wanted to be able to work full-time as an artist for so many years, and now that it's nearly upon me, I'm getting cold feet."

"You didn't pick the easiest of careers to break into. Artists are known for starving in garrets while waiting for that big break. You should have taken some classes in commercial art."

"That didn't interest me. I love to paint. I may have to watch my money carefully, but I can do that." She laughed. "It's not as if I grew up with Karen's bankbook."

"It's a good thing she has money. What can she do with a music degree? She's not getting a teaching certificate."

"I know. You know how Karen is, though. She floats through life and somehow always ends up on top. She'll probably be offered a job playing the piano in some elegant setting where she gets paid a fortune and can set her own hours."

"Can't you see her family if she takes any job at all?" Ryan grinned. "They don't have that in mind for her."

Chelsea glanced at him. Karen's parents had sent their daughter to college with the intention of her finding a good husband. A degree was of secondary importance. Until now Chelsea hadn't realized Ryan knew that. "She can be stubborn when she sets her mind to it."

"As stubborn as you?" He winked at her.

Chelsea grinned. "Not quite."

Half an hour later they arrived at Grapevine Lake and parked in a favorite spot. Ryan took an ice chest out of the trunk while Chelsea spread a quilt on the ground. "I hope you're hungry for bologna sandwiches."

"You cooked?" she teased. "Is it an old family recipe?"

"Go ahead and laugh. My sandwiches may not be inventive, but they're filling."

They sat cross-legged on the quilt, and Ryan handed Chelsea a sandwich and a beer. "I made enough to feed three. I thought Karen would be coming, too."

"I'll take one back to her. I'll bet I can even sneak in a beer as well. If someone catches me, I'll say I'm going to wash my hair in it."

"Do you suppose anyone ever believes that?"

"Probably not." She bit into her sandwich. "This really is good."

He tore open a bag of chips and put it between them. "Are you staying in Dallas for certain?"

She nodded. "I love it here. It's the closest thing I have to roots. Most Army brats love to move from place to place but not me."

"My parents expected me to come back to Colorado, but Dallas is my home now. My brother will probably settle down in Boulder once he's out of school. Assuming he ever graduates." Ryan grinned to show he was joking. His brother enjoyed learning so much that Ryan had said he would stay in school forever if given a choice in the matter.

"I know the sort of place I want to have eventually. A warehouse. You know, like you see in movies of New York. I could paint at one end and live at the other and never have to drive back and forth to my studio." She took a potato chip.

"It sounds perfect for you. But where are you going to

find a warehouse in Dallas that's in an area safe enough for me to let you live there?"

Chelsea smiled at him. "Maybe we could all live there and guard each other."

His eyes met hers. "I'm not so sure that would work out in the long run. Three would soon turn into a crowd."

She sipped the cold beer before asking, "Which two, then?"

"You and I could live together peacefully."

She slowly lowered the beer. "Yes. We could." Her heart started racing, and she looked away so he couldn't see what his suggestion was doing to her.

"Sometimes it's a relief for there to be only the two of us."

"You know you love being with Karen."

"Yes, but I love you, too."

Chelsea turned back to him. He had frequently said he loved them both, but never in that tone of voice. He was watching her closely, and his expression was one of love.

"You're so beautiful," he said softly as he reached out and touched her hair and let it trail like silk through his fingers.

"I think we'd better walk by the lake." Chelsea got to her feet. Karen also loved him. She couldn't let herself forget that.

After putting away the remnants of their picnic, they strolled by the water's edge. The sun was dipping low, gilding the high, thin clouds set against the pastel pink of the western sky. The gentle breeze had ebbed, and the glassy surface of the lake reflected the ever-changing palette of a picture-perfect sunset. "It's so beautiful here," she said with a content sigh.

"Why did you want to walk? The truth now."

She was aware of the warmth of his hand enclosing hers, and her fingers laced with his. "I'm Karen's best friend. What I was feeling wasn't in her interest."

"You and I are also best friends. Do you feel the same toward me as you do toward Karen?"

"Of course not." She laughed softly at the idea. "No, I feel entirely different about you."

He put his arm around her waist and slowed their steps. "Lately I find myself wanting to be alone with you, watching you when you laugh and playing back that picture in my mind instead of sleeping."

Chelsea wasn't sure how to respond. A part of her wanted to hold him in her arms and never leave him. Another part warned that Karen would be heartbroken if they began to love each other more than her. She looped an arm about him. She loved to touch him. His body was so lean and exciting. "I find myself thinking about you constantly, too."

They veered as they reached a marshy area and started back toward the car. The sun had slipped below the horizon now, and the sky and lake had taken on shades of deep purple and rose. Far away Chelsea heard a night bird calling in the trees.

They didn't speak until they were within sight of the quilt they had left spread on the ground. "I guess we ought to head back," Ryan said reluctantly. "It's almost dark."

"I suppose we should." She didn't want to leave either.

"Maybe another beer first. Talk."

"All right."

They sat on the quilt and gazed out at the water. The beer was cold in her mouth, but soon a comforting warmth was spreading from her stomach. "What if you can't find a job in Dallas?" she asked. "I'd hate for you to move away."

"You could move with me."

"I can see Karen's mother agreeing to that!"

"I didn't mean to include Karen."

Chelsea watched as he tossed their empty cans into the cooler and handed her another one. Almost inaudibly she said, "Karen loves you, too. Just as I do."

"I know. And I love her. But as you've told me many times, I can't have both of you. I have to make a choice." His face was almost lost in the encroaching darkness.

"Is that what you're doing? Making a choice?"

"Yes. I'm making a choice."

Chelsea drank the beer more quickly than she should. She had to think.

"Are you telling me I've picked the wrong one?" Ryan whispered.

"No," she answered without hesitation as she tried to read the expression in his eyes. "No. I'm wondering what I can say to Karen."

He smiled wryly. "Even when she's not here, she's still between us."

Chelsea tossed the empty can into the cooler. Ryan caught her arm and drew her closer. "I want to be with just you. At least for tonight."

Her heart was skipping in her throat, and he was so near she could scarcely think. What she felt for Ryan was stronger than her friendship for Karen. With a sigh, she went into his waiting arms.

He kissed her gently at first, then with increasing passion. Chelsea matched his ardor with her own. When he lay her back on the quilt and stretched out beside her, she pressed her body against his and entwined their legs to bring him closer still.

He left a trail of kisses from the warm hollow beneath her ear down the curve of her throat. Chelsea was sure he could feel the pounding of her pulse, an undeniable measure of the excitement she was feeling. She closed her eyes as his lips moved lower and lingered on the sensitive curve where her neck and shoulder met. As his fingers found the buttons of her blouse, a fleeting thought of Karen passed through her mind reminding her that she shouldn't let him do this; then it was gone. She loved Ryan, and she wanted nothing more than to give herself to him.

His lips followed his fingers as he exposed each inch of her skin. Chelsea trembled in her need for him, and was sure Ryan understood. He lifted his head and gazed into her eyes as his fingers found her breasts, bare now.

"If you want me to, I'll stop," he whispered.

Slowly she shook her head. "No, don't." She lifted her head to meet his lips, to taste his mouth.

She slid her hands beneath his pullover sweater and ran her palms over his taut skin. "You feel so good," she murmured between kisses. "I've wanted to do this with you for so long."

"I've wanted you, too. God, how I've wanted you!" The tremor in his voice revealed suppressed emotion. She knew he was struggling to hold back, to make their loving last. "Chelsea," he murmured, saying her name as if it were an endearment.

He brushed her blouse aside, and Chelsea caught her breath as his nubby sweater brushed against her nipples. Ryan held her close, burying his face in her hair. As his hands memorized her breasts, he said, "You're so beautiful."

"It's too dark to see," she teased as she kissed his ear.

"I don't need light to know your beauty." His fingers trailed down her stomach to the button on her jeans.

Chelsea started to help him, but he moved her hands away. "Let me," he said. "I've fantasized about this, and I want to do it myself."

After the button, he carefully unzipped her jeans and Chelsea lifted her hips so he could slide the pants off her legs. The night air was cold on her skin, but she didn't mind. She wanted to be aware of every possible sensation and to remember them all forever.

Ryan stroked her hips and down the curve of her thighs. His breath was ragged, indicating he was as excited as she was. Chelsea reached for the zipper on his jeans.

"Are you cold?" he asked as his hands moved over her.

"No," she whispered. "I don't think I'll ever be cold again." It was true. The touch of his hands and the sound of his voice were driving her to distraction. Then he lowered his mouth to her breast, and she realized she had only skimmed the surface of pleasure.

Ryan took her nipple in his mouth and suckled it gently, sending waves of desire thundering through her. He knew just how to touch and taste her to bring her to greater ecstasy. As she arched against him, offering him more of her body, his hand moved down her side and hips and found the warmth between her legs.

Chelsea had never made love before, but her body knew exactly what it wanted. She opened her legs to him, and her hand pushed his jeans down so she could touch the firm flesh of his buttocks.

Ryan shifted and kicked free of his jeans, then drew her panties away. When he lay back down and pressed against her, Chelsea drew in a sharp breath, surprised by the stimulating sensation of their bare flesh touching. She pulled his sweater over his head and tossed it onto the grass. Over his shoulder she saw a full moon free itself from a cloud bank. In the moonlight he was like a Greek god cast in silver. Almost in awe, she touched him, learning the planes and valleys of his muscles and sinews.

"You're beautiful," she whispered.

"So are you." He had lifted himself onto his elbow and was gazing at her as if he had never seen her before. "Chelsea, have I been blind all this time?"

She smiled broadly at him. She felt no embarrassment in his perusal of her body. She could tell he enjoyed seeing her and she was equally enthralled with him. Reaching out, she ran her fingers down his chest and over his flat stomach. "I always want to remember you like this."

"I don't intend to have you rely on memory. I want us to be together."

Chelsea put a fingertip against his lips. "No commitments, no ties. I want us to be as free as the wind, the moonbeams. That's the only way for it to work."

"I'll always remember you just as you are tonight, bathed in moonlight and looking at me with love in your eyes." Ryan stroked the hair back from her face. With one edge of the quilt in hand, he pulled it over them as he covered her body with his own. "I don't want you to be cold."

She ran her fingers through his dark hair. "There's no danger of that."

Again they kissed and Chelsea responded eagerly. As Ryan touched her intimately and knowingly, her desire spiraled upward and blossomed into ecstasy.

When he finally prepared to enter her, Chelsea was more than ready. Her breasts tingled from his touch, his kisses, and instinctively she knew he was about to fill a void she had never known existed. At first there was a flash of discomfort and she tensed. He stopped instantly and kissed her again. Chelsea soon forgot the discomfort and started moving with him, pulling him deeper and deeper into herself.

Ryan was in no hurry to finish, and each learned what pleased the other and what brought the other to the brink of satisfaction. When Chelsea thought she could stand the pleasure no longer, he quickened his movements and instantly her senses whirled upward and exploded. She cried out and held to him tightly. He pulled her ever closer, and with his one last thrust she knew he was experiencing the same release.

For a long time they lay in an embrace, neither wanting to move or speak. Chelsea had never felt more loved and protected and satisfied. It was as if a piece of her life had suddenly manifested itself and now encompassed him; a part of her would be absent if she wasn't with him.

He kissed her forehead and cuddled her head against his chest. As he stroked her hair, he said, "My fantasies didn't do it justice. I had no idea anything could be so wonderful."

She ran a hand over the now familiar territory of his chest and smiled contentedly. "Neither did I."

"You didn't tell me you had never made love before." His resonant voice was velvety in the darkness and seemed to caress her soul.

"It never entered the conversation." She lifted her head to smile at him. "I'm glad I waited for you."

"Chelsea, you're so precious to me. I never want to be

away from you. I want to take you home with me and make love to you for the rest of the night."

"Your roommate might object."

He sighed. "We could go to a motel."

"I have to go back to the dorm. Karen will be worried sick if I don't." Instantly she wished she hadn't given a thought to Karen.

"If I have to move away to find a job, will you come with me?"

"I'll always love you. That's what I enjoy about you, knowing that I'm free and you're free and that neither of us want to tie the other down."

"Does that mean you won't move with me if I have to go?"

"It means we can face that when it happens." She smiled at him, confident that she would follow him to the ends of the earth and positive he understood that. "We're like the passage in *The Prophet*. The winds blow between us, and we grow not in each other's shadow."

He was silent, and his eyes looked troubled.

"Is something wrong?" she asked.

"No. Nothing at all." He kissed her again and sat up.

She watched as he pulled his sweater on and reached for his undershorts and jeans. Something was bothering him, but she couldn't figure out what it was. Had he misunderstood what she meant by that? The passage she was referring to was about love and how to keep it free and alive. She realized she was growing cold, and pulled her blouse over her.

As she buttoned it he retrieved her panties and jeans, handed them to her. "I'll never have any regrets about tonight," he said as she took them.

"Neither will I. But, Ryan, I don't want Karen to know. Okay?"

"She has no reason to know." His face was enigmatic.

"Is there something I'm missing here?" she asked. "Tell me, what's wrong?"

"I asked you to live with me, and you said no. I didn't expect that."

"I can't live with you," Chelsea said reasonably. "I have to stay in the dorm, and so do you. We can't afford an apartment. Besides, neither of us wants to be tied down. You know that's true. Look how often we've said that. You still feel that way, don't you?"

"Sure." He looked away and finished dressing, then started folding the quilt.

"Ryan," she said, putting her hand on his arm to stop his movements. "Tonight was the most perfect of my life. I'll never forget it for as long as I live. You're wonderful, and I love you."

"I love you, too, Chelsea. I always will." Ryan looked as if he wanted to say more but didn't.

Chelsea took the quilt from him and finished folding it. She couldn't understand what was bothering him, so she decided she must be wrong about sensing it. After all, she knew Ryan as well as she knew herself. Their lovemaking had been a perfect and beautiful experience, one that she would dream about in nights to come. As he put the cooler back into the car, she smiled as her body remembered the ecstasy he had kindled in her.

Chapter Two

"Congratulations are in order, Mrs. Cavin." The doctor was grinning as he came back into the examining room and was peering down his nose through his half-lens bifocals at her chart. "You're pregnant."

Chelsea stared tight-lipped at him.

Still not making eye contact with her as he made additional notations on her chart, the doctor continued speaking. "I suspected that was what we'd find as soon as I heard your symptoms." He tilted his head back and leaned closer to the wall to consult a pharmaceutical calendar. "Hmmm. Let's see. Last period here. That'd make you due in about—"

"Are you positive?" Chelsea cut in. Even though she had expected him to confirm her worst fears, she found it difficult to believe.

"I haven't even given you a date yet. You see, I have to figure—"

"I didn't mean that, I mean are you positive that I'm . . . ?"

"Pregnant? Oh, why yes. Quite positive. This your first?"

She nodded, not trusting herself to speak further, and averted her eyes. A flood of conflicting emotions were tumbling about in her head, and a hard knot was forming like a lead weight in the pit of her stomach. She was pregnant!

"I'll want you on prenatal vitamins. You're a bit on the thin side. Don't gain too much, now. It's easier to keep it off than to take it off later." He chuckled and she glanced back to find him looking at her over the top rim of his glasses. "Now don't believe that old wives' tale about having to eat for two. Okay?"

"No." She stood and slung her purse strap over her shoulder. "No, I won't do that." Nausea was starting to rise, and this time it had nothing to do with her condition. As the doctor turned back to the calendar, she headed for the door, tossing him a goodbye over her shoulder.

He called after her that he hadn't given her a due date, but Chelsea didn't care; her world was crashing down on her, and she had to get away. The faster she walked, the more anxious she became, and by the time she reached the lobby she was running.

She burst outside and gulped in the cool spring air as her steps slowed to a fast walk. *Pregnant!*

Her mind rebelled. He had to be wrong! This wasn't happening to her!

Chelsea got into her battered old car and collapsed over the steering wheel. Hot tears stung her eyes, and a new rush of fear and anxiety threatened to close off her throat. She swallowed hard and closed her eyes even more tightly to staunch the pending flood. Pregnant!

She had to tell Karen. And Ryan. She dreaded telling both.

Ryan would marry her; she didn't doubt that. He was much too ethical and responsible a person to do otherwise. But she didn't want to be married. Not now. In two short months she would be graduating and starting a new life and her career. This was the time she had worked toward for so long! Just like every other young woman, she wanted marriage and babies—someday. But not now.

What would Ryan think?

And what would this do to Karen and to their friendship?

Chelsea and Karen had been best friends since first

grade at Buchanan Elementary. Karen had been so quiet and shy that she had needed Chelsea's more assertive companionship. Later, when they were old enough to date, Chelsea had found it much easier to talk to boys than Karen did, and more times than she could remember, she had stopped dating a boy for Karen's sake when she had learned that Karen had taken an interest in him. Ryan had been the exception.

At first it had been only friendship that drew the three together, but as time passed, both young women had fallen in love with him. Chelsea knew for a fact he was the only man Karen had ever loved, but this time she hadn't been able to step aside.

She was reasonably sure that Karen had never made love with Ryan—or with anyone for that matter—not with her shyness and her habit of confessing everything. Usually Chelsea had been equally open, often telling Karen much more than she wanted to hear, but Karen had no idea it had gone this far with Ryan. Chelsea had hoped Karen never would know.

Now that the doctor's words were sinking in, she felt curiously numb and decided this was what it felt like to be in shock. Dry-eyed, she pushed back from the steering wheel and brushed her long auburn hair away from her face. She should have used a phony name, she thought. Would the doctor try to contact her for a follow-up visit? She hoped not. She never wanted to see him again. At least he'd had the decency to call her "Mrs. Cavin," though she'd not included the title on the form she'd filled out before the examination and wasn't wearing a wedding ring.

Mentally she counted the weeks since that night under the stars. As the doctor had pointed out, she was thin and she wasn't tall, and that meant her pregnancy might be showing by the time she graduated. Her stomach roiled at the thought of what people would be whispering behind her back.

Telling Ryan about this was going to be one of the

hardest things she'd ever faced. Would he think she had done it to trap him? Nothing could be farther from the truth, but she knew some girls intentionally got pregnant.

With a groan Chelsea started her car and drove out onto Preston Road and into the Dallas traffic. First she had to tell Karen. This wasn't something she could handle alone. Together they would decide how to tell Ryan.

As she wound her way along the perpetually busy street, oblivious for the most part of the other cars, she let herself consider marriage with Ryan. He was an electrical engineering major and was determined to have a career in computer design. He had already sent out résumés, but so far hadn't received any responses. He wouldn't insist that she give up her art career for him and the baby, but Chelsea knew a baby would change everything. In time Ryan might come to resent them both.

And what about her own hopes and plans? Chelsea was an art major with an unusual talent, or so she'd been told by everyone who had seen her work. Even her professors had said she had the potential to go far. But creating required hours of uninterrupted work, sometimes far into the night. She couldn't maintain her concentration and tend to a baby at the same time.

When an alternate solution to this growing nightmare first came to her, Chelsea rejected it immediately. Even though she had always maintained a woman should have the right to choose whether to have an abortion or not, she had always said an abortion wouldn't be her choice. Nevertheless, the thought would not leave her. An abortion would solve everything.

By the time she reached the Southern Methodist University campus, she was growing used to the idea. It would be quick, from all she'd heard, and no one need know about it. A friend had had one a few months back; she would know who to contact.

Just when she thought the battle in her head was over, her conscience loudly argued that taking the easy way out was wrong, that getting an abortion was wrong—even if keeping the child meant the loss of her freedom. But freedom had always been very important to Chelsea.

Karen was in the dorm room they shared when Chelsea entered. Suddenly Chelsea didn't know where to begin.

"Hi. I've been wondering where you were." Karen held up a pair of designer jeans. "My mother sent these. Aren't they great? See? Rhinestones on the back pockets." Karen looked closer at Chelsea, and her smile faded. "What's the matter?"

Without a word, Chelsea sat down on her bed and motioned for Karen to sit opposite her. This was a part of the ritual they had established long ago when they were about to share confidences. If this weren't such a calamity, Chelsea could have smiled at remembering some of the private things they had shared over the years.

Karen sat down and stared at her. "You look awful. It's not something about graduation, is it? I told you to bring up your Qualitative Analysis grade!"

"This doesn't have anything to do with chemistry or graduation. At least not the way you mean."

"You're scaring me." Karen bunched the new jeans on her lap, and her gray eyes were large and worried.

"I went to the doctor."

Karen looked at her without a hint of comprehension. "You're not sick. Why would you go to a doctor?"

"If your classes didn't start practically at dawn, you'd have noticed I haven't been feeling well in the mornings." She couldn't meet Karen's eyes. "Every morning."

Karen laughed. "So what are you saying? You're pregnant?" The words flowed from Karen's mouth as carelessly as if such a thing were patently impossible.

Tears welled in Chelsea's eyes, but she fought them back.

Slowly Karen's smile faded. "You're not!" When Chelsea nodded, she said, "That's not possible! Tell me it's not!"

"Apparently it is."

For what seemed an interminable time Karen sat in

stunned silence. Finally, in a voice barely above a whisper, she asked, "Whose baby is it?"

Chelsea turned away and swallowed hard. "Ryan's."

The silence grew stony. At last Karen said in a stiff voice, "I didn't know you two were . . . you know."

"We weren't!" Chelsea reached out to cover Karen's hand. "We really weren't. Only once. That's all! I swear!"

Karen's gray eyes were fixed and unblinking as she stared at Chelsea as if she were a stranger and moved not a muscle to respond to her touch.

Chelsea pulled back her hand and looked away from her friend's penetrating gaze. "It was the night we went up to the lake. Remember? You had to stay home and study for that English Lit. test and didn't go. I came home late, and you were on my case for having drunk too much."

"I remember," Karen said. Although she was trying to keep the emotion out of her voice, Chelsea heard the strain.

"Well, we did more than drink." Chelsea stood and paced to the closet and back. "I didn't tell you because I thought nothing would ever come of it."

With a tremble in her voice, Karen said, "I can't believe Ryan would do this."

"It's not like he's a monk or something! Things just got out of hand, that's all."

"They wouldn't have with me." Karen sounded near tears. "I'd never have forgotten myself like that." For a few moments she was silent as Chelsea paced; then when she had her emotions in check, she flatly stated, "He'll marry you, you know. Ryan won't desert you."

Chelsea stopped and turned back to her. "That's just it. I don't want to be married."

Karen's mouth dropped open. "Not be married! You have to be. What are you going to do? Raise this baby alone? Ryan will insist on taking care of you."

"Don't you see? I care too much about Ryan to do this to him." She drew in a deep breath. "I'm not going to have the baby."

Karen jumped to her feet, her expression one of shock and disbelief. "What are you saying? I won't listen to this!"

Chelsea grabbed her arm. "You have to because I need your help. If I could manage this on my own, I would."

"You don't really think Ryan would let you go through with this, do you?"

"I'm not telling him anything about it—and neither are you. It's been hard enough telling you, knowing how you feel about Ryan."

Frostily, Karen said, "That apparently didn't matter much to you that night at the lake."

"Don't be like that. Listen to me. That's one reason I'm not having the baby. We love Ryan in our own ways, and he loves both of us. We've known this for a long time. I like things the way they are. If I tell Ryan about the baby, he'll think he has to marry me, and that will come between you and me as well. Admit it, Karen. Wouldn't it?"

Karen reluctantly nodded. "This is the worst thing that could have happened. The very worst!"

"That's why I'm going to fix it. No one ever needs to know about it but us." She reached in her jeans' pocket and took out a slip of folded paper. "I stopped by Jessica's room and got the name from her."

Karen took the paper as if it were tainted. "This is the name of an abortionist?" She stared at it. "I thought you said no one else would know but us. Now Jessica knows."

"No, she doesn't. I told her I needed the name for one of the girls in my sculpture class."

"Right. I'm sure she'll believe that. She'll probably be blabbing this all over the dorm."

"She won't. Karen, think about it. Jessica's been through this herself. She knows how something like this can ruin a girl's reputation. I'm just thankful I knew some-one to ask. I'm going to make an appointment right away. I can't wait. Every day makes a difference, Jessica says."

"Why are you telling me?"

"I need you to drive me there."

Karen backed away. "No. Don't ask me to do this. I'd do anything for you, Chelsea—you know I would. But I can't do this. You know how I feel about abortion!"

"I know, but what else can I do? I certainly can't ask Ryan to take me! You're my best friend."

Karen was quiet for a long time. "All right. I'll do it. But only because I can't think of another solution."

Chelsea went to the phone. She paused. "Am I doing the right thing? Can you think of any other way?"

"No. I can't."

Chelsea picked up the phone and dialed the number.

All the way back to the dorm Chelsea was silent and pale. Karen divided her attention between her friend and the freeway. "Are you sure you're okay?"

Chelsea nodded, not trusting herself to speak. It hadn't happened the way she had expected. The impact of what she'd done was only now sinking into her. She had gotten rid of Ryan's baby! "Promise me you'll never tell him. Promise!"

"I won't tell anyone. You know I keep all your secrets."

To help quell the queasiness, Chelsea tried to focus on the cars they were passing. "I should have gone to him. He should have had a say in this."

"It's a bit late to be thinking that. Besides, you know he would never have agreed to an abortion." Karen turned off Central Expressway onto the exit ramp that would take them to the college. "I think you were right to handle it the way you did."

"Really?" Chelsea looked at Karen for the first time since she'd joined her in the car. "I hope you're right. I didn't want to tie him down. I didn't want to ruin our friendship, and that would have. Me being pregnant could have ruined everything." She was having to tell herself this over and over. Now that it was done, she was bombarded with feelings of guilt and second thoughts.

"Ryan will never know." Karen turned onto the campus

street. "Like you said, this would have ruined everything. Now we can graduate like we planned and you can have your career. In time you'll decide to marry and you can have other children."

Karen's last statement hit a raw nerve, and tears coursed down Chelsea's cheeks. "Yes. That's true. There's no reason to believe I can't have more." She tried to laugh. "Lord knows, I'm fertile." The laugh ended on a sob.

Karen reached out and awkwardly patted her hand. "Don't cry, Chelsea. I can't stand to see you cry. If I let myself think for one minute that this was a mistake, I won't be able to stand it."

Chelsea shoved the tears off her cheeks with the back of her hand. "You're right. I made my decision, and it's too late to change it."

"How do you feel?" Karen asked hesitantly. "I'm sorry I couldn't go in with you."

"That's okay. I don't think they'd have let you, anyway. I feel okay, I guess." She didn't really. Nausea threatened to overtake her, but she hated to complain and didn't want Karen's sympathy, or anyone else's for that matter. It was important for her to be strong and handle this herself, just as she had handled all the difficult things in her life. Forcing a smile for Karen, she said, "I am a little tired. I think I'd like to lie down and rest for about a year or so."

Karen returned the smile, then resumed her solemn expression. "We're almost there."

Chelsea didn't try to keep the conversation going. Tears were too near, and she hated to cry.

The next few days were even more difficult. Chelsea sank further into depression and started cutting classes. She had avoided Ryan since that day in the doctor's office, making one excuse after another.

"He wants to know what's wrong with you. What am I supposed to tell him?" Karen asked. "He's worried about you. So am I."

"I'm fine. Tell him whatever you please. Just don't tell him the truth." She curled into a ball on her bed and drew the covers over her head.

"I told him you'd go to the movies with us tonight. It's *Star Wars*. I know you want to see it. Everybody who's been already says it's great."

"I can't go. What would I say to him?"

"You haven't talked to him since . . . you know." Karen sat on the bed beside Chelsea. "You can't keep avoiding him forever. What'll he think?"

Chelsea pushed the covers back and sat up. "How can I possibly talk to him as if nothing happened? One look at me and he'd know something is wrong."

"So you've lost some weight. I wish I could. Tell him you're on a diet." Karen wasn't overweight, but only because she watched every bite she ate.

"I don't feel like seeing a movie tonight. Maybe you and I can go tomorrow. You said you'd probably want to see it twice."

Karen shrugged her shoulders and shook her head. "You beat all. You know that?"

"I think I'm going to go see my parents." Chelsea looked at Karen for her reaction.

"After graduation, you mean?"

"No, now."

"You can't do that! Your father is stationed in Germany! What about school? We graduate in two months!"

"It doesn't mean as much to me as it did before. I need a change of pace."

Karen stared at her. "You can't just jump up and fly off to Germany!"

Chelsea didn't answer.

Karen's brow puckered in concern. "I have to go. Ryan will be waiting for me. Are you sure you don't want to come? It won't take long for you to get dressed."

"No, you go ahead. I know you hate missing the first of a show."

Karen paused in the doorway and with genuine sincerity

said, "You aren't going to do anything stupid, are you?"

"More stupid than I already have, you mean? No."

"It wasn't a bad decision."

Chelsea smiled sadly. "I meant I was stupid to get pregnant in the first place."

"I agree with that." Karen smiled. "I'll be in early."

All the way down the hall Karen had misgivings. Chelsea wasn't the type to harm herself, but Karen didn't like to leave her alone when it was so obvious that she was depressed. In all the years they had been friends, Karen had never known Chelsea to be really down for more than a day at a time.

As she had expected, Ryan was waiting in the foyer downstairs. "Where's Chelsea?"

"She's not coming."

A shadow of concern darkened his face. "Is she mad at me or something? It's not like her to avoid me this way."

She looked up at him and tried not to picture him lying naked with Chelsea by the lake. Since Chelsea had told her about that evening, she hadn't been able to enjoy the lake or to see Ryan without experiencing a stab of jealousy. Karen was determined to save her virginity until she was married, but that didn't keep her from being jealous of Ryan. Nor did it keep her from being angry at Chelsea for what had been done. Chelsea knew how much she cared for Ryan.

Karen realized she hadn't answered him. "No, she's not mad. I think she has a lot of reading and papers these days. Every time I come back to the dorm, she's there." This was true. She suspected that Chelsea was cutting more classes than she was admitting. "I'm worried about her," she found herself saying.

"Worried in what way?"

"She's been sort of moody lately." Karen felt she could tell Ryan that much. He already knew something out of the ordinary was going on with Chelsea.

"Maybe she's just dreading the end of school. Not me, though. It seems like I've been in school all my life."

"I know. That may be it. She said she's thinking about going to visit her parents."

"In Germany? Maybe we could all go. I probably won't have an offer to start work right away. We could use a vacation and I've never seen Germany. Have you?"

"No. I can just see me asking my mother if the three of us could go to Europe together! She wouldn't understand at all. She says we're together too much as it is."

"I don't think your mother likes me."

"She adores you. It's just that she thinks I should be spending time dating in the usual sense. She doesn't understand how Chelsea and I can both see you at once."

"We're friends." One of Ryan's heart-stopping grins split his handsome face.

Karen wondered if he had any idea how much she wished he loved her to the exclusion of Chelsea. They had kissed on the rare dates when Chelsea wasn't with them, and she had found it exciting. Karen had never been particularly fond of kissing, but the way Ryan did it was most enjoyable. She glanced up at him as he held open the door for her. If she had been carrying his baby, she wouldn't have done what Chelsea did. She would have seen to it that he married her. Sometimes men had to be manipulated into doing what was best for them.

The movie was all Ryan had hoped it would be, but he found his attention wandering. He was more worried about Chelsea than Karen realized. He knew she wouldn't have told Karen what happened that night at the lake, but he wondered if that wasn't the reason she was avoiding him. He hoped it wasn't. That night had been unlike anything he had ever experienced.

For a long time Karen and Chelsea had teased him about being in love with them both. He doubted that either knew how true that was. He loved Karen for her almost childlike innocence and the way she made him want to protect her from the world. With Karen he felt ten feet tall. But he also loved Chelsea's spontaneity and independence. She was like a prize that dangled just out of his reach, unattainable yet all the more desirable. Chelsea was far more complex than Karen, and she intrigued him to the point of distraction. The night at the lake had proven to him that Chelsea was the one he truly loved.

It wasn't just that she had made love with him, though he knew she hadn't done that lightly. With Chelsea he felt as if the stars had fallen from the sky and landed in his heart.

He glanced at Karen in the dark of the theater. Her eyes were fastened to the screen, and she was chewing popcorn slowly and absentmindedly. She was pretty, perhaps even beautiful. Ryan didn't love her any the less for his loving Chelsea more. He dreaded having to tell Karen that he had made up his mind. He didn't want to hurt her or destroy the friendship the three of them enjoyed.

Graduation was rushing upon them. That would be soon enough to tell Karen. He wanted to spend the rest of the school year just as they had in the past, the three inseparable, their friendship unaltered. Of course, there was the chance that Chelsea wouldn't want to be married—she was remarkably stubborn. And she had often told him she wanted freedom more than she wanted a commitment. But that had been before the lake.

After the movie was over, Ryan and Karen walked back to the dorm. The night was cool, so he put his arm around her shoulders to keep her warm. Karen didn't like to be cool, but as usual, she had forgotten to take a jacket. He and Chelsea were always teasing her about her needing someone to look after her all the time. She smiled up at him and matched her steps to his.

"When we get back to the dorm, I want you to go get Chelsea. I don't care if she doesn't have on her makeup or what she's wearing. Bring her down so I can see for myself that she's all right. Okay?"

Karen nodded. "I'll try, but you know how stubborn she can be."

"For some reason I can't stop worrying about her."

"You, too?" Karen looked up at him in surprise. "I found myself thinking about her all during the movie."

"Are you sure she's not avoiding me?" Ryan brushed Karen's pale blond hair back from her shoulder. She had let it grow longer than usual this year, and he liked it better, though she kept threatening to cut it again. She would never let it grow to her waist as Chelsea had.

"Why would she avoid you?" Karen asked, picking up the pace.

Ryan dropped the subject, content to ask Chelsea herself.

When they reached Mary Hay Hall, Ryan waited on the dorm steps while Karen went in to get Chelsea. Other couples arrived, and reluctant to say good night, lingered about in the shadows for one last kiss. Ryan ignored them, concerned that it was taking Karen so long to convince Chelsea to come out.

Suddenly, Karen came running out of the building, her eyes wide. "Ryan! She's gone!"

"What do you mean, she's gone?"

"Most of her clothes are missing!"

Cold dread settled in his middle. "That's not possible."

"I talked to the dorm mother, and she said Chelsea left about an hour ago. She had two suitcases with her!" Karen threw herself into his arms. "I think she's gone to Germany!"

"Why would she do that with graduation so close?" Ryan's mind was spinning. Chelsea was gone? "She can't leave for Germany with school almost over."

Karen shook her head. "I told you she said she wanted to visit her parents. That must be where she went!"

"It's not like they live across town! She wouldn't do this!"

Karen lifted her head, and he saw she was crying. "There's no place else she could be. She took almost everything she owns. Everything that would fit into suitcases."

"Where's your car? We have to find her!"

Ryan drove as Karen scanned the streets. They went first to Love Field where they learned that even for a connecting flight to Germany they would have to go to D-FW. Two hours later, after exhausting their efforts at the sprawling airport located between Dallas and Fort Worth, and finding no trace of Chelsea, they returned to Dallas and made one final fruitless stop at the downtown bus terminal. Chelsea had vanished.

Ryan was as upset as Karen. He had been imagining all sorts of terrible things befalling Chelsea, from kidnapping to amnesia. Karen was crying softly as they drove back to the dorm. Ryan parked her car and put his arms around her. "Don't cry. She'll be okay."

"But she was so depressed lately."

"You never told me that. You said she'd been moody."

"She didn't want you to know." Karen looked up at him as if there was more she wanted to say, but she lowered her face to his chest instead. "I can't believe she would go without leaving me a note or anything. She didn't even say goodbye!"

"I know. That's why I don't believe she'll be gone for long. Maybe she just went somewhere for the weekend."

"Without telling either of us? Never! Chelsea tells me everything. I'm positive she's on that plane to Europe— the one we just missed. It's stupid of the airlines not to tell you who's booked on the flight."

"I know." He held her closer and rested his cheek on the top of her head. He hurt as badly as if he had been physically injured, just knowing that Chelsea was gone. "Damn it! She could have at least said goodbye!"

"She hates goodbyes. Even short ones. She probably thinks she told me goodbye by telling me she wanted to see her parents. For Chelsea that sort of makes sense."

"She didn't tell *me* goodbye." Ryan couldn't hide the hurt in his voice. "I'd have thought she'd do that, at least."

Karen held him tighter, and he tried to tell himself that Chelsea was safe, wherever she might be and that he would see her again soon.

"Is there something I don't know about in all this?" he asked.

Karen paused, then shook her head.

Ryan wasn't sure he believed her, but he had never known Karen to lie to him before. All the same, it seemed odd that Chelsea or anyone would leave at this time of year and in this manner unless something was wrong. "If there's something I should know, I want you to tell me. Do you hear me?"

Karen nodded. "There's nothing you need to know."

Again Ryan was struck by doubts. But if there was something she wasn't telling him—a secret between the two friends—he might never find out what it was. He'd never known two people who were more loyal to one another.

Chapter Three

Karen and Ryan strolled along the bank of the lake, holding hands but not smiling. "I miss her so much," Karen said. "We've almost never been apart, you know."

"I know. But graduation is almost here. You'd have had to part before long, anyway."

"I don't see why. I have no intention of moving out of Dallas, and Chelsea could have painted here as well as anywhere else." She smiled sadly. "We used to say we'd rent one of those warehouses, like the ones you see in movies about New York. My piano would be at one end, and Chelsea's canvases at the other."

"Roommates forever." Ryan studied her face. "Is that all you really wanted?"

Karen shook her head. "More than anything I wanted to fall in love, get married, and live happily ever after with two perfect children. That's still my dream."

Ryan picked up a pebble and tossed it into the water. Ripples spread silently over the surface. "Chelsea wants to travel. She's afraid of being tied down."

"I know. I guess you'd have to know her parents to understand her attitude. They aren't anything like her."

"Yet she went to see them rather than finish out the year and graduate. I can't understand that." He sounded angry.

Karen put her hand on his arm to comfort him. She was tempted to tell him the real reason Chelsea had gone, but she had given her word. Suddenly it occurred to her that Chelsea's actions were tantamount to saying she wasn't interested in Ryan anymore. A plan began to form in Karen's mind. "I'm not sure she's coming back," she said.

"Have you heard from her?" he asked quickly.

"Yes." Karen sat on the bank and curled her legs under her. "I got a letter yesterday, and it said she's dropped out of school and may stay in Germany permanently. I can't believe she would throw away four years of education when graduation is so close." She glanced at him to see if her words had sounded believable.

Ryan sat beside her as if stunned. "Did she say why she left so suddenly? I've thought about it until I'm going in circles."

"No, but the return address on the envelope told me what town she might be in, and I managed to get her parents' phone number. It was too late to call her last night, so I waited until this morning. She wouldn't say why she left that way, only that she felt she had to and that she couldn't wait until graduation. I got the impression her mother may be sick or something and need her there. I don't know why she wouldn't tell me more. She's never kept anything from me before." Karen fell silent. She disliked lying, even when it would accomplish such an important end as the one she had in mind. But Chelsea had frequently stepped aside in the past when she'd learned Karen wanted to date a particular boy. Surely this was no different. If Chelsea really was in love with Ryan, wouldn't she have told him about becoming pregnant, have insisted that he marry her? Karen certainly would have. Surely what she was doing was justifiable.

"Why didn't you tell me this sooner? A letter. And a phone call."

"I told her you'd want to know, but she said it'd be better if I didn't mention to you that she'd made contact with me. She didn't make me promise not to tell you, though; and she said we aren't to worry about her."

"That's easier said than done." He threw another stone into the lake, obviously angry.

"I don't want you to hold this against her. It's just Chelsea. She's always marched to a different drummer. It doesn't mean she no longer cares for us."

Ryan squatted and rested his forearms on his knees as he stared out across the lake. "I come from steady stock. My parents probably never did an unexpected thing in their lives. Even my brother is dependable, but he's considered the wild one of the family."

"My family is like that, too." Karen pulled up a blade of grass and studied it in the sunlight. "Mother has her meetings and organizations. Daddy runs his company like clockwork. Dinner is on the table at exactly seven o'clock every night. Some people might find that boring, but I like knowing exactly what I can depend on. If I went to China, I'd still know my parents were eating at seven o'clock. It's reassuring."

"Chelsea is just the opposite. She wants to plan each hour as it happens."

Karen nodded. "I know. It's one of the things I find so hard to understand about her. I could never live with so much uncertainty. We really aren't much alike, even if we have been friends forever. Maybe that's why the friendship has lasted so long." She gazed thoughtfully over the water. "I always wanted to be like her—popular and self-assured. She's never lacked for dates. She can read something once and memorize it. I always have to try so much harder."

"There's nothing wrong with your memory. Your grades are good. And you're more popular than you seem to realize."

"Only because I work at my lessons constantly. As for being popular, I can thank Chelsea for that. I probably would have stayed at the dorm all the time if she hadn't been constantly dragging me to parties and out on double dates." Karen smiled at the memory. "I'm too shy. I always have been."

"You aren't shy with me."

"You're different."

Ryan looked at her and reached out to take her hand. Karen let her palm rest against his, measuring her fingers to his.

"You have longer fingers than Chelsea," Ryan commented.

"They come in handy in playing the piano. Chelsea's hands can't span an octave. They're stronger than mine, though. I guess it comes from stretching all that canvas and painting for hours on end. With all my practicing, you'd think my hands would be stronger, wouldn't you?" She studied her hands as if they belonged to a stranger.

Ryan was silent for several moments. "I think you underestimate your popularity. Chelsea tells me you turn down dates all the time."

"I don't want to go out with just anyone who happens to ask me. Do you think that makes me stuck-up?"

"No, just discriminating."

Karen looked along the lake. Where had Ryan brought Chelsea that night? Right here? She stood and dusted the grass from her jeans. "Let's walk."

He got to his feet and fell into step with her. "You and I are more alike than either of us are like Chelsea. Have you ever noticed that?"

She nodded. "We're both dependable. We know what we want in life. Chelsea's like a butterfly—beautiful to look at but impossible to tame."

"I know." Ryan smiled as he thought of their friend. "That's a good analogy."

Karen took his hand. "What am I like?"

Ryan thought for a minute. "You're more like a flower. You're beautiful, and I always know I can count on you being in the same spot."

"That sounds boring."

"Not to me. Chelsea's taking off like she did made me aware of something about her that I'd overlooked. If I'd married her, could I have expected her to be there when I came home, or would she be gone—off to Germany without any reason?"

"You've considered marrying her?" Karen asked a bit too quickly.

"I guess at our age that thought comes up about someone you date more than a time or two. We're almost out of college, it's time to consider settling down."

Karen wondered if he'd ever considered marriage with her, but was afraid to ask. Chelsea would have posed the question, but Karen wasn't that sure of herself. That was why she had to plan this move so carefully. It might be her only chance with him. They walked in silence for several yards.

"By the way, I've been scheduled for an interview," Ryan said.

"Have you? With whom?"

He grinned at her. "DataComp."

"Daddy's company? That's great! I'll tell him he has to hire you."

"No! Please don't do that. I want to get the job on my own."

"All right. If you insist." Karen made a mental note to speak to her father anyway. If he connected Ryan's application with the young man Karen spoke of so often, it would almost certainly sway him to offer Ryan the job. Karen saw nothing wrong in pulling a few strings to get what one wanted.

"I'd love to work there. It's the best computer company in Dallas, in my opinion—probably the best in this part of the country."

"I think it's the best anywhere, but I may be partial. Wouldn't it be great if you get that job? It'd mean you'd stay here in Dallas indefinitely."

"I may anyway." He smiled down at her. "I'm not in any hurry to leave."

"No?" Karen found herself smiling as warmth spread all through her. "I expected you to go back to Colorado to be near your family."

Ryan put his arm around her shoulders. "I have interests here."

She hoped he would elaborate but he didn't.

As Chelsea brushed her hair, she struggled to hide her growing frustration. Her mother was sitting across the room from her on the bed Chelsea used when visiting her parents, and she hadn't stopped talking since she'd come into the room.

"I do wish you'd cut your hair," Eileen Cavin said. "It's so long and looks so hot."

"I like it long."

"It's not flattering that way. Your face is shaped all wrong for long hair."

Chelsea studied her face in the mirror. It was small and heart-shaped with well-defined cheekbones. Her eyes were a dark brown and almond shaped. "What's wrong with my face?" she asked in concern.

"Why don't you let me make an appointment for you at the beauty salon here on base? If they cut your hair short and give you a permanent, it would be so flattering. Why, it hangs all the way past your waist!"

"Yes, I know," she said, trying hard to look pleasant. Chelsea had always considered her hair to be her best feature. "I don't want to cut it."

"By the way, your dad has someone he wants you to meet."

Chelsea met her mother's eyes in the mirror. "I'm not interested in meeting anyone."

"Don't be like that. He's a major and recently divorced. Richard says his being a major so young means he has a promising career ahead of him."

Chelsea had no intention of marrying an Army man. "One general in the family is enough," she said, to tease her mother into lightening up.

"Don't be flippant. Your dad has worked hard to be where he is, and I have, too. You know what I always say—he wears his insignias on his uniform, and I wear them on my heart."

Chelsea wisely made no comment.

"We were certainly surprised to see you on our door-step. And happy to see you, too. Just surprised that you didn't call and tell us you were coming. I still don't know why you made the trip so unexpectedly."

"I wanted to see you and Dad."

"But what about school?"

"I don't really need a college degree to be an artist. I've learned all I can there. I went to college to learn more about art, and I did exactly that. I don't see any reason to graduate."

"I disagree, but when have you ever listened to me? Your dad won't be happy. Not at all." Eileen frowned at Chelsea. "Don't tell him you've dropped out. It will set him off. I know it will. He thinks you're on holiday."

Chelsea nodded. Dropping out of college so near gradu-ation would be more than enough to send her father into a rage. She remembered how often during her childhood he had exploded in fury, often with little provocation. Her happiest times had been away from the house and out of his reach. So why, she asked herself, had she come here? "Maybe I did make a mistake."

"Of course you did! There's no doubt about it. Maybe if I call the school and talk to the dean, they'll let you back in. Richard is a general, after all. That carries a great deal of weight."

"Not in the civilian world. Besides, I don't want to go back." This wasn't entirely true. Chelsea was missing Ryan and Karen more than she had thought possible.

Eileen went to the window and looked down at the backyard. "You ought to meet this young man, I tell you. At your age, you should be thinking of marriage. Do you date anyone in particular in the States?"

"As a matter of fact, I do. His name is Ryan Morgan."

"You must not care too much about him or you wouldn't be over here. What's he like?"

Chelsea's voice softened. "He's intelligent and handsome. Tall, too. His major is electrical engineering. He wants to go into computer design."

"Whatever that is." Eileen didn't sound impressed. "I'm not so sure your father will approve of him." She glanced at her wristwatch. "It's almost time for your father to come home."

"I'll be downstairs soon."

Eileen left, and soon Chelsea heard the liquor cabinet open and shut. Eileen always fortified herself with a double scotch before Richard came home. Once he arrived, he matched her drink for drink.

Chelsea put her head down on the dresser. She wanted more out of life than her parents had. She didn't want to merely be a satellite for her husband, and she certainly didn't want to be trapped in a marriage in which alcohol was necessary before any communication could take place.

It had been a mistake to come here. She had wanted family around her and familiar arms to hold her as if she were still a small child. But her grandparents were dead, and her parents had never been particularly nurturing. Richard Cavin ran his family in much the same way he ran his Army post. Chelsea couldn't recall ever having been hugged by him. Her mother was less starched, but had almost no maternal instincts. She was more likely to find fault with Chelsea than to hug her.

In the drawer of the small writing desk in her room, she found some stationery and started a letter to Ryan. After a few lines she realized she couldn't mail it. The tone was much too sad and lonely. Nor could she tell him what was in her heart. She couldn't mention her real reason for needing space or that she realized now how much she loved him. These weren't things she should put in a letter, especially not when she wasn't positive that he felt the same way about her.

Instead of writing Ryan, she started to write to Karen.

* * *

Karen hurried to meet Ryan after her last class. When she reached his side, he hugged her. "You look happy today."

She nodded. "I got an *A* in English Lit.! The grades were just posted."

"That's great! Would you like to go to the lake and celebrate?"

Karen paused and looked away. "I really don't like going out there. Could we do something else instead?"

"Sure. You name it."

She thought for a minute. Ryan liked going to the lake because there was no admission fee; he had little money to spare. "Let's just go for a walk."

After passing the Hughes-Trigg Student Center, they turned down a street flanked by huge live oaks. After a while Ryan said, "Have you heard from Chelsea lately?"

"I got a letter from her today."

"Is she all right?"

"She's fine." Karen felt a little guilty for not having told him before he asked; she knew he was still worrying about their friend. But in the letter Chelsea had said she was coming home.

On one hand, Karen was glad and eager to see her. But since Chelsea had been gone, she had enjoyed having Ryan's complete attention, though she occasionally had experienced a bit of guilt for leading him to believe Chelsea might not return. Karen wasn't eager to share him again, especially now that she knew what the two had done at the lake. True, Chelsea had said it had only happened once, but Karen wasn't too sure.

Ryan took her hand and squeezed it in the affectionate manner she'd become accustomed to, and she told herself she was perfectly justified in not telling him Chelsea would come back. After all, Chelsea had removed herself from the running by just taking off for Germany.

Then there was the matter of the future. Karen's parents were upset with her for having spent four years in college without an engagement ring to show for it. Karen had known what was expected of her because her parents had told her on many occasions. "The best place to choose a good husband is in college," they'd said, almost in unison. That was why they had been willing to let her major in music, even though it would be next to impossible for her to earn her living in that field. No one, not even Karen, had ever expected her to get a job.

Karen had told her sister, Joyce, that she cared a great deal for Ryan, but that he couldn't seem to choose between her and Chelsea. When Joyce heard Chelsea had dropped out of school and gone to Germany, she advised Karen to strike while there was a chance, openly admitting she had had to push her husband Todd toward the altar, and that she was of the opinion this was universally true.

"In a way I dread college being over," Karen said. "I don't like changes. What if I never see you again?"

"I've already told you I intend to stay in Dallas."

"I know, but we won't have classes together. We may drift apart." She gazed up at him in the way she had found effective in getting and holding his attention. "I'd hate knowing I would never see you again."

"That won't happen."

"It's easy to say that now, but we can't be sure. What if DataComp doesn't hire you? You may have to move to California to get a job."

Ryan was quiet for several minutes. "You know I care too much about you never to see you again."

Karen sensed tears rising, and she let them fill her eyes. "I hope so, Ryan. Sometimes I think of being out there in the world, and it seems too large and unpredictable. I feel safe with you."

He stopped and drew her into the shade of one of the oaks. Karen stepped into his arms. As he gazed down into her eyes, he said, "I love you, Karen." He touched her hair and her cheek. "I couldn't stand it if I thought we wouldn't see each other again."

"You love me?"

"You know I do. I've told you this before."

"I know, but you always say it as if I were your sister. I need to know, Ryan. What do you mean by it?"

For a long time he didn't answer, and Karen was afraid she had come on too strong. She let the anguish show on her face and waited.

"I haven't made any secret of the fact that I care more for you and Chelsea than any other people I know. I love you both, in different ways."

"Chelsea is gone," Karen forced herself to say. "What if she never comes back, even for a visit?"

Ryan rubbed his thumb over the curve of her chin. "You're right. She may never return. And that leaves the two of us. If Chelsea cared as much for me as I thought she did, she would have told me goodbye. At the least she would have written me from Germany to explain why she left the way she did."

"You're right. So now there's just the two of us." Karen gently nudged Ryan in the right direction.

"What would you think about us getting married?"

Karen had dreamed about this moment all her life, but she had never thought the words would come like this. It sounded almost as if he were merely wondering what she thought of the idea. "Is that a proposal?" she asked in confusion.

He laughed softly. "Yes, I guess it is. I've never done this before. I guess I'm not very good at it."

Relief flooded through her. "You're wonderful at it. And yes, I'd love to marry you!"

Ryan looked down at her, and she wondered what he was thinking. Then he slowly bent to kiss her. Karen's thoughts were flying. Ryan had proposed to her! She was going to marry Ryan! She held on to him as if he were a lifeline, returning his kiss with more passion than she usually summoned. He had proposed! To her! Her guilt over Chelsea immediately vanished.

When he straightened, she hugged him, unwilling to let him go. "I didn't expect this," she said truthfully.

"Neither did I."

"I have so many plans to make! I'll tell Mother and Daddy as soon as I go back to my room. We'll need to find a place to live." She looked up at him. It seemed that sparklers were going off inside her. "I'm so happy!"

He smiled gently at her. "I couldn't let you face that big, scary world all alone, now could I? I don't ever want you to be alone or frightened. I can protect you from everything."

"I know you can. That's what I love about you."

"Are you sure you don't want to think about this for a while? I don't want to rush you into a decision."

She laughed. "You're not rushing me. I've hoped this would happen for months! I was just afraid that you cared more for Chelsea."

"She's gone. Like you said, she may never come back."

A twinge of conscience made Karen say, "What if she does? She might change her mind about staying in Germany forever. What if she does come back? What will you feel about me then?"

"My feelings for you won't change. It's important to me that I can depend on you. I don't want to walk on eggshells all my life, wondering if my wife will be at home or halfway around the world when I get off work. I can't imagine you doing such a thing."

Karen nodded earnestly. "I wouldn't even know how."

"You're the best choice for me. Most women wouldn't have waited so patiently for me to figure that out."

"I can see how you'd love Chelsea, too," Karen said loyally. "She's my best friend, and I know all her good points. As much as I like her, I have to admit I'm jealous of her at times. Life seems so easy for her. She always knows what to do and when to do it, and she doesn't seem to be at all afraid to make decisions. I admire her a great deal."

"I hope our getting married won't get in the way of our friendship with Chelsea."

Karen knew a pang of jealousy at the thought of her fiancé still wanting to be friends with another woman, but she tried to put the thought out of her head. "Chelsea will understand. Besides, she doesn't want to be married, at least not for a while. She's told both of us that. She wants a career first."

"Yes. I know."

Karen kept her arms around his waist. "Do you want to be with me when I tell my parents?"

"I will if you'd like. What do you think they'll say?"

"They'll be excited and happy for us. Daddy doesn't know you that well, but mother already thinks of you as one of the family. Wait until I tell Joyce!" Karen smiled up at him. "I don't want to wait. I'm going to call them as soon as I go back to my room."

"When do you want to look for a ring?"

"A ring! I hadn't thought of that!" Karen was practically beside herself with excitement. "What sort of ring would you like?"

"I don't know. I never really thought much about it. One with diamonds, I suppose."

Karen laughed. "Of course with diamonds, Ryan. I meant a solitaire or . . . Never mind. We'll see what we can find."

"Now it can't be a large one. I still don't have a job," Ryan cautioned her. "Later I can buy you a larger one."

"Never! I'm too sentimental. I want to wear the ring I'm married with forever. I wouldn't want a larger one." She thought for a minute. "Maybe we should get a plain band and add a nice ring later. No, I want to have an engagement ring." She could just hear the condescending tones of her mother and Joyce if she told them she had no engagement ring. They wouldn't consider her properly engaged and would think Ryan was pinching pennies. "Yes, definitely an engagement ring."

"Let's go shopping for one tomorrow. But I think you should tell your family first. I want to call mine as well."

"Won't they be surprised? What have you told them about me?"

Ryan grinned. "It was all good."

"A house!" Karen exclaimed suddenly. "Where will we live?"

"That will depend on what job I get. There's no point in looking for one here if I end up going to California."

Karen shook her head confidentially. "There's no chance of that now. You just proposed to the boss's daughter."

Ryan didn't seem to find that as amusing as she did.

Chapter Four

Chelsea threaded her way off the crowded airplane into the covered passageway that led into the D-FW terminal, happy to be home and anxious to get away from the airport. She shifted the weight of her bulky carry-on bag to her other shoulder and tucked her purse tightly under her arm as the crush of hurried passengers funneled through the narrow doorway and into the terminal itself. Once inside, she stepped out of the flow and scanned the crowd.

Karen was there as she'd hoped, jumping and waving to attract Chelsea's attention. Chelsea moved quickly toward her, breaking into a run for the last few yards. Karen grabbed her and hugged her.

"I could just wring your neck for having left like you did," Karen said as she held Chelsea at arm's length to look at her before hugging her again. "We've been so worried!"

"I've called and written," Chelsea protested. "It's not as if you didn't know where I went." Her eyes again searched the crowd behind Karen. "Are you alone?"

Karen's smile wavered. "Yes. I asked Ryan to let me come and get you by myself."

Chelsea was disappointed, but she hid it. "You look great! Graduating must agree with you."

"And that's another thing! You didn't graduate! If you had only talked to me instead of just going off . . . What on earth were you thinking of?"

"I don't know," Chelsea answered seriously. "I just had to get away, and I didn't think. You're right. You've always been my left brain." She smiled at her friend. "Remember what we used to say? I'm the right brain and you're the left one and together we have a whole brain?"

"Just don't leave like this again." Karen stepped back to look at her. "You look great. Germany agreed with you. I think you've even gained back some of the weight you lost."

"Maybe." Chelsea led the way through the crowd to the baggage claim area, answering Karen's questions about Germany and hardly able to get in a word of her own.

As they awaited the luggage, Karen finally wound down and Chelsea jumped in with a question of her own. "How's Ryan?"

Karen faltered for a moment, then answered, "Just fine."

Chelsea glanced more closely at her. "You sound funny. You two haven't had an argument, have you?"

"No. Chelsea—"

"Look, there go my bags. Here. Hold this and I'll be right back." Chelsea shoved her carryon at Karen and hurried to the baggage carousel.

When she had retrieved her luggage, she staggered back to her friend. "I wish you'd brought Ryan. I could use his muscles right now."

Karen took the bag Chelsea had under her arm. "I have your other things at my house. The stuff you left in the dorm."

"Thanks. I hope you've been wearing some of them. I left that blue blouse you like to borrow."

"I have. Chelsea, we need to talk."

"I know. It seems as if I haven't seen you for years instead of weeks!"

"It's been months, actually."

Chelsea led the way through the terminal, past the glass doors, and into the hot air outside. "It's already ninety degrees, I'll bet, and it's barely June." She looked back at

Karen. "Did you want to talk to me about anything in particular? You're acting oddly. You aren't still upset with me, are you?"

"No." Karen looked around. "This isn't the place. Let's go to the car."

Chelsea felt a growing apprehension. There was something Karen wasn't telling her.

They stashed the bags in Karen's trunk and soon were on Highway 183 headed east toward the Dallas skyline. "I made the phone calls as you asked," Karen said. "I found a garage apartment on Willow Lane not far from Sandhurst Street. It's small, of course, but there's a separate bedroom and living room, which you wanted, and it's cheap—and vacant. You can move right in. I'll take you by it on our way in."

"Cheap is good. At least until I get a job."

The houses along Willow Lane were owned primarily by young professionals on the way up, as were those on Sandhurst. It was a more expensive area than Chelsea would have looked in, though.

"I saw the apartment a couple of weeks ago. When you called, I knew it would be right for you."

"Why were you looking for a garage apartment?"

"I wasn't. I was shopping for a house." Karen parked in front of one of the brick homes. Down the drive Chelsea saw the garage and the rooms above it. "I found one on Sandhurst." She killed the engine. "Chelsea, there's something I have to tell you. Please, be happy for me."

Apprehension grew in Chelsea. "What's going on, Karen?"

Silently Karen held up her left hand. The diamond on it sparkled like cold fire.

"You're engaged! Why didn't you tell me? Who is it?" Chelsea caught Karen's hand and looked at the ring more closely. "It's beautiful!"

"Ryan gave it to me."

Chelsea looked up in confusion. "Then you're not engaged? But it looks like an—"

"I'm engaged to Ryan." Karen gripped Chelsea's hand as her friend began to draw back. "Please, try to understand!"

"You're engaged to Ryan? When did this happen?" Chelsea was numb, and she was grateful for that. Feeling would come back all too soon.

"He proposed a couple of weeks ago. We wanted you to be here when we told you. I thought it be best if I broke the news to you." Gray eyes searched Chelsea's face. "You know I've loved him for a year or more. I never made a secret of it."

"No. No, you never did." Chelsea responded automatically. Ryan had asked Karen to marry him? He loved Karen, not her?

"Please say you're happy for us. You're my best friend. I can't stand it if you're unhappy."

Chelsea squeezed Karen's hand, then withdrew her fingers. Her hand was cold, and there was a tightness in the pit of her stomach. "Of course I'm happy for you. My two favorite people are going to be married. That's great." She even managed a smile.

Karen relaxed visibly. "Thank goodness you understand! You'll never know how worried I've been. Ryan, too. You're so important to us both."

"We always said he would have to choose one day." Chelsea hoped her smile looked natural. It felt strained.

"Let's go see the apartment. Then I'll drive by the house we're buying."

Chelsea made herself get out of the car and walk with Karen down the drive. She no longer cared what the apartment looked like. If it had a roof to keep out the rain and enough space to set up her easel, she would take it. At the moment she only wanted a place where she could curl up and hide from the world until she could get accustomed to the idea of Ryan marrying Karen.

Karen introduced Chelsea to the woman who owned the apartment and got the key from her. Together they climbed the steps that went up the outside of the garage.

Karen was talking constantly, pointing out how near the apartment was in regard to shopping facilities, the desirability of the neighborhood, what sort of trees shaded the yard. Chelsea barely heard her.

The place was unimaginative but clean. There were windows on all the walls. It had a separate room for a bed. The main room was larger than Chelsea had expected because the kitchen was in one corner instead of in a separate room. She opened the bedroom door and glanced in. "I'll take it."

"That was quick! Don't you even want to see the bathroom?"

"There is one, isn't there?"

"It's through the bedroom. There's a shower, but no tub."

"That's okay. I prefer showers." Chelsea started back out, but Karen stopped her.

"Are you sure you don't hate me? I love him, you know."

Chelsea paused. She knew how much depended on her answer. "No. I don't hate you."

"What about Ryan?"

"I could never hate him."

"You love him, too, don't you?" Karen looked miserable. "Don't ask me to give him up."

Chelsea drew in a ragged breath. "I'd never ask you to do that. You're the one he picked. He never asked me to marry him."

"If he had," Karen persisted, "would you have said yes?"

"We'll never know, will we?" Chelsea met Karen's gaze evenly.

Karen was the first to turn away. In a forced voice she said, "I'll help you fix this place up. All it needs is some pretty curtains and some nice furniture." She hesitated and said uncertainly, "Will you be my maid of honor?"

"I've always said I would be." Chelsea knew she had to get used to the idea of Karen and Ryan as a couple. She would see them together for the rest of their lives. Avoiding their wedding would only make it obvious that she was in love with him, and that would hurt Karen. It might hurt Ryan as well. He had always said he loved them both. "I'd be honored to take part in your wedding ceremony, Karen." She smiled at her and held out her arms.

Karen hugged her as if she were drowning. "I was so afraid of how you'd take it. I wouldn't blame you if you never spoke to me again. If I didn't love him so much, I'd have turned him down so you could have him instead."

"You goose," Chelsea said through her tears. "If Ryan had wanted me, he would have asked me." The words made her hurt inside.

When Karen pulled away, Chelsea saw that she was crying, too. "Thank you," Karen said simply.

Chelsea didn't answer.

Chelsea avoided Ryan for several days. The longer she put it off, the more difficult seeing him seemed to be. The inevitable happened a week after Chelsea returned to Dallas.

Troy Green, the man Ryan had asked to be his best man, had recently moved into a house and was giving a party. The music from inside lapped over to the comparative quiet around the pool, and inside, despite the noise, Chelsea sensed Ryan's presence. It had always been this way between her and him. The three of them had called it "radar."

He was looking about as if searching for her. When their eyes met, he didn't look away for several seconds. By this time, Karen had also spotted her and was coming toward her. Chelsea refused to run away. Sooner or later, this meeting had to take place.

"Hello," he said, his hazel eyes searching hers. "It's been a long time, Chelsea."

She nodded, not yet trusting her voice.

"You see?" Karen said to him in a bantering voice. "I

told you she'd be here. She's not avoiding you, she's only been busy."

"That's right," Chelsea said. "It's taking me longer than I expected to settle in." This wasn't entirely true; she didn't own that much. But unpacking took longer when you were too depressed to do more than sit and stare at the walls most of the time.

"Is there anything I can do to help?" Ryan asked. His voice was deep and seemed to touch a fiber in her soul.

"No. I have to do this alone."

"Wendy Johnston is giving me a kitchen shower next week," Karen said. "I told her to check with you about the date."

"I don't have anything planned." Chelsea looked away from Ryan with an effort. "A kitchen shower? You're actually going to learn to cook?" She smiled at Karen.

"Now cut that out," Karen said with a laugh. "I can cook. Well, I *can.* "

Ryan and Chelsea exchanged glances as they both struggled not to laugh. "We know," Chelsea replied. "We've tasted your experiments."

"I've told her I'll have to get rich quick so we can afford to hire a cook," Ryan said with a fond glance at Karen that pierced Chelsea's heart. "I'm not sure how long I can survive on her eggplant casserole and tuna surprises."

"Well, they *were* a surprise, weren't they?" Karen countered. "That's all I promised about them, if you'll remember."

"I'll find you a cookbook—an easy one. There are some out now with only three ingredients. It will be like cooking with training wheels."

"Some friends you two are," Karen grumbled good-naturedly. She looked around the living room. "This place looks as if Troy has lived here for years. Look at all these hanging plants. I'll bet Wendy picked them out. They're practically engaged, you know."

"So I hear." Chelsea looked at the baskets that clustered in one corner and spilled out onto the latticed patio beyond. "They make a good couple. She's been crazy about him for years."

The music switched from "Disco Lady" to "Fooled Around And Fell In Love." Karen swayed with the music. "Finally! Something besides disco. That's all I ever seem to hear these days." She was pulling Ryan toward the space Troy had cleared for dancing when she stopped. "There's Wendy! I have to run and talk to her for a minute. You two dance together." Before either Ryan or Chelsea could reply, she was threading her way through the crowd.

Chelsea reluctantly looked up at Ryan. "You don't have to dance with me."

"I'd like to." He took her hand and led her onto the patio. "I don't want to fight the crowd, though."

The cooler breeze felt good after the packed room. Chelsea stepped into his arms, their steps matched perfectly, but the silence grew taut between them, and Chelsea saw no way to break it.

"I was worried about you," he said at last. "Why didn't you at least tell me goodbye?"

"I hate goodbyes."

"So do I, but I wouldn't have left you without letting you know where I was going and whether I would be back."

Chelsea tensed. "Karen knew. She must have told you."

"You didn't even write me."

"I'm sorry, Ryan. That was wrong of me. I had a lot to sort out, and I had to be alone to do it."

"You could have been alone without going all the way to Germany." His voice sounded strained.

Chelsea tried to keep her tone light. "I guess it turned out for the best. You and Karen needed some time by yourselves. I would have been in the way."

"No, you wouldn't."

Chelsea dared to meet his eyes. It was almost her undoing.

"Chelsea—"

"Ryan, don't. There are things that can never be said

now. You and Karen are engaged to be married. I'm her best friend. I want the two of you to be happy more than I've ever wanted anything else."

"You do?"

"Of course I do. How can you even ask?"

The music continued, but they had stopped dancing. Chelsea realized she was standing in his embrace only a few feet from the open patio door, and she pulled away. "I have to leave."

"Because of me?"

She hesitated. She knew Ryan, and she could recognize the pain and regret in his voice. The right words from her now might still bring him back to her. Guilt surged through her. "No," she said. "Because of me." Before she could waver in her determination, she ran around the house and to her car.

She got into the driver's seat and looked back the way she had come. He hadn't followed her. She hadn't expected that he would. He loved Karen, or he wouldn't have proposed to her. Maybe what she had seen as wavering in his decision had only been his regret over any hurt he had caused her. If she had acted on impulse, she might have destroyed her friendship with two people she loved more than she loved herself. In the future she would have to be more careful. Unable to face them again, she started her car and drove away.

Ryan watched Chelsea run from him and had to fight the impulse to go after her. If she hadn't made it so apparent that she didn't want him, he would have pursued her, whether he was engaged to Karen or not.

Self-loathing filled him as he looked back at the lighted room. He could see Karen talking to Wendy Johnston. She was moving her hands to illustrate some point, and she was smiling. He loved Karen. The problem was, he also loved Chelsea, and he didn't honestly know that he had made the best choice.

Certainly Karen needed him more. She had very little of Chelsea's stubborn independence and seemed too fragile and sweet to meet life's challenges head on. Chelsea didn't need anyone. Ryan had always wanted to be needed, and he was well suited to act as a woman's buffer against the world. It was how his parents had raised him. Karen would fit perfectly in his family.

So why did he long to go after Chelsea?

Just then Karen caught sight of him and came outside. "Where's Chelsea?" she asked.

"She left."

"So soon? We just got here."

Ryan walked to the pool and gazed into the azure water. "I don't know why. She said she had to leave and did. You know how she is."

"I'll call her tomorrow. Wendy has some really cute ideas for my shower, and as my maid of honor, Chelsea should be included in the planning." Karen frowned slightly. "You didn't say anything to upset her, did you?"

"Of course not. Why would I do that?"

"You wouldn't on purpose, but Mother says this may be a ticklish situation, what with you having dated us both and all." Karen looked up at him, her eyes filled with concern. "You don't regret choosing me, do you?"

Ryan sighed as he pulled her into his embrace. "Never. You don't ever have to ask me that again." He held her and thought how different she felt in his arms from Chelsea. Karen never put her entire body into a hug, and she could not be described as sensuous. "I chose you, and I don't regret it."

He felt her relax. "I'm so glad," she murmured against his chest. "I don't know what I'd do without you."

He noticed how soft and vulnerable she felt as he held her closer. Although taller than Chelsea, she gave the impression of being much smaller. She had a way of looking up at him through her eyelashes and of making delicate movements that caused her to seem as breakable as spun glass.

Ryan bent and kissed her. Karen seemed to enjoy it, but she didn't give herself to him with passion the way Chelsea would have. He hated himself for making the comparison.

Karen drew back and ducked her head self-consciously. "What if someone saw us out here kissing?" she said with a quick laugh.

"We're engaged. There's nothing wrong with kissing."

She glanced at the lighted room as if afraid of finding everyone crowded in the doorway to spy on them. "I know, but there's a time and place for everything."

Ryan told himself this meant she was reserving her passion for their marriage bed. This reassured him. After all, he had always known how shy Karen was and found it one of her charms. "Once we're married you won't have that excuse," he teased with a smile.

"We'd better get back inside. I don't want people whispering about us."

He kept his arm around her as they went back to the party. She was just shy. That was all.

Karen sat on her frilly pink and white bedspread and touched the rollers in her hair to see if it was dry yet. Her sister sat on the dressing-table stool and went over the names on the wedding list. "I hope we haven't forgotten anyone," Joyce said as a small frown puckered her brow.

"If we have, it's too late to do anything about it. The invitations were sent two weeks ago. No one can be added to the list now without knowing they were an after-thought." She unrolled one curler experimentally. Her hair was still damp, so she rolled it back up again. "My gifts are already arriving."

"I know. I looked in the guest room on my way in here. You can barely see the bedspread for the pile. You certainly won't need to buy towels for a while."

"Tell me about it! There's every color in the world in there. I'm never going to give towels for a wedding again."

"You should do what I did. Set some of them aside and use those as gifts when your friends get married."

"I couldn't do that. What if I gave them back to whoever gave them to me in the first place? No, I'll exchange them for something I really want."

"I drove by your house this morning. Ryan was there cutting the lawn."

Karen smiled and curled her feet under her. "Isn't that sweet? We're going to be so happy together. Don't you just love that house?"

"It's a nice starter house."

"A starter house?" Karen put her head to one side as she looked at her sister. "What does that mean?"

"It's the one you start with. Certainly you don't expect to stay in that house for the rest of your life?"

"Well, of course not." Karen hadn't thought about it at all. "Mother and Daddy have lived in this house all our lives."

"Yes, but it's certainly not the one they started with as newlyweds." Joyce laughed at the notion. "Mother says she wouldn't mind moving to something nicer, but it's just too much trouble."

Karen looked around the room. "I like this house."

"So do I, considering it's so old. Personally I would rather have something new. I can't see moving into a house that's older than I am." She laughed as if the idea were ludicrous. "Did I tell you that Todd and I are buying the property in that new addition behind the mall?"

"That's great! So you've decided to build after all?"

"That way I can have a house exactly the way I want it. The lot is near here, as well. Now that Mother and Daddy are growing older, one of us should live close to them."

"My house is just a few blocks away."

"I know," Joyce said with patience, "but that's your starter house. Remember? Who knows where you may end up by the time they need us?"

"You're smart to think so far ahead," Karen said. "None of this ever occurred to me."

"That's because I'm the oldest. It's my place to think about these things."

"You're lucky Todd doesn't mind. Some husbands wouldn't want to live so close to their in-laws."

Joyce smiled at her and winked. "I didn't actually tell him where the lot was until I was certain I wanted it. By then, he could hardly say no."

Karen's eyes widened. "What if he had hated the idea? What would you have done, once your heart was set on that particular lot?"

Joyce shrugged. "Todd lets me do pretty much whatever I please. He's really more interested in business and golf than in where we live. We decided a long time ago that he would take care of supporting us and I would see that we have a nice home for entertaining."

"You do that so well." Karen sighed. "I'll never learn how to do it. I don't have any self-confidence."

"You just need experience. Mother and I will teach you."

Karen lay back on the bed, and the rollers in her head poked at her scalp. "Do you think I'm anything at all like Mother?"

"Of course you are. We both look like her."

"No, I mean do you think I'll ever learn to handle my house the way you and Mother manage yours? You seem to do it so effortlessly. I have trouble remembering how to do place cards and when to send bread-and-butter notes or invitations. I know Mother taught me the same things she taught you, but I can't remember all of it."

"We aren't going to wash our hands of you just because you're getting married. We'll see each other practically every day and can talk on the phone as often as we like. If you have a question, you have only to ask one of us. It will be easier than you think."

Karen wasn't so sure. She was painfully aware of the fact that she wasn't as self-sufficient as Chelsea or as clever as Joyce about organizing her life. "Chelsea can help, too."

Joyce was quiet for a minute. "Karen, is it a good idea to be with Chelsea so often?"

"What do you mean? We've been friends forever. She's my maid of honor. Naturally I see a lot of her."

"Yes, but she did date Ryan, and you told me once that he seemed to like her better than he did you."

Karen sat up. "I was wrong about that, obviously. Besides, I trust them. Ryan loves me, and Chelsea wouldn't do anything behind my back."

Joyce didn't look convinced. "I'm sure you'd be the best judge of that."

"If you knew them as well as I do, you'd see how silly it is to suggest such a thing."

"I'm sure you're right. Mother and I just find it odd."

"Chelsea and I have discussed it, and she doesn't find it awkward. Neither does Ryan. I think I was wrong about the way they felt about each other." She smiled shyly. "Ryan certainly makes it clear that he wants me."

Joyce gave her a disapproving look. "I don't want to hear about it, I'm sure."

Karen tried not to blush. She never knew when she was making a social blunder. "I don't mean he's pressuring me to . . . you know . . . do anything before the wedding. He's not like that." Unbidden she remembered Ryan and Chelsea had done far more than kiss on at least one occasion. She didn't meet Joyce's eyes.

"Let me tell you something, little sister. Husbands are only men, and they can be led around by the nose if you know when to say 'no' and stick by it."

Karen stared at her. "You mean you refuse to sleep with Todd if he doesn't let you have your way? People really do that?"

"I wouldn't have put it quite like that, but yes. They're just overgrown boys. We have to look out for them."

"Not me. I could never tell Ryan what to do. He's so much smarter than I am in some ways."

Joyce frowned at her. "He's no such thing! Just because he's a man, you think he's got a corner on the brains market? No way. He's not from our crowd and if you'll forgive me for saying so, I don't think his family has had money for long. You can just tell."

Karen didn't answer. She knew Ryan's family had very little money at all and didn't pretend to have. He had worked summers to earn enough to put himself through school, but she didn't want anyone in her family to know about that. Karen rather liked the idea of making their own fortune, but she knew Joyce and Mother wouldn't see it that way.

Joyce nodded decisively. "It will be up to you to boost Ryan up the ladder. I've done the same for Todd. Do you think he was at all interested in the company before we married? Not a bit! He wanted to open his own CPA practice! Do you have any idea how long it would have taken him to get where he is today? Dallas is crawling with CPAs."

"Ryan is definitely interested in working in Daddy's business. He had applied for a job there before we were engaged. He understands everything there is to know about computers." Karen smiled proudly. "He's so smart, Joyce! I can't wait for you to get to know him better."

"The main thing is for him to make you happy." Joyce studied her polished nails. "And the best way for him to do that, is to be successful. Don't worry about it. Between Daddy looking out for him at work and us teaching you what to do socially, he won't be able to fail."

"Thank you, Joyce. I'm so glad you're going to help me." Karen decided she wasn't going to worry so often about her ability to handle her future. Someone had always been there to help her, and someone always would. It wasn't as if she had to manage on her own. "Let's go update the list of my gifts. Did you see the silver tray Aunt Eunice sent?"

As they left the room, Karen found she was no longer worrying.

Chapter Five

"Be still, Karen," Chelsea admonished for the tenth time. "I'll never finish your hair at this rate."

"Yes, do sit still," Cecilia Baker told her daughter. "We're running late as it is."

"They won't start without me," Karen said as she tried to keep from wriggling. Since they had arrived at the church, she had been a bundle of nerves.

"Don't be flippant," Cecilia scolded. "This is your wedding day. You should be less frivolous. This is a tremendous step you're taking."

Chelsea glanced at Karen's mother in the mirror. Karen had said her mother had expressed some doubts over her marrying Ryan. Knowing the Bakers as she did, Chelsea would have thought Cecilia would be thrilled over having her last daughter marry a man with Ryan's potential.

As if to explain her lack of patience, Cecilia said, "You're my baby. I can't believe you've already grown up."

Karen stood and hugged her mother. "Now don't start crying. You'll run your makeup. It's not as if I'm going halfway around the world. I'll only be on Sandhurst Street. I'll still see you every day."

"It won't be the same."

Chelsea drew Karen back to the stool. "If you don't sit down, you'll be late as always. It's probably bad luck or something to be late on your wedding day."

Karen smiled at Chelsea in the mirror. "Can you make me look beautiful, Chel?"

"You're already beautiful. I'm trying to make you look as if your hair is combed." Chelsea lifted a lock of Karen's pale blond hair and started teasing it into the bouffant style Karen preferred.

"I should have cut it."

"I told you that days ago," Cecilia said. "Didn't I tell you to make an appointment at the beauty shop?"

"I knew Chelsea would be here to do it for me." Karen looked at her reflection. She wore the white underwear she had purchased for this day, as well as the lacy silk slip made to go under her wedding gown. "I'm going to break out in hives! I just know it."

"No, you won't. Calm down and stop being so nervous." Chelsea combed Karen's hair unmercifully. "And stop moving around so much. I can't keep up with you."

"I hate my hair," Karen suddenly exclaimed. "I never realized it before, but it's hopeless. I'm going to cut it as soon as we're back from our honeymoon."

Chelsea kept her face impassive. She was trying hard not to think about the honeymoon. "Ryan likes long hair."

Cecilia glanced at Chelsea's long hair, then said, "He'll get used to it short. At your age, it's more appropriate. I'll make the appointment myself."

The door opened and Joyce hurried in. "People are already starting to arrive. Why, Karen, you're not dressed yet!"

"I'm not letting her off this stool until her hair is combed," Chelsea said with determination. She started brushing Karen's hair into a smoothly rounded style that curled up at her shoulders. The style was out of date, but it was flattering and Karen had been resistant to changing it.

"I hate my hair," she now told Joyce. "Does it look just awful?"

"Of course not. It looks exactly as it always does." Joyce went to the rack hanging at the end of the dressing room and got the wedding garter. "Here. At least put this on."

"Chelsea has to help me with that. She's the maid of honor."

"I'll never know why you were so insistent on having only one attendant," Cecilia said as she went to fluff the netting on the veil. "Joyce had a church full."

Karen's eyes met Chelsea's in the mirror. "I only want Chelsea." They exchanged a smile.

"My feelings weren't hurt in the least," Joyce said. "Even if I did include you in my wedding, Karen."

"There," Chelsea said with relief. "Hand me the hair spray and close your eyes."

She enveloped Karen's head in a nimbus of spray while Karen fanned frantically to find air.

Chelsea took the garter from Joyce and knelt to slip it over Karen's foot and up her leg to the knee. "Hurry," she said as Karen tiptoed over to see the garter in the short mirror. "I think I hear the music starting."

"It can't be! Joyce, run and see what's going on!" Cecilia went to the rack and started unfastening the wedding gown.

Joyce was back before they finished slipping the gown over Karen's head. "The music *has* started! I told you you'd be late!" She helped her mother and Chelsea pull the gown onto her sister.

"You're been eating too much!" Cecilia exclaimed as she tried to work the zipper up the track. "You've gained weight!"

Chelsea saw Karen's precarious confidence start to crumble. "I'll do that," she said quickly. "You straighten her skirt. Karen, hold your stomach in." She caught the zipper in her strong hands and pulled it up. "There. It fits perfectly."

Karen thanked her with a look. Chelsea wished she had been able to ban Cecilia and Joyce from the dressing room. They made Karen nervous under the best of circumstances. Karen's feelings of inferiority had certainly been fostered by the women in her family.

Chelsea got on tiptoe to put the veil on Karen's head. Karen then held it in place while she and Joyce spread the flowing net over the bride's back and shoulders. Karen was trembling so much the seed pearls and tiny silk flowers bobbed and nodded in the veil.

"Do I look all right?" she asked. She stared at her reflection in the mirror.

"Why didn't we think to bring a full-length mirror?" Joyce asked in exasperation.

"With the money we've given this church over the years, you'd think they would buy one," Cecilia complained.

"You look beautiful," Chelsea said.

Karen tried to smile, but she looked close to tears.

There was an impatient knock at the door, and Fulton Baker stuck his head in. "Aren't you ready yet? They want to seat the family."

"I'm coming," Cecilia and Joyce said, almost in unison.

"How do I look, Daddy?"

Fulton seemed to see her for the first time. For a moment he didn't say anything. Then he turned away as if to hide his emotion. "You look beautiful, sweetheart." To his wife and his other daughter, he added, "Come on."

Karen turned to Chelsea and took her hand. "It seems as if I ought to say so much, but I can't think how to put it. You've always been so good to me."

Chelsea found her eyes filling. "Don't do this or we'll both be crying." She thrust the white prayer book into Karen's arms. "This is borrowed, the garter is blue, the dress is new. What am I forgetting?"

"Something old." Karen's eyes widened. "I don't have anything old!"

Chelsea struggled to get her ring off her finger. "Here. This is old. It belonged to my grandmother."

"Come on!" Fulton said sternly. "We have to get down the aisle."

Chelsea and Karen hurried from the room and down the short hallway to the vestibule. As soon as they saw Karen coming, the ushers seated Ryan's mother and father, then

Cecilia. Joyce had already gone down to sit beside Todd and her son.

As soon as Cecilia was in the pew, the door beside the rail opened. Ryan and Troy took their places in front of the congregation.

Karen made a sound like a rabbit in a trap. Chelsea glanced at her over her shoulder and gave her an encouraging smile. She knew Karen was so shy, a walk down the aisle with everyone watching her was almost torture. Then the music grew louder and swept into the passage Karen had chosen for her entrance.

Chelsea looked down the aisle and saw Ryan watching her. For a dreadful moment she didn't think she would be able to go through with this. Then Fulton prodded her in the back and she stepped forward with a show of more confidence than she felt.

The aisle seemed a mile long. The Bakers were members of one of the largest churches in Dallas, and the entire congregation seemed to be in attendance. Chelsea felt all eyes turn to regard her, and an uncharacteristic shyness nearly overwhelmed her. Then she saw Ryan again and her courage returned. She was doing this for his happiness. Ryan's and Karen's.

She took her place opposite Ryan and Troy. For a dangerously long moment her eyes met his. Then he glimpsed the white satin of Karen's dress and his eyes turned back up the aisle.

Chelsea noticed Karen didn't look to right or left, only at Ryan. She, too, was drawing her courage from him. Her bouquet trembled visibly and she seemed pale enough to faint, but her steps didn't falter as she came to the altar. Fulton's face was waxy from suppressed emotion, and Chelsea wondered again if this marriage was as welcomed by Karen's family as she had assumed. Or perhaps Fulton, like Cecilia, was only reluctant to give up their remaining daughter.

The minister stepped forward and asked who brought this woman to be wed. Fulton made the correct response and put Karen's hand in Ryan's. For a moment he looked down into Karen's eyes, then turned away and took his seat beside Cecilia.

Chelsea only heard bits and pieces of the ceremony. Her heart was breaking and that claimed most of her attention. At the proper moment she took Karen's bouquet and gave her the ring she was to place on Ryan's finger. Karen's hands felt icy, and Chelsea thought she was going to drop the ring before she could get it onto his finger. As she made the responses, Karen's voice was wavering and almost inaudible; Ryan's was deep and sure.

Then it was over. Ryan lifted Karen's veil and kissed her gently. She ducked her head and smiled, overcome with shyness.

The organist broke into the triumphant march that would carry the newly wed couple up the aisle. Chelsea was almost afraid her own legs wouldn't propel her forward, but she met Troy at the center of the aisle and they followed Ryan and Karen up and out of the sanctuary.

When Karen and Ryan cut the first piece of wedding cake, Chelsea was glad the flash of cameras gave her a reason to blink and look away. Each tenderly fed the other a bite of cake; then they grinned self-consciously.

After most of the guests had been served cake and punch, Ryan removed Karen's garter and tossed it toward the unmarried males from both families. A young man Chelsea had never met caught it and was pounded on the back by his friends.

By refusing to think, Chelsea found she was able to get through the reception. Because it was to be held in the church hall, there was to be no dancing and only cake and punch were to be served. Chelsea kept busy, making certain that Wendy Johnston, who was serving the punch, had plenty of clean cups, and that the cousins who were cutting the cake had a supply of saucers. This wasn't really her job, but she had to keep busy.

The wedding cake was a tower of snowy perfection. Cecilia and Joyce had been in favor of one featuring a fountain and stairways connecting satellite cakes, but Karen had stood firm on this point. The resulting cake seemed to be made entirely of lace and flowers and was exactly the design Karen had told Chelsea she had dreamed of having since she was a little girl.

Chelsea had done all she could to be certain this wedding was what Karen wanted and not what Joyce wished she had done differently at her own wedding, or what Cecilia would do if she were the bride. It hadn't been easy. Chelsea was certain she had offended Cecilia and Joyce on several occasions, but Karen was delighted with the result and that was what Chelsea had intended.

Once, she made the mistake of looking directly at Ryan and found him watching her, his expression unreadable. She quickly looked away and pretended to be engrossed in conversation with one of the Baker cousins from out of state.

After what seemed like forever, Joyce found Chelsea and told her that Karen was on her way to the dressing room to change into her going-away suit. Chelsea hurried to help her.

Cecilia had already unzipped the wedding dress and was helping Karen out of it. Chelsea hung it carefully on the padded hanger and straightened the fabric so it wouldn't wrinkle.

"I'll take it to the cleaners first thing on Monday," Cecilia was saying to Karen. "I want to have it sealed so it won't yellow. Someday your daughter will wear it."

Karen laughed at the idea. "Talk about counting your chickens before they hatch!"

"Literally," Chelsea said with a grin.

Cecilia didn't find any humor in the comment. "It's an expensive gown. It would be a shame to wear it once and let it rot."

"I agree," Chelsea said with a smile at Karen.

Karen touched the gown wistfully. "My daughter. Someday I may have a daughter!"

"Get dressed," Cecilia ordered. "You can waste more

time than anyone I've ever known. No one can leave until you do."

Karen buttoned the ivory silk blouse and the powder blue suit she had selected. This wasn't an outfit Chelsea would have chosen, but Cecilia and Joyce had taken Karen shopping for it. The lines of the suit were more suited to the bone-slender figures of mother and sister than to Karen's rounded curves.

"Do I look all right?" Karen asked Chelsea nervously.

"You're beautiful."

The friends hugged, and for a moment Chelsea thought they both would cry.

"Are you okay?" Karen whispered.

Chelsea nodded before she could trust her voice. "I'm fine. Be happy, Karen."

"I will be."

Cecilia unwrapped Karen's arms from Chelsea's shoulders. "Stop that before you wrinkle your suit. There! See? You've wrinkled your blouse already."

Karen tucked it more tightly into her skirt's waistband, then ducked to see herself in the mirror. She patted her hair and grabbed her bag. She stood uncertainly as if she weren't too sure she was ready to embark on her new life. "I guess I'm ready," she said in a small voice.

"Hurry up. Everyone is waiting." Cecilia handed the bouquet to Karen and went to the door as if this was no more momentous an occasion than any other day.

Again Chelsea wondered if Karen's family was as fond of Ryan as Karen seemed to believe.

They went back to the reception hall, and Chelsea clasped her hands to keep them from trembling as Joyce marshaled the unmarried women in the wedding party. Karen stood on the stairs to the vestibule and glanced back over her shoulder to take aim. Then she turned her back and tossed the flowers into the air. Chelsea automatically put her hands up and the flowers landed in them. She stared down at them, not believing her eyes. Lifting her gaze, she saw Karen smiling at her and found she could return the smile.

With the others, Chelsea got a bag of birdseed—in lieu of rice—and went to toss it on Karen and Ryan as they left the church. Karen was laughing and shielding her face, and Ryan had his arm protectively around her as they ran to their car. Troy and the others had decorated it with shaving cream and shoe polish. A pom-pom of crepe paper in Karen's wedding colors adorned the antennae, while someone had tied tin cans together and attached the string to the back bumper. As they drove away, Chelsea heard the rattling of pebbles in the hub caps.

"They looked so happy." The voice came from beside her.

Chelsea turned to see Wendy Johnston, her hand in Troy's, her face wistful. She looked back at the car, now disappearing around a corner. "Yes. They did."

"I guess we'll be next," Troy said with a loving look at Wendy.

"Maybe not." Wendy smiled at Chelsea. "Chelsea caught the bouquet."

"Then she'd better hurry," Troy teased. "We've already set the date, and it's not that far away."

Chelsea smiled at them. "I'm so happy for you."

"I wanted to be a June bride," Wendy said as they went back into the church, "but this is the last Saturday in June and naturally I wanted to be in Karen's wedding. We've set our date for July the fifteenth."

"So soon? How will you ever be ready in time?" Chelsea wanted to talk about anything that would keep her thoughts away from Ryan and Karen.

"I've been planning and making arrangements for the longest time. You've just been too busy with Karen's wedding to have noticed. You'll be getting your invitation in a day or two."

Chelsea saw Cecilia and Joyce standing with their husbands and used them as an excuse to leave Wendy and

Troy. She had heard all the wedding plans she could handle for a while.

"Should I start cleaning the reception hall?" she asked Cecilia. "I don't think there's much that needs to be done. It will save having to come back and do it tomorrow."

Cecilia looked at her as if she had lost her mind. "We've paid the church janitor to do that. No, our work is finished."

"It went well, I think," Chelsea said.

Joyce nodded coolly. "As well as can be expected. You'd think Karen could have been on time for once in her life."

Fulton looked as if some of his color were coming back now that the wedding was history. "Ryan seems to be a good boy. I just hope she'll be happy."

"Of course she will," Cecilia said rather sharply. "What a thing to bring up at a wedding!"

Her husband gave her a look of dislike, but didn't comment.

Todd was wrestling with his namesake and trying to look as if the boy were only playing instead of deliberately misbehaving. "Are we ready to go? Todd, Jr., is wearing me out."

Joyce seemed aware of her son for the first time. "I suppose so. There's no sense in being the last to leave."

"I'll stay behind until everyone is gone, to be sure the church is locked," Chelsea volunteered. Though not eager to do so, she thought it only proper that someone stay, and none of the Bakers seemed willing.

"That's fine," Cecilia said. She finally gave Chelsea a smile. "Don't be a stranger, now that Karen is gone. You're still welcome in our home at any time."

"Thank you." This was more than Chelsea had expected from Cecilia. On more than one occasion, she had had the distinct impression that Karen's mother didn't particularly like her. "You know where my apartment is. Please drop by." At once she felt foolish. She couldn't imagine Cecilia or Joyce coming to a garage apartment for a chat.

At least, she thought, she had extended the invitation. Whether or not they accepted it was up to them.

After the Bakers left, the other guests didn't linger. One of the Baker cousins hung back and helped Chelsea clear the church. Thomas was from the Mississippi branch of the family, and Chelsea had known him slightly for several years.

"I'm glad we came to the wedding," he said as they checked the sanctuary to be certain it was empty. "Otherwise, I would have missed seeing you."

Chelsea smiled up at him. "You graduate from Old Miss in what, two years?"

"Three. I had to drop some of my courses."

She turned off the lights and closed the doors on the darkness. Thomas followed her to the dressing room.

"My parents have gone back to the hotel. Mom had one of her headaches and had to leave early. I wanted to see Karen and Ryan off, so I told them I'd take a cab. Do you know where the phone is?"

"I can give you a ride. Where are they staying?"

"At the Woodard Arms."

Chelsea looked around the room. A few coat hangers were lying on the floor. She picked them up and used a tissue to wipe the face powder from the dresser below the mirror.

"They looked happy," Thomas said as he followed her about. "Karen is so bashful, I didn't think she'd have a large wedding. I guess Aunt Cecilia wouldn't agree to anything less."

Chelsea didn't answer.

Thomas found the box Karen's corsage had come in and tossed it into the wastebasket as if he were on the basketball court. "Two points!" He grinned at her. "The other reason my parents left without me was that I told them I wanted to talk to you."

She looked at him more closely. "Why?"

"Because I like you and almost never get to speak to you."

"I'm really not at my conversational best tonight," Chelsea said as she went to the door and turned out the light.

"I thought we might go out for a drink."

"Are you twenty-one? That's the legal drinking age in Texas."

"I have a fake ID. But I look older than I am. I've only been carded once. How about it?"

The minister was coming toward them down the hall. He smiled and said, "You needn't stay. I have to check the lights and doors before I can leave."

She looked up at Thomas. "I'm parked out back."

Together they went to her car, and Chelsea drove them to a small bar she had frequented in college. The music was loud, the smoke thicker than she liked, but the crowd was her age and she felt safe here. It also had the reputation of being a place that didn't check IDs too closely. Thomas paid for their drinks, and she sipped her gin and tonic as she watched the couples on the small dance floor.

"Where do you think they are by now?" he asked casually. "Karen and Ryan, I mean."

"I have no idea. Let's dance."

"I'm not very good at dancing."

She faced him squarely. "What are you good at?"

Thomas grinned slowly. "I can't show you here."

Chelsea paused. She had never let a man pick her up like this and knew exactly what Thomas was hinting at. One-night stands had never interested her. But what did she have to lose? "My apartment is a few blocks from here."

He took her hand. "Let's go."

On the drive to her apartment, Chelsea regretted having invited him. She liked Thomas, but she had never thought of him in a romantic way. Certainly she hadn't encouraged him sexually. But the man she loved had just married her best friend, and she wasn't up to enforcing her standards tonight.

When they were inside, Chelsea made them another drink while Thomas looked around her apartment. Her bed was in the main room, along with what little other furniture she owned. She had draped apple green and white fabric over the windows instead of curtains, and the world was shut out by Venetian blinds. The hardwood floor was bare except for a braided rug in shades of green and blue; the walls were covered by her paintings.

"You do nice work," Thomas said as she handed him his drink.

"Thank you." She refrained from pointing out that "nice" was tantamount to "cute" in her vocabulary and that neither were compliments. She knew her work was good. Thomas's opinion wasn't relevant.

"What's in there?" he asked, gesturing toward the closed door.

"The dungeon." She smiled as she opened the door. "Actually, it's where I paint. I love to paint, but I'm not fond of smelling oil and turpentine constantly." The odors drifted past, and he wrinkled his nose.

"It's pretty strong, isn't it?"

"I'm used to it." She closed the door again.

Thomas stepped up to her and put his arms around her. Almost as if she were watching it happen to another person, Chelsea saw him bend and kiss her. She kissed him back. She felt nothing, so she kissed him again. Thomas seemed inspired even if she didn't.

She finished her drink more quickly than would have been prudent under other circumstances, and this time his kisses began to stir her. As his hands roamed over her, she stepped out of her shoes. Thomas reached behind her and lowered the zipper on her dress. For a moment Chelsea considered changing her mind. He would leave if she said he should. But she didn't want to be alone. Not even if it meant having sex with a man she didn't love or particularly want. At least someone would have his arms around her. For a while she could forget.

Chelsea shrugged out of her dress and let it puddle about her feet. Thomas was awkward so she unfastened her bra and tossed it aside. He put his hands in her panty hose and pushed them down.

Naked, Chelsea drew back the bedspread and lay on the sheets. Thomas shucked off his own clothes and was soon beside her.

His bare skin touching hers finally sparked some excitement in Chelsea. She ran her hands over him, trying to awaken her senses and to shut out everything except what was happening. Thomas kissed her lips, then her breasts. Slowly Chelsea's body started to respond.

When he came into her, she murmured in eagerness. This was what she needed. Something, anything, to make her feel alive and not a mere husk. She moved with Thomas, trying to lose her thoughts and the cold loneliness that still haunted her.

Thomas proved to be an energetic lover if not an accomplished one. Long before she was ready to reach her climax, he shuddered and collapsed on top of her. For a while he lay like someone dead, then he rolled to one side.

Chelsea wondered what he would say if she asked him to give her the same satisfaction.

"That was great!" he said between breaths.

Until he spoke Chelsea hadn't realized they hadn't exchanged a single word since their first kiss. Instead of chasing away her loneliness, the sex made her feel more isolated than ever.

"I guess I ought to go," he said at last. "I don't want my parents to wonder about me being gone all night."

"No. We wouldn't want that." She wondered if Thomas was staying in their room. If not how would they know when, or if, he came back to the hotel? "I'll call you a cab."

"That would be great. Thanks." Now that it was over, he seemed ill at ease.

Chelsea was glad he would be on his way back to Mississippi early the next morning. At least she wouldn't have to see him again soon. Tonight had been a mistake, and she was eager to have it all behind her.

Using the bedspread as a sarong, Chelsea got up and

went to the phone, while Thomas braved the smells of paint and went through to the bathroom. Chelsea then curled up in a chair and waited. In a few minutes she heard the cab pull up in the drive. "Your ride is here," she called out.

Thomas came back into the room and shrugged into his suit coat. He wadded his tie up and put it in his pocket. At last he looked at her. "Thanks, Chelsea. This has been great. I'll never forget tonight."

"Neither will I. You'd better hurry, or the cab may leave."

He kissed her on the forehead and left. Then she went to the door and automatically turned the locks. At least, she told herself, she now knew what wouldn't ease her broken heart. Just any man wouldn't do, not when she was in love with someone.

She went into the painting room and turned on the lights. Her canvases stood there in varying stages of completion. Slowly, as if they were the work of some stranger, she walked among them and viewed them dispassionately. They were all good. Some were even better than that.

Chelsea went back into the main room and tossed the spread back on the rumpled bed. She pulled on a pair of paint-stained jeans cut-offs and a tee shirt. Getting back into the bed she had shared with Thomas didn't appeal to her, and she was wide awake any way.

She went back to her easel and started painting. She worked with sure, quick strokes. As the painting began to unfold, she finally found the surcease she had wanted. For hours she painted, not stopping to rest or to think. When the morning light brightened the windows she stopped and let her brush hang from her tired fingers. The seemingly endless night was over.

Her body ached from painting all night, but until this moment she hadn't been aware of it. Chelsea cleaned the brushes and went back to the bed. She tossed her paint-smeared clothes on the vinyl squares that designated the kitchen floor and lay down. The air was cool on her naked body, but she was finally tired enough to sleep. She was even tired enough not to dream.

As her mind wound down, Chelsea told herself this was the answer. She had to put all her energy into her art, to become as good as she possibly could be. Her career would demand large chunks of time, but in art she could express herself, resolve her loneliness. Someday she would be good enough, rich enough and famous enough, so that her broken heart wouldn't matter.

On this resolve, Chelsea finally slept.

Chapter Six

Even though the house was small by her family's standards, Karen loved her new home. It was rose-colored brick with white trim and dark green shutters on the front windows, and it sat on a square of lawn that had been landscaped by its former owners. The neighborhood had been part of a development, and of the five floor-plan variations, Karen's house had the largest and, in her opinion, the nicest.

The place had three bedrooms and a den as well as a living room and a separate dining room. Ryan had argued that it was larger than they needed, but Karen had held firm in her decision to buy it. She was positive that he would be glad in the long run. She had often heard her father say that real-estate investment was a smart move.

Karen discovered she enjoyed working in the flower garden that curved with the front walk and then wrapped around the house. Although she knew next to nothing about plants, she liked to buy the colorful flowers that abounded in the Dallas nurseries and to experiment with planting them.

"Karen, what on earth are you doing?" Cecilia asked as she and Fulton came around the house. "I've been ringing your front doorbell for the last ten minutes."

"Have you? I didn't hear anyone drive up." She got up from the ground and self-consciously wiped her grimy palms on her jeans. As usual, her parents were dressed as if they had just come from some important meeting. Karen couldn't imagine her mother ever getting down on her knees and digging in the dirt.

"What are you doing? Planting more flowers?"

"I found these this morning. Aren't they pretty? The tag says they need full sun, but I thought I'd try them around here. Do you think sun for half a day will be enough?"

"I have no idea. I'll send Juan over to take care of them. He can work miracles with gardens."

"But I want to do this myself." Karen looked doubtfully at her mother and then back at the garden. "I guess he could do a better job, couldn't he?"

"Of course. It's what we pay him to do." Cecilia gave the garden a dismissive wave. "Let's go inside where it's cool. I detest Dallas summers."

"So do I," Karen said quickly. "Spring is my favorite time of year."

Fulton opened the back door for them, and Karen went to the sink to wash the soil from her hands as her parents went into the living room. She caught her reflection in a mirror and remembered that her hair was drawn back in an unattractive ponytail. With a groan she pulled it free and tried unsuccessfully to pat it into order. Of all the days for her parents to drop by, this was one of the worst.

She stuffed her shirttail into her jeans as she hurried into the living room. Cecilia looked her over from head to toe and didn't smile. "I could go change if you don't mind waiting," Karen said uncertainly. She had intended to work in the garden all afternoon.

"We won't be here long." Cecilia leaned forward to pick up the crystal owl on the chrome-and-glass coffee table. "This is pretty. Where did you get it?"

"Ryan bought it for my birthday. I know it's not until tomorrow, but I just couldn't wait to open it. Don't you just love it?"

"It's nice." Cecilia put the owl back down.

"Ryan is working out well in the company," Fulton said. "I'm impressed with the boy."

Karen relaxed and gave him a smile. "I knew he would. He's so smart! There's nothing Ryan can't do."

Fulton smiled indulgently. "At this rate, he'll work his way up the ladder in no time. Someday he and Todd will run the company."

"I hope you don't intend to retire anytime soon," Cecilia said. "I'm not ready to have you around the house all the time."

"No, no. I'm not going to retire for years yet. And when I do, you'll seldom see me. I'm going to spend all my time on the golf course." He smiled as if he considered this amusing banter. None of the Bakers was gifted with a sense of humor.

"I think it would be fun to be retired," Karen put in. "You wouldn't have to work all day and could do whatever you please."

"I leave that up to your mother," Fulton said. "I'd rather stay busy."

"If you tried to do half what I do every day, you'd collapse from exhaustion," Cecilia shot back. "To hear you talk, I sit around all day and do nothing."

"I'm glad you came by," Karen said quickly. She could sense tension building, and she had always been the peacemaker in the family. "I was going to come over to see you later."

"Actually, we've brought you a birthday present," Cecilia told her. "It's out front."

"My present is out front? On the porch, you mean?" Karen went to the door and opened it. "I don't see anything."

"Look in the street," Fulton called out. "It's red."

Karen's eyes widened. "Not a car! You bought me a car?"

Her parents came to stand with her in the doorway. "Not just a car. It's your first BMW. Now that you're grown, it's time you had something respectable. Besides, your old car is starting to get some miles on it. We thought you'd like to trade it for this one." Fulton put a hand on

Karen's shoulder, a rare gesture of affection for him. "I hope you like the color."

"I love red!"

"It looks rather flashy to me," Cecilia said, "but the salesman says that's the most popular color this year."

"A BMW! I can't believe it!" Karen crossed the lawn and bent to look in the car's windows. "My very own beemer!"

"If you'll give me the keys to your car, I'll drive it to the dealership. We left our car there."

"You know your father," Cecilia said. "He loves to be dramatic."

"I wouldn't say that." Fulton frowned at her. "I just didn't see any sense in driving both cars over, then driving Karen's back. This is more logical."

Karen opened the car door. "It smells so new!"

"It should. I ordered it specially for you. Look at the glove compartment."

Karen touched the interlacing initials. "You had it monogrammed! Oh, Daddy, this is the most perfect gift I've ever had!"

"What about me?" Cecilia asked. "I chose the interior colors, after all."

"It's simply perfect!" Karen hugged them both. "I've never had such a lovely gift. I can't wait to show it to Ryan."

"He may be late today. We've had some problems with one of our biggest clients." Fulton looked thoughtful as he added, "I left it in his hands. I want to see how he handles it."

"Is that fair? I mean, you know what you're doing, Daddy, but Ryan hasn't been there long."

"I know. But if he's to run the company someday, I have to be certain he's capable of working under pressure." He smiled benevolently. "Besides, I had to pick up the car or your mother would never have let me hear the end of it."

Karen sat in the BMW and ran her hand over the glove-soft leather upholstery. "I love it! Ryan will be so pleased."

"Just remember, we bought it for you. Don't let him take it to work and leave you with that relic he drives," Cecilia cautioned. "We want you to have reliable transportation, and this will look so much nicer when we attend functions."

"Thank you, Mother." Karen couldn't believe how fortunate she was to have such generous parents. They had always equated love with money and this proved they loved her a great deal.

"Whose car is that in the drive?" Ryan asked when he came in from work. His tie was loose, and he looked tired.

"Guess!"

He kissed her on the forehead. "I can't guess. We don't have company, do we?" he asked in a whisper. "I'm too tired to think. You wouldn't believe the kind of day I've had."

"It's mine!"

For a minute Ryan stared at her. "You bought a car?"

"It's not just a car," she said in imitation of her father. "It's a BMW. Mother and Daddy bought it for my birthday." She went past him and out to the driveway.

Ryan hesitated, but tossed his suit coat and briefcase onto the entry table. "Karen, you can't accept a car as a gift."

"Don't be silly. Of course I can. I already have." She put her head to one side and smiled up at him. "Do you want to go for a drive?"

Ryan walked around it. "This is a top-of-the-line model. Do you have any idea what a car like this costs?"

"I could hardly ask them that. It's a gift. For my birthday," she repeated. "You don't seem pleased."

He came to her and draped his arm over her shoulders. "Honey, try to understand my position. I can't afford to buy you anything like this. Hell, we probably can't even afford the insurance on a car this expensive."

"Of course we can. We have to have good transportation."

"There's nothing wrong with your old car. It's only four years old and in perfect condition."

"No, it's not. The air conditioner is acting up. Besides, Daddy took that car as a trade-in for this one."

Ryan looked at her, then went to peer in the garage door. As she had said, the car was gone. He tried to control his temper. "Karen, this is too much. Don't I have a say in what cars we drive?"

"You're just being silly. My beemer is a gift. You don't have to pay for it."

"But I want to buy our cars. I want us to decide, together, when we'll trade in cars and what kind we'll buy. Do you know what the insurance will run on this car?"

"No, I don't, and I think you're being mean. Mother and Daddy ordered the beemer especially for me. As far as that goes, they bought my old car, too. That gives them the right to trade it if they please."

"Not if the car is in your name. Whose name is this one under?"

"Mine, of course. Otherwise it wouldn't be a gift, now would it?" She frowned up at him and stepped away.

"I'm going to call your father and discuss this with him."

"You can't do that!"

"Why not?"

"He'll think we aren't appreciative. You'll hurt his feelings."

Ryan didn't know what to do. He wasn't looking forward to an altercation with his new father-in-law and boss. He had noticed that the Bakers weren't that fond of him, but he had hoped to have reasonably smooth relations with them. "This makes my gift look pretty small, doesn't it?"

"No," Karen said hastily. "I love that little owl. I put it

on the coffee table so every one can see and admire it. Mother said it's very pretty, and you know what good taste she has."

Ryan circled the car. This was more than a mere gift. It said that Karen's parents knew he couldn't support their daughter in the way they wanted her to be supported and that they were going to do things their way in spite of him. He wondered if he was misjudging them because he was so tired. "I guess this was just too big a surprise. You caught me off guard."

Karen came to him and hugged him. "I knew you'd see it my way after you thought about it for a while. And guess what! I've made something special for dinner. Taco meatballs!"

Ryan had to smile. Karen was trying hard to learn how to cook, but most of her efforts were more inventive than digestible. "Sounds good," he said loyally. "I noticed you were cooking the minute I walked in the door."

"I'd better go in and check on them. We can go for a drive later, if you'd like."

"Okay." He decided it would be more politic to let the matter drop about the car. After all, he knew Fulton wouldn't take it back and Karen would be hurt and disappointed if he made an issue of the gift. All the same, he was resentful.

They went into the house, and Ryan went to the coffee table and picked up the crystal owl. When he'd bought it, he had considered it an expensive gift. It had come from a prestigious jewelry store, and he would be paying for it for months to come. Now it seemed dowdy and ridiculous. He put it back down.

As he crossed the room he called to Karen in the kitchen, "I see you've been planting again. I think you're starting to get the hang of it."

She was silent for a few minutes. "Actually, Juan came over and did that for me. Mother didn't want me getting so hot and dirty when he would do it better anyway. He's going to mow tomorrow."

"I planned to mow the yard on Saturday." Ryan frowned at the neat row of flowers that rimmed the patio. They no longer looked so good to him. "Tell your mother thanks, but no thanks."

"You know I can't do that." A clanging sound came from the kitchen. "I hope you're hungry for jalapeños. I put them in the rice as well."

"I love jalapeños." He had a feeling this was going to be one of their more adventurous meals. Fortunately, he had a strong stomach and enjoyed spicy foods. Karen seemed to put peppers in nearly every dish.

"I asked Chelsea over for dinner. I hope that's okay. She called when I was putting the meatballs in to bake, and I asked her to come and try them."

"That's fine." Ryan was glad he wasn't face to face with Karen when she gave him this news. He was ambiguous about seeing Chelsea these days.

As Karen's best friend, Chelsea was over often, but she usually avoided being there when he was home. This hurt because it seemed to prove that she had never cared for him in the first place. On the other hand, he found himself as drawn to her as he had ever been. Perhaps even more so.

Ryan hated himself for feeling this way. Karen loved him and tried hard to be a good wife. She kept the house spotless and insisted on being the one to pay the bills on the first of the month. She had been adorable when poring over the checkbook and trying to devise a system for filing receipts and records. For the most part she was a perfect wife.

He went to their bedroom and hung up his suit coat, then pulled off his tie. As he undressed, he looked at the bed they shared. Karen was a better wife than she was a lover.

It wasn't a matter of expertise. Karen simply didn't like to make love. She tried to hide it from him, even faked orgasms to please him, but he could see through that and was hurt because she felt it necessary. He had tried to talk to her about it, but the subject embarrassed her so he had given up. After only six weeks of marriage Karen was starting to avoid him in bed.

At first he thought she was really interested in late movies. Then he discovered she was only stalling off bedtime so he would fall asleep before she came to bed. That had really hurt and still did. Ryan had tried everything he could think of to please her, but it wasn't so much a matter of how he did it as that he wanted to do it at all. Karen found lovemaking a turn-off, something to be endured only out of love for him. Lately he seldom tried to initiate it. As a result, she had stopped staying up so late in front of the TV, and Ryan was experiencing a high degree of sexual frustration.

No, he didn't look forward to seeing Chelsea. His memory of her sexuality was all too clear and painful under the circumstances. She had not only enjoyed lovemaking, she had elevated it to an art form.

To get his mind on safer subjects, Ryan dressed in jeans and went into the kitchen to help Karen with dinner.

Chelsea arrived on time and with a plate of sopapillas. "I didn't know what to bring. I guess these will go with anything that has jalapeños in it." She looked at Ryan. "Hello."

"Hi." He reached past Karen and took the plate from Chelsea. "I'll take these into the kitchen."

"I'm afraid it's going to be another disaster," Karen said gloomily. "The meatballs look a little strange."

"They'll taste fine, I'm sure. Let's see them."

They followed Ryan into the kitchen, and he put the sopapillas on the counter. Chelsea and Karen went to the oven and bent to look inside.

"They do look a little odd," Chelsea said carefully. "Is that the size you're supposed to make them?"

"I wasn't sure. I thought if I made them small, the meat would stretch further."

Ryan laughed. "Like cutting a pizza into fourteen slices instead of twelve?"

Chelsea laughed, but Karen only looked puzzled. "Exactly. What's funny about that?"

"Never mind. I'll set the table." Chelsea went to the cabinet where Karen kept the plates and took out three. She opened the drawer beneath and said, "Where's the silverware?"

"I moved it. It's in the drawer by the refrigerator now."

"How can you find anything if you keep rearranging the kitchen?" Chelsea found the knives and forks and went to the oak table.

Ryan got out place mats and set them on the table so Chelsea could put down the plates. The dining-room table, like all the other furniture in the house, was the result of a shopping spree Karen had gone on with her mother and sister. Ryan hadn't received a bill yet, but he was concerned.

"I like the table," Chelsea called to Karen. "Where did you find it?"

"At Bendyll's. It's where Mother and Joyce always shop. They carry such good quality things."

Ryan saw Chelsea's expression as she touched the table top. She, too, knew the prices of the furniture Bendyll's carried.

"Take a good look," he suggested. "Once the bill comes, you may never see it again."

Karen came into the dining room, carrying a bowl of rice. "Don't pay any attention to him. He's been like that ever since he came in from work."

"Did you see the BMW in the driveway?" Ryan asked Chelsea.

"How could I miss it? Whose is it? Joyce's?"

"No, it's mine." Karen smiled as she put the rice on the table. "It's my birthday present."

Chelsea turned to Ryan.

"Don't look at me," he said. "It's from her parents."

"Karen? A BMW? Wasn't that awfully expensive?"

"Oh, for goodness' sake. You sound exactly like Ryan. It probably was, but it's what they wanted to give me. It's not as if they can't afford it."

A small frown puckered Chelsea's forehead. Ryan said, "I'll get the meatballs."

As he left the room, he heard Chelsea whisper, "Karen, are you sure you can afford all this?" He didn't catch Karen's reply.

It hurt Ryan that Chelsea knew they were living beyond their means. He was a proud man, and he wanted to be able to buy anything his wife wanted. If Karen had been willing to wait, they would have acquired these things without his having to worry about payments.

It also bothered him that Karen was determined to compete with her parents and sister in the area of possessions. Not that she didn't have good taste. Every piece of furniture was well chosen and of fine quality. As she said, it would probably outlast them and become heirlooms. But, cost aside, he wasn't sure the style pleased him. The furniture was formal and had little personality, in his opinion. He would have preferred something with more character. Karen didn't understand that.

He put the meatballs in a bowl and carried them back into the dining room. Karen and Chelsea had their heads together, and when he entered they moved apart. He had the distinct impression that Chelsea was telling Karen she was making a mistake in trying to live beyond their means.

"Not that bowl," Karen said as he put it on the table. "Can't you see we're using the ones Mother gave us?"

Ryan hadn't noticed. They had picked out pottery in an old-fashioned floral design, but Cecilia had given them a complete set of rather formal dishes in shades of rust and navy. Ryan thoroughly disliked them, even if they were more masculine than the roses Karen had preferred. "A bowl is a bowl."

"Give it here." Karen laughed in Chelsea's direction. "I have to do everything myself if I want it done right."

Chelsea stared at her as if she couldn't believe she had heard her correctly. Karen hurried out without noticing.

"She has her own ways of doing things."

"Tell me about it. I lived with her for four years." Chelsea moved around the table to the place where she usually sat. She looked as if she wanted to ask something but knew she should mind her business.

Karen came back carrying the bowl that matched the rust and navy dishes. "There now. Let's eat before it gets cold. Otherwise, we may lose our nerve."

Ryan heaped his plate as the food came around the table. Before the marriage, the three of them had found countless things to talk about. Now the silence felt uncomfortable. "How's the painting coming along?" he asked.

"You make her sound like a house painter," Karen said with a laugh. "You're supposed to call them 'canvases.'"

"They're progressing just fine." Chelsea glanced from one to the other, then turned her attention to her plate. "I had an interview with a gallery owner yesterday, and he says I'm promising and probably marketable."

"I'd say you are! I love your canvases." Karen frowned at the idea of anyone not being rapturous over Chelsea's paintings. "You should take them somewhere else."

"He's agreed to hang three of my pictures on consignment. That's more than I've been offered before."

"I like your work," Ryan said. "It's unique."

Chelsea laughed. "I know. That's the problem. I seem to be neither fish nor fowl in the art world. My instructors used to say I was bent on developing my own genre."

"There's nothing wrong with that," Karen said firmly. "It's good to be different sometimes. If you ask me, you'll be rich and famous someday."

"I'll settle for famous."

"Wealth is important, too," Karen said emphatically. "Money buys everything."

"Maybe not everything," Ryan said somewhat testily.

"Everything of any importance," Karen maintained. "Name one thing that doesn't cost something."

"Love," Ryan and Chelsea said in unison.

Karen laughed. "You two! I meant some possession, like furniture or dishes. Or a car. I know you can't buy love."

Ryan grinned at her. "On the other hand, you can rent it."

"Now you're being silly." Karen bit into a meatball and wrinkled her nose. "This is really bad, isn't it?"

"I've tasted worse," Chelsea hedged.

"The cabbage casserole was definitely worse." Ryan made another attempt to chew the meat. "Is it supposed to be crunchy?"

Karen put down her fork. "I'm sorry. I guess I made them too small and overcooked them as well."

"That's okay. Vegetarian is healthier anyway." Chelsea pushed the meat aside and took more rice.

"You can't just eat rice and corn bread. What kind of a meal is that?" Karen objected. "I'll go order some pizza."

"No, no. This is good. And we have sopapillas for dessert." Chelsea pushed the rice bowl toward Karen. "There's plenty of rice."

"I know," Karen said dismally. "I always make too much."

Ryan reached out and covered Karen's hand with his. "It's okay. Rice and corn bread is good. Do we have a can of pinto beans? I'll warm them up and that's all we need."

"We don't have any." Karen put more rice on her plate and reached for a wedge of corn bread. "I'm glad you're being such good sports about this."

"We're used to you, and we love you any way," Chelsea said with a teasing grin. "We can use the meatball marbles for a fast game of Wahoo after dinner."

Karen gave her an exasperated look, but Ryan could tell she was mollified. "I started to invite someone else tonight. I'm glad now that I didn't."

"Who?" Chelsea asked.

"Bill Jenkins. He's moved back to town and works for Daddy."

"You mean Bill Jenkins with the big ears? The one who played the tuba in high school?"

"His ears aren't that big, and he's still single."

"I don't want to meet single men. I'm not interested."

"It's not like you'd be meeting him. We went to high school together. It would be more like a reunion," Karen insisted.

"Not interested. Thanks anyway."

"But Chelsea, you can't hole up in your apartment all the time and never see anyone. How will you ever find a person you want to marry?"

Chelsea paused before she answered. "I'm doing just fine, Karen. I see you two all the time, and Wendy Green has been over since her wedding."

"I saw her, too. Do you think she looks happy? Maybe she was just tired."

"She's looked happy to me," Chelsea said. "Why wouldn't she be? She's a newlywed."

"It seems funny to call her Wendy Green instead of Johnston. It's like saying my name is Karen Morgan. It's just strange. I thought about hyphenating my name. I still may."

Ryan looked at her. "This is news to me."

"Well, Joyce did it. She's been Joyce Baker-Smyth ever since she and Todd were married. Would you really object if I do that?" She stared at Todd as if she had never expected opposition.

"Of course I would. There's nothing wrong with my name. Baker-Morgan sounds pretentious."

"You think my sister is pretentious?"

"Would you pass the rice?" Chelsea interrupted hastily. "I just can't seem to get enough of it."

Ryan let the matter drop, but he was uneasy. Karen seemed determined to become a clone of her sister, and he didn't like Joyce. "Let's talk about it later," he said to Karen as he handed Chelsea the bowl of rice.

Karen rolled her eyes at Chelsea as if she thought Ryan wouldn't notice. As Chelsea pretended not to notice, Ryan wondered if Karen really was as soft and gentle as she had seemed during their courtship. Lately she had become very assertive, at times almost aggressive in her determination to have her own way. These days he saw more of her mother and sister in her than he would have thought possible. They had had more than one argument, and he had discovered Karen had a temper that she had previously kept hidden. He was discovering he hadn't known her nearly as well as he believed.

Chapter Seven

As the days of summer passed, Chelsea discovered it wasn't easy being a professional artist. One of the paintings she was exhibiting at the gallery sold, and she had some encouragement in that, but the others simply hung there.

When her savings began to dwindle, she started painting quick, commercial canvases on a small scale. These sold easily, though for little money. "I hate doing these pictures," she told Karen.

Karen looked at the group of canvases Chelsea was framing to take to her outlet. "I love them! Especially this one with the roses. If it were in blue and green, I'd buy it for my den."

Chelsea gave her an exasperated glance. "When was the last time you saw a blue rose, Karen? Look toward the back. I think there's one back there you'll like."

Karen sorted through the pictures, being careful not to rub one frame against another. "Is this it? The one of the lake?"

"That's the one." Chelsea looked critically at the painting. It was skillfully done, but was a scene that could be captured by any camera. She picked up another canvas and started fitting it into a frame.

"What lake is this?" Karen asked, tilting her head to the side.

"It's an imaginary one. I did it here in the apartment."

"It's not the one we used to go to?"

"I suppose it's a composite of it, but I didn't have a particular location in mind. Do you want it?"

"No, I'll take the one of the roses. How much do I owe you?"

"I can't charge you. Just take it."

"That wouldn't be fair. How much would you get if you sold it to a stranger?"

"My share would be twenty-five dollars."

Karen took her checkbook out of her purse. "It's too cheap. You know that, don't you?"

"Yes, but twenty-five dollars is more than zero. I'd rather sell a dozen paintings to tourists or home decorators than not sell one of the really good ones in the gallery. I have to pay the bills, after all."

"I just hate money."

Chelsea had to laugh. "Since when?"

"Since I had to start managing it. Ryan can be so stingy. I saw a gorgeous dress at The Shady Lady in the Galleria, and he said I can't buy it."

"The Shady Lady is awfully expensive."

"I suppose. I've always shopped there, though." Karen rolled her eyes. "He's still up in the air over what I paid for the furniture."

Chelsea made no comment.

"If it were up to him, we'd be living out of orange crates and cardboard boxes and sitting on the floor."

"You're sitting on the floor now."

"That's entirely different. This is an artist's garret."

"It is?"

"It's like one. It's okay to sit on the floor here. I just couldn't do it at my house." She laughed. "Can you imagine Mother and Daddy sitting on the floor when they come over?"

Chelsea chuckled. "Or Joyce and the Todds."

"Maybe Todd, Jr., but I don't think Big Todd's legs bend that way."

"Is that what you call him now? Big Todd? He doesn't fit the name. Joyce is taller than he is."

"Only when she wears heels. But she always wears them." She looked around the small apartment. "Do you ever get claustrophobic in here?"

"Not really. The room I paint in is much smaller. The windows help. The best part is that I can afford to live here. I thought for a while I wasn't going to make it."

"Of course you will. You have lots of talent. Haven't I always said so?"

"You're partial."

"Ryan says so, too."

"Thank him for me." Chelsea had almost reached the point where she could hear his name without experiencing physical pain.

"Thank him yourself. I'm not speaking to him."

Chelsea stopped tapping nails into the picture frame. "You've had an argument?"

"This certainly isn't the first one. Just because I don't tell you, doesn't mean we don't fight. This one started over the dress at The Shady Lady and branched out from there. Ryan is so quiet these days. He wasn't like this when we were all running around together."

"I can't imagine him being quiet for long. Is he working too hard?"

"He's not working any harder than Daddy always has. Daddy says Ryan's well liked at work. I guess he's just quiet at home. He says he's worried about money." Karen made it seem like the most unlikely possibility.

"Maybe he is. I don't know what your furniture cost, but anyone can see it's not inexpensive. And I know those shoes you bought last week cost an arm and a leg, because I was with you when you bought them."

"I can't go barefoot. Besides, they're perfect with my going-away suit."

"You already had shoes that went with it. And how often do you wear that suit? I haven't seen it on you since your wedding."

"I'll wear it more often now that I have nicer shoes. You sound just like Ryan." Karen held the canvas of roses at arm's length. "How will this look in my dining room?"

Chelsea wondered if Karen's twenty-five-dollar check would exacerbate what was already a strained topic with Ryan. She decided to tear up the check and not tell Karen. She could afford to give her a painting. "It'll be fine. I think that wall by the door to the living room would be just the spot."

"You know," Karen said a bit too casually, "I don't like being married as much as I thought I would."

"You don't? It's what you've wanted all your life."

"I know. I'm not saying I regret marrying Ryan. It's just that we had so much more fun when we were single. You must still be going to parties and having dates. All I do is sit at home."

"I'm not leading the carefree life you seem to believe. I stay here most of the time. That's how I'm able to finish so many canvases. I have to work long hours in order to find the time to paint the works that could make a difference in my career."

"That makes me feel a little better. You could come over more often, if you'd like. I get bored watching so much TV."

"You and Ryan need time together. You're still newlyweds."

"I don't feel like a newlywed. And we have too much time together. It puts thoughts in his head that I don't care for."

"Such as?" Chelsea finished the framing and reached for another canvas and frame.

"Sex. I don't see how anyone could enjoy it. I certainly don't."

"Karen, you shouldn't be talking to me about this."

"Who else can I talk to? Mother? I'm convinced Joyce and I were virgin births. Mother and Daddy never so much as kiss or hold hands. And from all accounts, Joyce feels the same way I do. At least, she and Todd have separate bedrooms now."

"They do?"

"She says it's because he snores, but I think it's more than that. It's not that Ryan doesn't try, I guess. At least that's what he says he's doing, but I just don't care for it. I think it's like escargots. Some people like them and others can't stand them."

"That's not a comparison I would have chosen. I hate escargots."

"And I hate sex. What I don't understand is why everyone says it's so great. I'm hoping I get pregnant. At least then I'll have a baby to show for it."

"I can't discuss this with you."

"But, Chelsea—"

"No! This is between you and Ryan."

Karen sighed. "I suppose you're right. I do tend to talk too much at times. I guess I'll learn to put up with it." She stood and reached for her purse. "Do you want to go shopping?"

"Thanks, but I have the rest of these canvases to frame and deliver. Maybe next time." She wondered if Karen was heading for the expensive shops, given Ryan's concern about their finances. She told herself it was none of her business.

When Karen left, Chelsea stopped hammering and leaned back against her bed. Karen disliked sex. That meant Ryan must be frustrated and hurt. He wasn't one to force himself on anyone. She hated to think of him unhappy, even if the alternative would cause stabs of jealousy. The only way she could bear to think of Ryan married to someone other than herself was to believe he was happier than she could have made him.

As Christmas neared, Chelsea's sales increased. Three of her better paintings were bought, and she developed a nostalgic, Victorian-type line for the inexpensive canvases that shoppers snapped up. For the first time she was able to breathe when it was time for bills to be paid. She had a reply now to her parents, who were urging her to give up the silly notion of being an artist and get a "real" job.

She had fallen into the habit of having dinner with Karen and Ryan at least once a week, at her house or at theirs. In her new burst of prosperity, Chelsea bought steaks and Ryan cooked them on the little hibachi on her tiny porch while she and Karen put together a salad and baked potatoes in the microwave.

"This looks pretty," Karen said as she set the card table and put folding chairs around it. Chelsea had hidden the table beneath a tie-dyed cloth and had made matching cushions to pad the chairs. "You'd never know this isn't a real table unless you look close."

"It *is* a real table," Chelsea said patiently. "It's just not a wooden one. I'll have one someday."

"You're so good at fixing up things like this. I wish I had your talent. I would never have thought of this."

"Will you check the bread? I think I smell it burning."

Karen went to the oven and levered open the door. "We're just in time." She grabbed an oven mitt and put the tray of bread on the cabinet. "This all smells so good! I just can't seem to stop eating these days."

Chelsea smiled at her. Karen had gained several pounds since her wedding, but she was still beautiful. "The butter is in the refrigerator."

Ryan opened the door and came in carrying the platter of steaks. "I hope your part is done. The steaks are ready."

"Perfect timing." Chelsea took the potatoes from the microwave and dropped them gingerly into a pink bowl. None of her dishes matched—she had bought them at garage sales—but they all had a rose pattern. The result was eclectic but pleasing.

"Is this a new plate?" Karen asked as she sat at her customary place.

"Yes, I found it at a sale last Saturday. It's my favorite."

"Mine, too." Karen reached for the salad. "I love your place, Chelsea. It's fun to be here."

Ryan gave her an amused look. "We could get rid of those ugly navy and red plates and head for the flea market."

"You know we can't do that." Karen passed him the salad bowl. "Mother gave us those dishes. Besides, they're expensive."

Chelsea buttered a slice of bread while she waited for the platter of steaks to reach her. "I had an interesting phone call just before you came."

"Oh? Was it from a man?" Karen leaned forward expectantly.

"No, it was a greeting-card company. The owner's wife bought one of my Victorian pictures, and he's interested in buying some for a new line of note cards."

"Great!" Ryan smiled at her encouragingly. "You're going to do it, aren't you?"

"I almost have to. I can't afford to turn down any sale. He hasn't mentioned a price. I'm do to several paintings and show them to him. Keep your fingers crossed. I never thought of going into commercial art, but this fell into my lap."

"You're too picky," Karen said. "This way more people can see your pictures. Personally, I like the Victorian ones best. I don't always understand the others." She looked around the table. "I have some good news, too."

"You didn't find another sale, did you?" Ryan asked, only half joking.

"Of course not. I went to the doctor today." She paused for affect. "I'm going to have a baby."

Ryan stopped chewing and stared.

Chelsea managed not to choke on her iced tea. "You're pregnant? Are you sure?"

"I'm positive. The baby will be here in June." She beamed at them. "You're not saying anything, Ryan."

"I didn't expect this. Are you sure there's no mistake?"

"I said I'm sure. You could at least look pleased."

Chelsea glanced from Ryan to Karen. "I think he's in shock. This was such a surprise!"

"We said we were going to wait," Ryan said. "We can't afford a baby now."

"It's not coming now. It won't be here until next summer. You'll earn plenty of money by then." She gave him a warning look and tightened her lips. "Don't spoil this for me, Ryan."

He finally smiled. "I don't want to ruin anything. I know you're happy. And I'm happy, too. It's just a surprise, that's all."

"Joyce said you'd be unhappy."

"You told Joyce before you told me?"

"I went to her doctor. The one she used with Todd, Jr. She says he's wonderful."

"What's wrong with our regular doctor?"

"Nothing, but he's not a specialist. I want the very best for my baby."

"Our baby," Ryan corrected quietly. Karen didn't notice.

She turned to Chelsea. "You'll have to help me put together a layette. And I'll need a bassinet. And a cradle. And a rocking chair. I want to sit and rock her for hours."

"Or him," Chelsea reminded her. "Of course I'll help you."

"And you'll be the godmother, of course. You will, won't you?"

"Does your church recognize godparents?"

"No, but you'll be one unofficially. I'm so happy! I'm going to have a baby! Someone who will love me better than anyone else in the whole world. Someone I can love with all my heart."

Chelsea avoided Ryan's eyes and told herself that Karen was only speaking in superlatives because of her excitement. "I'll find you a name book."

"Yes! We'll have to decide on exactly the right name." Karen looked at Ryan. "Unless you want to have a junior."

"No, thanks. I'd rather the baby have its own name."

"I might want to name it after myself if it's a girl," Karen said. In inspiration she said, "We could call her Karen Chelsea Rae Morgan. The Rae would be for Ryan."

"That would be too confusing. I'll buy the name book first thing tomorrow," Chelsea said with a laugh.

Karen continued to chatter away though the rest of the meal, but Ryan barely spoke at all. These days Chelsea could see what Karen had meant about his silences. Ryan didn't look happy. And he seemed particularly unhappy about the pending birth.

In the weeks that followed, Ryan became accustomed to the idea of being a father. As Karen blossomed with her pregnancy, he forgot he hadn't been enthusiastic at first. They went through lists of names, none of which seemed exactly right and a few of which would doom the child to a life of ridicule.

"We have to decide," Karen said as she pored over the worn and dog-eared book. "She'll be here before we know it."

"I never knew it would be so hard to name a baby. I like a lot of names."

"Yes, but most of them sound wrong with 'Morgan.' I love the name Mandy, or maybe Tammy, but that's so many *M*'s with Morgan. What about Candy? Not short for Candace, just Candy?"

"This may be a son, remember. What about Jason or Josh?"

Karen wrinkled her nose. "I couldn't possibly call a tiny baby such grown-up names. Maybe Jamey."

"He won't be a baby forever. We have to pick something that he or she will can age with."

Karen shook her head. "I'm not sticking my daughter with some stuffy name. Maybe Cyndy, with two *Y*'s or Kely with one *L.*"

"We're not naming this baby something she will have to spell aloud for the rest of her life. K-E-L-Y could be Keely or Kelly."

"Keelie," Karen said thoughtfully. "No, it doesn't go with Morgan." She pulled at the maternity top and tried to arrange it more comfortably. "I'm already hot. Mother says I'll just die this summer. Even Joyce feels sorry for me."

"I wish they'd quit telling you war stories. Can't they see they're only frightening you?"

"I have to know what to expect. I told the doctor I want to be put to sleep when the time comes. I don't want to go through labor awake." Karen frowned petulantly. "He refused to agree."

"He's the doctor. He knows what's best for you."

"He's a *man*. What could he possibly know about having a baby?"

"He told me he expects you to have an easy labor."

"That's the most ridiculous thing I ever heard of. He can't possibly know that. Joyce said she thought she was going to die. That was when she decided Big Todd was going to sleep in another room."

"Todd's a fool to agree to that."

Karen ducked her head and fingered the hem of her blouse. "Actually, I was going to ask you to do the same thing."

"What?" Ryan frowned at her. "I'm not moving into another bedroom."

"Just until the baby is born and I feel better. I can't sleep with you beside me."

Ryan tried not to show the pain her words gave him. "Absolutely not. We're married and we're going to sleep together."

Karen's mouth set into stubborn lines. "I don't want to make love anymore."

"What are you talking about? Up until last night I hadn't touched you in weeks."

"Last night was terribly uncomfortable. You don't have a baby squashing you all the time."

"I tried to be careful. I thought maybe you enjoyed it."

Karen shook her head petulantly. "I didn't. If you really loved me, you'd want to do what I ask at a time like this."

He sighed and ran his fingers through his hair. "Karen, you act as if no woman ever survived having a baby. Pregnancy is a condition, not an illness. I asked your doctor, and he said there's nothing wrong with us making love for several months yet."

Her mouth dropped open. "You asked my doctor a question like that? How could you?"

"He knows we do it," Ryan said with exasperation. "This isn't a virgin birth, for pete's sake!"

"How could you embarrass me like that?"

"Because you told me after your last office visit that he said we shouldn't. I was curious."

"You were checking up on me, you mean! Todd would certainly never do this to Joyce!"

"I'm not Todd, and I wouldn't have married Joyce if she were the only woman in the world. You used to like to be kissed and held, before we were married. What happened?"

"I knew then that you respected me and that it wouldn't go any further. That's not true now." Her voice rose, and her eyes flashed angrily. "Now you're all over me!"

"Most wives like to make love," he retorted, his own anger rising. He felt guilty about last night because he had known Karen wasn't eager to make love and he had pretended not to notice.

"Well, I don't! And how would you know? Have you been asking all our friends?"

"Certainly not. In my opinion, I think you should be seeing a counselor as well as a medical doctor. It's just not right for you to dislike having me touch you."

"Oh?" she said in stinging tones. "Maybe it's because you're not any good at it."

The words seemed to pierce Ryan. He stared at her in disbelief.

"You don't like to hear that, do you?" she demanded, seeming to enjoy his pain. "Well, it's the truth. You're no good in bed, and I hate to have you fumble around on me. It's disgusting."

"You're going too far," he said in a tight voice.

"It's about time you started taking the credit for it. You're always thinking the problem is with me! I might like it if you were any good!"

The doorbell cut off his reply. Ryan turned away while Karen went to answer it. Was Karen right? Maybe he really was a bad lover. Did anyone ever really know? He had made love with women before Karen, and they had seemed pleased. With Chelsea it had been like a love song. But then Chelsea had gone away and hadn't even told him goodbye. After that night on the lake, he had expected things to be different between them, not that she would disappear. Certainly he hadn't made love with her simply because they had been drinking beer and the night was right. Had she left because she hadn't enjoyed it and didn't want to repeat the experience?

He closed his eyes. It was best not to think about that night at the lake with Chelsea. Not if he wanted to keep his sanity.

Behind him, he heard voices and recognized one as Chelsea's. Ryan hurriedly crossed the room and went out the back door. He couldn't face her right now. Not after all Karen had said.

Chelsea saw him leaving and said, "Have I come at a bad time?"

"You couldn't have picked a better one. We were having a fight."

"Not again! I'm so sorry. Is there anything I can do?" She saw Ryan cross the yard toward the garage. He looked as if he were weighted down by sadness.

"No, it's something we have to work out." Karen glared after him. "I told Ryan I want him to move into the spare bedroom, and you'd have thought I asked him to move to China!"

"You didn't! Karen, why would you do such a thing?"

"Because I can't sleep in the same bed with him. I keep waking up and then I can't go back to sleep. It's so irritating! Besides, I don't think it's a good idea for us to make love right now. Not with me pregnant and all."

"Did your doctor say that?" Chelsea looked at her in concern. "Nothing is wrong, is there?"

"Probably not." Karen didn't meet her eyes.

"Is there something you're not telling me?"

"Doctors don't know everything! It can't be good for the baby to be jostled around like that. And I look so ugly now. I'm fat and cumbersome. I don't want anyone to see me."

"You're not fat, you're pregnant." Chelsea was being kind. Karen had put on several extra pounds every month.

"I don't care. I don't want him to touch me."

Chelsea sat on the couch and Karen lowered herself into the chair beside her. "Karen, I really think you're making a mistake. Ryan loves you, but you've been pushing him a lot lately. I haven't wanted to say anything because it's none of my business, but—"

"That's right. It's none of your business," Karen snapped. Then tears welled in her eyes. "I'm sorry, Chelsea. What makes me say things like that these days? I said some awful things to Ryan, too. I feel as if I'm going crazy!"

Chelsea reached out to pat her shoulder. "You're not crazy. Just pregnant. I guess your hormones are running wild or something."

"I suppose so. I seem to be in a bad mood all the time." She looked out at the back yard. "Where do you think Ryan went?"

"I don't know. I think I heard him drive away."

Karen sighed. "I seem to mess up everything. This should be the happiest time of my life. I have a wonderful husband, and we're going to have a perfectly beautiful baby. I should be happy."

Chelsea shook her head. If she were in Karen's place she would be ecstatic. Certainly she would never have Ryan sleep in another room. "Once the baby is here, you'll feel like your old self again. You'll see." She hoped that was the way it would be.

Chapter Eight

June dragged by for Karen, and therefore for Chelsea and Ryan. As the days grew hotter, Karen became more uncomfortable and her moods darkened.

"I hate being pregnant," she told Chelsea. "I'm never going to do this again. Joyce told me I'd feel this way."

Chelsea kept her opinion of Joyce to herself. "It'll be over soon. The baby's dropped and is in position. It can't be much longer."

"I'm already past my due date." Karen flexed her swollen feet and surveyed them from her position on the couch. "I look like a blimp."

"You know you're supposed to stay off your feet. Didn't the doctor tell you to take it easy?"

"Yes, but I can't let my house go to seed. Ryan can be so messy. You don't know what it's like to have to live with a man."

"His apartment was always cleaner than our dorm room."

"Maybe so, but I have to work all the time to keep the house the way I want it. After all, you never know when you might have company, and I'd just die if someone saw my house in a mess."

Chelsea looked around. The den, like the rest of the house was perfectly clean. It could be a showroom display in a furniture store for all the wear it showed. "You're a great housekeeper. I've never seen anything out of place, let alone dirty."

"That's because I work at it all the time. It's not like your place, where a person would expect to find things scattered about. Artists don't have to be as neat as everyone else. It's not expected."

Chelsea looked at her with amusement. "It's a good thing we're friends. You have a peculiar way of putting things at times."

"Did that come out wrong? I'm sorry. I meant it's okay if your apartment needs dusting or whatever, because you work there as well as live there and artists are supposed to be messy."

"Don't try to fix it, Karen," Chelsea said with a laugh. "You're only making it worse. Where's Ryan?"

"Who knows? I think he went to have the car inspected. It's almost the end of the month." She heaved a sigh and rested her hands on her bulging stomach. "I'm never going to have this baby. What if I'm not pregnant at all, just bloated? That happened to Queen Mary."

"That was in the sixteenth century. You're pregnant." Chelsea was accustomed to having to reassure Karen. "If you ask me, it has affected your mind."

"You're probably right." Karen tried to haul herself off the couch. "Do you want any lemonade? I'm so thirsty in hot weather."

"Stay put. I'll get it for you." Chelsea went into the kitchen. She was there so often, it was almost as familiar as her own. Opening the refrigerator, she said, "I don't see the pitcher. Are you sure you have lemonade?"

"I'll bet Ryan drank the last of it." Karen sounded perturbed. "He's so bad about that."

Chelsea opened the freezer. "I'll make some more. It won't take but a minute."

Karen came to the door and stood with her feet braced apart and her hands on the small of her back. "I don't see how women lived through pregnancy before air conditioning. Is it hot in here to you?"

"No, you could hang meat in here. Didn't I tell you to stay on the couch? You can't keep your feet up if you're standing on them."

"I can't stay put. I feel so restless." Karen went to the table and straightened the bowl of artificial fruit. "The baby has been kicking so much I feel bruised inside."

"I can't imagine how that feels."

"I hope for your sake that you never know. Pregnancy is so uncomfortable!"

"Are you sure you're not exaggerating? You think you have pneumonia every time you have a head cold," Chelsea reminded her. "I'd hate to be your doctor."

"Ryan says 'Pregnancy is a condition, not a disease,' " Karen said in imitation of him. "If only he had to go through this."

"He's right. You're just spoiled."

"A fine friend you are." Karen watched Chelsea make lemonade from the frozen concentrate. "Add some sugar to that. Okay?"

"It's already sweetened."

"I know, but I like more sugar in it."

Chelsea kept her opinion to herself and added sugar to the lemonade. She put ice in two glasses and poured lemonade into them.

"Thanks," Karen said as she took the glass. She tasted it and went to the sugar bowl.

To Chelsea the drink was already syrupy sweet. "Should you be using so much sugar?" she asked as Karen added two liberal teaspoons.

"You're sounding like Ryan again. I'll lose weight after the baby comes. This may be the only time in my life that I can indulge myself." She got the sponge wet and wiped the already-spotless cabinet top.

"You're becoming a cleaning fanatic," Chelsea observed.

"I like everything to be just so. It makes me feel good to

see my house in order, so clean it sparkles. Ryan doesn't understand. He says I'm obsessive. I guess he read it in some book." She laughed deprecatingly.

"Are things better between the two of you?"

"I suppose. Marriage is boring, really. Once the baby is here, it will be more fun. I'm sure I'll spoil her rotten."

"Why are you so positive it's a girl?"

"I don't know. I'm just sure. I haven't even picked out a boy's name."

"What did you decide on for a girl?"

"Bethany. No middle name. What do you think?"

"I like it. I think you should have a boy's name, too, however."

"It's taken me nine months to pick this one. We don't have time to work out a boy's name. At least I hope we don't." She patted her middle. "I feel as if I'll be pregnant forever. It's been an eternity already."

"I'm going to the farmers' market. Can I pick up anything for you? I hear the peaches are particularly good this year."

"Peaches would be wonderful. I can make a cobbler. And if you see anything else I'd like, get it as well. Do you want money now?"

"No, pay me after I get back." Chelsea put her glass in the sink. "Will you be all right alone?"

"Of course. It may be days before I go into labor. Weeks!"

"It won't be that long. I'll be back in a couple of hours."

"I'll be here."

When Chelsea returned an hour later, Ryan was sitting with Karen. "What are you doing home?" she asked when he opened the door.

"She called me at work. I think this is it."

Chelsea put down the bags of produce. "Karen? How do you feel?"

"Terrible!" She looked up at Chelsea. "I'm afraid."

"Did her water break?"

Ryan shook his head. "She says she's having contractions. I'm trying to time them, but she keeps forgetting to tell me when it's over."

"It's not easy," Karen said testily. "You could be a little more understanding." She gripped the arms of the chair as another contraction started.

"They're five minutes apart." Ryan stood. "I'll get the suitcase."

"Do your Lamaze breathing," Chelsea said. "Go hahahaha."

"You go hahahaha. I'm hurting!" Karen's face was pale, but it seemed to be more from fear than from pain. "How much worse do you think it will get?"

"How should I know?" Chelsea put her hands on Karen's arms. "Let me pull you up. We can be going to the car."

Awkwardly Karen made her way across the den. She paused at the back door until another contraction passed. "What's keeping Ryan?"

"As soon as I get you into the car I'll go see. Does he know where your suitcase is?"

"I put it at my side of the closet beneath my winter skirts."

Chelsea saw that Karen was safely in the car, then ran to the bedroom. Ryan was on his knees looking under the bed. When he saw Chelsea he said frantically, "I can't find the suitcase. She keeps moving it."

She hurried to the closet and soon found it. "Let's go!"

They ran out to the car. Chelsea followed in her own car, and they arrived at the hospital together. Ryan ran to get a wheelchair while Chelsea stayed with Karen.

"I'm going to die! I know I'm going to die!" Karen gripped Chelsea's hands in panic. "Why did I want to have a baby? Chelsea, will you take care of Ryan?"

"Of course I will, but you're not dying. We'll be laughing about this tomorrow."

"Never! I'll never laugh again!"

Ryan came back with an orderly pushing a wheelchair. They helped Karen into it and started back to the hospital. Ryan stopped at the desk to check Karen in and to send word to her doctor that she was in labor.

"Where's Ryan?" Karen demanded as they went down the polished halls toward the elevator. "Why isn't he with me?"

"He's calling the doctor. Calm down."

By the time they reached the fourth floor, Karen was convinced that she would never make it to her room. Chelsea kept reassuring her and promising to stay with her for as long as possible.

"I'd rather have you with me than Ryan. He's the reason I'm in this fix," Karen said in a peeved voice. "I think men should have the babies since they like making them so well."

Chelsea glanced at the orderly who was trying to pretend not to hear. "Hush. You're making a scene."

"I don't care. What's keeping Ryan so long? He's coming with us, isn't he?"

"Of course he is. I told you to come by the hospital and take care of all the paper work ahead of time, didn't I? You never listen to me."

"I'm a terrible person," Karen agreed, suddenly contrite. "Chel, do you think I'm going to die? Do you think the baby will have all her fingers and toes?"

"Everything will be fine." Chelsea was finding Karen's panic contagious and was having to fight hard not to succumb. "Breathe, Karen. Go hahahaha."

Ryan found them after Karen had changed into a hospital gown and was in bed. She glared at him as she tried to breathe the way she had been taught in Lamaze class.

"How is she?" he asked.

"She's doing fine."

"The doctor is on his way."

"He'd better hurry! The nurse said I'm already dilated far enough to have this baby," Karen retorted.

"You are? That's great! Didn't I tell you that you have

nothing to worry about? You're going to have an easy delivery."

That was the wrong thing to say. Karen gripped the bed rails and hurled angry words at Ryan until the contraction subsided. Chelsea hadn't known her to be so vitriolic. Ryan looked as if he had heard it all before. He took Karen's hand.

"Squeeze my hand when you need to. Did you bring something to focus on?"

"It's in my suitcase."

Chelsea opened it and found a small china dog. "Is this it?"

"Yes. Put it on the tray there." Karen stared at the dog as she worked her way through another contraction. "They're coming closer. Go call the doctor again, Ryan."

"He's on his way. If I call, it will slow him down."

"If he's really on his way, how could he hear the phone?" Karen reasoned. "Are you sure he's coming?"

"Positive. Breathe."

Karen gripped Ryan's hand and glared at him as she puffed her way through the contraction. "I'm never going to have another baby. Do you hear me? Never!"

"That's fine with me. Let's just get through this one."

The doctor arrived twenty minutes later. Chelsea stepped out into the hall with Ryan while he examined Karen.

"Oh, my lord! We forgot to call Mr. and Mrs. Baker!" Chelsea exclaimed. "I'll go do it." She ran down the hall in search of a phone.

When she returned she said to Karen, "I called your parents. They'll be here as soon as your mother changes her clothes."

"They're not on their way? What about Joyce?"

"Your mother is going to call her."

"What if I have the baby before they get here? My water broke, and the doctor says it won't be long now." In her eyes was terror. "He gave me some Demerol, but it hasn't helped at all."

"Give it time, Karen. It hasn't had time to take effect yet." Ryan held her hand tenderly. "You're going to be all right. The doctor said so."

"Chel, stay with me. Promise you won't leave."

"I'm not going anywhere."

Suddenly Karen's eyes widened and the contractions seemed to be unending. She screamed out for someone to get the doctor.

When she and Ryan were taken to the delivery room, Chelsea was left to pace alone in the waiting area. She couldn't hear Karen now, but her screams as she had been wheeled down the hall had been unnerving. Karen had the lowest pain threshold that Chelsea had ever seen, and fear was making it worse. What if Karen wasn't all right? Chelsea had never been with anyone in labor before. She struggled not to panic herself.

Suddenly Ryan came running through the double doors. He was grinning as he grabbed Chelsea and swung her around. "It's a girl! We've got a daughter!"

Chelsea tried to catch her breath. "Is Karen all right?"

"She's doing great!" He didn't turn her loose but held her almost fiercely. "God, Chelsea! I was so worried! I was afraid she might be dying and it would be all my fault!"

She held him, aware of the vulnerability he wouldn't show Karen. "She's okay. The doctor said she's fine. You just told me so."

He finally released her. "I've got to get back in there. It's a girl!"

Chelsea laughed as her eyes filled with tears. "I'm so happy for you! Go hug her for me!"

Ryan ran off, and Chelsea wondered if he realized how long he had held her. Every second had been an eternity to her. She silently cursed herself for having enjoyed it so much—especially when Karen had just given birth to his daughter. Chelsea felt so guilty she wanted to leave.

At that moment the elevator doors parted and Cecilia and Fulton Baker came toward her. Seeing them, she smiled and wiped at her tears. "It's a girl! Ryan just came out and told me."

"So soon? I thought we'd have hours to wait yet." Cecilia started toward the double doors.

"You can't go in there," Chelsea said quickly. "They'll bring the baby by on her way to the nursery. We can see her through the glass."

"How's Karen?" Fulton asked.

"Ryan says she's fine."

"I should have been here," Cecilia said reproachfully. "Why wasn't I called earlier?"

"There wasn't time. She had an easy labor and a fast delivery."

"There is no such thing." Cecilia lifted her chin as if she knew more about birthing babies than Chelsea ever would. "All labor is hard and delivery is hell. Pure hell."

Fulton looked away as if the subject embarrassed him.

"At any rate, the baby is born and Karen is all right." Chelsea refused to let Cecilia dampen her mood. "Little Bethany has arrived! I can't wait to see her."

"They're not really naming her that, are they?" Cecilia wrinkled her nose. "I was hoping for something with a bit more class."

"I like the name." Chelsea was rapidly tiring of Cecilia looking down her nose at everything. "It's the only name both Karen and Ryan liked."

"Yes." Cecilia's tone implied that was reason enough to change it. "At least Karen is all right. Has the doctor been out?"

"Not yet." Chelsea tiptoed over to look through the glass and toward the next set of doors. "I think I see Ryan coming this way."

Ryan and a nurse came through the doors. In his arms he held a bundle of cloth, and it took Chelsea a minute to realize he was holding the baby.

"They're not letting him carry it to the nursery, surely," Cecilia gasped.

"He was in the delivery room. He's wearing a sterile gown." Chelsea leaned forward eagerly.

Ryan glanced at them all, but his eyes smiled only when they focused on Chelsea's face. Carefully he lifted the blanket to show them the pasty-colored baby in his arms. Her eyes were shut and her little red mouth opened to let out a shriek of protest as she waved her tiny arms and legs.

"She's beautiful!" Chelsea exclaimed. With every breath the baby grew pinker. White-blond hair, almost too pale and fine to see, capped her head.

"She looks exactly like Karen when she was born," Cecilia said. "Doesn't she look like Karen, Fulton?"

"I guess." He grinned at the baby. "She's got a set of lungs on her. And look how long her feet are!"

"She's the image of Karen." Cecilia smiled at Ryan, willing to include him in her magnanimity.

The nurse said something to Ryan, and he followed her toward the nursery, never taking his eyes off his tiny daughter and looking as pleased as if he had personally invented babies.

Chelsea was suddenly tired. Although she was happy for Ryan and Karen, seeing him holding their baby touched a part of her that she had tried to wall off. She found herself wondering what her baby would have looked like—hers and Ryan's. Would it have been as adorable as this one? Trembling, she made an excuse to the Bakers and left before seeing Karen. She took the elevator down and was almost running by the time she reached her car.

As the days went by Chelsea tried to bury herself in work. She had interested a gallery in hosting a one-woman show for her, so she was trying to finish some new canvases to take the place of completed ones that might sell. After her more commercial pictures, these were both refreshing and exacting. Working on them gave her less time to think. They also gave her an excuse to avoid invitations to Karen and Ryan's house.

Karen was determined to be the perfect mother. She read all the current books on babies and could converse on every aspect of caring for a newborn. Chelsea knew next to nothing about babies, so this made their conversation rather limited. Karen's every thought now seemed to revolve around homemade baby food, eye-hand coordination exercises, and formula. Karen had drawn the line at breast-feeding. Whether the doctor thought it a good idea or not, she was set against it and wouldn't even discuss it.

"I found this black and white mobile," Karen said as she set it to twirling slowly above the baby's bed. "You wouldn't believe how difficult it was to find one. Everything is in pastel colors. Babies can't see pale colors."

"Now how do we know that?" Chelsea challenged. "Babies can't talk."

"I'm sure the people who research these things have ways of determining it. Since black and white are such sharp contrasts, the baby can see them easily." The zebras and penguins rotated to a tune, and the baby's eyes did try to follow them. "See? She's already learning to see them."

"Bethany is a genius. I'm sure of it." Chelsea reached down to touch the baby's soft arm. "Her skin is like velvet."

"I've been doing leg exercises with her, too." Karen reached down and bent Bethany's legs in a gentle motion. "It's supposed to develop early coordination."

"You may be sorry you're doing this when she's running around and into everything."

"I've already put her name on the list for the Montessori preschool. There's a waiting list a mile long. Mother says it's the best way to go with her."

Chelsea laughed. "Karen, she is only two weeks old! You're already signing her up for school?"

"I want to be certain of getting her in. I want my baby to have every advantage." Karen regarded the baby thoughtfully. "I'm having second thoughts about her name."

"Too late now. You had nine months to make up your mind. What's wrong with 'Bethany'?"

"Nothing. It just has such an old-fashioned sound to it. Mother and Joyce say it might hold her back with her peers."

"That's just plain silly." Chelsea reached down and lifted the baby. Bethany looked about with interest. "It's a pretty name, and it suits her. I've never seen such a beautiful baby."

Karen gave her a long look. "Chel, do you ever think about . . . you know?"

Chelsea put the baby on her shoulder and turned away. "No. It is time for her bottle?"

"Not yet. I just wondered. You love Bethany so much I just can't help but think about your abortion. I know you must regret it every day of your life."

"No," Chelsea replied honestly. "I don't. It's bothered me more since Bethany has been born, but I can't honestly say that I would have done anything differently. I couldn't have. It would have been wrong for all of us."

"Well, I'm just glad I never had to make a decision like that." Karen touched Bethany's soft hair. "I wouldn't have cared if it upset Ryan or not. I'd have told him he had to marry me. Wouldn't we, Bethany? Yes, we would." She coaxed a reflexive smile from the baby by stroking her tiny cheek.

Chelsea didn't want to pursue the subject. "Where's Ryan tonight?"

"Working late as usual. He seems to come home later every night. I was hoping the baby would change all that, but he says Daddy isn't doing the work so someone has to do it. Imagine! Daddy got along fine before Ryan worked there. I think he's just making excuses."

"He seems tired lately. I know he would rather be with you and Bethany."

"I suppose. If it were me, I'd tell Daddy to do his own work."

"Having your father-in-law for a boss can't be easy."

"Come in the kitchen. It's time for Bethany's bath."

"I can't stay. I have some canvases in the car. I'm on my way to the gallery."

Karen looked disappointed. "You'll be back later, won't you? I get lonesome here all alone. Bethany is wonderful, but she sleeps a lot."

"I'll try, but don't count on me. I have to discuss the coming show, find out which canvases he wants to display and where they're to be set up. Then we have to talk about publicity. I may be busy all day. I've never done my own show before, and I'm not sure what's involved."

"Okay, but you're coming for dinner tomorrow. I'm not taking any excuses."

"All right. Tomorrow. I'd like that." Chelsea handed the baby to Karen. "Be good, Bethany. I'll come back and play with you tomorrow."

"You know, I'm sure she understands some of what we say," Karen said in a marveling tone. "Look at her smile."

Chelsea laughed as she let herself out. Karen was certainly enjoying motherhood. Chelsea was glad to see it. She hadn't been entirely sure Karen would adjust to an infant's demands.

The gallery wasn't far away, located in a new shopping center that was attracting a great deal of business. The gallery was in the corner where the lines of shops met. If a person didn't know it was there, it was easy to overlook it. Chelsea parked and took her paintings out of the trunk. None of them were large, so she had no trouble carrying them into the building.

She was met just inside the door by the owner, a congenial man in his late fifties. Alfred Bane took the paintings and carried them to his office in the back. A younger man was there, and he looked up when Chelsea entered.

"I want you to meet my son-in-law, Jason Randall. He has a gallery downtown. You might say this is a family business. Jason, this is Chelsea Cavin. You've heard me speak of her, I'm sure." Bane uncovered the paintings and started setting them up so he could study them.

Jason came around the desk and never took his eyes off Chelsea. "I've heard a great deal about you. Is this your first one-woman show?"

Chelsea nodded. "I have to confess, I'm a little nervous."

"There's no need to be. You do good work. Very original."

"Thank you." She watched Bane nervously. "I can bring some others in a day or two, but they're not dry enough yet to travel."

Bane glanced at her as if he had almost forgotten she was still there. "These are fine. I like your use of color. It's riveting. Simply riveting."

"Do you have anything you could place in my gallery?" Jason asked.

Chelsea turned to him. "Yes, of course. That is, if Mr. Bane doesn't object."

"No, no," Bane said with a wave of his hand. "It's all in the family. The exposure would be good for you." He pointed to a canvas done in deep greens shot through with pure yellow. "This one is hypnotic. What do you call it?"

"That's *Might Have Been.*" Chelsea had started it the day she'd learned Karen was pregnant. It held all her hurt and lost hopes. Until now she hadn't wanted to show it to anyone.

"Magnificent. Simply magnificent. I may have to buy it myself."

She smiled. "It's for sale."

"I can't believe I've never met you or seen your work," Jason said. He was watching her, not the canvases. "Have you been in this area long?"

"Yes, but I've only been exhibiting for a short while. I was in college and then I had to get settled. These are some of the first canvases I did for exhibit." She was not about to mention the inexpensive Victorian works she sold for a song to tourists and do-it-yourself decorators.

"I'd like to see more of your work. Would it be all right

for me to come by your studio sometime?" Jason gazed into her eyes, and his smile was infectious.

Chelsea hadn't been looked at with such interest in a long time. "Yes," she said with a smile. "I'll give you the address. I'd like to show you my other canvases. Say, tomorrow afternoon?"

"Tomorrow is perfect."

She gave him her address and phone number. It wasn't until after she'd left that she recalled Bane had introduced him as his son-in-law. Was Jason married? That must mean he had only the paintings in mind. Chelsea felt a bit foolish for having read more into his smile and intent gaze than was intended.

Chapter Nine

Jason Randall arrived at Chelsea's apartment at the appointed time. She felt unaccountably nervous about his being there, but she attributed that to her attraction to him. Jason had been in her thoughts more than she liked to admit. He was tall and attractive, though she couldn't classify him as handsome, and his hair was as dark as his eyes. She had reflected several times that it was a shame he was married.

He moved around her tiny living room, gazing raptly at her paintings and ignoring the bed in one corner, the kitchen in another. When she took him into the room she used for painting, he didn't bother to mask his excitement.

"Fantastic!" he said as he lifted a canvas she had finished the day before.

"Careful of the paint. It's still wet."

Jason had obviously been around art in progress before, because he was holding the canvas in such a way that his fingers never touched the paint. "Tell me about this one."

"I call it *Reverie*. I started it a couple of months ago when a friend of mine was expecting her first child."

"It looks lonely." His black eyes searched hers unexpectedly.

Chelsea looked away, afraid she had let her emotions show. "It was a lonely time for me."

He put down the canvas and came to her. "I can't imagine you ever being lonely."

His words surprised her. "You don't know me. How could you possibly know whether I'm ever lonely or not?"

With a sad smile, he said, "I don't know you, but I feel you and I are a great deal alike." Without explaining, he turned and picked up another canvas. "This shows a great deal of promise."

"Thank you. I still have a lot of work to do on that one. I'm not satisfied yet."

He went to the canvas on her easel. "All your work has a note of sadness."

"There's no reason why it should," she said defensively. "I'm not a hermit. I have friends, and I wouldn't say that I'm particularly lonely."

"No?" He looked back at her as if he knew better.

"No more so than anyone else."

"I understand what you mean. You can be lonely even in a crowd." He came to her, but stopped short of touching her.

Chelsea didn't want his closeness to be exciting, but her pulse quickened. She refused to back away.

"I'm lonely myself. I can recognize it in others."

"Since Mr. Bane is your father-in-law, I assume you're married to his daughter."

Jason turned away. "Technically, yes."

"Isn't that like being a little bit pregnant? Either you're married or you aren't."

"I'm married, but we're separated." He held up his left hand to show her he wasn't wearing a wedding ring. "We're getting a divorce."

"Mr. Bane didn't act as if there were bad feelings between you."

"We have a business relationship. We're trying not to let my separation from Audrey effect our business interests."

"I shouldn't think that would be possible."

"It's amicable, as divorces go. I don't hate Audrey, and she doesn't hate me. We just don't want to be married any longer."

"Are there children?"

"No. If there were, matters would be considerably more complicated. No, we never had children." He looked away and she wondered if he was more deeply hurt by the separation than he was willing to admit. "That's my primary regret. I wanted children."

"I know," Chelsea said in commiseration. "I'm so happy that my friend, Karen, has a baby, but at times," she laughed self-consciously, "I'm almost jealous."

He looked back at her, and his dark eyes seemed to bore into her soul. "I've felt exactly that way! Everyone of our friends has a family, and I feel I've missed out on so much. Little League games, school plays, recitals. All the things my friends seem to take for granted."

"I love to hold little Bethany," Chelsea said, voicing her feelings for the first time. "She's so tiny and cuddly and warm and soft. When I pick her up it's as if she snuggles down in perfect trust that I won't drop her or frighten her in any way."

"Where do babies get such complete trust?" Jason asked with a sad smile. "At least you can hold her. It's harder for a man. It's not considered manly to want to hold a baby."

"I don't know. I think gentleness and caring are attractive in a man."

"Do you?" he asked with interest.

"I'm talking too much. I have a bad habit of doing that." She went to a canvas that stood against the wall. "Did you see this one? I was trying to capture the essence of sunset. Not just the colors, but the way it makes me feel."

"You're very sensitive. I thought you might be." He took the canvas from her and studied it. "I want to hang several of these in my gallery."

"Do you?" She had driven by the gallery earlier that day and had discovered it was in an affluent section of the city. To have paintings exhibited there could be important to her career.

"I have a number of clients who would be interested in your work. The one who comes immediately to mind has a villa in South America. He's filling it with important paintings, for investment purposes. He would be excited by your work, I'm sure." He went back to the one called *Reverie*. "And I want a friend of mine to see this one. She's an interior decorator."

Chelsea put her head to one side. "Oh?"

"Viola Pearson is one of the best in Dallas. She's terribly exclusive and audaciously expensive."

Phantom thoughts of her "inexpensive" art left Chelsea's head. She was glad she had thought to hide those works in the closet before he arrived. It wouldn't do to let someone like Jason know she had ever prostituted her talent. "I'd like to meet her."

Jason came back to her. "You know, you're fascinating."

She tried to laugh. "I'm not. I'm as ordinary as they come."

"No, you're not. Don't ever let me hear you say that again." As before, he stood so close to her, she thought he might be about to touch her. "I want to know more about you. Where did you come from? What's your background?"

Chelsea led him back into the living room and poured them coffee before she curled her feet under her on the couch. Jason sat beside her. "I've been in college until recently. SMU."

"It's a good one."

She smiled in agreement. "My father is in the Army so he and my mother traveled quite a bit. I usually lived here in Dallas with my grandparents. They wanted me to have an American education and more stability than Army life offers. But I was able to go abroad from time to time, so I've studied art under teachers in England and Spain."

"Oh?"

"They weren't painters you would have heard of. Dad didn't intend for me to become an artist, and he was never stationed in a place that would give me access to a really great teacher. But I learned a lot of different techniques and approaches."

"I think you may have developed some of your own, as well."

She smiled. "Yes. I love to paint. I always have. When I'm painting, I feel omnipotent." She laughed. "I know that sounds silly."

"Nothing you say is silly."

Chelsea looked across the room at a painting hanging on her wall. Seriously she said, "It's as if I become more than I really am. As if I become part of my art. I lose myself and all track of time. Karen—the friend I mentioned earlier—swears she's carried on conversations with me and I've never heard a word that was being said."

"That's the concentration all great artists have."

"I would hardly call myself great."

"Not yet, but you will be. The depth of feeling in your canvases promises to become imperative. When you reach that point, you'll have greatness."

Chelsea studied his face to see if this was all a pack of lies. "You really think I have that capability?"

"Yes, I do. Otherwise I wouldn't say it. What do I have to gain by paying you empty compliments? I've already said I want to hang your work in my gallery. I don't do that just to make an artist feel good. If I did, I'd lose my credibility and be out of business in a month."

"True. You have to uphold a certain standard. It's just that I've never been sure of my talent. There's a vast difference between being better than average and in being an artist. I'm too close to my art. I can't be objective."

"I can." Jason pointed to the canvas she was studying. "I can see depths in your colors and an intensity of feeling that doesn't come along every day. It almost shimmers with life."

Chelsea wasn't so sure she agreed with that comparison, but she knew better than to argue the point with a gallery owner. If he saw something that impressed him she would be foolish to talk him out of believing in it.

"How do you achieve that clarity?"

"I mix my own painting medium. It's a combination of Damar varnish, sun-thickened linseed oil, and Venice turpentine."

"Never tell anyone the secret. It's one of your marks of individuality." He turned back to her. "I wish I could take some of the sadness out of your eyes."

Chelsea didn't know how to answer. Did it show so plainly, or was this something he had hit upon by accident? "I'm not sad. You're mistaken."

"No, I'm not." He leaned toward her slightly, then stopped. "I think I had better go."

She hadn't expected him to say this. "So soon? I mean, I'm glad you came by. I wish I had other paintings to show you. Of course, I would have brought them to your gallery. You didn't have to come here to see them."

He reached over and took her hand. "I didn't come only to see the paintings. We both know that, don't we?"

She had no answer.

"That's why I should leave. I've seen the canvases. If I stayed it would only be to see you."

She couldn't look away from his dark eyes. Few people had ever made her feel this way. She wasn't drawn to him on an intellectual level, but physically she felt as if a forest fire were raging inside her. "Yes. I think you'd better go."

He didn't rise. "I really am separated. I'm not lying about that."

"I believe you." His left hand looked as if it hadn't worn a ring in a long time. Maybe not ever. She looked back at his face.

"May I see you again?"

"Of course. I'll be bringing the paintings to your gallery toward the end of next week. They'll be dry by then."

"I meant may I see you socially?"

Chelsea found herself nodding.

"Say, tomorrow night?"

"Tomorrow?"

"I understand if you're seeing someone else." He

reached up and touched her cheek. "I don't think you are, though. Not with all that unhappiness in your eyes. Let me take your sadness away."

"I'd love to see you tomorrow." She could barely think with him so near. Her body was urging her to do things that caused her thoughts to fly in all directions.

Jason leaned closer and kissed her lightly on the lips. Chelsea couldn't move. She had never expected the interview to take this turn, and she was amazed at herself for wanting to fall into his arms.

On numb feet she walked with him to the door. On her tiny porch he paused as if reluctant to leave, then turned away. Chelsea watched him go down the steps, then stepped back inside and closed the door. She didn't want to repeat the mistake she had made with Karen's cousin on the night of the wedding. She had never been one to hop into bed with a man just because it seemed to be a good idea at the moment. But Jason had come along at a time when she was unusually vulnerable, and he had said all the right things.

She went to her bathroom mirror and studied her face. What sadness had he seen there? Or was this just a line he used on all women? Now that he was gone, she could see how effective it would be. Everyone had some hidden sadness, and it was both flattering and exciting that a near stranger could detect it and want to remedy it.

"He's good," she murmured to her reflection. "I'll have to be careful with this one." But she wasn't so sure she meant it. Whether Jason had seen it or not, she was lonely and at times she desperately needed to feel a man's arms around her. He was getting a divorce so no one would get hurt. Her eyes were thoughtful as she went back into her painting room.

"No. Don't set me up with anyone else," Chelsea said firmly to Karen.

"But it's so awkward having an uneven number at a

sit-down dinner." Karen frowned at Chelsea, then at Ryan. "I don't often have such an elaborate affair. It wouldn't hurt you to humor me."

"Actually, I've started seeing someone," Chelsea said with a smile.

"You didn't tell me! Who is he? Do I know him?"

"No. He owns a gallery downtown. His name is Jason Randall."

Karen smiled broadly. "I like the sound of him. Tell me all about him."

"I met him through the Bane Gallery. Mr. Bane is his father-in-law."

" 'Father-in-law'! He's married?" Karen regarded her with alarm. "Chelsea!"

"No, no. He's not married. At least he won't be much longer. He's getting a divorce."

"I think that's just awful!" Karen looked at Ryan. "Isn't that awful, Ryan?"

Ryan wasn't smiling. "Chelsea's a grown woman. She can make her own decisions."

"In a matter of weeks, maybe months, Jason will be single," Chelsea argued. "They've been separated for a long time. It's not as if he's living with her."

"How long have you been seeing him?"

"It's been almost a month."

"And you never told me? Chel, I'm hurt!"

"I didn't know it would amount to more than a few casual dates. I saw no reason to tell you. Lately, it's become more than that." Chelsea looked over at Ryan. Their eyes met and held, and she felt miserable inside. She hurriedly looked away. He had no right to make her feel guilty.

"How much more?" Karen was still frowning. "He may be separated, but technically he's still married."

Chelsea ignored the question. She wasn't about to tell Karen in front of Ryan that she and Jason had become lovers. "May I bring him to your party? I want you to meet him."

"I suppose so. Yes, I want to meet him." Karen shook her head. "It's just taking me time to get used to the idea, that's all. Does he love you? Is it serious?"

"Maybe." Aware of Ryan's gaze on her, she refused to look in his direction. "It could be serious." Against her will, she turned her eyes toward him.

"I think I hear the baby," he said abruptly, and left the room.

Karen paused to listen. "I don't hear anything." Then she leaned toward Chelsea. "There's something you're not telling me. What is it?"

"I care a lot for him. Maybe more than I should."

"What does that mean? You're single and not getting any younger. Don't look at me like that! You know what I mean. I want you to find somebody, fall in love, marry him. I want you to be as happy as I am."

Chelsea smiled, but her heart was still with Ryan. Had he left the room because of the conversation? She was sitting near the door to the hall, and she hadn't heard Bethany cry out. Neither had Karen. "I could fall in love with Jason. He's good-looking and exciting, and he fascinates me. He owns a very prestigious art gallery."

"Forget your career! That doesn't have anything to do with falling in love with him, does it?"

"Of course not." But Chelsea wondered why she had lumped Jason's business in with the attributes she found desirable about him. "I'd never date someone in order to further my career. But I do have to make a living, and my art is so much a part of who I am. His interest in art was the common ground that brought us together."

"That's true. I can't wait to meet him. I'm upset about his being married, though. Wouldn't it be better to wait until he's really divorced? You're always hearing stories about a man claiming he's getting a divorce when he really isn't."

"You've been reading *Reader's Digest* again." Chelsea laughed. "Jason isn't lying to me. A relationship has to be built on trust, or it's not worth having."

"Have you ever been to his house or apartment or whatever?"

"No, but that doesn't mean anything. He takes me out for dinner and dancing. If he were married, he'd be reluctant to take me out in public."

"Dallas is a big city," Karen said, concerned. "If I were you, I'd insist on seeing where he lives. Or with whom."

"You worry too much." Chelsea refused to let Karen see the seed of doubt she had planted. "Once you meet him, you're going to feel ridiculous for having said half these things. You'll see."

The next few weeks were like a dream to Chelsea. Jason was ardent as a lover, almost insatiable. His desire for her knit up the scars she had suffered over Ryan's marrying Karen. They had few conversations, but that was fine with Chelsea. At the present she had more need to feel desirable as a woman. Soon she truly believed she had fallen in love with him.

Although Jason had been unable to attend Karen's dinner party, Chelsea convinced him, more or less against his will, to meet her friends one Saturday.

"See?" Chelsea whispered to Karen as they put together an informal lunch. "Isn't he all I said he'd be?" She looked out the window to where Jason and Ryan were standing in the yard and talking.

"He's very nice."

"Nice? A head of lettuce is nice. Jason is sexy!"

Karen looked out the window. "He's good-looking."

Chelsea frowned. "You don't like him?"

"I don't even know him." Karen tried to laugh off the question. "Will you get the potato salad out of the refrigerator? I hope everyone likes it. I made a boat load."

Chelsea opened the refrigerator door and took out the covered bowl. "I think I'm in love with him," she said. "I'm pretty sure he feels the same way about me. Should I take this out to the picnic table?" Although September had arrived, it was still hot enough to wear summer clothes and to appreciate air conditioning.

"Yes, we're eating out there. How can you know so soon that you're in love with him? You've only known each other since July."

"What do you have against him?"

Karen stopped slicing tomatoes onto a plate and stood with her knife poised as she thought. "When will his divorce be final?"

"I'm not sure. The last time I asked, it had been bumped back on the docket. I don't ask very often. It upsets him."

Karen turned to her. "Don't you think that's a bit strange? I mean, if he wants to divorce this woman, why would he be upset over talking about it?"

"How should I know? I've never been divorced." Chelsea didn't want to admit that she had wondered the same thing. "Besides, what could he hope to gain by lying about it?"

"He could gain you as a mistress."

Chelsea frowned at her. "I never thought of myself in that term."

"Well, isn't that the name for it?" She went to Chelsea. "I just want you to be happy. I'm afraid he'll hurt you."

"Nonsense. Jason doesn't have a bad temper. He's certainly not violent, and he'd never hurt me."

"I don't mean physically, and you know it."

"Karen, I just told you that we're in love. I'm probably going to marry him."

"Has he asked you?"

"Not in so many words, no. But like you said, we've only known each other for a short while. Neither of us want to jump into something permanent until we know if it'll last." She started taking the cover off the potato salad bowl. "I was hoping you'd stop worrying once you met him."

Karen shook her head. "I had hoped so, too. I don't know, Chel. There's just something about him. It's not anything I can put my finger on, but it's there, nonetheless. You know, like a sound you can't quite hear."

Chelsea laughed. "How can you be aware of a sound you can't hear?"

"You know what I mean. There's just something about him I don't trust."

"Well, get over it. I love Jason, and if he proposes I'll say yes." Chelsea spoke with confidence to overcome her own doubts. "He's exactly what I should have in a husband."

She carried the bowl outside and smiled at the men. Ryan didn't return her smile, but Jason did. She went over to them. "It's almost ready. Karen says she hopes you like potato salad, because she made enough to feed an army."

"I do." Jason looped a familiar arm about her shoulders. "Ryan was just showing me where he wants to put a garden."

Ryan turned away. "You know how Karen is about planting things. Or to be more exact, how she likes to give Juan something to plant."

If Chelsea didn't know him so well, she wouldn't have noticed the strain in his voice. She wondered if he and Karen were arguing. That might explain Karen's reluctance to like Jason. When Karen was angry, she was angry at everything. "I'll go back in and help Karen. I just wanted to get a hug."

Jason dropped a kiss on her forehead and released her. For some reason Chelsea wished he hadn't done that in front of Ryan. As she went back to the house, she questioned her feelings. She loved Jason, and Ryan loved Karen. What could possibly be wrong with Jason's kissing her?

When Chelsea was back inside, Ryan said carefully, "She's a special lady."

Jason glanced at the back door. "Chelsea? Yes, she is."

"We were hoping you could come to the party we gave a few weeks ago. Chelsea said you had to work."

"That's right. Weekends are difficult for me. Today is an

exception. I'm usually freer with my time during the week."

"I'm surprised at that." Ryan started back to the covered patio. Jason walked beside him. "I would have thought a gallery owner would do most of his work during the week. Chelsea says she usually sees you then."

"On weekends I sometimes travel to other places in search of art for my gallery."

"Oh? I don't know much about the gallery business." Ryan smiled to relax Jason's guard. For some reason, Jason seemed to be weighing every word before he spoke it.

"It's pretty much like any other business, I suppose."

"Would you say Chelsea has more talent than the average artist?"

"It's hard to say. She's good. If she weren't, I wouldn't hang her canvases in my gallery. But I've seen better."

Ryan smiled as if he couldn't care less. "I've always thought she was exceptionally talented."

"There's so much more to art than something pleasing to the eye. Truly great art has something I call heart."

"And Chelsea lacks that?"

Jason nodded. "Don't tell her I said it. She's good, but she lacks depth."

"That's strange. She told us you think her art is the best thing since sliced bread."

Jason winked at him and grinned. "If it makes her happy, why not let her believe that? As I said, she's better than average, and she hasn't reached her full potential, probably."

"So why let her think she has?" Ryan kept his voice calm, but he was watching Jason carefully.

"Like I said, it makes her happy. When she's happy, I'm happy. If you get my meaning." He winked again.

Ryan controlled his impulse to hit the man, but he knew in that instant that his reservations about Jason were right. The gallery owner was only using Chelsea.

The door opened and Chelsea followed Karen out with

the rest of the picnic fare. "It's ready. Let's eat before Bethany wakes up from her nap." She smiled at Karen. "We almost never have a chance to eat a complete meal without one of us having to jump up and change her or feed her or hold her or something."

Jason sat with his back to the yard, and Chelsea slid onto the bench beside him. Ryan saw Jason's arm move and knew he had his hand on Chelsea's leg. Knowing how Jason really felt about Chelsea the move made Ryan's temper rise. He practically shoved the plate of sandwiches at the man.

Jason took one and then handed the plate to Chelsea.

"I'm going to the beach next weekend," she said to him. "Want to come with me? I've rented a house, and I plan to lie around all weekend."

"You know how busy I am then. I can't come."

"Where exactly do you go to search out this art?" Ryan asked. "I'd have thought the artists would contact you."

"Usually they do. But I also hear of art shows and attend them. Occasionally I find something interesting."

"At an amateur show?" Karen asked. "I would think that would be a waste of time. Is it really worth your while?"

Jason smiled at Chelsea as if they had an understanding that Karen couldn't grasp. "I find art in some surprising places."

Chelsea poked at him. "He's always teasing me about my apartment and it being filled wall to wall with paintings. I'll move one of these days. Maybe I'll rent that warehouse Karen and I used to say we'd own. What about it, Jason? Would you like to share a warehouse with me? Karen has become married and respectable, so I can't count on her to lead a bohemian life."

He laughed and patted her leg.

Ryan noticed he didn't answer the question. "Yes, Jason. What about that?" Ryan asked innocently. "You could help Chelsea stretch canvas and smell all those paintings in the making. That should be a gallery owner's dream—having his own private artist."

Jason gave him a calculating look, and Ryan smiled guilelessly. Still Jason made no commitment.

Chelsea glanced at Ryan, then back at Jason. "He's right, you know. I could send paintings to work with you and save the trip downtown." She laughed and bumped his arm in a joking manner. "We could call it a garret and pretend to be starving. Think what good press it would make for my artist's profile."

"Sounds too permanent to me," Jason said lightly. "Besides, I like your apartment in spite of my complaints about it."

Ryan saw Chelsea and Karen exchange a look, and some of the sparkle went out of Chelsea for a while, but soon she was her old self, making jokes and laughing along with everyone else. Ryan wondered how he could tell her what he had found out about Jason without hurting her too badly. Karen had once told him that Chelsea had a knack for picking men it would be best to avoid. Now he saw what she had meant.

Chapter Ten

Chelsea managed to find a parking space on the crowded street outside Jason's gallery. She maneuvered her car into it, wishing she owned a smaller car that would be easier to park. That was out of the question as long as she intended to transport canvases, however.

The air had turned cool, and she enjoyed the respite from the past summer's heat. Windows had Halloween trappings, the feel of autumn was in the air, and Chelsea's step was brisk as she went into the gallery.

A man came to meet her. "May I help you?"

"I'm Chelsea Cavin. I have some paintings on exhibit here."

"Of course. Forgive me for not having recognized you." The man gave her a smile, but he looked no more welcoming.

"That's all right. I come in so seldom it's not surprising that you didn't know me. Is Jason here?"

The man regarded her for a moment before saying, "No, he isn't coming in today."

Chelsea frowned slightly. "Are you sure? I left a message that I need to pick up my canvases for a show in Waco."

"I gave him the message. He said to give you whichever canvases you want."

"I had expected him to be here." She tried not to feel so

disappointed. "This is an important show for me. I thought he might help me choose what to take."

"I'm sure I can help you with that." The man's demeanor was coolly polite as if he wished he didn't have to talk to her.

"That's not really necessary." She went to her nearest painting. "Has there been any interest in this one? It's been here for a while."

"No, I'm afraid not." He didn't sound sorry, and he glanced at his watch as if he wished she would finish her business and leave.

Chelsea had only seen this man on one other occasion, but she had the distinct impression that he disliked her. She told herself that was ridiculous. "I may as well take it. I don't want to leave one hanging until everyone notices it's not selling."

"You'll want to take the one on the back wall as well. For the same reason." He walked away to remove that painting.

Chelsea glanced at him as she unhooked the painting from the hanger. Why would Jason keep on someone who was so unpleasant? For that matter, why wasn't Jason here? Perhaps his salesman hadn't given him the message at all.

From the half-dozen canvases she had there, she chose four. While the man removed the others from the wall, she went out to her car to get the quilt she used to keep the paintings from being scratched in transit. When she returned she found a couple had come into the store and were asking about her painting that the salesman was removing from the wall. Chelsea wasn't close enough to overhear the conversation, but it was easy to see that the salesman was directing their attention to another canvas against the far wall.

Chelsea frowned and went to him as the couple moved away. "Weren't they asking about my painting?"

"Originally. They're now looking at that one over there."

Giving him a long look, Chelsea went over to the couple. "Hello. My name is Chelsea Cavin. I saw you looking at my painting." She nodded in its direction. If you have any questions, I'd be happy to answer them."

The woman smiled. "It's a shame it's already sold. It's exactly what we're looking for."

"But it's not sold. I only asked that it be removed so I can take it to an exhibit." She steered the couple back, and they bought her work on the spot.

After they were gone, Chelsea went over to the salesman. "Why did you try to block the sale of my painting?" She was barely able to keep her anger under control. She needed every penny she could get.

"You're mistaken." He regarded her with pure dislike.

"I intend to tell Jason about this." She enfolded the remaining three paintings in the quilt and carried them out to the car.

As she drove back toward her apartment, her anger built. She pulled into a service station and went to the public phone booth. Jason had never given her his home number, but she had never needed it. During the day she could always find him at the gallery, and at night he was frequently with her.

There were two Jason Randalls listed. She knew by the voice that the first wasn't the man she sought. The second number was answered by a woman.

For a minute Chelsea was too surprised to speak. "I must have the wrong number. I'm looking for the Jason Randall who owns an art gallery?"

"Yes. Just a moment." The woman put the receiver down, and Chelsea heard her call Jason to the phone.

His voice sounded familiar and relaxed. "Hello?"

Chelsea found herself gripping the receiver so tightly her fingers were growing numb. "Jason? Who was that?"

"Chelsea? I didn't expect you to call." A guarded note

leaped into his voice, but was gone when he said, "Did you get the paintings you wanted to take to the exhibit?"

"Yes." She could hear children's voices in the background. "I must have caught you at a bad time. I didn't realize you had company. I can hear children."

Jason paused for a beat. "Yes. They'll be leaving soon. It's no problem."

"That man you have working at the gallery gave me a problem. While I was there, a couple asked about *Interlude,* and he told them it was already sold. Luckily I was there to explain to them that it wasn't. They bought it, but wouldn't have if I hadn't been there."

"So it's been sold? Wonderful!"

"Didn't you hear me? Your salesman tried to block the sale. I can't help but wonder how many times he's refused to sell paintings. He could be costing us both a great deal of money!"

"I'll have a talk with him first thing tomorrow." Jason sounded a bit too impersonal, as if someone were listening to his end of the conversation. In a lower tone, he added, "I'll call you tomorrow."

In spite of her desire to trust him, Chelsea's uneasiness was growing. "You never mentioned that you were expecting company today. And why would a guest answer your phone?"

"Yes," he said as if responding to her previous statements for someone else's benefit. "I'll look into the matter about the sale of your painting. If he's not doing his job right, I'll see that there's no problem in the future."

"What's going on, Jason?"

"I'll talk to you about it tomorrow. Goodbye."

Before she could speak, she heard him hang up. For a moment Chelsea stood holding the dead receiver. Then she hung up and looked in the phone book again. When she found the listing for Jason Randall she wrote down the address.

It took her a while to locate the street because he didn't live anywhere near the section in which he had claimed to reside. This neighborhood was similar to the one she lived in, not one of the exclusive sections. This didn't bother her, but she wondered why he had lied. And why she had been willing to take so much on faith before now.

The street was quiet and had brick houses of varying colors but similar designs. It was the sort of street where children rode bicycles and where the landscaping lacked the polished touch of a professional gardener.

She found the house and let her car roll to a stop. Jason was in the front yard, on his hands and knees and working in a flower bed. A woman worked beside him in old jeans and a faded blouse. As Chelsea watched, two children, a boy and a girl, ran out of the house, circled the only tree and raced back inside again.

The woman sensed her presence and looked up, shading her eyes against the sunlight. In one hand she held the packet of bulbs she and Jason were planting. She said something to him because he glanced at her and then looked over his shoulder at Chelsea. When he recognized her, he froze and the expression on his face was a mixture of anger and dismay.

Chelsea's world dropped out from under her. The domesticity of the scene tore at her. Jason and his wife weren't separated at all.

She peeled away from the curb, her only thought to get as far away from there as possible. Somehow she found her way home, though she had no memory of getting there. She ran up the steps and fumbled with the key, unable to see through her tears.

Jason had lied! He was still married!

The enormity of what she had discovered threatened to crush her. It all made sense now. He wasn't available on weekends because he was with his wife and children then. That was why he had asked her not to call him at home. It was because his family was there, not because he was rarely in the house as he had told her. Chelsea felt like a fool. She had fallen for the oldest line in the world.

She fell onto her bed and curled into a tight ball around

her pillow. The tears flowed unchecked. No wonder Jason had never talked to her about their future. No future was possible. As Karen had once said, she was his mistress. Nothing more.

She lost track of time and was startled when someone knocked loudly on her door. When she answered it, Jason was there.

"What the hell did you mean, coming by my house like that?" he demanded as he pushed past her.

Chelsea glared at him. "You told me you were separated and that you would soon be divorced! You're still living with her!"

"What does that have to do with it? You must have known that!"

She stared at him. "I believed you!"

"Nobody is that naive." Jason paced the length of her apartment and back. "I told you never to call me at home. What the hell did you think I meant?"

"I thought you meant that you wouldn't be there! I believed you!"

He made an angry sound in his throat. "Thank God Audrey believed me when I said you were a stranger looking for another address! Do you realize the trouble you could have caused me? Do you have any idea what you've done?"

"Me! Don't you assume any blame in this? You're the one who pursued me, with your lies about being alone and needing me as much as I needed you. Why did you lie to me?"

"Women like to hear those things. I've never met a woman who didn't like to see herself as a paragon of pain and misery. You didn't really believe all that crap, did you?"

"You knew I did!" She went to him and glared up at him. "You even said you loved me!"

"And I do. In a way."

Chelsea took a step back. She felt as if he had hit her. "Leave, Jason. Now. Don't come back."

"You don't mean that. You said you love me."

She lifted her head defiantly. "And you believed me? It seems I'm not the only naive one in this room." She was lying, but she wasn't about to admit that her heart was breaking.

Jason frowned at her. "We can forget all this happened. Just don't ever do it again."

Chelsea's mouth dropped open. "That's why your salesman acted the way he did! He knows you're married and that you're seeing me! That's it, isn't it?"

"I'm going to tell him to mind his own damned business. What I do is no business of his."

She backed away as embarrassment flooded through her. "Get out of my house, Jason! Now!" She went to the door and yanked it open.

"Now, Chelsea, you're upset. I don't really blame you." He was trying to hide his anger behind a conciliatory smile. "If you really believed me, you didn't mean any harm. I was wrong about that." He spread his hands, palms up. "How was I to know you're such an innocent?"

"I guess the same way I was supposed to know you're a bastard! I'll be better able to recognize one in the future."

A muscle knotted in Jason's jaw, but he didn't give in to his anger. "Close the door and come here. There's no reason for us to argue over this. Now we've cleared the air. Let's make up."

"Make up?" she exclaimed. "Aren't you listening? I have no intention of making up! I never want to see you again!"

"You're not thinking this through." His smile vanished. "I've opened a lot of doors for you. I can close them just as easily."

"I don't believe you," she said bluntly. "You can't blackmail me into having a relationship with you."

"No? It's time you grew up, Chelsea. All that purity and innocence may be charming, but this is the real world. Everyone has his price. We all pay our dues. If you want

to get on in the art world, you'll play the game like everyone else. Otherwise, you're finished. It's that simple."

"You're lying again. My paintings are good. I don't
need to sleep with you in order to sell them."

"No, but you do if you intend to sell them in any gallery
worth mentioning. We're all acquaintances, you see. All it
takes is a word from me and you won't be exhibited."

"That's not true. Why would your competitors listen to
you?"

"Because none of us likes to be involved in a lawsuit. All
I have to tell them is I have reason to know your paintings
are being copied from another artist's work and a lawsuit
is pending. You'll be dropped like a hot rock."

"You're lying!"

"No, I'm not. I've seen it happen before."

Chelsea was so angry she was trembling. "If you don't
leave, I'm going to call the police."

Jason hesitated, then realized she meant it. He strode to
the door and brushed roughly past her. "You'll be sorry
for this," he threatened. "You're going to wish you had
listened to me before all this is over!"

"No way." She slammed the door in his face and locked
it. From the other side she heard a string of curses, but
Jason left.

She went to her couch and sat on the far end, her legs
drawn up so her forehead could rest on her knees. She felt
sick inside. After a while she heard another knock on her
door, but she ignored it. When she heard a car drive away,
she opened the door and found the other two paintings she
had left at Jason's gallery. She took them inside and put
them away. A heavy numbness pervaded her.

In the next few days Chelsea discovered Jason hadn't
lied about everything. His father-in-law called from the
Bane Gallery and told her he was returning her canvases.
Bane was genial, but much cooler than he had ever been
in the past. Chelsea tried to explain that it was a lie about

her pirating another artist's work, but that seemed to further convince Bane it was true.

Her exhibit in Waco was canceled the day before she was to have delivered the paintings. Chelsea was furious with Jason for what he was doing to her and with herself for having been so gullible. Every gallery she approached with her work politely turned her away. If it hadn't been for her inexpensive Victorian paintings, she wouldn't have made enough to make ends meet.

"Chel, what's wrong with you?" Karen asked as she bounced Bethany on her knee.

"Nothing. I don't know what you're talking about." Chelsea hadn't told Karen about Jason. She didn't want to hear that her friend had tried to warn her.

"It's depression. I've read about the symptoms. It seems like everybody has it these days. It's like an epidemic."

"That's probably it." Chelsea held out a rattle to the baby. Bethany grabbed it and tried to stuff it in her mouth. "I'll get over it."

"Is it because the Waco exhibit was canceled? I don't see how they can do that to you. I mean, wouldn't they know ahead of time if they're going to be painting the walls that week? How can they run a business like that?"

"Painting?" Chelsea had almost forgotten the excuse she had given Karen for not attending the exhibit she had been so eager for. "Yes. You'd think so." She looked around her apartment. Almost every surface was covered with paintings. "I need to find a new place to exhibit. They're starting to stack up on me."

"Jason won't hang any more?" Karen expertly wiped the drool from Bethany's lips. "I think she's teething."

Chelsea regarded the baby who was concentrating on getting the rattle in her mouth. "I need to branch out. Maybe I'll try some galleries in Fort Worth."

"You need to diversify. That's what Daddy always says."

Chelsea smiled at her. "Maybe so."

"We've been worried about you. You haven't been over in a while. Are you leaving your phone off the hook?"

"At times."

"I wish you wouldn't do that. I try to call you and all I get is a busy signal. What if I really needed you for something?"

"Sorry. I didn't want the phone to interrupt my concentration." She also hadn't wanted to take a chance on answering it and finding Jason at the other end. She was more lonely than ever and wasn't sure her anger was still strong enough for her not to agree to see him again.

"There's something you're not telling me. Chel, I can always tell. Out with it."

Chelsea studied her as she sat back down on the couch. At times Karen's perception surprised her. At others, it took a house falling on her to get Karen's attention. "It's nothing. Isn't it early for Bethany to be cutting teeth?"

As she hoped, the question diverted Karen's attention. For the next hour Karen explained teething and told Chelsea all the clever things the baby had done in the past week. Chelsea was glad to have the conversation on a safer subject.

Karen left when it was time for Ryan to come home from work, and Chelsea went into her studio and stared at the canvases. She hadn't been able to work on an important one since her argument with Jason. When she heard a knock on the door, she considered ignoring it, but then changed her mind and answered it.

"Ryan!" She stepped aside to let him inside. "What are you doing here?"

"I wanted to talk to you. Is it okay?"

"Sure." She gestured at the couch and chairs. "Karen just left a few minutes ago."

"I called Jason's gallery and learned he's no longer exhibiting your work. What's going on?"

Chelsea sat beside him and picked up a throw pillow to cuddle in her lap. As she ran her fingers along the seams, she said, "We don't see each other anymore."

"Since when? Karen didn't tell me about it."

"She doesn't know." She looked up at him. "Why did you call the gallery?"

"I wanted to buy a gift for my parents' anniversary."

"I'd have given you a painting."

"I know. That's why I called the gallery. The man I talked with was hardly polite when I told him what I wanted."

"That would be Jason's primary salesman. He doesn't care for me."

"What happened?" Ryan's voice was soft and deep.

Tears sprang to Chelsea's eyes. "Don't be nice to me. I'm tired of crying, and you'll get me started all over again." She puckered the pillow, then hit it. "I don't want Karen to know about it, but I found out Jason is married."

"You already knew that."

"I mean *really* married. As in living with her. He's not getting a divorce at all. And there are kids. I saw them running out of the house." Tears spilled out of her eyes, and she impatiently brushed them off her cheeks. "I was such a fool! I feel so stupid!"

He was silent for a while. "I can't say I'm sorry to hear you're no longer seeing him. I didn't like him any more than Karen did."

She sighed. "Why didn't I listen to the two of you? I thought I knew what I was doing, but I was so blind! Now that I know he was lying, it was all there in front of my face! All I had to do was think and I'd have known he was feeding me a line! Why do I have to learn everything the hard way?"

Ryan reached out and pulled her against him. "It's okay. Nothing catastrophic happened. Let him go."

Chelsea rested her cheek against his chest and listened to the calming beating of his heart. "It's catastrophic in a way. He's had me blackballed from all the best galleries in Dallas."

"Can he do that?" Ryan held her protectively.

"He's done it." She closed her eyes. "I needed to be

held. How did you know how much I needed to have somebody hug me and tell me the world hasn't come to an end?"

"I know you pretty well." He stroked her hair gently. She could feel his breath warm against it.

Chelsea relaxed against him. "Karen will never let me live this down. She never liked Jason. She told me he wasn't to be trusted. Why didn't I listen to her?"

"You thought you were in love, I guess. We all make mistakes." He sounded almost as sad as she did.

She raised her head. For a moment they didn't move. Then Chelsea pulled away and sat up. "I shouldn't have let you do that."

"Do what?" he asked in a forced voice. "All I did was hold you. It's no more than Karen would have done."

"But you're not Karen," she said softly. Not trusting herself, she got up from the couch and said, "Thanks for coming by. I guess I needed a friend more than I realized."

"No problem." He stood and went to the door. "Do you want me to tell Karen for you? I'll see that she understands she's not to rub it in. Not that I think she would."

"No, I'll tell her." Chelsea didn't want Karen to know Ryan had been there. Nothing had actually happened, but in Chelsea's heart and mind something momentous had almost occurred. "I'll call her as soon as you leave."

He paused at the door. "Are you sure you're all right?"

"Yes." She managed a smile. "Karen has already diagnosed me as depressed, but I'm not suicidal. This happened a week ago. I'm getting used to it now."

"If you need me, all you have to do is call."

"I know," she said softly. He turned to leave. "Ryan," she said. "Thanks."

He turned and smiled at her. "Anytime."

She closed the door behind him and pressed her cheek against it. The embrace had happened so naturally. Had he meant it only as a friendly gesture? Was she reading more into it than was meant?

Chelsea groaned and put her back against the door. She

had to believe Ryan had only platonic feelings for her. Otherwise, she couldn't continue the friendship. Unfortunately, she hadn't felt platonic at all when he had stroked her hair so gently, the way he used to before she had run away to Germany.

She went to the sink and washed her face. Such thoughts were only going to lead to trouble. She had just screwed up monumentally with Jason. She couldn't afford to do the same with the friendship she shared with Karen and Ryan.

Going to the phone, she dialed their number. When Karen answered, Chelsea said, "I have something to tell you about Jason."

Chapter Eleven

"There's someone I want you to meet," Karen said as soon as Chelsea was in the door. "You're really going to like him."

"I don't want to meet anyone." Chelsea went into the den and sat in the chair nearest the window.

"Now don't be like that. What are you going to do? Mope about Jason forever? It's been over a month."

Chelsea leaned her head back against the chair in exasperation. "I loved him. Or at least I thought I did. I don't know which it was anymore. But I'm not ready to meet anyone. . . . Who is it?"

Karen smiled as if Chelsea had given in. "It's one of my cousins from Oklahoma. He didn't come to my wedding, so you've never seen him before. I couldn't believe how good-looking he is now! As a child he was so skinny!"

"No way. It's not that I don't like your family, but even if we *did* hit it off, he'll go back to Oklahoma and I'll be here in Dallas."

"I thought you said you didn't want a real relationship. I thought this would be perfect. You can date him a time or two, then he'll go away and leave you alone." Karen's forehead puckered in her effort to understand.

"Even if I wanted to date, I would seldom have time. I've had to work part-time, and I'm usually scheduled for hours the other employees want off. When I'm not at the

Burger Barn, I'm painting. Even the little Victorian pictures take hours to do, you know."

"I think it was mean of Jason to have you blackballed. Can't you sue him for defamation of character or something?"

"What's the point? I'd have to prove I never copied anyone's work, and how can I do that? It would be easy to prove I had, but the reverse is nearly impossible. Besides, I keep hoping I'll find some gallery Jason didn't reach. I just don't want the adverse publicity."

"I knew I didn't like him the minute I saw him. Didn't I tell you? I just wish you'd listened to me."

"Don't start, Karen."

"Well, I want you to be happy, don't I? You're like a loser magnet. Every Jason in the state seems to bump into you. There was Bryan Nivens in college. Remember him? He used you to pass *three* classes. And Will Olsen? We won't even go into that!"

"Why is it you can't go to the grocery store for milk without a list, yet you can recall every mistake I ever made? You have a rare talent. You really do."

"I think it's good to remember things like that. You're not as likely to make the same mistake twice. You could use a better memory, Chel."

"Why bother when I have you?"

"Have you ever been attracted to a single man who was good for you?"

Chelsea looked at Karen, then turned away. There had been one. "Probably not."

From down the hall came an infant's cry for attention and Karen went to get Bethany, leaving Chelsea to gaze unseeingly out the window. There had been one good man in her life, but she had been stupid enough to lose him forever to her best friend. The depression she had fought for weeks settled about her.

Karen came back with Bethany. When the little girl saw Chelsea, she gave a squeal of delight and struggled to get to her. Karen put her on the floor, and Chelsea held out her hands. Then Bethany crawled across the carpet and threw herself into Chelsea's arms.

As she hugged the child, Chelsea said, "She's getting around really well now. I told you this is a genius baby." She rubbed her nose against Bethany's, and the little girl laughed and patted her cheeks.

"Bethany, can you tell Aunt Chel our surprise?" Karen asked.

"What surprise?" Chelsea sat Bethany on her knee and played patty cake with her hands.

"Bethany is going to be a big sister."

Chelsea looked up sharply. "What? You're pregnant?"

"I just found out this morning. That's why I wanted you to come over."

"What did Ryan say?"

"I haven't told him yet."

"Karen, your husband is supposed to be the first to know." Chelsea looked at the baby on her lap. "Isn't this awfully soon?"

"I suppose so, but I want to get it over and be done with it. I don't like being pregnant. Two babies. That's all I'm going to have. It's what I've always wanted."

"I know. Obviously Ryan is in agreement."

Karen lowered her eyes.

"Karen? He *is* in agreement, isn't he?"

"He doesn't know anything about it yet. He thinks I'm still taking my birth-control pills."

"Oh, no! He wasn't planning on it?" Chelsea stared at her. "You shouldn't have done this!"

"Well, I don't know why not. After all, I'm the one who gets pregnant and goes into labor and everything. Not him! It should be my decision."

"But he's your husband! This is something you should have decided together!"

"It's too late now. I've already done it. I thought you'd be happy for me." Karen looked like a petulant child.

"I am happy for you, but—"

"But nothing! Ryan will be happy. You'll see. Every man wants a son."

"You don't know it will be a boy. There aren't any guarantees."

"I just feel this one is a boy. That's what I always wanted—a boy and a girl. The perfect family."

"Does your mother know?"

Karen's expression clouded. "Not yet. I'm not going to tell her for a while."

"She's going to notice before long. You know how early you started to show with Bethany." Chelsea let the baby chew on the gold locket she wore around her neck. "You'll have to tell her before then."

"I know that!" Karen bit at her fingernail before she thought, then jerked it out of her mouth. "Will you go with me to tell her?"

"Me? That's Ryan's place!"

"I know, but to tell you the truth, Mother isn't that fond of Ryan."

"She's not? How can anyone not like him?"

"You know how stubborn he can be. I keep telling him to give in to Mother now and then but he won't do it. They had an argument over whether Bethany should be allowed to have a night light or not."

"I can't see that it hurts."

"That's exactly what Ryan said. Mother says we're spoiling her to the point where we won't be able to do anything with her in a few years."

"It doesn't spoil a child to love them. What will be gained by letting her be afraid at night?"

"Have you been talking to Ryan about this? You're using the same argument he used."

"No, this is the first I've heard about it."

"Anyway, Ryan won't back down, and you know Mother never gives in, so I'm caught in the middle." Karen sighed. "Because I have to live with Ryan, Bethany has a night light, but when I know Mother is coming to visit, I hide it."

"Bethany is your daughter. If you and Ryan want her to have a night light there shouldn't be any discussion about it. I don't think you'd be so afraid of the dark today if you'd had one when you were little."

"You're probably right. But it's so hard to stand up to Mother. I've never been able to do it successfully."

Chelsea watched Bethany try to gnaw through the locket. "Your family won't be pleased by your news."

"I know. So you see why I don't want Ryan to help me tell them? They might hate him after this."

"I doubt that. Okay, I'll go with you. But you owe me for this one."

Karen smiled. "I know. I've always been able to count on you."

That night Ryan was tired when he came in from work, and he wanted nothing more than dinner and a quiet evening. But he became suspicious as soon as he saw the candles on the table. "We don't have company coming, do we?"

"No, of course not. I just wanted tonight to be special, that's all."

He smiled. He was tired, but never too tired for what Karen's words might imply. Their lovemaking had become more frequent lately, and he was beginning to hope that Karen would eventually learn to enjoy it. He put his arms around her. "Where's Bethany?"

"I asked Chelsea to baby-sit for a while tonight."

"This is sounding better and better," he said, his smile broader now. "Let's skip dinner."

"I've been cooking all afternoon."

He bent to kiss her. Karen returned the kiss, but pulled away as he became more passionate. It was a familiar reaction.

"I have something to tell you." She stepped out of his arms and led him into the den. "Sit down." She sat on the couch, and he lowered himself beside her.

"We've never done it in here," he said as he tried to kiss her on the neck.

"Ryan, be serious." She put her hands on his chest and pushed him away gently but firmly. "What would make you the happiest man in the world?"

"For you to stop pushing me away." He grinned at her and tried to pull her back into his arms.

"I should have known you wouldn't be serious. Never mind." Karen crossed her arms over her chest and half turned away.

"Okay. You have my attention. What is it?" He tried to keep the disappointment from his voice.

Karen smiled at him. "I have some wonderful news. I'm pregnant!"

Ryan was silent for several minutes. "Pregnant?" he finally said.

"Now don't look at me like that. If I waited for you to decide the time is right, we'd never have another baby or we'd wait until Bethany is practically in school."

"Or until we can afford it." His anger was rising, and he wasn't sure he could block it. "Karen, why did this happen? I thought you were taking birth-control pills. I called in a prescription for you last month!"

"I know. I didn't want to tell you that I had stopped taking them. I knew you'd be mad."

"Damn right, I'm mad! What about me, Karen? Why didn't you consult me about whether or not I wanted another baby? This is too soon!"

"I knew you'd yell at me! That's why! Lately you get mad at everything!" She turned away from him, her posture rigid and her words clipped. "I want two children, a boy and a girl. If I waited for you to agree to another child, I'd never have it."

"Then you did this on purpose? It wasn't some slipup?"

"Yes, I did! I'm surprised you didn't figure it out. I've been throwing myself at you for the past month!"

Ryan drew back. Her words cut too deeply. "I should

have known you had your own reasons to let me touch you."

Karen threw him a glare. "Well, I'm sorry if I don't like to be pawed at all the time. I can't imagine any woman liking it. I think the ones who say they do just say it to make their husbands feel better. I think it's disgusting."

Ryan bit back his retort. He turned away and went to the window to stare sightlessly into the back yard. No matter how many times he heard Karen's opinion on love-making, it hurt him.

"I'm due in July. My babies will be thirteen months apart."

"And you think this is a good idea?"

"I didn't expect it to happen so quickly," Karen admitted. "I had heard it takes several months after you get off the Pill to become pregnant. I guess we just got lucky."

Ryan didn't turn to look at her. "We'll have two in diapers at the same time. Bethany will barely be walking by then."

"Nonsense. She started to crawl early. She'll be on her feet soon."

"I just wish you had discussed it with me."

"You would have tried to talk me out of it!"

"Of course I would have! If for no other reason than because this is too soon for you to get pregnant again. Not to mention our finances!"

"There you go on money again! Is that all you think about?"

"Karen, we have to pay our bills! Now we'll have more medical costs on top of everything else."

"We have insurance!"

"Our insurance won't pay for the doctor's visits, just the hospital costs. It won't buy formula or a baby's bed—we'll have to have another one, you know—or baby food." He ran his fingers through his hair in frustration. "If only you had let me have some say in this."

"I had to do it this way. I love babies! And I hate being pregnant. I wanted to get it over with as quickly as possible. That means I had to have them close together." She added, "This is my last one."

"You're only twenty-three. For all we know, we may end up with a house full." In his depressed mood, this seemed likely. If Karen decided she wanted more, he obviously couldn't stop her.

"No way. I want a boy and a girl. Just two. No more."

"It may be another girl," he pointed out. "Don't get your mind set on it being a boy."

"It's a boy. I just know it." She ran her hand over her stomach. "After this one, I'll lose the extra weight I put on. There wasn't much point in losing it before. I knew I'd only put it back on as soon as I became pregnant again."

Ryan looked at her as if he had never seen her before. "I really don't matter to you, do I?"

"Of course you do," she said impatiently. "You know I love you."

"No, I don't. I used to think you did, but I'm not sure anymore. One thing is for sure, you love yourself more."

"Now you're being ridiculous. Look at all the things I do for you. I've been cooking all afternoon! I keep the house in perfect condition!"

"I'd rather eat sandwiches and have clutter from time to time. I'd love to put my feet on the furniture and eat on TV trays occasionally! I don't want gourmet meals! I want you to kiss me for once without putting your hands on my chest so you can push me away if it lasts too long! I want you to be spontaneous! Just once I want you to initiate lovemaking!"

"There you go again! I should have known you'd bring the conversation back to that. Is sex all you can think about?"

"It wouldn't be if it happened more often!"

"I'm pregnant! Obviously it's happening often enough!" She raised her voice to a strident level. "You knew what I was like before you married me!"

"No, I didn't." He turned away again. "You had a few surprises in store for me."

"Well, you may as well make the best of it." She glared at him and tossed her head to show him how little she cared for his opinion. "I told Chelsea you'd be like this. That's why I asked her to keep Bethany. I don't want our child to hear us fighting."

Ryan looked at her over his shoulder. "You told Chelsea before you told me?"

Karen avoided his eyes. "She's my best friend. Besides, I had to give her some reason for baby-sitting on a week night."

"What did she say about our blessed event?" He couldn't keep the sarcasm out of his voice.

"She said I should have let you be in on the decision. But she's wrong! She's never been married. How could she know what it's like? Besides, she didn't tell you about—" Karen suddenly stopped and her eyes grew round.

"She didn't tell me about what?" he asked suspiciously.

"Nothing. Never mind."

"About what, Karen?" He could tell that whatever she was keeping from him was something he needed to know about.

She walked to the other side of the room and kept her back turned to him. "Chelsea's been pregnant. It happened just before she ran away to Germany at the end of college."

"What?" He had to struggle to comprehend what she was saying. "Chelsea was pregnant? She never told me."

"Of course she didn't! It was your baby!" Karen wheeled around to face him. "There! It's high time you knew! Do you know how difficult it's been to keep this from you for so long?"

Ryan felt as if his world had dipped out from under him. "My baby?"

"From that night at the lake," Karen shouted, venom in her voice. "You remember that night, don't you, Ryan? The night I'm not supposed to know anything about?"

"Why didn't she tell me?"

"She didn't want you to know. She got rid of the baby

and went to Germany. That's why she didn't tell you goodbye!"

"I don't believe you!"

"Ask her!"

He went to her. "Why are you telling me this? Why now?"

"Because I'm tired of you always asking what Chelsea would think about this or that. I'm tired of seeing you two laugh together and of remembering that you actually *slept* with her!"

"You and I weren't engaged then. I was dating you both." He felt sick inside. Sick and numb.

"That doesn't excuse it. She should have thought about me and how that would hurt me. Sometimes I can't stand to be around her for thinking of what she did with you. She was my best friend even if she did behave like a slut!"

"Don't say that about her!" Ryan stared at Karen. "I'll never understand you. Why do you invite her over if you feel that way about her?"

"I don't have a lot of friends." Her voice rang out shrilly. "If I didn't see Chelsea, I wouldn't have any at all."

He stared at her. "Then you don't care about her?"

"I didn't say that. I can usually put what happened out of my head." Karen lifted her chin angrily. "But not always. Maybe now you'll understand why I hate for you to touch me! You touched her first!"

"But you married me!"

Karen came to him, her gray eyes dangerously narrowed. "I wanted to be married. That's why I went to college in the first place! I wasn't dating anyone else, school was almost over, and my parents wanted a son-in-law. You were the one that asked."

Ryan's numbness was being replaced with a keen pain. "Then you never loved me?"

"I loved you! I loved you as much as you deserved. I knew you would make a good husband. And this way, Chelsea wouldn't have you."

"You can say that and tell me she's your friend?"

Karen smiled maddeningly. "Yes, I can. I care more for her than I do for you. We've always been friends. We always will be. It's the way I want it."

"What if I tell her all you just told me?"

"She won't believe you. I'm the best friend she's ever had. And you'd have to admit to her that you know she aborted your baby. What do you think that will do to her? She won't be able to stay friends with you, once she knows you're aware of it."

He realized she was right, but he was having trouble grasping all of it. Chelsea had been pregnant with his baby. "Why didn't Chelsea tell me?"

"She knew you'd insist on being married, and she didn't want to marry you. You know Chelsea. She doesn't want to be tied down. I doubt she'll ever marry." Karen shrugged. Ryan had the impression she was actually enjoying this. "I drove her to the place where she had the abortion and brought her home again afterward."

"I don't believe you."

"I can take you to where it happened."

Ryan turned away. He felt sick to his stomach.

"So I don't want you touching me ever again," Karen said decisively. "I want you to move back into the spare bedroom and stay there."

"Don't worry. I'll be glad to." He turned and left the room. If he stayed he would say more than he wanted to.

As he went to the bedroom and started yanking his clothing out of drawers, he considered divorcing Karen. It would be the end of his job. More important, she might be able to prevent him from seeing his children. Karen, and her parents, would be capable of doing this. Until now he hadn't realized how vindictive she could be. Yes, he might never see Bethany again. Or the new baby.

Ryan sat on the bed and stared at the pairs of socks in his hands. He had fathered a baby with Chelsea and she had never told him! She had destroyed it without ever so much as telling him it existed!

Tears stung his eyes, and he had to fight hard to keep

from shedding them. As he packed, he tried to make sense of all he had learned. Knowing Chelsea as he did, he thought it was most likely that she hadn't told him because she wouldn't have wanted him to feel trapped into a marriage. He had never convinced her that he loved her. It was an omission he had regretted for a long time. If she had known he loved her, she might—she would—have reacted differently.

He thought of her going through that painful decision alone and he hurt for her as well as for his loss. Her impulsive act—and knowing Chelsea, it was impulsive—had ruined three lives. If she had stayed in the States, he wouldn't have thought he loved Karen more. What he had seen as Chelsea's rejection of him had weighed heavily in his decision to marry Karen.

He carried an armload of clothing into the spare room and dumped it on the bed. He felt so sick inside, he wondered if he was coming down with something. Was it possible to feel this ill from sadness? He wouldn't have guessed it.

Divorce again crept into his mind. He could leave Karen and never look back if it weren't for Bethany. He didn't know the unborn baby yet. He might not love it as much. Even as the thought formed, he knew it wasn't true. Not when he had loved his first born so easily and dearly.

But Chelsea was single. What if he left Karen and went to her? Would she have him?

He had a lot to think about in the next few days.

Chapter Twelve

As spring approached, Karen decided she had to have a new house. She enlisted Chelsea to help her look.

"Are you sure this is the right street?" Chelsea asked as she looked out the car window. "These places must cost a fortune."

"Ryan makes good money. Besides, he needs to ask Daddy for a raise and this will encourage him to do it." She pulled into a drive behind a realtor's car. "She's already here. I was afraid Bethany would make me late."

Chelsea removed the baby from her car seat. "It's not her fault. She's not old enough to potty-train yet." She smiled at the little girl. "Right, honey?" Bethany crowed happily and swatted at Chelsea's face with a chubby palm.

They went up onto the narrow porch and greeted the realtor who had been watching for them. Karen introduced herself and Chelsea, then went into the house. It was exactly what she wanted.

There was a formal living room and dining room. Wallpaper in a white-on-white design was above the wainscoting. The windows were large, and the place was sunny. She disliked the draperies, but that was a small problem.

"It's certainly big!" Chelsea said. She had put Bethany on her feet and was holding her hand to balance her. Bethany hadn't been walking for long and was still unsteady on her feet.

"My family is expanding," Karen said, stating the obvious. At seven months she was larger than at full term with Bethany. The doctor had promised her it wasn't twins, but her mother wasn't so sure and told her so often. "You did say there are four bedrooms, didn't you?"

Mrs. Haroldson nodded. "Yes, they're upstairs."

Summer hadn't arrived yet, but the house was uncomfortably hot to Karen. She had begun to actively hate summers. Why did both of her babies have to be born during the hottest part of the year?

"The den is in here." Mrs. Haroldson pushed open a door to reveal a sunken room lined with bookshelves at one end.

"The carpet is awful."

"It's been well lived on, I'm afraid."

Karen looked at Chelsea. "What do you think so far?"

"It's beautiful, but it's so big!"

Karen crossed the room and found the kitchen beyond. It was sunny, and the appliances looked new. All the cabinets and countertops were eggshell white; the sink was stainless steel. "I like this. Don't you think I could turn out some good meals in here, Chel?"

"You'd certainly have room enough." Bethany broke free and toddled about gleefully. "Bethany seems to like it."

Karen smiled at her daughter. At times she was almost embarrassed by the amount of love she felt for her. She couldn't imagine loving anyone more. Absently she touched her stomach. What would her son be like?

She went to the window and looked out at the back yard. "It's not very large, is it?"

"Not for this neighborhood. Personally, I think that's one reason the house is still on the market. People who want a four-bedroom house generally need a larger yard." Optimistically the realtor added, "There's room for a swing set and sandbox. You can't see the patio from here, but it has a barbecue grill and room for a table and chairs. It's practically a room, except that it's outdoors."

Karen opened the back door and found herself on the

patio. It was as nice as the realtor had indicated. "How odd that you can't look out on it from the kitchen."

"You could put in a glass door," Mrs. Haroldson suggested. "And the den windows overlook it when the drapes are drawn. There's a door in that room that leads to it as well."

Karen made no comment, but she liked the house better all the time. "Let's see upstairs."

She was puffing for breath by the time she reached the second floor. "I can see I won't be running up and down these all day!"

"Once you're used to it, they'll be nothing," Mrs. Haroldson assured her. "I have a two-story myself, and that's the way it was with me."

Chelsea was carrying Bethany again, and Karen said, "You're being awfully quiet."

"I'm trying to take it all in. My apartment would fit in the den."

Karen wished Chelsea hadn't said that. She didn't want the realtor to think she couldn't afford this house. "She's an artist," she explained to Mrs. Haroldson, hoping this would be explanation enough. "We were roommates in college."

"This is the master bedroom," Mrs. Haroldson said as she stepped aside.

Karen went into the large room and tried not to show her admiration. The room was as sunny as the rest of the house, and she could see two walk-in closets. Across the room was a dressing area that led to a bath. She stepped in and saw that it, like the kitchen, was all white. "Beautiful! I can put any color in here."

"I understand there are hardwood floors under the carpet on this floor," Mrs. Haroldson said. "Naturally I prefer carpeting myself, but you could have it taken up if you wanted."

"I love carpeting. Not this color though. Who on earth would have wanted to live with this awful shade?"

"I have no idea what goes through the mind of some people. It could be changed."

Chelsea looked at the carpet. "Perhaps it just needs a good cleaning. That would be far less expensive. I don't think it would be so bad if it were cleaner and if furniture were on it."

Karen looked at the sunken tub and said, "I'd want it for this bathroom alone. There's plenty of room for all my things in here."

"This house is unusual in its number of bathrooms. There's a half-bath off the den and three full ones up here."

"Three?"

Mrs. Haroldson led the way down the hall. "These two bedrooms are connected with a bath, making them a suite. The other one is down there in the hall next to the fourth bedroom."

Karen went into the first bedroom and turned in a circle. "Would you like this to be your room, Bethany? All your toys could go in here." The connecting bath was much smaller than the one in the master bedroom, but it was quite large enough and was also white.

"The house was built by a rather wealthy plumbing contractor," Mrs. Haroldson was saying. "That's the reason for all the baths, I suppose."

"You can never have too many." Karen went into the adjoining bedroom. "This will be perfect as a nursery. Or maybe I'll put Bethany in here and the baby in the other room. That's closer to my bedroom."

They went back into the hall and into the last bedroom. Karen eyed it critically. This would be Ryan's room, and she knew it was important that it be one he would like. Otherwise he might refuse to buy the house. Like the other rooms, it had a walk-in closet and large windows. Someone had built shelves along one wall, and there was room enough in here for a desk if he wanted one, as well as his bed and perhaps a reading chair.

"The rooms are certainly large," Chelsea said from the doorway.

"Yes, that's the charm of this house. I think it more than makes up for the small backyard," Mrs. Haroldson said cheerfully. "This room could also be used as an upstairs den or an office."

"No, we'll need it as a bedroom."

Chelsea glanced at her, but Karen pretended not to see. She hadn't told Chelsea that Ryan no longer shared her bedroom. Chelsea would tell her she was wrong, and Karen didn't want to have to argue the point. Also, she felt a bit guilty about telling Ryan Chelsea's secret. She didn't want Chelsea to fish an admission out of her.

They went downstairs and Karen glanced in the rooms again. "This is exactly what I want, Chel. And it's not far from Saint Anne's. That's the best school in Dallas, according to Joyce, and she should know. After they leave the Montessori school, the children will attend Saint Anne's."

"A private school?" Chelsea asked. "I thought they would go to public school like we did."

"Private is better. Saint Anne's even has its own football team. Can't you see us now? Cheering as my son makes a touchdown and Bethany jumps up and down as cheerleader?"

Mrs. Haroldson smiled indulgently. "Your daughter is certainly lovely. I can tell she'll be a heartbreaker in a few years."

Karen smiled at Bethany who was ensconced in Chelsea's arms. "She's such a good girl. I only hope the next one will be so well behaved." She glanced around again. "My husband will have to see it, of course, but I'm sold."

"That's just wonderful. Could he see it tonight? I'm afraid another couple is also interested in it, and I'd hate to see you lose it."

"We'll be by as soon as he gets home from work."

Goodbyes were said, and they went to the car. As she strapped Bethany into the car seat, Chelsea said, "You shouldn't have seemed so eager. If she tells the owners, they may not come down on the price."

"I didn't think of that. I just couldn't help but love it, and I've never been good at keeping my feelings secret. Whatever it costs, though, it's worth it. Have you ever seen a more beautiful house?"

"Never," Chelsea said honestly. "Karen, I know it's none of my business, but can you afford a house like this?"

"It may be a strain for a while," she admitted reluctantly. "But we can stay here for the rest of our lives. It's even nicer than Joyce's house!"

Chelsea stared at Karen as she fastened her seat belt. "What difference does that make? What if Ryan doesn't like it?"

"He will. I'll make him like it! Chel, I have to have this house! It's my dream home."

"Maybe you ought to look at some others as well. Some smaller ones."

"I'm in a smaller one now, and we're practically living on top of each other."

"If you'd like, I'll keep Bethany tonight so you and Ryan can look over the house without having to keep up with her."

"That would be great. Bethany, can you thank Aunt Chel?"

Chelsea put her hand in the baby's "She knows I love her. She's a lucky little girl to have three adults that adore her."

"Yes. And I can hardly wait for her little brother to be born." As she drove Chelsea back home, Karen was deciding the color of the drapes she'd buy for the windows in her new house.

"I like it well enough, but it's too expensive," Ryan said as they drove home from seeing the house. "I don't think we'll even qualify for the loan. They're based on salary, you know."

"I'll talk to Daddy. I'm sure he'll help us out. You ask for a raise tomorrow, and I'll see if he'll provide the down payment and closing costs. Once we're in, we'll manage."

"You aren't going to ask your father for money. I don't see how you can even suggest such a thing." He kept his eyes on the street, but his mind was reeling. "Why did you have the realtor to show you such a big house?"

"I happened to be driving by and saw the For Sale sign in the yard. I've watched for a house in that neighborhood for months! That one is almost too good to be true! It's always been my favorite."

"How can I make you understand? We don't make enough money to live in a place like that."

"I'm not stupid, Ryan. I know it's going to be tight for a while. I'm willing to make sacrifices. We don't have to have steaks as often as we do. I can even cut back on my clothing allowance. After all, a housewife doesn't need a closet full of expensive dresses every season." She smiled at him. "See? I can be logical."

He shook his head. "It's going to take more than that, I'm afraid. Maybe you should consider getting a job."

"I have a job. I'm raising my children and keeping your house," she said in a tense voice. "We've been over this before."

"We may need two salaries to make the payments on a place like that."

"Then you'll have to moonlight. Raising children is a full-time job. You have no idea how busy I am." She sounded hurt that he would suggest she seek employment. "Besides, I'm seven months pregnant. No one would hire me now, and I couldn't possibly leave my new baby for several months. If we can make the payments for that long, we can make them indefinitely."

Ryan didn't answer.

"Well? You know I have a point there."

"Karen, we can't afford that house."

"You're just being mean. I talked to Mother about it and—"

"Your mother knows about it?"

"I saw no reason to keep it a secret. I took her by there this afternoon. We couldn't get in, of course, but we peeped in the windows and she suggested a honey beige for the draperies in the living and dining rooms. Do you like honey beige?"

"I have no idea what color that is."

Karen smiled and reached out to pat his hand. "I know. That's the way men are. Don't worry. Mother and I will see to everything. She says she's sure Daddy will give us whatever money we need. And it's not so much farther from her house than the one we live in now."

Ryan knew he was beaten, and he hated it. "Karen, why does it have to be like this between us? We could have been so happy."

"I'm happy now." She sounded wounded. "It's cruel of you to say you're not happy with me. That's one reason this house is so important to me. I thought you'd like it and that you'd be proud of me in it. I can be such a good hostess, Ryan. I was brought up to know exactly how to entertain."

"I'd be proud of you in a hovel. The house has nothing to do with it. I'm talking about what's happened between you and me."

She turned her head to gaze out the window. "I have no idea what you mean. I love you as much now as when I married you. We have two—almost—beautiful children, and soon we'll have a house we can be proud of. I don't know what else you can expect."

Ryan wondered if Karen could possibly be that obtuse. Neither of them had mentioned the argument that had put him, permanently, in the guest room; it seemed to have completely left her head. Not for the first time, Ryan wondered if Karen wouldn't benefit from seeing a psychologist. She didn't seem to think like everyone else.

After her outburst about Chelsea and the venom in her voice, Ryan had expected there to be some difference in her attitude toward her friend, but he couldn't see any change at all. Karen still spoke of Chelsea as if there was nothing in the relationship out of the ordinary, she still invited her to dinner or to visit at least once or twice a week. When they were together, Ryan couldn't see any indication that Karen wasn't as close to Chelsea as she had ever been. The implications were chilling.

What did Karen really feel about anything or anyone? Ryan was becoming more and more suspicious that all Karen's affections were more cerebral than heartfelt. Cerebral wasn't a word he would have associated with Karen. Did she feel any spontaneous affection? For anyone? He almost hoped he never found out.

Karen and Ryan spent the Fourth of July with her parents. Holidays with the Bakers had become a part of their life, and Ryan was learning to adjust. Joyce and the Todds were there as well, and Todd, Jr., soon had Bethany in tears. Ryan resisted the urge to spank him soundly and rescued his daughter. The day went as other holidays had since he and Karen had been married.

That night Karen was restless. She couldn't sleep, and the sound of the TV woke Ryan. He came to the living room to see what was the matter with her.

"I didn't mean to wake you." She rubbed the small of her back and irritably turned the TV off. "I guess I ate too much barbecue."

"Could it be the baby?"

"I'm not due for another week. Bethany was late. I assume this one will be, too."

"Not necessarily. The doctor told you it could be any time."

Karen stood and went to the patio door. "I wish the papers would be finished on the house. I want to be moved in before our son gets here. I haven't even been able to get into the house to paint the nursery."

"You have no business painting. Besides, you can't climb a ladder in your condition. If he comes before we move, I'll take care of all of it. He'll never know the difference."

"I don't see how you can be so blasé about our family life. It would suit you fine to just stay right here."

"Yes, it would." Ryan had stopped trying to humor her. Karen, difficult under ordinary circumstances, was impossible when she was pregnant. "The baby could have my room, and I could move back where I ought to be."

"I'm not going to talk about that." She rubbed her back again. "That felt almost like a contraction. Maybe I *am* in labor."

Ryan glanced at his watch and went to the phone. "Tell me when it happens again."

He could tell he'd wakened Chelsea, which wasn't surprising considering the hour. "I think Karen may be in labor."

"I'm on my way!" The phone went dead in his hands, and he hung up.

"She's coming."

"There! I'm doing it again."

Ryan consulted his watch. "It may be a false alarm, but I'm taking you to the hospital. If we're wrong, we can always come home again. Go get dressed."

He went to his room and pulled on jeans and a shirt. Karen didn't seem too pleased that the baby might be coming, but he felt a surge of excitement. During this pregnancy he had been reticent, but now that the baby was about to arrive, he was glad.

He went into Bethany's room and looked at her. She was asleep amid a flock of stuffed animals, her round cheek pillowed on a teddy bear, her chubby fist clutching her favorite doll. Her blond hair made a halo about her head, and she seemed angelic. As he gently touched her cheek, Bethany sighed and cuddled the doll. His love for her was so pure and so simple and so all-consuming it made him ache. He would gladly battle dragons for this small child.

Karen came into the room, and they stood gazing down

at their daughter. Ryan put his arm about Karen's shoulder. At moments like this he knew it was worth all the bad times.

"What do you suppose is keeping Chelsea? My water broke in the bathroom. This is definitely it!"

Before he could answer, they heard a soft knock on the door. Karen hurried to answer it. Ryan paused long enough to pull the sheet over Bethany's shoulders.

Chelsea had dressed hurriedly. She wore no makeup and looked younger and more vulnerable because of it. "Are you okay?" she asked Karen.

"So far. The worst part is still ahead of me." She gripped Chelsea's hands. "I wish you could be with me!"

"So do I, but I have to stay with Bethany. Ryan won't leave you."

Karen glanced at her husband. "My suitcase is beside the bed."

He went to get it and returned as Karen was giving Chelsea last-minute instructions.

"Will you just leave?" Chelsea asked with a laugh. "I know what Bethany likes for breakfast as well as you do. Go!"

Ryan took Karen's arm and helped her to the car. When he slid into the driver's side, Karen clutched his arm. "I'm afraid!"

"There's nothing to be afraid of. You had an easy, safe delivery with Bethany, and the doctor has told us this one may be even quicker."

"Easy! Sure, you can say that! You didn't have to go through it." Karen's fingers were like ice on his arm. "What if I die?"

He started the car. "You're not going to die. A few hours from now we'll have another perfect baby and you'll be resting and happy."

"What if something is wrong with the baby!" She stared at him in the darkness as he backed out of the drive. "What if he's missing arms or legs or is retarded?"

"We'll love him just the same. Everything is fine. You have no reason to worry."

"But what if—"

"Karen, calm down. You're working yourself into a frenzy for no reason at all."

She sank back in the seat and glared straight ahead. "I'm glad this is my last one! I hate being pregnant! You can't have any idea what it's like. Giving birth is hell! I don't care what the doctor says. It hurts!"

"I know. But look at the result. We'll have the baby we've been waiting for these last nine months." He drove toward the hospital. The streets were almost deserted, and he was going faster than he normally would have.

When the building was in sight, Ryan relaxed slightly. He was nervous, too, but didn't want Karen to know. He parked by the emergency doors and had an orderly come out with a wheelchair for Karen while he went to check her in.

Chelsea couldn't sleep. She tried watching TV, but nothing interesting was on so she went into the kitchen and made coffee. It seemed strange to be here in Karen and Ryan's house when they were gone. She wasn't sure what to do with herself since she hadn't thought to bring the book she was reading.

She went down the hall to be sure Bethany was sleeping soundly. The little girl was fast asleep and breathing deeply. Chelsea tried to imagine what the new baby would look like. Karen was positive it would be a boy. Chelsea hoped Karen was right since she wanted a son so badly. Ryan didn't seem to have a preference as to its sex.

Chelsea left Bethany's room and started back down the hall to the den. An open door drew her attention, and after a pause, she went in.

This was the spare bedroom, but obviously someone was using it. She turned on the light and knew the belongings had to be Ryan's. For a moment Chelsea only stared.

Then she went to the end of the hall and looked into the master bedroom. There was no sight of any masculine apparel or belongings. Karen's gown and robe were on the foot of the bed, her jewelry boxes and trinkets were on the dresser, her clothes took up the entire closet.

Chelsea was stunned. She knew Ryan had slept in the extra bedroom during Karen's earlier pregnancy, but his things had remained in the master bedroom. Now they had all been moved. Karen and Ryan were no longer living in the same bedroom and the separation seemed to be a permanent one.

Suddenly she felt embarrassed, as if she had learned something shameful about them. She turned out the light and left Karen's room. At Ryan's door she paused. Why had they decided to live this way? She knew it had to be at Karen's instigation, but why had Ryan agreed?

To still her thoughts, she turned off the light and went back to the den. Since neither had mentioned the change in sleeping arrangements to her, she knew she couldn't talk to Karen about it. Part of her was even glad to know Ryan was no longer sleeping with Karen, but it was a part that she wished had remained unacknowledged. The arrangement must be temporary, in spite of appearances, a case of convenience for the last months of Karen's pregnancy. Nothing more.

But Chelsea remembered Karen's insistence on having a four-bedroom house and how she had told the realtor that all the rooms would be used as bedrooms, none as an upstairs den. Unless Karen believed she was carrying twins in spite of her doctor's assurances, since she was adamant that she didn't want another pregnancy after this one, didn't that mean that she intended to continue sleeping apart from Ryan?

Chelsea couldn't imagine wanting to do such a thing. There were nights when she ached all over for a mere caress from him. When imagining the sound of his voice, the memory of his loving were tortures in her loneliness. If she were his wife, he would never spend a single night out of her bed.

The hours dragged by. Midnight came and went. Chelsea found a book in the den and tried to read it, but her mind kept returning to Karen and the baby, Ryan and his lonely bedroom.

At four in the morning she heard the sound of a key in the lock and hurried to the front door. Ryan was there, and he was grinning. "It's another girl! Wait until you see her, Chelsea. She's as beautiful as Bethany."

"A girl? Was Karen disappointed?" She could tell he wasn't.

"I don't think she will be after she gets used to the idea. What do you think of the name 'Ashley'?"

"I like it. I didn't know you had a girl's name picked out."

"We didn't. Ashley was my idea."

"I like it. Karen's all right?"

"She's great. The baby was born over an hour ago. I should have called, but I was afraid the phone would wake Bethany. That's why I waited to tell you in person." His eyes, full of happiness, searched her face. "She has dark hair. So far, at least. We have a blond and a brunette."

"I'm so happy for you." Chelsea laughed from the excitement. "I can't wait to see her."

"She's several ounces bigger than Bethany but the same length. The Bakers are still at the hospital. I think they're disappointed over her not being a boy."

"They'll get over it."

Spontaneously Ryan hugged her. "A baby girl! I still can't believe it!"

Chelsea wanted to stay in his arms. "I have coffee made. I couldn't sleep."

"I'd love some. There's no way I can go to bed tonight. I'm too excited."

They went into the kitchen, and Chelsea got a cup for him. Ryan opened the pantry and took out a box of doughnuts. "Junk food," he said. "Just what we need."

They went into the den and sat on the floor facing each other, their legs folded under them. Chelsea took a doughnut and bit into it. "Bethany's been asleep the whole time. I hope the new baby—Ashley—is as good as her big sister." Chelsea laughed. "How funny to think of little Bethany as a big sister!"

"Did I say she has dark hair? The Bakers weren't too pleased about that, either. Mrs. Baker says it will fall out and come in blond."

"I'll bet it doesn't. I'll bet she stays dark like you."

"I hope so. I feel outnumbered in that family. If you know what I mean."

"I know exactly. I like Karen, but her family is overbearing in a lot of ways." She licked her fingers. "These are good doughnuts. I haven't had one in ages. We used to practically live on them in the dorm."

Ryan studied her face. "Those days seem like forever ago."

"That's a good way to put it. It seems like that to me, too." She looked into his eyes and wondered if he was happy in his marriage. It was a question that she could never ask him. "It's as if we were different people then."

"Do you ever wish you could go back?"

She found herself nodding. "There's so much I would do differently."

"Me, too." His voice was husky, and his eyes were darkening with unexpressed emotion. "So very much."

She was afraid to ask him to explain. "I ought to go. You're home now to watch Bethany."

"Don't go. Not yet."

A pulse raced to life inside her. Did he mean his words to sound so caressing?

Slowly Ryan lifted his hand and put it on her neck so that his thumb stroked the line of her chin and his fingers were hidden in her hair. Chelsea couldn't have moved if she had wanted to. And she didn't.

He leaned toward her, and Chelsea met him halfway. At first his lips were gentle on hers, as sweet as a memory.

Then the kiss deepened into something that held more than mere passion.

Chelsea kissed him back, not caring if it was wrong. Not even remembering that he belonged to Karen. All her hidden love for him exploded inside her, and at that moment, she would have given herself to him without hesitation. His fingers laced in her hair and he kissed her as he had when they were lovers and there was no impediment between them.

With a ragged breath, Chelsea drew away. She leaned her forehead against his chin, her eyes closed as she gathered the strength to stop what they were about to do. He pulled her into his embrace and held her, not speaking.

After what seemed like an eternity, she said, "We can't do this."

"I know." He didn't release her.

Chelsea lifted her face until she could meet his eyes. For a long time neither spoke. They merely gazed into each other's eyes as they touched gently, almost fearfully.

Slowly, painfully, Chelsea pulled back. "I don't want to stop," she admitted in a whisper. "I'm going to hate myself tomorrow for having done this."

"No. It was my fault." His eyes were dark and haunted. Chelsea wondered how long he had wanted to touch her, to kiss her. "It won't happen again."

"There's so much I want to say. And I can't say any of it."

"I know. I feel the same."

"What are we going to do?"

Lines settled over his face, and he looked so tired she wanted to hold him and comfort him. "Nothing. We're not going to do anything at all." He drew back and let his hands fall into his lap. "You ought to hate me for this."

She shook her head. "I could never hate you."

He ran his fingers through his hair as he did when he was frustrated. "Can you believe what I've done here? Karen is in the hospital with my baby. Our daughter is just down the hall. And I kissed you!"

"You didn't do it alone." Chelsea reached out and touched his hand. Her fingers closed over his, and she waited for him to look at her. "No one will ever know."

"Will that make it okay?" He sounded almost angry. "Will that get the memory of you out of my mind?"

"I have to go. If I don't leave now . . ." There was no need to finish the sentence. He understood. She rose and went to the door. Pausing, she looked back. "We have to pretend tonight never happened. For Karen."

"I know."

But Chelsea would never forget—and he wouldn't either.

Chapter Thirteen

"Did you two have an argument while I was in the hospital?" Karen asked Chelsea.

"No, of course not." Chelsea turned away and pretended to be searching for Ashley's rattle.

"He says the same thing, but I don't believe either of you. Do you know you haven't been in the same room since I came home from the hospital? You never come to dinner anymore, and Ryan always has to work on the days you come over."

"You're imagining things." Chelsea held the rattle over the baby and jiggled it gently. Ashley's eyes searched for it, and she waved her plump arms while Bethany tried to climb into Chelsea's lap and get the toy for herself. "It's probably a symptom of postpartum depression."

Karen looked thoughtful. "Do you think so? I've heard it can do some strange things to a person's mind."

"What else could it be? You know Ryan and I never argue." It caused her pain to speak his name so casually, especially to Karen. She had been riddled with guilt since the night she'd kissed Ryan. She knew him well enough to know he was undergoing the same misery. That was the reason they had avoided seeing each other. The memory of the kiss was still too new.

"If that's all it is, I feel silly for having mentioned it." Karen laughed and picked up the baby. "Thank goodness

I won't be going through this again. Having my tubes tied was the smartest thing I ever did."

Chelsea took Bethany into her lap and let her play with the long braid that hung over her shoulder. "I got a job today. One that will pay more than the Burger Barn."

"You did? I thought you would go back to painting."

"What's the point? I can't get into a gallery, and the Victorian paintings are starting to top out. I find I can't paint at all lately." She smoothed the child's hair. "Nothing creative is flowing."

Karen hugged Ashley. "I guess I'm creating for both of us these days. So where will you be working? Tell me about it."

"It's with Spenser Construction. Their main office is downtown, and I'll be a receptionist. I won't get rich on what they've agreed to pay me, but I'll be able to pay my bills and have some money left over for a change."

"What do they construct? Houses?"

"No, it's commercial construction. They're doing that office building that seems to be made of black glass."

"That's beautiful! I never thought of you as being interested in buildings."

"I'm not. All I have to do is answer the phone and route calls to the proper office. If someone comes in for an appointment, I send them to the right place. I make coffee. It's not glamorous but that's okay. I need a break from painting."

"Sometimes I wish I had a job," Karen said thoughtfully. "But it never lasts for long. Besides, can you picture me telling Mother and Daddy I want to go to work? They would think I had lost my mind."

"Lots of people work, Karen," Chelsea said dryly.

"I know, but they've always said I'm not suited for it. I think they're right. I'm much better at being a mother." She smiled at her children and leaned forward to kiss the baby. "Ryan talked to the realtor, and we can move in this weekend. Isn't that wonderful?"

"Yes, it is. But do you feel up to moving? You just had a baby."

Karen laughed. "I won't be doing any of the moving myself, of course. When Daddy's company relocates people to Dallas, they pay for their moving expenses. He says he's going to have the company they use move us as well. He says it's a bargain for the company, really, since we only have to go a few blocks. I won't have to lift a finger."

"I'll come and help you unpack after I get off work," Chelsea offered, though she wondered if this was a good idea. Ryan would almost certainly be there.

"There's no need. Mother is sending over the woman who works for her. I'll just sit around and tell her where I want things. Thanks for the offer, though."

Chelsea glanced at her watch. It was past time for Ryan to get off work. "I have to run. I have a dozen things to do before I start work. I didn't realize how often I wear jeans and tennis shoes until I started looking through my closet this morning."

"I wish I could go with you. Be sure and get a couple of skirts in a neutral color. I know how you are. You dress like a Gypsy. Red doesn't go with everything. It's best to have colorful blouses and neutral skirts. You can switch them around that way."

"I'll keep that in mind." Chelsea kissed the two children goodbye and left. The Dallas heat made the air shimmer as she went to her car. She had stayed too late. Before she could open the car door, Ryan pulled into the drive. She hesitated. It was one thing to avoid him, another to hurry away without so much as a word.

He got out of his car and gazed at her across the drive. He came over to her. "Hi. I haven't seen you lately."

Butterflies sprang to life in her middle. "I thought that would be best."

"Probably." His voice was quiet, and he looked as if he wasn't sleeping any better than she was. "How are you?"

"Fine." She made herself smile. "I got a job today. It's with Spenser Construction. I'll be a receptionist."

"You'll be good at that. You've always liked people."

Silence stretched out between them. Neither could say what was really in his or her mind, yet neither wanted to leave. "How are you?" she asked at last. "You look tired."

He grinned, but it didn't reach his eyes. "Nobody sleeps much with a new baby in the house. We put her in the room with Karen, but I still hear her and get up at night."

Chelsea pretended she hadn't heard the reference to Karen's being in one bedroom and his being in another. She had wondered if that would change now that the baby was born. Apparently it hadn't. "She's beautiful. Such a good baby."

"Thanks. Did Karen tell you we're moving this weekend?"

"Yes. She said it would be compliments of the company."

He nodded. "I don't feel right about it, but I couldn't do it all myself and Troy is on vacation." He smiled again and avoided her eyes. "I guess that's one of the benefits of having married the boss's daughter."

"It could be worse."

His eyes met hers for a long time. At last he said, "I guess I'd better be going in."

"I have to leave, too."

"Chelsea, don't stay away," he said in a lower voice. "Seeing you and not touching you is difficult, but not seeing you is worse."

She nodded, not trusting herself to speak. She wrestled open the car door and got into the baking heat inside. As she started the engine, she didn't look in Ryan's direction. He might see the tears in her eyes even through the dusty windshield.

Spenser Construction was located in a copper-glassed building the company had built. It was a huge operation, Chelsea soon learned. Not only did they handle construction, but they had interior decorators and a realtor who specialized in commercial sales. The rest of the building was leased to lawyers, accountants, and financial consultants.

Chelsea was glad to see the women she would be working with were generally friendly and that several were willing to help her get settled into the new job. The work wasn't difficult, but there was enough to keep her occupied, actually enough work to have justified hiring a switchboard operator as well as a receptionist.

One of the first people she met was Sheila Stanford, who was personal secretary and receptionist in the inner office of Lorne Spenser, the owner of the company. Sheila was nearing middle age and was both attractive and intelligent. The rumor around the coffee pot was that she had been, and some said still was, Spenser's lover.

"He can be a bear to work for," Sheila said over coffee one morning when she and Chelsea were alone. "He has moods, you know? I've been with him so many years we're practically like a married couple."

"Is he married?"

"Lorne? No way! He was once, years ago, but he's more married to the company than he could be to any woman."

Chelsea remembered the rumor and decided it could be true. She knew he was in his mid-forties, young for a CEO, but old enough to be Sheila's contemporary. "I've been here two weeks, but I haven't met him yet."

"He's been on location in Waco and hasn't been into the office. He rarely takes on a project of his own these days. I guess he needed a break from the usual grind. He's a good architect, you know. That's how he got where he is in such a short time." Sheila added, "His father was in construction, too, but on a smaller scale."

"I hadn't realized Mr. Spenser is an architect. I thought he only hired them."

"No, he started as an architect and added the construction part after he was established. He says it's sort of one-stop shopping here. We can design, build, and decorate an office building—even sell it without going outside this building."

"It sounds efficient."

"It is. Lorne has a fortune invested in this company, but I'm sure he's making it all back and then some." Sheila put down her coffee cup. "I'd better get back to my desk. I've got some letters to type up." She laughed. "You wouldn't believe how many tapes he mails me to transcribe. I think he'll be opening his own post office next!"

Chelsea smiled and turned to answer the phone. The morning had been quieter than usual. It was rare for her to be able to have an entire conversation without an interruption. "Good afternoon. Spenser Construction Company." As she punched in the line the caller wanted, she wondered if she would ever learn to like office work.

The following week Sheila called in sick. A virus was sweeping the town, and Sheila had it. "I'll cover for you," Chelsea said. "Just stay in bed and drink lots of liquids."

That day and the next were nightmarish. Chelsea had already been too busy. Now she was handling Sheila's calls as well. A packet of Spenser's infamous tapes arrived, but she didn't have time to transcribe them. She got one of the secretaries in the pool to take care of them. When they were done, Chelsea took them to Spenser's desk.

As she was leaving, she almost ran into a man she had never seen before. He frowned down at her. "What are you doing in my office? Where's Sheila?"

"You must be Mr. Spenser. I'm Chelsea Cavin. Sheila is out sick, and I'm taking her place."

"You work here? I've never seen you before." He looked less angry now that he knew she was an employee.

"I've only been here a short while. I'm the receptionist."

He stroked his smooth-shaven chin. "I remember Sheila saying something about the other one quitting. I didn't realize she had filled the position." He finally smiled and instantly became handsome. "She pretty well runs my life."

"I'll get out of your way." Chelsea tried to ease past him.

"There's no hurry. I like to get to know my employees."

"There's no one up front to watch the phone."

He went to his desk and punched an inner-office number. "Sue? Can you cover the front desk for a while? Thanks." He hung up. "Have a seat, Mrs. Cavin."

"Ms. I'm not married." She sat on the leather chair facing the desk.

"How do you like working here?"

"It's taking me a while to get the hang of it, but I enjoy it." It was a small lie, but one she felt was prudent when speaking to her boss.

"That's good. I guess when Sheila hired you, she told you about all the benefits. The insurance, the paid vacations after twelve months of employment?"

"Yes, sir."

He smiled at her again and made a steeple of his fingertips. "We aren't so formal here. Can't you call me Lorne?"

She didn't know what to say. "All I've ever heard anyone but Sheila call you is Mr. Spenser."

He laughed. "I like you. You say what's on your mind, don't you?"

"Unfortunately, yes." She smiled in return. "But I'm not outspoken to clients. I can be tactful."

"I'm sure you can." He swiveled a quarter turn in his chair. "You're not married. Is there a boyfriend?"

"No. Why do you ask?"

"I'd like to ask you out, and I was wondering if anyone would mind."

Chelsea didn't know what to say. "I'm not sure that would be a good idea since I work for you. Isn't that sort of thing frowned upon?"

"Are you afraid the boss will find out?"

She stood and went to the door. "I also don't want you to get the idea that I'm willing to sleep my way into raises and special favors. I don't think it's wise for you to ask me out."

He seemed intrigued. "I wasn't inviting you to have an illicit affair. Just dinner."

Chelsea flushed. "I'm sorry. That was rude of me. It's just that I thought . . ."

"I know. I watch old movies, too. No, this is only for dinner. I like to get to know the people who work for me. If you were a man, I could ask you to dinner and you wouldn't think anything about it."

"That's true. I hadn't thought of it in that way. All right, I'd like to have dinner with you."

"Great. How about tonight?"

She laughed. "So soon? Fine. I don't have anything planned."

"We can leave from the office then."

She nodded. "I'll be looking forward to it."

As she went back to her desk, she found she really was interested in getting to know him better. It only made sense if they were to work together indefinitely.

After work, Chelsea hung behind as the others left for the day. Lorne was one of the last to come down the hall. "I'm running late," he said in apology. "I had to call a man about the building we're doing in Waco. He was long-winded."

"No problem. Sheila tells me you're the architect on that job."

"Yes, it's been two years or more since I tackled a job myself. Every once in a while I have to do one, just to keep my hand in. Maybe you'd like to see it when it's closer to completion."

"I'd like that."

As they went down in the elevator, Chelsea had the impression that several people noticed and were speculating about her leaving with Lorne. If he noticed, he didn't mention it. They crossed the inlaid marble of the lobby and went into the hot sunlight.

She knew where he parked. She had to pass his car slot

every day when she was vying with others for space in which to leave her car. Today his Mercedes was there. It was maroon with a black interior, and when he opened the door, she noticed it still smelled like cars do in a showroom.

Lorne went around to the driver's side. Chelsea had seldom ridden in so expensive a car and she was impressed in spite of herself.

He drove them to a restaurant halfway across town. "I hope you like seafood. I think this is the best place to go if you're hungry for shrimp."

"I love seafood."

Once they were seated Chelsea found she was intimidated by the restaurant. It was much more exclusive than any she had ever been in. Nervously she glanced at the skirt and blouse she had worn all day. Thanks to Karen, she had learned to dress conservatively and tastefully for work, even if she still preferred to look like a Gypsy at home.

After they ordered, Chelsea said, "I didn't expect dinner to be quite so extravagant. I find it hard to believe you do this with all your employees." Her eyes met his levelly. "This is just dinner, isn't it? Tell me I haven't made a mistake I'm going to regret."

"Would you really regret it so much if this were more of a date than a company dinner? Am I that repulsive to you?" He smiled as if he knew that wasn't the case.

"You could never be described as repulsive. It's just that I need this job, but I don't need it enough to compromise myself. Your intentions could create some complications in my life."

He laughed. "You certainly don't mince words. It's refreshing. My last receptionist was willing to do just about anything. I didn't take her up on any of it, incidentally."

Chelsea studied his face. Lorne was handsome when he smiled and looked romantically sad when he didn't. His dark hair was liberally threaded with gray and his eyes were a chocolate brown. In some ways he reminded her of

Jason Randall, but Lorne wasn't married. "You're an interesting man," she said at last. "I find I'm having to stay on my toes around you."

He leaned forward, and his eyes were no longer as teasing. "You interest me, too. In a way I wish we had met before you started to work for my company. Then my moves might not be so suspect."

She smiled. "What moves did you have in mind?"

"You're already willing to believe the worst of me. I know this is a strange consolation, but your position in the company doesn't exactly have an unlimited ceiling. It's not as if you could sleep your way up our corporate ladder even if that were your intention from the start."

"What are you trying to tell me?"

"That we could date—assuming you're willing—and it wouldn't matter in your job one way or the other. Our raises are more or less standard for the first few years, and frankly, receptionists don't last long with us."

"They might if you hired a switchboard operator. You're probably working them to death."

"I'll look into it. You're the first one who told me what the problem may be. I appreciate that."

"For some reason you bring out the blatant honesty in me. I'm not usually this outspoken. I'll probably worry the rest of the night about having said too much and about whether you'll fire me tomorrow."

"I can promise you that I won't. No, I want to keep you around. In fact, I'll want you around for quite a while."

Going out for dinner after work became their habit in the following weeks. By mid-August Chelsea knew her name was being linked with Lorne's around the office. Some of the secretaries started avoiding her at the coffee pot, and others made a point of being friendlier than ever. Chelsea wasn't too sure she liked either change. Her friendship with Lorne had nothing to do with how he treated his employees, but none of them seemed to believe that.

Sheila was cooler toward Chelsea, and this led Chelsea to believe that she most probably had been Lorne's lover. Whatever might have been was in the past, however, because Lorne was falling in love with Chelsea.

She knew it before he told her. He found excuses to stop by her desk several times a day and frequently lingered to talk even when they both had other work to do. When he learned she had been a professional artist, he started asking her opinion of color schemes and designs, and Chelsea was uncomfortably certain that he wasn't endearing her to his staff of decorators by doing so.

Lorne was single-minded in his courtship of her. He was an accomplished dancer, and their conversations were quick and interesting. He saw to it that she was entertained at every turn. Chelsea had never been pursued by a man to whom money was no object. She began to see how Karen could have been spoiled by her parents' wealth.

Eventually, she introduced Lorne to Karen and Ryan. Unlike her attitude to Jason, Karen was wholeheartedly in favor of Lorne. Ryan was less enthusiastic, but Chelsea could understand that. It hurt her to take Lorne to their house the first few times because she knew the effect it was having on Ryan. But she had to get on with her life, just as he was with his. There was never any consideration of Ryan leaving Karen, nor would Chelsea have encouraged him to. Therefore, the sooner he became used to the idea of her seeing Lorne, the better it would be for both of them.

One night, after leaving Karen and Ryan, Lorne was quieter than usual as he drove Chelsea home. "Is something wrong?" she asked.

"No, no. Nothing at all. I was just thinking about your friends. They seem to have it all, don't they?"

Chelsea was silent for a minute. "It seems that way."

"Do you ever wish to have what they do?"

She jerked her head around to look at him. Had he

somehow learned what she and Ryan felt for each other?
"What do you mean?"

"They have a nice house, two beautiful children, even a
dog."

"The dog was Karen's idea." Chelsea smiled at the
memory. "She decided the girls needed a pet. I don't think
he's working out well." The dog refused to be house
trained so Karen had delegated him to the back yard, and
the girls almost never got to see him. The poor creature
spent his days digging up grass and his nights barking at
invisible intruders. Karen was already talking about getting rid of him.

"I want to show you something."

Instead of driving to her house, he turned in the opposite direction. Soon they were in a neighborhood not far
from the one Karen now lived in. The houses here were
among Dallas's finest. Lorne pulled into a drive and
stopped the car.

Chelsea leaned forward to look out as he came around
to open her door. The house was huge, much larger than
the one the Bakers owned. Enormous trees were in the
yard, and the gardens, with their discreet lighting system,
were beautifully maintained.

They went up the front walk. Chelsea paused on the
porch. "This is where you live?"

"Yes. I want you to see it."

She had wondered where he lived and why he had never
taken her there. Now she understood. This house would be
enough to sway most people's attitudes. Until this moment
she hadn't really grasped how wealthy Lorne was. He had
wanted to be sure she was interested in him, not his money.

The house was as beautiful inside as it was on the outside. Lush carpeting cushioned their footsteps. Potted
plants stood in niches and corners, looking as if they were
attended by florists. The furnishings were elegant, though
more formal than Chelsea would have chosen. She knew
Karen would be perfectly at home here.

Lorne took her through all the downstairs rooms, and

they ended up in the study. "This is my favorite room," he said, watching her enigmatically.

Chelsea went to the bookshelves that lined every wall. Many of the editions were bound in leather. In one corner was a draftsman's table with an orderly array of paper and pencils. A mahogany desk dominated the opposite corner. Several chairs upholstered in oxblood leather stood about the room. "I can see why it would be. I think it would be my favorite as well."

"So you think you could be happy here?"

She laughed. "Who couldn't be? It's like a palace!"

"There's more to the house than appearances. I go along with it."

She looked at him. "I don't think I understand."

Lorne came to her and put his arms around her. "I'm asking you to marry me, Chelsea."

For a long moment she was silent. Warring emotions tore at her. Could she marry one man knowing she loved another? On the other hand, she and Ryan had no future. Instantly her decision was made. "I'd love to, Lorne."

He bent and kissed her. His kisses excited her, but they didn't drive her to ecstasy as Ryan's did. Chelsea tried as hard as she could to stop making comparisons. She returned his kiss, hoping to drive the demons out of her head by concentrating on him.

"You haven't said that you love me," he commented when he straightened and held her in his embrace.

"Nor have you said that to me."

"I do love you, Chelsea. I'm not good at saying it. That's a failing of mine, I know, but it doesn't mean I don't feel things. I want to make you happy."

She drew in a deep breath. "I'm falling in love with you, Lorne. It would be a lie to say that I'm already there. But I care for you, and I would make you a good wife."

He seemed to be thinking that over. "It's good enough for me. In time you'll love me as much as I do you."

"I'm sure I will." She held him fiercely. "You'll never

know how much I want to love you and to have nothing but you on my mind."

"I haven't been in love in a long time," he said almost to himself. "I didn't ever expect to be again."

She wondered if he was remembering his first marriage. He never spoke of it. If Sheila hadn't told her that he had been married before, Chelsea would never have guessed it. "I've been in love before, too. Once."

"You're still in love with him? That's why you don't love me?"

She shook her head. "I've always believed that you can love more than one person. Maybe several. I don't know. I think I'm just afraid of getting hurt."

Lorne kissed her again. "I'll never hurt you, Chelsea. We're both adults and neither of us expects undying romance. I find that refreshingly sensible in you. I know we haven't dated long, and this must seem too sudden to anyone looking on, but I've got both feet on the ground. I know what I want, and I want you. It's a gamble that your love may not grow as fast as I'd like it to, but I'm willing to take that gamble."

She smiled up at him. "Then I think we should be married and let the rest of the world go hang itself. If no one else understands, that's not our problem."

"Set the date. But don't make it too long an engagement. I don't want you to get cold feet."

Chelsea stood on tiptoe to kiss him. The demons at war inside her weren't stilled, but she was determined that they would be in time. She had to get on with her life, and Lorne was the perfect solution to her problems. In time, she told herself, she would come to love him so much that she would no longer see Ryan in her dreams.

Chapter Fourteen

Chelsea went alone to tell Ryan and Karen the news of her impending marriage. "I wanted you to be the first to know. Lorne has proposed, and I said yes." She met Ryan's eyes as Karen squealed and ran to hug her. He looked as if he had been struck. At the sight of Ryan's pain, tears rose in Chelsea's eyes.

"I'm so happy for you!" Karen gushed. "Have you set a date? What did your parents say? Oh, that's right! You said we're the first to know. I'm so excited! Aren't you excited, Ryan? I really like Lorne! I mean I *really* do."

"We haven't set a date yet." Chelsea wished she could go to Ryan and put her arms around him. "He asked me last night."

"And you didn't call me?" Karen asked, as if amazed that Chelsea hadn't needed to tell her the news immediately.

"I thought it would be best to tell you in person." Chelsea pulled away from Karen and smiled at her. "I knew you'd be excited."

"Excited isn't the word! I'm simply beside myself! Will your parents come for the wedding, do you think?"

"I don't know."

"Well, if they don't, I'll help you plan everything. It's going to be a big affair, isn't it? Say it is! Big ones are so much prettier, in my opinion."

"I'd rather it be small, personally."

"If your parents can't come, who'll give you away?" Karen looked at Ryan. "I know! Ryan can do it."

He turned away.

"No, I don't think that would be a good idea," Chelsea said quickly. "I don't need anyone to give me away. I've been living away from my parents for years. It's not like I'm leaving their household for his."

"But someone *has* to do it. I know! Maybe Daddy will. Would you like that?"

"Maybe. I haven't thought any of this through. Like I said, it only came about last night."

"Lorne will be the perfect husband for you. I knew it the minute I saw him. Didn't I tell you so, Ryan? I never felt that about Jason, but Lorne impressed me right away."

"I should have asked you and saved the effort of figuring it out for myself," Chelsea teased.

"We have to drink to this. I'll be right back." Karen hurried from the den.

Chelsea and Ryan were left alone, for the first time since the night he'd kissed her in this very room. They looked at each other across a gulf wider than the space that separated them.

"Do you love him?" Ryan asked.

Chelsea turned away, unable to answer, afraid of what she might say.

He came to her and made her face him. "Do you love him?" he repeated, unable to hide the pain in his voice and eyes.

Silently she shook her head. Lying to Karen was one thing, but it was another to lie to Ryan. "No. I've told him that."

"He must love you a great deal if he wants to marry you when you've told him you don't love him. Why would a man want to do that?"

She had never thought of it in that way. "I don't know. I suppose it's because he believes I'll grow to love him in time. I like him. It's not as if I don't care for him at all."

She couldn't bear the look on his face, and she felt treacherous tears start to well up.

"You're making a mistake," he said. Gently he reached out and brushed a tear from her cheek.

"No, I'm not. I can't live on crumbs forever. Do you have any idea how hard it's been for me these last two years?" She was whispering in case Karen was on her way back into the room, and she couldn't keep the hurt from her voice.

"Yes. I know exactly how hard."

"I doubt it. You haven't visited my husband's house and baby-sat our children."

"Not yet at any rate."

She frowned up at him, and clenched her hands into fists to keep from throwing herself into his arms.

"You two are being awfully quiet in here," Karen said as she came back into the room. She was carrying a tray with three wine glasses. "I thought for a minute Chel had left." She came to them and held out the tray for each to take a glass.

Chelsea surreptitiously brushed her tears away.

Karen took her own glass and put the tray aside. "I know it's early in the day, but as Daddy says, the sun is over the yardarm." She lifted her glass toward Chelsea. "Here's to your happiness." She glanced sharply at Ryan. "What's wrong? Don't you want to toast Chelsea?"

He raised his glass. "To Chelsea's happiness," he said.

The wine tasted bitter in Chelsea's mouth.

"I just love this house!" Karen said in a whisper as she followed Chelsea down the hall, each of them carrying a box of Chelsea's belongings.

"It's impressive, all right." Chelsea balanced the box to open the bedroom door. "Just bring that in here."

"Are we all alone? I'd have thought Lorne would employ a maid."

"A woman comes in on Monday, Wednesday, and Friday. She's off today. That's why I had to go by and get a house key from him."

Karen put her box down on the floor beside the dresser. "My goodness! Just look at this room! It makes my house look like a hovel."

Chelsea glanced around as if she hadn't paid that much attention to the room until now. "It's beautiful, isn't it?" The bed was mounted on a dais and seemed huge. The headboard was gleaming brass and was polished to a brilliant shine. The other furniture was massive oak with brass fittings. One wall was solid glass and overlooked the private backyard.

"I'm just so glad you didn't move in with him before the wedding," Karen said as she went to the window. "I know it's none of my business, but I think that's cheap, somehow."

Chelsea smiled at her but didn't voice her opinion on Karen's standards.

"This way, you can leave for the wedding from your own house and come to this one afterward. It's just nicer that way. More traditional."

Chelsea started putting her clothing into the empty drawers. "I feel overwhelmed by this place, to tell you the truth. I like my little apartment. I know where everything is. If I hear a noise in the night, I can open my eyes and see virtually my entire house. Here, I'll have to creep up and down stairs."

"But here you'll have Lorne to protect you," Karen pointed out. "Having a husband is much nicer in every way." She went to the door and looked down the hall. "What's in the other rooms?"

"Guest bedrooms. Go look, if you'd like."

Karen soon returned, her eyes wide with wonder. "I've never seen so many nice things in my life! Lorne must be as rich as a king!"

"Probably."

"Aren't you glad to be marrying into a fortune? Naturally, you're more interested in Lorne than in his money—I don't mean that you aren't—but you must feel *something* about it. I mean, look at all the months you weren't sure if you'd be able to pay your rent."

"I'd say those days are gone forever. I'd be lying if I didn't admit that I'm glad for that. Scraping for every cent isn't fun. But money isn't everything."

"I know, I know. I've heard it all before. Money can't buy happiness. But it can certainly rent it for a while."

Chelsea laughed. "True."

Karen sat on the bed and bounced experimentally. "You can have several children in a house this size. Are you going to start a family right away?"

"We haven't discussed it."

"You haven't? You should. Or better yet, plan it yourself. I've found that's the best way."

Chelsea didn't answer.

"If you have a baby right away, our children will be in school together. I can get you information on Saint Anne's. Wouldn't it be fun to watch our children grow up together? If you have a girl, they might be best friends just like we were."

"I don't know if Lorne even wants to have children." She sat back on her heels and smiled. "But I'd like to have a baby. I love Bethany and Ashley. A baby of my own would be wonderful, and I'd like a large family. As an only child, I was lonely so often."

"I don't know what I'd do without Joyce. We weren't close as girls, but now that we're both married, we talk often and go places together. I want my girls to be close like that."

"Will you bring up another box? I want to get everything moved in this afternoon if I possibly can."

Karen left and Chelsea heard her go downstairs. She stopped unpacking and stood up. Everything seemed to be going so fast. At times she felt she didn't have time to take a breath or process a thought before the wedding would be upon her.

She and Lorne had decided there was no point in a long

engagement so their marriage day had been set for mid-September. In less than a week they would be married. Was she doing the right thing?

Her parents had been glad to hear of her engagement. Though they wouldn't be able to attend the wedding, she and Lorne had decided to honeymoon in Germany so he could meet them. Chelsea hoped this trip would wipe that last one out of her mind. Karen's father had agreed to give her away in her own father's absence, and Chelsea thought this fitting since she had spent so many years coming and going from the Baker house. Fulton Baker was almost like a father to her.

Karen had wanted a huge wedding, but Chelsea had held firm on that point. She wanted a small, intimate affair with only close friends in attendance. Karen would be her matron of honor, Ryan would be the best man. Lorne had surprised her by asking Ryan to do that, but he'd had no close friend to ask. Sometimes Chelsea wondered why Lorne had so few friends, but it wasn't something a person could ask. She decided it was because he had been buried in his work.

She no longer worked at Spenser Construction. As soon as she'd agreed to marry him, he had suggested that she might want to turn in her resignation. Chelsea was glad he wanted her to do that. She had never adapted to the work, and the other women had continued to vacillate between being cool to her or too friendly, once they'd learned she was dating the boss. Sheila Stanford had stopped speaking to her altogether.

For the past couple of weeks Chelsea had concentrated on finishing the canvases she had started and preparing to become Mrs. Lorne Spenser. She hadn't realized how many roots she had put down until she had to make lists of places where she would have to change her last name and services she would have to cancel or switch to her new address.

She had seen very little of Ryan in the last few weeks but she was glad of that. Marrying Lorne was best for her. She was convinced of that. If she remained single and lonely, she was afraid of what might eventually happen between Ryan and herself. Karen was her friend and she was loyal, but she was also human. As Lorne's wife, she would be far less tempted.

"What are you doing? Are you waiting for me?" Karen asked as she brought up the last of the boxes.

"What?" Chelsea glanced at her in surprise. "Sorry. I guess I was just daydreaming."

Karen smiled and sat beside her on the floor. "I don't blame you a bit. If I was about to marry a man like Lorne Spenser, I'd probably be walking around with my head in a cloud all the time."

Chelsea bit back her retort. It was none of her business if Karen took Ryan for granted. As she opened the box, she said, "I don't think all this is going to fit in these drawers."

"Well, we can't bring your furniture. Can you see it in here?"

"Not in a million years." Chelsea had shopped in thrift shops and at garage sales, and her furniture looked it. "See if you can find any other empty drawers."

Karen went around the room, opening and closing drawers. "He's neat. I like that. You can't believe how messy some men can be. Joyce and I were talking about that the other day. Would you look at this? He even folds his underwear. I think it's been ironed!"

"You're kidding!" Chelsea went to the drawer Karen had opened. "You're right."

"I guess that's the advantage of having a really good housekeeper. I have to do everything at my house. Ryan says we can't afford help." She shook her head dismally. "I can hardly wait until we have money."

"I suppose I could move some of Lorne's things over and put my nightgowns in here. The drawer is almost empty. Maybe I ought to ask first."

"No, just do it." Karen took the underwear and stacked

it neatly on one side. "There. Will that give you enough room?"

"Perfect."

"I wish Ryan could see this." Karen went to the middle of the room and turned in a full circle.

"I can't think of a reason in this world why he would want to see Lorne's bedroom."

"It would put our house in perspective. He's always going on about it being too large and about us not having enough money. Daddy gave him a raise after I talked to him and explained about the house. Then he got a bonus because of Ashley being born. If he knew I still get my allowance, he'd have a fit!"

Chelsea looked over at her. "Your parents still pay you an allowance?"

"Only until Ryan can afford to provide spending money. Mother says I shouldn't have to suffer just because I married someone with no money."

"You sound as if Ryan is working at minimum wage. He makes a good salary. He's bound to."

"He does. And he's good at his work. Daddy told me so. It's just so hard, starting out from scratch. You're lucky. Lorne already has this house and is established in business. You'll never have to scrimp and save."

"I've done enough of that these past few years to make up for not doing it now."

"Yes. You've paid your dues, as Daddy says. I'm just so happy for you!"

"That's everything in this load. Let's go back and get the rest."

"Thank goodness it's mostly things to hang and stuff for the bathroom. There aren't any more drawers left." Karen followed her down the stairs. "I hope we haven't forgotten anything about the wedding. I double-checked on the chapel and your dress this morning, and everything is all set. You're to pick up the dress this afternoon. Don't forget to do it. Will you remember?"

"I think I can be trusted with that," Chelsea said with a smile.

"Try it on! Don't just pick up the box and walk out. If anything is wrong, they'll have to fix it right away."

"I will."

"I wish you were taller. You could have worn my dress. Mother would have been beside herself, but I would have loaned it to you."

"Thanks, but I'd rather have my own."

"Of course you would. This way, you can pass it down to your daughter."

"I'm going to shorten it and wear it as a cocktail dress."

"That's so practical! I could never do that. Not my wedding dress. I'd feel so strange going to a party in it!"

Chelsea looked around as they went through the living room and to the front door. "It's going to take me a long time to get used to living in a place like this."

"It wouldn't me! I'd adjust right away. I love it!"

Chelsea made sure the door locked behind them and told herself she wouldn't feel like an intruder there forever.

The wedding was small but beautifully done. Chelsea was glad to have avoided the hassle and strain of a large wedding such as Karen's. She dressed in the same room Karen had used, but when it was time for her to walk down the aisle, she went to the small chapel at the back of the church.

Karen preceded her down the aisle. Ryan and Lorne were already there by the rail. For one dreadful moment Chelsea had to fight the urge to burst into tears and run away. Then Fulton Baker took her arm, and she walked down the short aisle to stand beside Lorne.

He was handsome in his dark blue suit. Because her dress wasn't elaborate, they had decided he would forgo a tuxedo. His eyes were warm as he gazed down at her. He repeated the minister's words as if he had memorized them. Chelsea's voice wasn't as sure. Lorne hadn't wanted a wedding band, so only one ring was involved. The one he had bought for her was a circle of diamonds that caught the light and sparkled like cold fire.

After the ceremony, Lorne kissed her, and Chelsea smiled up at him. She had made the right choice. She was sure of it. They walked up the aisle, husband and wife.

The reception was held at the Bakers' since there were so few invited to the wedding. Chelsea had the curious sensation that all of it was unreal. That she was dreaming and would soon awake. That the diamonds on her left hand and the man at her side couldn't possibly mean she was married. It had all happened so quickly, and she felt no different.

Ryan was at the reception, of course, but he stayed in the background. Twice Chelsea caught him watching her, but he looked away with a smile. She knew how he was feeling and wished she could do something for him. She could remember her pain when he married Karen and how bereft she had been. If she could spare him that misery, she would have done so.

They left the Bakers' house and went straight to the airport. Karen stood apart and watched Lorne check in their baggage for the flight. This was her husband. Her name was Chelsea Spenser now, not Cavin. Tonight and every night for the rest of her life, she would lie beside Lorne. It still seemed like something in a dream.

They boarded the plane and Chelsea buckled her seat belt dutifully. Lorne was waiting until the last minute to fasten his. She heard the plane's engines and smelled the scents peculiar to airplanes and told herself that flying was perfectly safe whether she enjoyed it or not.

"So it's over," he said as he took her hand. "I was afraid you'd back out at the last minute."

"Were you? I wouldn't have done that."

"Just the same, I was worried." He stroked her hand. "I wish we weren't spending our first night together in the air with fifty other people."

She laughed. "So do I."

"All day I kept thinking, tonight's the night. I felt like a teenager." He laughed. "I thought this evening would never arrive."

"It seemed to fly by to me. It was as if I blinked and discovered hours had passed. Karen was a nervous wreck! She must have phoned me a hundred times in the past week."

"We can settle down now. All the rushing is over."

She laced her fingers through his. "I have a confession to make. I hate to fly."

"Then why are we going to Germany? I could meet your parents another time."

"It may be years before they come back to the States. Flying hurts Mom's ears, and her blood pressure isn't good lately. I want them to meet you."

"My parents have been gone for so long, it seems odd to think I have another set now. And these are almost my contemporaries."

She smiled. "I forget at times that you're older than I am. That's never been an issue with me."

"I've felt every year lately. Karen exhausted me with her endless lists and plans."

"That's not because of your age. She exhausts me, too. That's just Karen."

"Incidentally, I have to be out of town for a few days when we return from Germany."

"You do? Where are you going?"

"To Austin. I'm bidding for a project there. It's a big deal, and I have to go down myself to be sure it's handled correctly."

"Can I go?"

"I think it would be best if you didn't. I'm going to be in meetings all day, and you'd be bored. You and Karen can go shopping or something. I know you'll have a lot to tell her about Germany."

"Sure. That's fine." Chelsea tried not to feel disappointed.

"It will give you a chance to adjust to my house without me under foot."

"I adjust easily," she assured him. There was no reason to tell him she was rather afraid of being alone in the huge house.

"I'll leave you a list of things you'll need to do while I'm gone. When to pay the housekeeper, for instance."

"Lorne, I wouldn't mind if you're at meetings all day. I could take the car and go shopping there as well as I can in Dallas."

"I'm not driving down. I'll fly." He looked at her as if driving had never occurred to him.

"Oh. Won't you rent a car while you're there?"

"Chelsea, you can't go on business trips with me. That's just the way it is."

"Okay. I was only asking."

The plane's engines revved up, and she felt a mild jolt as it started to taxi. She looked out the window at the passing runway and tried to tell herself the trepidation she felt was due to the pending flight, not her new marriage.

The plane turned and began its take-off approach. Chelsea gripped the arms of the seat and tried to breathe deeply. Lorne finally fastened his seat belt and took a magazine out of the seat pocket before him to read. The plane bounced as it went faster; then Chelsea's middle seemed to drop away as it left the runway and lifted into the air.

Her ears felt the pressure, and her heart was pounding as the plane banked and started on its journey. She told herself for the thousandth time that planes flew every day and she was perfectly safe.

After several minutes she started to relax and glanced at Lorne. He was leafing calmly through the magazine. The stewardess stood and explained the oxygen masks and safety procedures to the passengers. Chelsea tried to memorize every word, though she had heard them all many times. Lorne seemed not to be aware of her at all.

By the time they had leveled out at traveling altitude,

Chelsea felt a little better. "Karen is in love with our house," she said to make conversation.

"Is she? That's nice. I built that house in seventy-five."

"I never thought about that. I suppose you would build your own house, wouldn't you? No wonder it doesn't seem to be like any other I've ever been in."

"Houses of that size don't follow tract plans," he said as if it bored him to have to point that out.

"No, of course not." She felt out of her league. Every place she had ever lived had had a duplicate floor plan a few doors away.

"I suppose it's too big, but I wanted one that would be a good investment as well as beautiful. When I decide to sell it, I'll make a good profit."

"Sell it? You'd move?"

"Someday. You wouldn't want to stay there forever, would you?"

"I guess I've always thought of moving in regard to finding a larger place. The only house larger than that one is Buckingham Palace! Karen says we'll have to have a drove of children to fill the bedrooms."

Lorne looked uncomfortable.

"I like children," she said quickly, "but I don't really want a drove." When he made no comment, she said, "Why are you looking like that?"

"Chelsea, I guess we should have discussed this before, but I don't want to have children."

She stared at him. "Well, I don't necessarily want to have them right away either. I'd like us to be together and alone for a while."

"I don't ever want them. I guess I should have told you this before, but I feel so strongly about it that I forget having them is a possibility in marriage."

"You don't ever want children? Not even one?"

"I've had a vasectomy."

"Oh."

"I'm sorry I didn't tell you. It slipped my mind."

"That's okay. It just surprised me, that's all." She took

an airline magazine from the pocket before her and started
to leaf through it.

He didn't want—couldn't have!—children. Anger
flooded through her. After all the rush and strain of the
past few days, this topped it! She wanted children, but he
hadn't thought it important enough to tell her that they
were out of the question? She exerted all her willpower not
to tell him exactly what she thought about his omission.

With a great effort, she calmed herself. It was a disappointment, but there were benefits to this marriage. Life
with Lorne would be exciting enough to banish Ryan from
her thoughts forever. That was worth any sacrifice.

Still, she felt a great deal of resentment as they winged
toward Europe, and she decided not to tell Karen that
children were out of the question. She didn't want to have
to defend her husband on an issue on which she disagreed
with him.

Chapter Fifteen

"I wish you had told me ahead of time that Lorne wouldn't be coming." Karen was frowning as she removed the plate from the table. "I made lasagna, and my recipe is perfect for four people."

"I'm sorry. I didn't know until I called the office. He forgot to tell me he'd be late. Or maybe Sheila forgot. Since I married Lorne she hasn't been at all friendly toward me."

"Was there something between them?" Karen asked. "You know, an office romance?"

"I've heard there was. It's certainly not something I can ask Lorne."

"If I thought there was something between my husband and another woman, even if it was in the past, I'd ask."

Chelsea didn't answer for several minutes. "Karen, can I talk to you about something?" She looked around to be certain Ryan was still down the hall with the girls. "Do you think it's odd that Lorne is working late so often these days? He never did when we were dating."

"Well, you didn't date all that long." Karen put away the plate and placed a trivet on the table to hold the lasagna. "Your entire courtship only lasted a couple of months." She looked more closely at Chelsea. "Why are you wondering?"

"When I called to see why he was late, Sheila answered the phone."

Karen pursed her lips thoughtfully. "She's his secretary, after all."

"I know." Chelsea shook her head. "It's probably just my imagination."

"Of course it is. Why, you're still newlyweds."

"Yes. I suppose we are." Chelsea didn't want to admit to Karen that she didn't feel like one. Wasn't the honeymoon period supposed to last longer than the trip? She felt more lonely now than she had before she married Lorne.

"Suppose you are what?" Ryan asked as he came into the room.

"It doesn't matter." She didn't want Ryan to know how things were between her and her husband.

"I got the girls into bed."

"Good. Now maybe we can eat in peace." Karen handed Chelsea two glasses of tea to put on the table.

"It's too bad Lorne couldn't make it," Ryan said. "Is he working late again?"

"He loves his work," Chelsea said in a controlled voice. "I would have thought construction would have fallen off this close to Christmas, but I guess I was wrong."

"I'm surprised the weather hasn't held it up. That ice storm last week had everything at a standstill." Ryan took his own glass of tea to the table. "I couldn't get into the office for two days."

"It didn't hold Lorne back. He called a cab and off he went." She hoped she didn't sound as angry about that as she felt. She had spent the day worrying about his safety, and he had finally called to say he was sleeping in the office because conditions were so bad on the freeway. He hadn't come home until the third day.

Ryan gave her an assessing look. "I would have thought the roads would be worse in the morning than after vehicles had tried to get through on them all day."

"So would I." She turned away to get the salt and pepper. "Karen, where did you hide the salt and pepper this time?"

"In the cabinet closest to the sink."

Chelsea went into the kitchen, then turned to find Ryan had followed her. He caught her arm. "Are you okay?"

"Of course I am."

He studied her face and then shook his head. "I know you too well."

She tried to smile. "I guess I expected more out of married life than was reasonable."

"If you ever need me, call me. Day or night."

She nodded. His offer to help almost brought tears to her eyes. Before Karen could wonder about their absence, Chelsea hurried back into the dining room with the salt and pepper shakers. "I wish you'd stop rearranging that kitchen."

"It's big, but not very convenient," Karen told her. "I thought at first it would be heavenly to have a really big one, after the little one in our first house, but this one has cabinets in odd places. I guess a man designed it." She laughed.

Chelsea glanced at Ryan and wondered if he objected to Karen's increasingly derisive comments about men. If he did, he gave no sign.

"Are you coming to our Christmas party?" Chelsea asked as Karen passed her the lasagna.

"I wouldn't miss it. I love that house!"

Ryan laughed. "I guess you see where you rate, Chelsea. She coming to see the house—and you."

"Oh, you know what I mean," Karen said with a wave of her hand. "Chel, I love the way you've decorated it for Christmas."

"Thanks. It was fun having an unlimited budget. I'm tempted to keep the tree up all year just so I can continue to enjoy it."

"It's beautiful. I don't see how you think of the things you do. I really don't. If I tried to put together a tree like that, it would just look tacky. I guess your major in art is paying off."

"Do you ever paint these days?" Ryan asked.

"No. Lorne says it's too smelly. And he's right, of

course. Oils may be beautiful to look at, but living with the smells of oil and turpentine is an acquired taste."

"It certainly is," Karen said as she wrinkled her nose. "It used to almost turn my stomach in the dorm, and you almost never painted there. To smell that every day would be more than I could stand."

"Couldn't you close off one of the unused rooms upstairs?" Ryan asked. "I know how you love to paint."

She looked away as if it didn't matter. "They all have wall-to-wall carpeting, and that would be ruined the first time I dropped or spilled something. Besides, I'm tired of painting. It's not as enjoyable when I know I can't exhibit any of the canvases."

"That's not fair," Karen said. "I still think you ought to sue Jason for having you blackballed like he did."

"In time it will be forgotten. Since Lorne doesn't want me to paint anyway, there's no point in pushing it."

"How are you spending Christmas?" Karen asked. "Are you going to Germany?"

"No, I guess we're staying home. Lorne has no close family still alive. It'll be a quiet one."

"I think those are the best. We'll be surrounded by family as usual. There are times I wish I could sneak off and hide for a few minutes." Karen reached for another slice of garlic bread. "This will be Ashley's first Christmas. And probably the first one when Bethany understands what's going on."

"Take lots of pictures and give me the negatives."

"Chel, you ought to have a baby of your own, the way you love my girls. I thought you might be pregnant by now."

Chelsea laughed mirthlessly. "I've only been married three months!" she hadn't told anyone that Lorne wouldn't be fathering any children. "Besides, I have yours to love."

"It's not the same. Not the same at all."

Ryan was watching her silently. Chelsea wished he

didn't have that uncanny ability to follow her thoughts. He could read her like a book.

"I don't know what I'll wear to the party," Karen was saying. "I guess I can still fit into that red wool with the white collar. It's going to be tight, though."

"What about your navy dress?" Chelsea asked. "That's pretty on you."

"I don't know. I've worn it everywhere. Maybe I'll buy something new." She looked across at her husband. "And don't say we can't afford it. I need new clothes from time to time. You don't want me to look dowdy."

"I like the navy, too." Ryan gave Karen a steady look. "No one at this party will have seen it."

"He just doesn't understand," Karen said to Chelsea. "Men can wear the same old suits to work or parties, or anywhere, and nobody notices. It's not the same with a woman."

"I haven't decided what I'm going to wear yet either." Lorne had told her to buy something new, but Chelsea was reluctant, especially since Karen couldn't afford to do the same and would be certain to notice.

"Clothing has never meant enough to you," Karen observed. "You have a position to uphold now, just as I do. We can no longer go around dressed just any old way."

Chelsea looked down at her pullover sweater and jeans. "I'm still me, Karen. I haven't changed."

"I know. I'm just suggesting that maybe you should. I never wear jeans around the house anymore. You never know who might drop in."

Ryan smiled wryly. "Has anyone but your mother or Joyce dropped in on you since we've been married?"

"That's not the point, Ryan. You see?" she said to Chelsea, "Men can't understand."

"Then I must be a man, too, because I don't see any reason to change my lifestyle just because I have money now."

"I should have known you two would gang up on me. You always have." Karen frowned at them both.

"I know," Chelsea said in sudden inspiration. "Let me buy you a dress for Christmas. That will solve everything." As soon as the words were out of her mouth, she knew she had made a mistake. Ryan's expression became closed, and Karen started telling her that she couldn't allow a friend to do any such thing.

Chelsea was discovering that wealth could cause more problems than it resolved.

The Christmas party was formal, catered, and exactly the sort of gathering Chelsea had always chosen to avoid. Karen loved it. "These little sandwiches are wonderful. I wonder what they are," she said as her eyes swept the room. "You have to give me the name of your caterer."

"You'll have to ask Lorne. He arranged for the refreshments. Or Sheila did, to be more exact. I just got dressed and came down the stairs."

"You look beautiful, by the way. Is that a new dress?"

"Lorne gave it to me. I wouldn't have bought black for a Christmas party."

"It's gorgeous!" Karen ate another of the tiny sandwiches. "I can't believe all the people that are here. Your guest list must include everyone that's important in the city. I feel flattered that we're here."

"Don't be silly. We're friends. I'd never have a Christmas party without you and Ryan." She smiled across at him. Since they arrived, he was unusually quiet. Chelsea knew it was because he had never seen her—or Lorne's— house and that he hadn't believed Karen's descriptions of it. Chelsea was a bit embarrassed by its ostentatiousness.

Lorne came over and smiled down at her. "Have you spoken to the Maxwells? They said they haven't seen you at all tonight."

"Then I suppose I haven't spoken to them." Chelsea tried to keep the barb out of her voice. Just before their guests had arrived, her husband had instructed her on how she was to mingle and that she was not to talk only to Karen and Ryan. "Where are they?"

"It's the couple over by the punch bowl. You must remember them. She's the tall brunette."

"I'll be right back," Chelsea said to Karen and Ryan.

She threaded her way through the crowd until she reached the Maxwells' side. "I'm so glad you could come."

"We were just admiring what you've done with your house. Who decorated for you?"

Chelsea smiled. "No one. I did it myself."

"Not really!" Mrs. Maxwell said in disbelief.

"I'm a professional artist. At least I was. I guess you'd say I'm in semiretirement now."

"You're way too young to retire," Mr. Maxwell said as he sidled a bit too close. He had been standing by, and consuming the contents of, the punch bowl. "Isn't she too young, dear?"

"I'm sure she meant it only as a figure of speech," his wife said.

"I painted the Victorian miniatures on the tree and wreaths, and I sewed the lace fans. I'm not as good with a needle as with a paint brush, but I like the effect of lace and brocade."

"Good heavens! You mean these actually are home-made ornaments?" Mrs. Maxwell exclaimed. "I would never have guessed it."

Chelsea wasn't sure whether her guest had meant these words to be as barbed as they had sounded. "Yes. If you'll excuse me, I see someone I haven't greeted yet." Chelsea edged into the crowd and managed to find Karen and Ryan again.

Karen had discovered the piano in the alcove between the living and dining rooms. She was running a hand over it as if stroking a pet. Chelsea opened it. "Play for us."

Karen blushed and hesitated. "I couldn't! In front of all these people?"

"Please. I love to hear you play."

Karen sat on the stool and ran her fingers lightly over the keys. "It has a beautiful tone!"

"Lorne keeps it tuned even though neither of us play."

Karen's deft fingers began a rippling piece of music that had always been Chelsea's favorite. Ryan smiled proudly. His wife's talent wasn't strong enough to have taken her on the concert circuit, but she was a better than average pianist. Several guests stopped talking and came over to listen.

Chelsea was proud of her friend. This was the old Karen she had known in school. Shy and sweet, but transformed by her music. Her eyes met Ryan's, and for the first time in a long time she didn't see masked unhappiness in his face. He had once said that Karen was more than herself when she was seated at a piano. It was the only time she wasn't self-conscious.

Her fingers moved deftly over the keys, flowing from one song into another, mixing popular with classic. She seemed tireless, her repertoire almost unlimited.

Lorne came to Chelsea and took her elbow to guide her away from the piano. When they were out of the crowd that was gathering, he said, "Tell Karen to stop playing."

"What?" she asked with a laugh. "Why would I want to do that?"

"Because she's a guest here. Not the entertainment. I've hired a man to play. He's arrived late, but he's in the other room fuming because she's playing some of the music that was part of his program."

"To bad," Chelsea said stubbornly. "He should have arrived on time. I like to hear Karen play. So does everyone else."

"They probably think she's hired to do it."

Chelsea shook her head. "That's ridiculous. If I were visiting someone and a person started to play the piano, I'd assume my host had a talented friend."

He smiled coolly. "Yes, but these people aren't used to the social whirl of living in a garage apartment. They expect paid entertainment. Your friend is making a fool of herself."

The blood left Chelsea's face. She wouldn't have felt worse if he had slapped her. It wasn't the first time Lorne had spoken to her cruelly, but she hadn't thought he would do so at a party in their home. She glanced around to see if anyone had overheard them. Fortunately no one was near.

Chelsea turned on her heel and went to the piano. Surreptitiously she glanced at the faces of the people gathered to hear Karen play. They looked politely bored, as they might if they were listening to music played by a paid musician.

She caught Ryan's arm and pulled him away. Quickly she told him what Lorne had said. "I'm sorry. I don't how to put it more tactfully."

Ryan lifted his head and glared around the room. "Where is he?"

"Please, don't cause a scene. Not now. I'm furious with him. When everyone goes home, we'll discuss this, I promise. Just find a way to get Karen from the piano before someone goes over and treats her like hired help."

He thought for a minute. "Call the house and get Bethany on the phone. I'll tell Karen she had the baby sitter call to say she misses her. That should do it."

Chelsea hurried to do as he had said. She chatted with Bethany until Karen came to the phone. With a smile, she then gave her the receiver. "It seems Bethany misses you."

Karen took the phone, her face all smiles.

Chelsea and Ryan stepped away so they could talk. "I'm so embarrassed! I didn't want to tell you what Lorne said, but I didn't see any alternative."

"I'm as upset about what he said to you about your garage apartment standards as I am about the business with Karen." Ryan frowned down at her. "Does he talk to you like this all the time?"

"No, no. Of course not." She hoped he believed it. "It's

just that he didn't want Karen to be embarrassed and he's short on tact."

Ryan obviously didn't believe it. Chelsea had never been adept at lying. "Are you sure you're happy? That he treats you okay?"

"What can I do, Ryan? Leave him because he has an abrasive edge I never noticed before we were married? That's an overreaction, isn't it? After all, marriage comes with downs as well as ups."

"I know that as well as you do."

Chelsea glanced back at Karen. "I suppose you'd better leave, much as I hate to suggest it. If someone asks her to play at their party or inquiries about what she charges, she'll be upset."

"If I know Karen, she'll insist on leaving as soon as she gets off the phone. You know how she is about the girls."

Karen hung up and came over to them. "I hate to do this, but would either of you mind if we make it an early evening? Bethany wants me to come home. She says the sitter is having trouble getting Ashley down for the night and that her tummy hurts. I think I should be with them."

"I understand." Chelsea walked with them to the door. "I'll help you find your coat."

When they were gone, she felt mixed emotions. Now she didn't have to worry about Karen's feelings being hurt, but she was left with a houseful of strangers to entertain. Karen and Ryan had been the only friends of hers Lorne had agreed to invite.

She went back into the living room and started mingling the way Lorne had wanted her to do from the start. She had never been good at it.

"Such a lovely party," one elderly woman said. "Your pianist was exquisite. You must give me her name."

"I'll call you tomorrow," Chelsea said evasively. She could just imagine what Karen would think if she actually gave her name and phone number to someone who wanted to hire a pianist. She maneuvered a way into the crowd.

The pianist Lorne had hired was at the piano, and Chelsea was wryly amused to see that he wasn't as talented as Karen. Almost no one was listening to him. Instead people were standing in tight knots the way they had before the music had started.

Chelsea bumped into the Maxwells on her way around the room. Mrs. Maxwell trapped her before she could get away. "I was so dismayed to hear you're moving. Have you found a buyer for this house?"

"It was a stroke of genius to have a party as an open house, of sorts," her husband said. "A stroke of genius!"

"Moving? We aren't going anywhere. The house isn't for sale." Chelsea smiled at them in confusion. "Where did you get the idea that it is?"

"Why, from Lorne, of course." Mrs. Maxwell looked more confused than Chelsea felt. "He told me not ten minutes ago that you're moving to Austin and that he hopes to sell the house as soon as possible."

"You must have misunderstood him."

"No, no. I heard him, too," Mr. Maxwell said. "He said you're moving. He's opening a new branch in Austin and wants to be in town with it."

"Excuse me." Chelsea turned away and started searching for her husband.

She found him at the table in the dining room, overseeing the new offerings being put out by the caterer. "There you are!" he said. "I'm having to do your job for you."

"Lorne, what's this about our moving to Austin?" She waited for him to deny it.

"I meant to talk to you later. I'm opening a new branch there, and I have to be on hand to see it gets off to a good start."

For a moment she could only stare at him. "You're selling our house and we're moving to Austin and you didn't bother to tell me?"

"Hush! Keep your voice down." He glanced around and frowned at her.

Chelsea turned and left the room. She heard him call out to her, but she didn't stop. Anything she said to him had better be said when their guests had gone. Not speaking to anyone, she went through the crowd, up the stairs, and into their bedroom. Once inside, she locked the door and sat on the edge of the bed.

Moving! Her mind couldn't take it in. Austin was hours away! It was halfway across the state!

She was too shocked for tears or coherent thought. She knew only that her evenings with Ryan and Karen and the girls would soon be things of the past. Finally the tears came. She couldn't choke them back. She stood and went to her closet. She didn't care if she had a houseful of guests or not. For her the party was over.

She undressed and put on a nightgown, not caring what she took from the drawer. The numbness was going away and in its place was misery. She went into the bathroom and removed her makeup and brushed her hair, then braided it. She didn't want to leave it loose and tempt Lorne into lovemaking. Not tonight.

Going back to the bed, she considered calling Karen, but decided against it. Karen would be busy getting the girls into bed, and Chelsea wasn't too sure she wanted to talk just yet. The shock was still too new.

She pulled back the covers and went to bed, leaving the room in darkness. Lorne would be angry, but she didn't care. If anyone had a right to be upset, it was her.

In the last few weeks he had started making unkind remarks to her about her lifestyle and about the unsuitability of her friends. Often when she told Karen and Ryan that Lorne was working, he was at home and refusing to spend the evening at their house. Sometimes when she came home, she found him gone. She didn't enjoy being alone in the huge house, but lately she had found that preferable to sharing it with him.

She curled into a tight ball under the covers, her misery almost a physical pain. Silently she cried into her pillow. If she moved to Austin, she wouldn't see Ryan or the girls for months. Perhaps for years if Lorne kept her as close to home as he had in Dallas.

She hadn't gone more than a few weeks without seeing Karen since they had met in the first grade. And part of her pain was the knowledge that she wouldn't see Ryan. Chelsea hated herself for feeling this way about Karen's husband, but she couldn't help it. Since marrying Lorne, she saw marriage in a different light, and she wanted Ryan more than ever. Did Lorne know that? Impossible! Chelsea had been careful to give no sign that she was still in love with Ryan.

So Lorne didn't have jealousy as a motive. That meant he had done this because he didn't care enough about her to tell her he wanted to sell the house and leave town.

Chelsea wondered how she had managed to get herself into such a predicament. Short of divorce, there was no way to change things. She hoped she would be asleep before the guests left and Lorne came to bed. Otherwise, she was certain she would say things she might later regret.

Chapter Sixteen

When Chelsea awoke the next morning, Lorne's side of the bed was still empty. She sat up and tried to organize her thoughts. Had it been a nightmare? Even as the thought formed, she knew it hadn't. Lorne had put their house up for sale and was moving her to Austin without so much as consulting her.

She pulled on her robe and went downstairs, expecting to find him asleep on the couch. The house was empty. Panic began to fill her. Where had he gone?

Everywhere she looked there were remains of the party. Dirty glasses stood on every surface, along with dessert plates and crumpled napkins. The candles had burned down to stubs and the carpet looked littered.

"Lorne?" she called as she searched the rooms again. "Lorne, are you in here?"

She heard the front door opening and ran into the living room to see him coming into the house, still wearing the suit he had worn the night before. "Where have you been?" she demanded.

"Out. You chose to go to bed in the middle of my party, and I chose to go out." He looked at her with distaste. "There's nothing you can say to me that will excuse your rudeness."

"*My* rudeness? What about you putting our house on the market without so much as mentioning it to me? I had to find out from a guest! What were you going to do? Wait until some realtor arrived with prospective buyers and have her explain it to me?"

"I should have known you'd overreact." He went to the stairs.

"Where are you going? We have to discuss this!"

"No, we don't." He paused to look back at her. "I own this house. I have a right to sell it if I choose. My business is taking me to Austin. As my wife, you're going with me. It's that simple."

She went to the foot of the stairs and held onto the bannister. "Don't my feelings matter to you at all?"

"What would you have me do? Forestall a multimillion dollar deal until I can talk it over with you? I'm to build a mall in Austin that will be larger than the Galleria. I have to be there to see it's done the way I want. I don't want to fly back and forth, and I certainly don't intend to stay in a hotel for the length of time it will take to finish the project. Especially since I expect more work to come my way once people in Austin see what I'm capable of. We have to move."

"You could have said that to me days ago. You didn't have to let me find it out from strangers." She held onto the newel post so tightly her fingers went numb.

"I honestly didn't think it would matter to you." He didn't sound contrite at all—only mildly curious as to her reaction. He turned and started up the stairs.

"Wait a minute! Where have you been all night?"

"Out." He didn't stop.

"Damn it, Lorne! Out where?"

He turned and gave her a cold stare. "I have no intention of answering that. Last night you embarrassed me on every count. You insisted on inviting your friends who— even you will admit this—had nothing in common with those on my guest list. Karen made matters worse by playing the piano as if she thought this was amateur night. Then you topped it all off by going to bed when we had guests in the house. That's unforgivable."

"Karen played far better than the man you hired,"

Chelsea retorted. "As for them not fitting in, I'm glad they don't! The other guests were insufferable bores! No one seemed to be able to talk about anything but stocks and parties. Don't those people have real lives?"

"Quite real. Just not as pedestrian as the life you were accustomed to before I married you."

"And that's another thing! I'm tired of hearing how you found me in the gutter!"

He smiled maddeningly. "Didn't I?"

"Listen, Lorne! You're a contractor, not royalty. Granted you're rich and you've bought your way into society, but that doesn't put you on a level above me!" Chelsea stormed up the stairs to him. "You owe me the respect of telling me where you spent the night!"

He glared at her. "Do you really want to know?"

Chelsea's confidence crumbled. "You were with a woman?"

"I would hardly have spent the night with a man, now would I?"

She threw herself at him, and he caught her wrists. Angrily she struggled to get free.

"I'm going to let it go this time," he said, his voice measured and cold. "But from this point on, you're not to question me. If I feel like staying out, I'll stay out. If not, I'll be here."

"Then the same goes for me."

He shoved her away from him with all his strength. She fell hard against the wall, then onto the floor. Dazed, she stared up at him.

Lorne knelt in front of her and lifted his finger warningly. "You're expendable, Chelsea. Remember that."

"Why did you marry me?" she whispered. "You don't love me."

"Nor do you love me. You were quite clear about that, if I recall. I enjoyed the challenge. I've always wanted what I couldn't get." He stood. "But now I have you, and I'm not so sure I want you." He turned and walked away.

Chelsea sat there, trying to comprehend all that had

happened. Slowly she got up and went back downstairs. She sat on the couch in the den until she heard him leave the house, then went upstairs to dress.

"What do you mean you're moving?" Karen exclaimed. Ryan stared at Chelsea.

Chelsea avoided their eyes. "That's right. We're moving to Austin."

"When?" Ryan asked.

"As soon as the house sells, I suppose. I don't really know. We haven't decided yet," she added. She was too proud to let them know how matters really were between Lorne and herself.

"You never told me you were considering such a thing," Karen protested.

"It all depended on Lorne getting the contract to build that mall. I know I told you about that. It's to be bigger and better than the Galleria, if you can imagine such a thing. You'll have to come down; we'll go shopping in it."

Karen looked as if she were about to cry. "I've never lived apart from you. Not in another town!"

"We'll survive. Lorne's phone bill will go through the roof, but that can't be helped. And we'll visit. It's not like we're moving to the ends of the earth. Austin is only an hour away by air. I can fly up here to visit from time to time." She had no idea whether Lorne would agree to that, but she couldn't bear the separation if he didn't. She looked at Ryan to see how he was taking it.

"Something's wrong here," he said slowly. "If you were considering a move, you'd have told us, first thing."

"Lorne wanted to keep it secret until it was certain. I'm telling you now. I only found out myself last night."

"But your house is so pretty!"

"Karen, it's too big. I hate being there alone. It's like sleeping in a museum. Besides, I'm sure the one in Austin will be similar to it." She wondered if she would have any say in the choice of houses. Had he already bought one and not mentioned it?

Bethany came running into the room and tackled Chelsea at knee level. She gingerly sat on the floor to hug the little girl. She was still finding sore places from her fall and knew she had several bruises on her back and hip. "I'm going to miss you," Chelsea said, her voice breaking. Bethany regarded her solemnly, not comprehending what was going on.

"I wanted you to live close enough for our children to grow up together. I wanted them to be best friends," Karen protested.

Tears rose before Chelsea could stop them. "So did I," she whispered. She tried to smile at the child. "But it's not going to be that way."

"You have no say in it?" Ryan asked. "Why not?"

She brushed tears from her cheeks. "Of course I have a say in it. It's just that Lorne's work is taking him to Austin. He would hardly move there and leave me behind."

When Bethany left her lap and headed down the hall at a fast trot, Chelsea found it difficult to get off the floor and tried to cover it.

Ryan held out his hand, and she took it. "I guess I'm getting old," she said with an attempt at a laugh.

He made no comment, but was watching her closely. Chelsea wished she could confide in them and ask their advice, but her pride prevented it.

"Do you know when you'll be going down to look for a house?" Karen asked as she walked Chelsea to the door.

"Not yet. Lorne is going down this coming week. Maybe he'll start looking then."

"Without you?" Karen sounded shocked. "I'd never let Ryan do that. Lord knows what he might decide upon!"

"Buildings are Lorne's business. I can trust his judgment. Look at the house we're in now."

"Are you saying you won't have a say about your house?" Ryan asked. "That he may buy one before you see it?"

"No, of course not." Chelsea managed to smile convincingly. "He may do the preliminary searching, that's all. He wouldn't buy a house without showing it to me first." She wondered if this was true. "I have to be running. I have a dozen things to do. I'll see you both in a day or two."

"Come for dinner on Monday if Lorne is out of town. Call me."

Karen waved goodbye and closed the door. "I just can't believe it! Chelsea is moving away!"

"Did she seem odd to you?" Ryan was frowning slightly.

"Odd in what way?"

"I'm not sure. It was as if she wasn't telling us everything. And she had trouble getting off the floor. I had to pull her up."

"That doesn't mean anything. I'm on and off the floor all day long, chasing the girls. Chelsea isn't used to it. That's all."

"She's never had trouble getting off the floor before."

"Ryan, what on earth are you getting at? I'm worrying about losing Chelsea and all you can think about is whether or not she's as agile as she was a year ago."

"I'm not happy to hear she's moving either." It was true. He felt as if he were about to lose a part of himself. "But maybe it's for the best," he said, thinking aloud.

"How can it possibly be?"

"Change is good for people," He couldn't admit how much he dreaded the separation. But if Chelsea stayed, would they be able to keep their distance from each other? She was far too tempting. With her gone, he hoped to rekindle the love he and Karen had once shared.

"Well, that's the most coldhearted thing I've ever heard," Karen said angrily. "I'm losing my best friend, and that's all you can say? That you're glad she's going?"

Ryan sighed. "Let it go, Karen. I don't want to fight with you today."

She started berating him, but he tuned her out. He had become proficient at doing that.

* * *

The house Lorne bought was almost a clone of the one they had left behind. Chelsea went from one echoing room to another. "I'll get lost in here," she commented.

"No, you won't." He was inspecting the house with his builder's eye to be certain all the improvements he had requested had been carried out.

"I wish I had been able to help you pick it out."

"I thought you would rather huddle in Dallas with your strange friends for as long as you could." He no longer bothered to pretend to care for her feelings when they were alone. "Besides, I knew what I wanted."

Chelsea frowned at him. "Lorne, we need to talk."

"Not again, surely."

"I think we should get a divorce."

He looked at her as if she had finally managed to surprise him. "A divorce? No."

"Why not?"

"For one thing, I just bought a house. Because it was purchased after our wedding, and because Texas is a community property state, I would owe you half of it."

"I wasn't after your money before we married and I'm not after it now. You can keep the house."

"In the second place, it's not good for my business."

"What?" She stared at him.

"I'm moving in larger circles these last few years. Several people have told me I would do better if I had a wife. Someone pretty who could entertain clients and charm them into doing business with me."

"That hardly describes me."

"I know. But you can be trained."

"I don't need your permission to divorce. Not under Texas law."

"You've already looked into it? My, my, you're full of surprises today. That would be a huge mistake, even for you. My lawyers would see to it you don't get a dime. I could even bring Ryan into it."

"Ryan?" she exclaimed. "What are you talking about?"

"There needn't be real grounds. As often as you're with them, a good lawyer could prove infidelity. That would sway the judge to my side. You'd come out looking like a gold digger and a tramp."

"I don't care about that."

"No? I wonder if Karen would see it differently. And Ryan's boss. It's his father-in-law, isn't it?"

Chelsea drew back. "Are you blackmailing me?"

"Certainly not. I'm only explaining to you that you're going to regret a hasty action like divorce."

She looked at him with curiosity. "Why, Lorne? Why do you want to keep me when we don't love each other? You could find another wife to entertain your clients, if that's all you want from me."

"I'm a busy man. I don't have time to waste on courts and lawyers. You're pretty, and will look good on the society page. Besides, I find it more convenient to have a woman living in my house than to have to go to some other place whenever I want sex."

"You disgust me! How can you ever hope to have me want you if you treat me like this?"

He smiled. "I've told you. I always want what I can't have. If you're trying to refuse me, that puts you back in a more interesting category. For a time, at least."

She kept the room between them. "I don't have to put up with this!"

"Don't you? Are you that anxious to go back to working in some dead-end job or to trying to sell paintings no one wants to exhibit?"

"I should never have told you about that."

"No, but you did, and if it worked once, it will work again. I can keep you from working as an artist forever, if I like. All it takes is a word in the right ear." He smiled. "Perhaps I could even convince—what's his name?— Jason Randall to aid me in my venture."

Chelsea turned away. She no longer let him see her cry. "I hate this house."

"That doesn't matter." He glanced at his watch. "I'm leaving. Stay here and wait for the movers. See that nothing is scratched or broken. I'll be home around nine tonight."

She made her face a mask. "Where are your offices? You never told me. I don't know how to call you if I should need you."

"You won't need to call me for anything, now will you? I can't be answering foolish questions during working hours." He went to the front door and didn't look back at her, leaving Chelsea to wonder how she had gotten herself into such a mess.

For the next two years Ryan did his best to put Chelsea out of his mind, or at least to think of her only in a platonic manner. It wasn't easy. Without Chelsea's softening influence, Karen listened entirely to her mother and Joyce, two women who did not have a high regard for men. No matter how hard Ryan tried, he couldn't please his wife.

Instead of Chelsea's fading in his memory, he found her smile and her memories invading his thoughts, and his dreams of her were extremely erotic. They left him feeling shaken by a longing his wife would never have understood.

He still slept apart from Karen. As their relationship had long since begun to fray, he was often glad for the respite. Karen nagged him and was so strident, he wouldn't have minded a separate house as well as a separate bedroom.

His only consolations were his daughters. Bethany at four was adorable, and Ashley believed he hung the moon. When he came home from work, they ran to greet him with squeals and laughter and he gladly lavished love upon them.

In Karen's defense, she was a good mother. He had to give her that. It was only that she had no interest in being his lover or even his friend. She seemed to feel they were separate species who happened to share a habitat, and that was enough for her.

By the fall of 1983 Ryan was nearing his twenty-ninth birthday, and for the first time he began to be aware of the march of time. He would be thirty soon, yet he wasn't living the life he had foreseen when he was in college. True, he worked for a prestigious company and had been given raises on a regular basis, but Karen frequently told him this was only because his boss was also his father-in-law. Unlike Todd, who used the Baker connections whenever it was convenient, Ryan didn't willingly ride on the family coattails, and a good look at his marriage told him it was in even worse shape than he had thought.

"Karen, we've got to do something. We're drifting apart and I don't like it."

She looked up from her needlepoint. "Drifting apart in what way?"

"Think about it. Are you happy? Really happy, I mean?"

"Of course I am. I have no idea what you're talking about." She went back to her sewing.

He sat beside her on the couch. "Remember what it was like in college? We had so many dreams. Don't you miss them?"

She moved away almost imperceptibly. "College was a hundred years ago! Don't wrinkle my skirt."

"We were going to set the world on fire. I was going to revolutionize the world of computers, Chelsea was going to give Michelangelo a run for his money, and you . . . What were you going to do, Karen?"

"I have no idea. I think I wanted to be a wife and mother. So I got my dream." She gave him a smile. "Would you like meat loaf for dinner?"

"No. I hate meat loaf. Didn't you want anything more than a home and children? What about your music?"

"I only majored in music because they expected me to major in something. I got my degree—which is more than Chelsea can say—and that appeased my parents. I could make a pot roast, I suppose. There might be time to thaw one out."

"I'm not interested in dinner," he said in exasperation.

"You will be in about three hours."

"Let's get a sitter and go out for dinner. And to a movie. Better yet, let's go dancing."

"I don't want to go dancing. The music is so loud in those places, and most of it doesn't have a tune anymore. How do kids sing along with it, do you suppose? We could always sing with our music!"

"How about a movie?"

"I'd rather watch TV. If we go out, I'll have to dress up."

"You're already dressed." He couldn't understand why she would have to change. Karen always looked as if she were expecting company. She even freshened her makeup during the day.

"I couldn't possibly go out in this old dress. What movie did you want to see?"

"I don't know. Let's just ride over to the mall and see what's playing."

Karen sighed as if this were asking too much. "You go. I'll stay with the girls." She frowned and jabbed her needle into the fabric. "I was at the community center all afternoon to plan that fund drive. I'm too tired to go out again. Besides, I doubt we can get the sitter on such short notice. You know how teenagers are."

"Okay. Let's put the girls to bed and play a game."

"What sort of game?"

"I don't know. Gin?"

"I hate gin. If you want to do something, go do it. You don't have to take me along when you leave the house."

He studied her profile. "That's not the point, Karen." He took the needlepoint from her and put it aside. "Our marriage is in trouble. We seldom go anywhere together. You have your interests, and I have mine. We don't have any together."

"That's ridiculous. We have the girls."

He thought for a minute. "Maybe we should have another one. It might be a boy this time."

Karen stared at him. "I can't have another baby."

"Of course you can. You're only twenty-eight."

"I know exactly how old I am, thank you."

He took her hands and smiled at her. "Wouldn't you like to have another baby around the house? Ashley's two years old and talking. She's not a baby anymore. I miss the midnight feeding and even the diapers. What do you say?"

"I told you I can't have another baby. I had my tubes tied."

"What?" He thought he had misunderstood her.

"I told you."

"No, Karen. I would have remembered a thing like that. You had your tubes tied? When?"

"When Ashley was born, of course. I told you I only wanted two children and that she would be the last."

"You never told me about having your tubes tied! Karen! How could you do something like that? Why wasn't I consulted?"

"Chelsea knows. I thought I told you."

"Chelsea knew and I didn't? Can it be reversed?"

"I doubt it. Even if it could, I don't want to be pregnant again." She reached for her needlework. "Besides, this is only a four-bedroom house. We'd need another bedroom if we had another child."

"Not if I moved in with you. Where I ought to be."

"We're not going to discuss that."

He snatched the fabric from her hands and threw it onto the floor. "Listen to me, damn it! I'm tired of you making all the decisions around here! Maybe Todd and your father will put up with it, but I won't. I don't want to be the undisputed head of the house, but I insist on us being equal. I've let matters slide and tried not to cause waves, but I'm sick of doing it! I think it's time I caused some waves! Maybe even a storm!"

"You're overreacting. I didn't expect anything else from you." Karen's voice rose sharply. "It's just like a man to want everything his way! Naturally you'd want a houseful of children! You don't have to go through the misery of pregnancy and the pain of having them!"

"Neither do you! You took care of that, didn't you!" He left the couch and paced angrily to the window. "What hurts me is that you didn't even tell me. You didn't tell me!"

"I thought I did! Things were so hectic then. Ashley was brand new and Bethany was barely walking. I had my hands full. I couldn't remember everything!"

"Everything? This isn't the same as forgetting to buy milk at the store or overlooking an appointment! You had yourself sterilized and forgot to mention it?"

"Well, whether I told you then or not, you know now. So let's just drop it. The girls are in the back yard, and if they come in, they might hear you."

"Karen, this is too much!"

She maddened him by smiling. "At least it keeps you out of my bedroom."

He stared at her. "I haven't set foot in your bedroom in a long time. What's it been? A year?"

"I don't know. I didn't mark it on the calendar."

"I want you to get into counseling. There's something wrong when a healthy young woman doesn't ever want to make love."

"Maybe you're the one who needs counseling."

"I know what I need, and it's not that," he retorted. "Not many husbands would stick around as long as I have. Maybe I'm a fool to have done it."

"Go ahead and threaten me! I don't care. You'll never leave me. If you do, Daddy will fire you and I'll never let you see the girls again! You don't want that. Now leave me alone. You're giving me a headache."

Ryan glared at her, then stalked down the hall. He pulled the suitcase out of his closet and began to pack for the weekend. He had to get away before he said something to Karen that he would regret. Her threats weren't empty ones. That was why he still lived with her.

He knew where he was going without even thinking about it. By the time he got to Austin he might be calmer. At any rate, he had to see Chelsea. He had to know whether she was happy. If she wasn't, that would make his decisions more clear.

When he left, Karen asked where he was going, but he ignored her. He didn't want to give her the ammunition of knowing he intended to see Chelsea. He went out back and told the girls goodbye, promised to bring them something, and left.

Chapter Seventeen

"What are you doing in Austin without Karen and the girls?" Chelsea asked as she motioned for Ryan to come into the house. "Are you here on business?"

"I'm here to see you," he said with the smile she remembered so well. "It's been a long time."

"Yes." She knotted her fingers together to keep herself from throwing her arms around him. "A long time. You look wonderful."

"So do you. Married life must agree with you."

Chelsea smiled but made no comment. Few things had agreed with her less than married life. "Come in. Have a seat." She called out, "Maria, will you bring us some coffee in the morning room?"

"Maria?"

"She lives in. Over the garage. Lorne says that's more convenient for us. Her husband takes care of the yard."

"Nice. You've moved up in the world." He sat on the green and white wicker couch and looked out at the yard. "It's a good thing Karen hasn't seen this house. She still talks about the one in Dallas."

"Lorne seems to have an affinity for over-sized houses." She smiled at the woman who was bringing in a tray of two mugs and a coffee urn. "Thank you." As the woman left, Chelsea said, "How are Karen and the girls?"

"Fine. The girls are wonderful. I wish you could see them. Bethany is getting tall and never stops talking. Ashley is quieter, but she's more likely to get into mischief. They keep us busy." He took the mug of coffee and watched as Chelsea poured one for herself. "How are you?"

She sipped the coffee and found it too hot to drink. "I'm fine. Too bad you missed Lorne. He's out of town." She kept her voice expressionless. "He's in Dallas all this week."

"Why didn't you come with him?"

She shrugged. "I'm too busy." The truth was, he hadn't asked her. He had, in fact, told her she wasn't welcome.

"Am I keeping you from something?"

"No. Nothing at all." She curled her legs under her and regarded him. "It just occurred to me. You'll be thirty in a few weeks. It doesn't seem possible."

"I wish you hadn't reminded me." He put his coffee cup on the side table at his end of the couch. "The big Three-O."

"Don't let it get you down. You get better looking every year." She hadn't intended to say that. She sipped her coffee again and burned her lip. "So why did you come to see me?"

"I had forgotten your directness," he said with a laugh. "Can't friends visit without a reason?"

"You never have before."

He leaned forward and rested his forearms on his knees. "I'm thinking about leaving Karen."

Chelsea put down her coffee and bent toward him in concern. "You're not! What's happened?"

"Nothing new." He tried to smile and failed. "Did you know she had her tubes tied when Ashley was born?"

"Yes, didn't you? She told me she had talked it over with you."

"You may have noticed that Karen isn't averse to bending the truth when it serves her."

Chelsea was shocked. "She lied to you? About something like that?"

"No, she just omitted telling me anything about it."

"Surely you noticed the scar. I'm sure it's not large, but it's not invisible."

He looked away as if the answer were embarrassing to him. "No, I haven't."

She remembered the separate bedrooms. "I'm sorry, Ryan."

"So am I. I wanted more children. Turns out I like to be around them and I miss having a baby in the house."

"You could adopt."

"Can you really see Karen agreeing to that? No, this goes beyond her having her tubes tied and not telling me. It's something that's been eating at me for years."

"I don't think you should tell me." Chelsea glanced toward the open door. More than once she had had the unsettling idea that Maria was spying on her. Silently she went over and looked into the other room, closed the door. "I don't want Maria to overhear," she said in explanation.

"Karen has changed. So have I. But we changed in opposite directions. She's no longer the girl I married. In fact, she's more like her mother and sister every day."

"She's sounds the same on the phone."

"It's easy to fall back into old patterns when you're talking to someone you don't speak with often. Our house is like a showcase. You can't live in it. If I put down a book, she closes it and puts it away before I can pick it up again. Do you have any idea how irritating that is?"

"Yes. I lived with her for four years in the dorm."

"I like a clean house, don't get me wrong. But this is ridiculous! I feel as if she's going to inspect my fingernails before I can come inside! No house with two small children in it should be that clean!"

She could hear his frustration. "Is it really the house that's the main problem? I can talk to her about that."

He was silent for a long time. "No. That's not the main problem." He shoved his fingers through his hair in the familiar gesture she remembered so well. "We aren't sleeping together."

"Not at all?" she asked.

"It's been a year." He gave a shaky laugh. "I can't believe I'm telling you this."

"It won't go any further. You know that."

"That's why I didn't see that damned scar. I haven't made love to her but twice since Ashley was born. She's always insisted on the room being completely dark. Both times I felt like a rapist."

Chelsea reached out and took his hand. "I'm so sorry," she whispered.

He looked at her, and she saw tears standing in his eyes. "I guess I shouldn't have told you."

"Yes, you should." She was trying to put her personal feelings aside and think of what would be best for Ryan. "Are you really leaving her?"

"I don't know." He turned away.

Chelsea shared his misery. If he had been certain, she would have gone to him in the blink of an eye. "You stand to lose a lot. Your job for starters. Mr. Baker has never struck me as a man who's long on forgiveness. Especially not when it comes to Karen. She's always been his favorite."

"I know. I doubt he would even give me the customary notice. He makes his own rules." He sighed. "There are other jobs. The real clincher is that Karen will keep me from seeing the girls. I don't know if I can stand that."

"She can't do that legally. You'd have visitation rights."

"Yes, but enforcing them is another matter. Several divorced men have told me horror stories about trying to see their children. With the Bakers' money, Karen could hide Bethany and Ashley so I couldn't find them. She could even leave the country with them."

"I can't picture Karen going that far."

"She wouldn't need to. There are ways of preventing visitation. According to my friends, ex-wives can be very creative."

There was no need for Chelsea to ask whether Karen would be capable of such cruelty toward him. She knew Karen could be completely self-centered and totally convinced she was in the right. "Would she do that to the girls? They love you."

"All the more reason to keep them away. She's said that she'll turn them against me if I leave. The subject has come up before."

"I had no idea it had gotten so bad."

He sat back and rested his arm along the back of the couch. "It happened gradually. At first I thought Karen was just having trouble adjusting to married life. That she would learn to enjoy lovemaking." He stopped talking abruptly and pretended an interest in the garden beyond the large windows.

"It's not your fault." She didn't dare elaborate.

Ryan met her eyes, and she saw the pain he couldn't disguise. "I wish I believed that."

There was a discreet knock, and Maria opened the door before Chelsea could answer. "Pardon, Mrs. Spenser. I just wanted to know if I should set an extra plate for dinner."

"No, Maria. I'd rather not eat tonight, either." She waited until the woman was gone. She hadn't been fooled by the interruption. Maria had wanted to know what was going on behind the closed door. She was glad she hadn't been touching Ryan as she had been about to do before Maria had come in.

"What is she? Your watchdog?" he asked wryly.

"No, she's Lorne's. I can't have a conversation with anyone without feeling she's eavesdropping."

"I'd fire her."

"I tried that once. Lorne rehired her."

He gave her a steady look. "Is it like that with you?"

"I don't mean to sound as though he's impossible to live with," she said hastily. "We just don't have the same taste in hired help."

"So you're happy with him?"

Chelsea looked away. "Everything's fine."

"I don't believe you."

She stood and went to the window, then smiled sadly.

"I've imagined you coming here, saying these things. In my fantasy, it was so easy to know what to say."

"I'm asking if you're happily married. That's not a difficult question."

"Yes, it is. It's the hardest question I've ever been asked. You just told me if you leave Karen you stand a chance of never seeing Bethany and Ashley again. That you'll lose your job. You'll lose everything. So yes, I'm happily married."

"I still don't believe you."

She turned to face him. "Ryan, don't ask me this! I'm not strong where you're concerned. I never have been."

He rose. "I didn't come here to cause you trouble. I never intended that."

She wrapped her arms around her body. Inside she was hurting. "If I tell you it was a mistake for me to marry Lorne, what will you do? Leave Karen? Never see your children again? Lose everything? Lorne has money, and money is power. I don't know whether he's as influential as he says, but he would be far more vindictive than Karen. If I were to leave him for you, you might not be able to find a job in Dallas. Not a job you'd want. That would mean moving away, which would make it even more difficult for you to see the girls."

"But I'd have you."

It was as if no distance separated them. Chelsea gazed at him and felt her heart break. "And you wouldn't have Bethany and Ashley. I can't allow that to happen. Not when I know how much you love them."

"Maybe Karen is bluffing. Maybe I can have it all."

She slowly shook her head. "You know you can't."

"Having you would be enough."

Tears brimmed in her eyes, and she tried to blink them back. "It would be for now. But what about in ten years? Some day you might regret making that choice."

"Do you really think I'll stop loving you in only ten years?" he asked. His voice was soft, but she could hear the hurt in it. "I won't stop loving you in a hundred years."

"You'll always love Bethany and Ashley, too." She was glad he was intelligent and sensitive enough not to say they could have children of their own. No child would ever take the place of Bethany or Ashley, no matter how much he loved it.

"Is Lorne good to you?"

She turned away. "Of course."

"Look at me and say it." He came to her and gently took her arm to make her face him. "Chelsea?"

"I don't know. How do you measure it? I live in a house that's practically a palace! He's generous about my wardrobe, my jewelry. We take trips to Europe. I drive a new car that's more expensive than the house my grandparents lived in. I never want for anything."

"I didn't ask about his bankbook."

"No. I'm not happy." She looked up at him sharply. "What difference does that make? One thing I've learned about life is that you don't have that many choices. And if the choice is there, the price may be too great. There's a price on everything. If I have you, the price is your daughters. Do you think for a minute I could live with that?"

"I can't believe we have no choice." He sounded almost angry. "That's not the way it is!"

"Yes, it is!" She reached out and touched his arm. "Ryan, think about the girls. If you're not there, they'll grow up to fit perfectly into the Baker family. Do you want that for them?"

"No." His voice was husky with emotion. "I don't want that. It's why my marriage with Karen isn't working. She's too much like her family. I don't think anyone in that entire family has ever been happily married."

"And you can't forget that as much as you love them, the girls love you. What will it do to them if you leave them?"

"What will it do for them to hear Karen and me fighting the way we do? The argument goes both ways."

"I know. I can't make the decision for you. It's up to you whether you leave or not. But I can't be the reason.

The girls love me, too. So does Karen. It would hurt them all to know we chose each other over them."

Ryan was quiet for a long time. "Was it a mistake for me to come here?"

"No. We had to have this talk. Until now, I had hoped it would all somehow go away and that we could turn back the clock. That you and I might somehow be together. Now I realize too much has happened to us both. It's a dream I can't hang onto."

"Chelsea, what happened in college? Why did you really go to Germany?"

She closed her eyes and tried to control her thoughts. "Who knows?" she said as lightly as she could. "You know how I was. I just took it into my head to go."

"That's the only reason?"

She knew she could never tell him the truth about that. Knowing how he loved his children, she could never hurt him by telling him he might have had one more. That they might have married if she hadn't been so impulsive and so determined to avoid a permanent relationship. "That's the only reason."

For a long time he said nothing. Then he said, "I guess I'd better be going. I have a long drive back."

"You're leaving now? You're not staying the night in town? It's a long drive back."

"I don't think it would be wise for me to stay in Austin. Not knowing that Lorne is out of town and that you won't leave him."

"You're right of course. And Karen will be worrying about you."

"Maybe."

"She will. We both know her that well. She's not as cool and as collected as she likes to pretend. Inside, she's hurting over this as much as you are."

"You think so?"

Chelsea nodded. "I know it. You have to remember, she's a product of the Baker family. They frown on the more tender emotions. Go back to her, Ryan. Stay with her and try to work things out."

"And if I can't?"

She drew in a deep breath. "Then come and tell me."

They gazed into each other's eyes, both hearing what hadn't been spoken. If he couldn't work it out with Karen, Chelsea would be waiting for him.

"Goodbye," he said at last. "Take care of yourself."

"I always do." She stepped into his arms and allowed herself one forbidden embrace. Before it could get out of hand, though, she stepped away and said, "Drive carefully."

He left.

When Ryan arrived at his house, he sat several minutes in the car, trying to decide if this was a good decision or not. Slowly he got out and carried his suitcase to the door. No lights were on. He didn't know whether Karen was there or not. She might have gone to her parents in tears. He was so exhausted he almost didn't care.

He put his key in the lock and opened it. Karen had been hurrying to the door, and she stopped when he came in. They looked at each other.

"You came back," she said at last.

"Yes." He shut the door and put his suitcase on the floor.

"I was afraid you wouldn't."

"I nearly didn't."

"Where did you go?"

He shook his head. "That doesn't matter. I'm home now. I guess the girls are asleep?"

"At this hour? Of course. Ashley cried because you weren't there to tuck her in." Karen stood there stiffly, rubbing one hand against the other.

"What about us, Karen? I don't want to come back if there aren't going to be some changes."

"Can't we sit down and talk about it?" She came nearer,

and he could see she had been crying. "I could make some coffee."

"No, thanks. I've been drinking coffee all night. I won't sleep as it is."

They went into the den and seated themselves. "I didn't mean to make you cry," he said awkwardly. "I didn't think you would."

"How can you say that? I love you, Ryan. I was afraid you had really left me. I've been crying ever since you went out the door." Her voice quivered, and she ducked her head.

"I honestly didn't think you cared enough to miss me. Karen, we have to change some things. I don't want a divorce if it can be avoided." On the way home from Austin, he had thought about what Chelsea had said. He cared for Karen, though he didn't love her as he once had. He loved his daughters wholeheartedly, however, and whether she was happy or not, Chelsea was financially secure. Too many lives would be turned upside down if he divorced Karen.

"I don't want one either." She looked at him, her expression miserable. "I was so afraid you wouldn't be back. I'll try harder, Ryan. I really will! It somehow got out of hand. That's all. We said too much."

"It's more than that, Karen. I've been faithful to you. But you can't expect me to be celibate forever. I'm willing to have separate rooms if that's what you want, but I can't live like a priest."

"I could get into counseling," she said in a small voice. "Maybe there really is something wrong with me."

"I'll go with you, if you like. I've heard marriage counseling works if both people are willing to make changes. I won't put too many demands on you. I'm willing to be patient."

"I'll try so hard, Ryan. You'll see."

He reached out and took her hand. As it lay in his, he studied it. "In some ways we've changed so much, but your hand is still the same. I always thought you had the most beautiful hands I've ever seen."

She knelt on the floor beside his chair and leaned her forehead on his thigh. "I'm so sorry for all of it, Ryan. I've said so many things to you that should never have been spoken. While you were gone, I thought of all of them and wished I could take them back."

"I want to ask you one thing, and I want you to tell me the truth. Did you lie when you said Chelsea had an abortion?"

She shook her head. "It's the truth. I should have talked her out of it. I still feel guilty about it. But I wanted to marry you, and I knew she would get you if she told you she was pregnant."

"You told me you wanted me primarily because you didn't want her to have me."

"That part was a lie." She looked up at him, her face puffy from crying. "I loved you. I still do. Naturally I didn't want her to have the man I wanted, but I was only trying to hurt you when I put it that way."

"Well, it worked."

"God, Ryan, I've made so many mistakes." Her voice was small and helpless. "In the last few hours I've come to see them all. That's why I'm willing to go into therapy."

"I'll ask around and find a counselor. We'll see if we can glue it back together somehow."

Karen came into his arms and he held her, letting her cry softly on his shoulder. He closed his eyes and held her tightly, wishing he could love her with all his heart or that he could walk away from her unencumbered.

Neither was possible.

Lorne came home on Friday, and he handed Chelsea a gift-wrapped box.

"What's this? It's not my birthday or our anniversary," she said as she opened it.

"I haven't bought you anything lately. I thought you'd like it."

Inside the box she found a delicate bracelet with diamonds sprinkled among the gold links. "It's beautiful! Lorne, you shouldn't have."

He smiled. "I could take it back if you like."

She laughed as she snapped it onto her wrist. "I love it."

"How was your week?"

"Fine," she said smoothly. Since Ryan had only come to the house once, she thought it unlikely that Maria would mention him to Lorne. At least she hoped that was the case. "And yours?"

"Busy. I'm worn out. The negotiations worked out in my favor, though, so it was worth the trip. Next time you can go with me."

"All right. I'd like to see Karen." She was surprised at how well she could conceal her feelings from her husband when Ryan could see right through her defenses.

"I won't be going for a while though. Maybe you'd like to fly up next week."

She looked at him thoughtfully. "I can't go then. The charity horse show is scheduled for next weekend, and I've agreed to serve on that committee."

He shrugged. "Whatever. Don't say I never offered." He picked up his bags and carried them toward the stairs.

Chelsea watched him in confusion. She never knew how to read him either. Why had he bought her a bracelet that was so expensive and then offered to let her fly to Dallas when he so recently had been adamant about her not going with him?

The next day it became clear. Chelsea rarely called Lorne at work, but she was at the committee meeting and had to verify a date for one of the women concerning the coming horse show. As soon as his secretary answered, she recognized the voice. "Sheila?" she asked.

There was a long pause. "Yes. Did you want to speak with Lorne?"

"No. I'll talk to him when he comes home tonight."

Chelsea hung up and sat staring at the phone. Before his week-long trip to Dallas, his secretary had been a young woman with a husband and baby. Sheila had returned to Austin with Lorne.

Chelsea unfastened the diamond bracelet and put it in her pocket. As soon as she reached home she was going to put it away and never wear it again. Lorne was still full of surprises, she reflected. She had thought he no longer had the ability to hurt her. She had been wrong.

Chapter Eighteen

1992

"Happy anniversary," Patricia Norlock said as she lifted the champagne glass in the air. Her husband repeated the toast.

Chelsea glanced at Lorne, then smiled. She drank silently. After twelve years of marriage, she no longer had any false beliefs that the next year would be any happier than the previous ones.

Lorne drank the entire glass. His hair had gone almost silver now, and fine lines creased his face. At fifty-seven he looked at least ten years older.

The party had been his idea, as were all their parties. Chelsea had many acquaintances in Austin, but no one she really considered a close friend. Lorne had discouraged her from developing friendships, saying that she always chose people who would embarrass him socially. So she had begun to keep her distance, rather than to have her husband humiliate her or her acquaintances at gatherings. He had done that to discourage her from having relationships.

This one, at least, was a small party. Only five couples were in the house. By Lorne's standards, this was intimate. Chelsea glanced around the room, making sure Maria was keeping glasses filled and finger foods on the trays. Her eyes automatically overlooked Sheila.

In the past few years, Lorne hadn't tried to keep the woman in the background, and Sheila was glorying in what she considered to be her triumph. She was invited to all Lorne's parties and often served as a second hostess. Chelsea no longer cared.

She reached up and touched her hair. Lorne had been after her to cut it, but she was holding firm on that issue. She liked it long. As a compromise, she wore it in a sleek bun almost all the time. If Lorne disliked it and said that at thirty-seven she was too old to have long hair, she didn't care. Her locks were still a glossy auburn, and she considered them to be her best feature.

Maria came into the room and began to fill the champagne glasses again. Chelsea wished the maid was not so efficient at that. Lorne was too fond of this beverage and to Chelsea's practiced eye, he had already exceeded his limit.

Lorne had invested in two savings and loan banks, both of which had collapsed in the past few months. Chelsea wasn't sure what their financial status now was, because her husband refused to tell her, but she knew his fortune had been greatly diminished. His increased drinking proved to be a reliable barometer of his financial situation.

"It's a lovely party," Patricia said as she stood by Chelsea. "No one gives parties quite like you two do." Her eyes followed Sheila, who crossed the room to stand beside Lorne.

Chelsea knew Patricia, like many other wives in their circle, was wondering whether Sheila was Lorne's mistress as gossip said, and if so, why was she in Chelsea's house. Patricia was too well bred to ask, and Chelsea never volunteered information. "Thank you. I'm so glad you and James could come."

"Twelve years! In our crowd that's almost a record," Patricia said with a laugh.

Chelsea smiled and didn't reply.

"James told me about the Houston project. I was so sorry to hear it fell through."

Chelsea didn't betray her surprise with so much as the blink of an eye. "That happens. Houston is so far away, I was almost hoping it might. Lorne is gone so often as it is." In her mind she was wondering what this would mean to them. She knew he had been counting on that project to put him on his feet again. She looked across the room to where he was holding out his glass for Maria to refill with champagne. He was drinking heavily, even for him.

"I don't know how he does it," Patricia said in a lower voice. "James says Lorne can drink him under the table and you'd never know he had a thimbleful."

"My father says Lorne has a hollow leg," Chelsea said. He had also commented that practice makes perfect. Neither of her parents liked Lorne, and they barely concealed the fact. Because of that, she seldom heard from them. In fact, it wouldn't have surprised her to find that Lorne had told them outright not to contact her or to interfere in his marriage. That was Lorne's style, especially now that he was drinking.

She knew he was an alcoholic, but the one time she had tried to convince him to get help, he had become violent and had slapped her so hard she had fallen. After that, she let him drink as much and as often as he pleased. To her, his health wasn't worth her being battered.

As she watched, Lorne swayed and caught himself. She glanced at Patricia and wondered if she had noticed. This woman wasn't a particular friend of hers, though James was probably Lorne's closest friend. Still, her comment about Lorne being able to hold his liquor might have been meant to convey that he was not doing so now. Chelsea could always tell when he was drunk. As she watched, he raised the glass uncertainly to his lips, his movements the overly precise ones of a drunken man.

"It's getting late. I think we had better be going," Patricia said. She had noticed.

"Must you? It can't be that late." Chelsea dreaded the end of a party. If Sheila and Lorne had plans, she waited until everyone was gone and they left together. If he didn't leave with Sheila, Lorne demanded his rights with Chelsea. Alcoholism hadn't diminished his desires, only his abilities.

"No, no, it's nearly midnight. We have to relieve the baby sitter. You're so lucky not to have children. Sitters are almost impossible to find, and they charge an arm and a leg these days." Patricia whispered to Maria as she passed, and Maria went to get the Norlocks' coats.

"We're so glad you came." Chelsea noticed that the others were also preparing to leave. Sheila was accepting her wrap from Maria. Lorne helped her into it. She smiled up at him. At least, Chelsea thought, he was loyal to Sheila.

As their guests shook hands with Lorne and said good-bye to each other, Chelsea went to stand beside her husband. She tried to ignore the fact that Sheila was at his other side and was saying farewells as if she, too, lived in the house.

James helped Patricia into her coat, and they, too, came to the door. "It was a good party," James said as he gripped Lorne's hand.

"I wish you wouldn't go," Lorne said plaintively. "It's early yet. Chelsea, tell them it's too early to leave."

"We'd like to have you stay longer," Chelsea said dutifully.

Lorne frowned at her as if she had said just the opposite. "Don't listen to anything she says," he said in drunken confidence to James. "It's early!"

Patricia put her hand on her husband's arm. "Remember the sitter, James?"

He sighed. "I have to drive the sitter home."

Lorne winked broadly. "I'll bet you hate having to do that. Right, James? Tell me, what's she look like? Is she one of those cute, perky ones or the slinky kind that acts as if she'd like to get you alone for five minutes?"

"You're just awful!" Sheila laughed and punched his arm. "Isn't he awful, James?"

Patricia gave Lorne a cold smile.

Chelsea tried to pull Lorne back. "You know you're just teasing," she said. Patricia struck her as a jealous woman. "Let them go if they must."

Unexpectedly Lorne turned on her and shoved her backward. Chelsea cried out as her feet went out from under her. Then she landed so hard she lost her breath.

Patricia shrieked and ran to her. She helped Chelsea sit up and pulled her skirt down over her exposed legs. "Are you all right?"

Lorne swayed above her. "I'm sorry. I didn't know you were standing so close. You know I was just kidding. Tell them I was kidding, Chelsea. I wouldn't hurt you for anything in this world." He held out a hand to help her to her feet.

Chelsea ignored his offer of help. Carefully she sat up and then stood. She was too embarrassed to look Patricia in the eye.

"Are you all right?" Patricia asked. She leaned over to Chelsea in genuine concern.

"Yes. Yes, I just fell. That's all."

"We have to go," Patricia said to James. "Now."

James looked almost as uncomfortable as Patricia. He glanced from Lorne to Chelsea to Sheila. "Yes. We'll see you in a day or two." He shook hands again with Lorne and left.

Chelsea sat shakily on the arm of the nearest chair.

"I should go, too," Sheila was saying. She opened the door Lorne had shut and glanced at Chelsea. During the entire confrontation she hadn't said a word to Chelsea. " 'Bye, Lorne."

"I'll see you later," he said. She hurried out.

Chelsea buried her face in her hands. He wasn't leaving with Sheila.

"Well, I hope you're satisfied. You managed to embarrass me in front of my friends again," Lorne said as he came to her.

"You shouldn't have pushed me. I lost my balance."

Her voice was faint. She didn't want to be alone with him. Not when he was in this mood.

He grabbed her arm and yanked her to her feet. "I saw you talking to James earlier! What did you say to him?"

She refused to look at him. "I told him the champagne came from Fidel's. He was asking me where I bought it."

"He could have asked me that!"

"He could have asked Sheila, too!" Chelsea lifted her head. Maybe she could bluff her way out of the situation. Sometimes that worked. "If you want to talk about embarrassment, what about you inviting her to our house and her acting as if she were the hostess?"

"She's a damn sight better at it than you are! I must have been crazy when I married you! You tricked me! That's what it was! You married me for my money!"

"No, I didn't. But right now I can't remember why I did marry you."

Lorne drew his hand back and struck her. Chelsea didn't see the blow coming and was caught squarely on the cheek. Lights seemed to explode, and her ears were ringing as she fell. Fearing what was coming, she curled into a ball and tried to protect her stomach and face from his blows and kicks. She heard someone crying out and realized the screams were her own.

After what seemed to be forever, Lorne staggered to the front door. Without getting a coat or saying goodbye, he left, slamming the door behind him.

Chelsea stayed where she was. She hurt all over, and was too miserable to try to stand. When she felt hands on her, she flinched in fear.

Maria was bending over her, her face puckered in concern. "Mrs. Spenser? Can you stand up?"

Chelsea wasn't sure. Slowly she tried to uncurl.

"Should I call an ambulance?"

"No," she said quickly. If she made this public, Lorne might beat her half to death next time. "No, I don't need an ambulance. Just help me get up."

Standing was more painful than she had expected. She

had trouble straightening. "I'm okay, Maria. Thank you."

The woman guided her toward the stairs. "I'll help you up to your room. You need to rest. That's all."

Chelsea felt an overwhelming gratitude toward Maria for her kindness. Until tonight Maria hadn't seemed to care about her at all. But until this night the woman hadn't been in the house when Lorne had taken out his anger on her.

The more Chelsea moved, the worse she felt, but she knew no bones had been broken, no internal organs had been damaged. She had had cracked ribs and bruised organs before.

Once they were in her bedroom, Chelsea said, "Bring me my suitcases, Maria. The ones I take on trips."

"You're not going to leave, are you? Mr. Spenser won't like that at all."

"Just bring me the suitcases." Chelsea sat on the edge of the bed. She doubled over and hugged herself. The pain was bad. The humiliation was worse. She could no longer lie to herself. Lorne's abuse was increasing. This time he had shoved her in front of people. At last he had pushed her too far.

Maria helped her pack. All the while Chelsea listened intently for the sound of the front door opening. Lorne never came in the back way, and the other door made a sound she was certain she could hear in the bedroom. She had listened for it on too many occasions.

When she had gathered everything she wanted to take, she had Maria call Juan to help carry Chelsea's things to her car. Chelsea wasn't sure how much time had passed. Usually Lorne would be gone all night, but not always. If he came home and found her packed and leaving, he would hurt her far worse than he had already.

Chelsea didn't allow herself to relax until she had driven out of the neighborhood. Would he come looking for her? He would expect her to head for Dallas, to the north. She drove south, toward San Marcos. Neither of them knew anyone there.

At the first place that looked clean, Chelsea stopped for the night. She was too exhausted to take more than her overnight bag inside. In her room, as she passed the mirror she hesitated.

Her cheek was swollen and bruised. There was an angry abrasion above her left eye. Slowly she leaned forward and studied her reflection. She wanted to remember it. She would never make excuses for him again. Too often she had blamed his abuse on alcohol, or had believed that she had goaded him into hitting her.

She pulled off her clothes and showered. The bathroom mirror revealed more bruises. She tried to scrub off every trace of Lorne. Afterward she fell into bed naked and willed herself to sleep.

"Bethany, will you take the roast out of the oven?" Karen asked as she carried the broccoli to the table. "Ashley, leave the rolls alone. I saw that."

Ashley gave her a smile and waited until Karen's back was turned before taking another roll from the platter. Bethany poked her. "If you don't stop that, you'll weigh a ton."

"No, I won't. I'm like Dad. We could eat all day and not gain."

Karen heard them and said, "No arguing, you two. Come to the table. Ryan? Come and eat."

Bethany took the roast out of the oven, and her stomach rebelled. Resolutely she ignored the hunger pangs. She carried it into the dining room and put the dish on the trivet her mother had placed in readiness. As she took her place she tried not to look at the food.

Ryan came in and smiled at her, then at Ashley. "This looks good. Did you girls help your mother cook it?"

"Yes, they did," Karen answered for them. "I don't know what I'd do without them." She passed a bowl of potatoes to Bethany, who handed it on to Ryan without taking any.

"You're not eating potatoes?" Karen asked. "I fixed them just the way you like them."

"I'm on a diet." Bethany shook her head at the roast as well. "I only want tea."

Ryan frowned at her. "You've lost enough, honey. Any more and you'll blow away."

Bethany frowned. "I've looked at myself in the mirror. I'm *huge.*"

"You wear a size seven," Karen argued. "That's not huge in anyone's opinion."

"My arms are still too big. And so are my legs. I'm only going to lose a little bit more." She sipped her iced tea and hoped it would keep her stomach from growling. The idea of putting food into her body was revolting to her.

"Maybe I should go on a diet, too," Ashley said, looking down at her body. "What do you think?"

"You're perfect." Ryan glanced at Bethany again. "Are you sure you're feeling all right? I haven't seen you eat in weeks."

"I ate last night," Bethany argued. "Remember? I cooked that ham?"

"Yes, but I didn't see you eating any of it."

"I ate bites as I was fixing the vegetables. Mom, you do that, too. I've seen you. I ate."

Karen frowned slightly. Weight was a sensitive subject with her. Over the years she had become decidedly plump. Bethany thought her mother grossly fat, and was determined not to look like that herself. Of the two girls, Bethany had always gained weight faster than Ashley, but she had decided at the beginning of this school year that she was going to do something about that.

At first it had been difficult. Then, as time went on, she found she wanted to eat less and less. Now, the only time it bothered her was at the beginning of a meal. Already her hunger was slackening. Just watching the others consume the meal was enough to kill her appetite. Bethany hated to watch others eat or to think of the digestive process at all.

She was thirteen now and starting to get interested in

boys. She had noticed that the most popular girls were invariably the thin ones, who looked like the models in magazines. This proved to her that fat was something she didn't want in her life. To reinforce her decision, she cast a glance at her mother. Karen layered butter on a roll and then focused all her attention on eating it.

"May I be excused?" Bethany asked.

"If you're not going to eat, at least sit there and keep us company," Ryan said. "I never see you anymore."

"Maybe if you didn't work late every night," Karen said coolly.

"We've been unusually busy. I don't like it either."

Karen made a noise that showed she didn't believe him. "Ashley, did you do your homework?"

Ashley nodded, but didn't make eye contact.

Bethany knew what that meant. Ashley always did her homework in school before the tardy bell rang in the mornings. Sometimes she didn't do it at all. "I got a ninety-eight on my English test," she said.

"That's good," Ryan said with a smile. "How about you, Ashley?"

Ashley gave her sister a glare. "We didn't get the papers back yet."

Bethany smiled. She knew better.

"Have a roll and butter?" Ashley asked Bethany a bit too innocently.

"No, thank you. I don't want to eat cholesterol and white flour," Bethany said in a self-congratulatory tone. "Neither should you."

Ashley added more butter to the roll and ate it with obvious relish. Bethany looked away. To keep up her will-power, she concentrated on the bulge she had discovered on her inner thigh that very afternoon. Ashley had said it was just a muscle, but Bethany didn't want to take any chances. It could be fat.

"I found a new diet in a magazine," Karen said. "You can eat all the grapefruit and cantaloupe you want, but no starches. I may try that."

"Those diets aren't healthy for you," Ryan said. "Some of them can do more harm than good."

"That's easy for you to say." Karen reached for the broccoli and cheese. "It sounds perfect for me. Would you like to go on it with me, Bethany? You like cantaloupe."

"She diets too much as it is." Ryan frowned at Karen and gave her the look that parents seem to believe their children can't interpret.

"What's for dessert?" Ashley asked.

"Chocolate cake." Karen started on her second helping of roast. To Ryan she said, "I suppose you'll be late again tomorrow night?"

"Yes. I'll have to work late every day this week and probably next week as well. By then Beall will be back from vacation and can take some of the load."

"You'll find something else to keep you away from home."

Bethany tried to ignore them. Her mother had been finding fault with her father for as long as she could remember. Sometimes she wondered why he put up with it. Bethany had decided she would leave home as soon as she graduated and never come back. Being there was just too depressing.

Ashley finished and took her plate to the kitchen. She returned with two slices of cake. "Want one, Bethany?"

"Don't tease your sister if she's on a diet," Karen said automatically. "Here. Give it to me. I'll eat it."

Ashley gave the other piece to Ryan and went after one for herself.

"Now may I be excused?" Bethany asked plaintively.

"Sure," Ryan said. He watched her go, and the nagging worry returned. She was much too thin already. To Karen he said, "I wish you wouldn't encourage her to diet. Have you taken a good look at her lately?"

"She's slender," Karen said with a shrug. Her eyes didn't meet his.

"You've noticed it, too. I think we should take her in for a checkup."

Karen glared at him. "When do you propose *we* do this? I have something scheduled every afternoon this week. I can't take her to the doctor."

"Damn it, Karen, this is more important than whatever it is you and Joyce have planned."

"Oh? I'll let you be the one to tell the Toys for Tots group or the Heart Association. That's where I'm going to be. I'd say both those are rather important. Of course you'd know best. You always do." She cut into the cake on her saucer.

Ashley came back in time to hear the last part. "Toys for Tots? Can I go with you?"

"*May* I and no, you can't. You have to be in school when we're meeting."

"I could do something after school, couldn't I?" Ashley frowned as she slid back into her chair.

Karen looked across at Ryan. "Besides, I don't see any reason to take Bethany to the doctor. She never misses a day of school, and her grades are practically perfect. She just took after your side of the family. All of you are skinny."

Ryan ignored the jab. "I'll find time to take her."

"Oh? So you can get off for that but not to come home on time? That's good to know, Ryan. I'll keep that in mind."

He stood and tossed his napkin down beside his plate. He could take only so much family togetherness. It was no surprise to him that Bethany disliked mealtimes and wanted to avoid them. He would do the same if it wasn't for Ashley.

As he passed the door on the way to Bethany's room, the doorbell rang. He opened it. "Chelsea?"

She stepped into the hall light, and his mouth dropped open. "What's happened to you? Were you in a wreck?"

She was already on the verge of tears, and at his questions they spilled over. "Is it all right if I stay here for a while? I've left Lorne."

"Is that Aunt Chel?" Ashley called out as she came

running into the room. She stopped and stared. "What's wrong with your face?"

Ryan made a quieting motion. "Go get your mother, honey. We need to talk to Aunt Chel in private." He took Chelsea into the den and shut the door. "What the hell happened to you?"

"I ran into a door?" she said with a feeble attempt at humor. "I think that's the standard excuse."

"I'm going to kill him!"

"No, you're not." She caught his arm as he reached for the phone. "I don't want him to know where I am. I'll find a lawyer tomorrow and start divorce proceedings."

"You look terrible." He couldn't stop staring at her bruised and swollen face.

"Thanks. You always know what to say to lift my spirits." This time her smile was almost genuine. He could tell the effort hurt her.

"You should see a doctor. Let me drive you to the hospital."

"I don't need to go there. This happened last night. I'm fine." She looked up as Karen came into the room. "I'm fine," she repeated. "Don't look at me like that."

Karen stared at her in undisguised amazement. "Lorne didn't do that, did he?"

"Yes, he did. I've left him. I want to stay with you for a few days. Just until I can find a place. Know of any garage apartments for rent?" she asked wryly.

"How can you joke at a time like this?" Karen demanded.

"If I don't, I'll cry, and I'm tired of crying. It's all I've done for twenty-four hours. Do you have any aspirin?"

Karen hurried out to get it for her.

Chelsea met Ryan's eyes. "Promise me you won't do anything stupid. He's not worth it."

Ryan felt sick inside. "I can't believe anyone would hurt you like this! What the hell happened?"

"I stepped too far out of line, I guess." Chelsea shook her head. "I can't explain it. It started so gradually. At first it wasn't enough to divorce over; then it was too much for me to admit. Last night he scared me. I thought he was going to kill me."

"He's done this before and you stayed? You didn't tell me?" He glared at her as he stood and paced to the window. "You should have him arrested!"

"If I do, he'll come after me when he's released. They don't keep them forever, you know. I pressed charges once, and I'll never do it again."

"That's crazy! I'll press charges myself!"

"They won't let you."

He went to her and knelt in front of her. Looking into her face was painful. He wanted to take her into his arms and hold her. Never to let her go. It was as if the past twelve years had never happened. "Chelsea," he said, his voice filled with the pain he felt for her.

She touched his face gently. "I'm all right."

They heard Karen returning with the aspirin and water. Ryan pulled away. Chelsea accepted two tablets and swallowed them. "Thank you. May I stay here? I can go to a hotel if it's too much trouble."

"I won't hear of such a thing." Karen sat on the arm of Chelsea's chair and put her arm around her friend's shoulders. "You'll stay here where I'll know you're safe. He won't dare look for you here."

Ryan wondered if this was as much of a surprise to Karen as it was to him. She didn't seem all that startled now that the initial shock was over. "You can have Ashley's room. She won't mind sleeping with Bethany."

Chelsea smiled and nodded. She seemed close to tears again. "Would you mind if I go lie down? I'm exhausted."

"Of course you are! Ryan, bring in her things. I'll go get her settled in."

Chelsea handed him her car keys. As he went outside, he told himself that Chelsea was right. If he went to Austin, found Lorne, and beat the crap out of him, Lorne wouldn't be the one to end up in jail. And as pleasurable as it would be to pound Lorne's face to a pulp, it wasn't worth getting arrested over. All the same, Ryan enjoyed the fantasy of what he would like to do to the man.

At least, he told himself, Chelsea was back where he could keep an eye on her. She would be safe now. He tried not to think about the divorce and how that would leave Chelsea free.

Chapter Nineteen

Chelsea knew she couldn't stay with Karen and Ryan for long. Aside from the feelings she and Ryan still had for each other, there was the possibility that Lorne would cause trouble for them. She knew he would know immediately where she had gone upon leaving Austin.

She started her search for a place to live the day after she arrived. Karen was against it, saying she should at least wait until her bruises had faded, but Chelsea wanted to be on her own long before that. More than once she had found herself wondering what Lorne was doing and whether she had somehow caused him to hit her. These thoughts frightened her. She wanted roots of her own in Dallas, so she would be stronger in her determination not to return to Austin. She also made an appointment with a counselor to help her overcome the battered-wife syndrome.

At first she looked at houses, but she soon ruled them out. She was tired of living a structured lifestyle. She wanted to rediscover who she was and live to please herself.

The realtor reluctantly showed her a warehouse. It wasn't too far from Karen's house, in an area of Dallas that was established and safe. It had once been an automobile dealership. Downstairs there were doors large enough to drive a car through, along with small offices. Behind these was the area where the cars had been repaired and repainted. Upstairs was one huge room with windows that overlooked the streets in front and behind the building and the adjacent alley.

"I'll take it," Chelsea said. It was perfect. She could rent out the ground floor and have some income. The loft was perfect for a live-in studio. The windows let in plenty of light, and she would have privacy from the business below because stairs led up the side of the building to an outside entrance to the upper floor.

She held her breath until the papers were signed. Between the money she had taken with her and the diamond bracelet she had sold that morning, she had enough for the down payment. At least, she thought, Lorne had been generous in his gifts of jewelry. By the time she sold the rest, she might have enough to buy the building outright. It wasn't expensive, not gauged against her recent luxurious lifestyle.

"You bought a warehouse?" Karen asked when she went back to the house. "Are you out of your mind?"

"Not anymore. Don't you remember? It's what I've always said I wanted to do—have a loft studio, live at one end, and paint at the other."

"But we were teenagers when you wanted that!"

"I'm going back to painting. I have to have a studio. Wait until you see it. I can even rent out the downstairs to a mechanic and have some money coming in on a regular basis."

"This gets worse and worse. You can't possibly live over a garage!"

Chelsea laughed. "Yes, I can. It's where I started out. Remember? At least this garage and apartment are bigger. You just have to see this place."

"I can hardly wait." Karen didn't sound enthusiastic.

Chelsea looked up as the girls came through on their way in from school. She smiled and spoke to them, but when they left, she said, "Has Bethany been sick?"

"No, she's just been dieting."

"But she's rail-thin! Are you sure she's all right?"

"Ryan is after me to take her to a doctor, but there's no need. I think she's too thin, too, but she doesn't seem to be sick. Her grades are up, she has lots of energy. She's mentioned wanting to be a fashion model, and they have to be skin and bones."

"She's that, for sure!"

"Speaking of dieting, I'm going to join the health club at the mall. Would you like to go with me?"

Chelsea wrinkled her nose. "I hate saunas and exercise machines."

"So do I, but it makes you feel so pampered to have a rubdown and I'll enjoy the steam room and pool."

"Maybe I'll go later. Right now, I have enough on my hands just getting settled in. I saw a lawyer this morning and have started divorce proceedings."

"So soon? What did he say? Why didn't you tell me that first instead of about the warehouse?"

Chelsea looked at her hands knotted in her lap. "It was harder than I expected. I'm not sure I'm doing the right thing."

"You've got to be kidding!"

"Lorne is so immature in some ways. You don't know him as I do. Sometimes he's like a little boy. I think he needs me more than he realizes."

"Did you also make an appointment with a counselor? You need someone to talk sense into you. Lorne is a grown man with a vicious temper. There's no little boy hiding in there."

"I made the appointment. I'll keep it. Anyway, the lawyer was interested as soon as I told him who it is I'll be divorcing. It seems Lorne went against him in court for a payment dispute some years back. The lawyer still has hard feelings toward him. He says he'll get everything he can—especially since the makeup doesn't hide my bruises. He says I should take pictures."

"That's a good idea. I'll take them myself."

"He says that way I'm not as likely to change my mind,

that I'll have a reminder. It seems he's dealt with battered wives before."

"I don't understand you. I really don't. You're stronger than any woman I know. Why would you need a reminder not to go back to him?" Karen frowned as she poured them both another cup of coffee. "It wouldn't take anywhere near this much for me to leave him."

Chelsea shook her head. "I'd have said the same thing once. It's different when you find yourself in the situation. It's not clear anymore what you should do. You make excuses for your husband and put the blame on yourself. You think it will never happen again. But of course it does."

"You need psychiatric help."

"I know that. That's why I made the appointment." Chelsea smiled as she sipped the coffee. "And that's why I came to you. I knew you wouldn't let me do anything stupid."

"Ryan and I will keep an eye on you. You can depend on that."

Bethany came down the hall and passed through on her way to the den. Soon Chelsea heard the TV come on. She couldn't keep the worried frown from her face. "Karen, maybe Bethany should be seeing this counselor, too."

"What on earth for?"

"Now come on, you can't tell me you think she lost all this weight on a normal diet and for ordinary reasons. She looks like a refugee from a prison camp. Her jeans hang on her!"

"You sound like Ryan. That's all he can talk about lately. Bethany's too thin, she looks too sickly, she's destroying her health. Frankly, I'm tired of hearing about it! I think it's his way of pointing out that I need to lose weight."

"I don't care if you lose weight or not," Chelsea objected. "I'm worried about Bethany! You've heard of anorexia. Everyone has these days!"

"Anorexia? Bethany? No way." Karen didn't sound too

convinced in spite of her firm words. "She eats supper with us. Three days ago I bought a gallon of that chocolate chunk ice cream she especially likes, and she ate the whole thing!"

"Did she throw up afterward?"

"That's disgusting! How would I know?"

"Please, Karen. Do it for me. Get her to a doctor and then to a counselor."

"All right. I'll make an appointment for her next week. But you and Ryan are going to feel ridiculous when you hear there's nothing wrong with her."

Chelsea was relieved. Perhaps Karen didn't see anything wrong with her daughter since she was with Bethany every day, but since Chelsea hadn't seen her for a while, the changes were frightening. Karen might insist that her daughter was energetic, but in Chelsea's opinion, the girl seemed depressed and listless. At least now she would get some help with whatever was bothering her.

Chelsea rose and said, "I have some more jewelry I'd like to sell. I guess I'll take it to the same jeweler."

"I wish you wouldn't sell all those pieces. Someday you'll want them and they'll be all gone."

"I think it's best for me to get rid of all the nicer reminders of Lorne. Besides, I want to pay for my new house and the divorce could take forever. If he contests it, it may drag on, and I need cash now."

"All right. If you say so. But we won't let you starve, you know."

"I know. Do you want to come with me to the jewelers?"

"No, I'm on my way to the health club. If I put it off, I may weaken."

When Chelsea went to her room to get the other things she intended to sell, Karen told the girls goodbye and left. The drive was a short one, and she could always just stop going to the health club if the workouts proved to be too strenuous. Just because she was purchasing a membership didn't mean she was honor-bound to keep attending.

She had been there before with Wendy Green and had enjoyed the experience. Wendy had lost all the weight she had put on in the last few years, and she looked young and pretty again. Karen didn't know if it would work for her or not, but she was willing to give it a try. Her bathroom scales had prompted the action.

She went to the office and talked to the woman in charge of memberships. After hearing about the packages offered, Karen bought the one that gave her unlimited access to the equipment and the freedom to go every day if it suited her. It cost more, but the woman assured her it was worth every penny.

After she wrote out the check, Karen was taken to the back room and given a leotard and tights in her size. She cringed when she put them on. Her street clothes were chosen to hide the bulges and rolls. Here everyone wore exercise wear. Reluctantly she came out of the dressing room to rejoin the woman. Beside her stood a young man who looked more like a Greek god than a mere mortal.

"This is Hank Farley, one of our best instructors. Hank, this is Karen Morgan. She's new to our program."

Hank smiled and reached out his hand. Karen put hers in his. "It's good to meet you, Karen. We'll be working together. I'm looking forward to it."

"Thank you," she murmured. Outside of movies, she had never seen anyone built like this man. He wasn't tall, but he looked as if he could lift a truck. His face was boyishly handsome. She found herself wondering how old he was and whether he was married.

They went to the wall, and Hank showed her how to stand and pull against the stirrup-like handles to firm her torso. To demonstrate, he put his hands over hers and helped her pull at the right angle. Karen realized she was staring and tried to get her mind on the exercise. It wasn't easy.

Hank took her all over the gym, showing her how to use the equipment safely and to the best advantage. "Don't try to do it too quickly," he advised. "You'll just hurt yourself and have to build up all over again. I'll be here anytime you come in, as long as you call for an appointment. Otherwise, I may be with another client."

"I'll remember to call." She had a fleeting thought that she might be making a fool of herself, and she looked away.

"Good," he said in a softer voice. "Be sure you do that." He gave her that smile that made her feel young and thin. "To the showers now. When you finish, wrap the towel around you and come into the massage room."

Karen did as he said. She showered quickly and told herself not to be foolish. Hank was sexy and he made her blood reach the boiling point every time he smiled, but she was almost old enough to be his mother. It wasn't a pleasant thought.

She wrapped the towel around her and found the door to the massage room. To her surprise, he was there waiting for her. "You do this, too?"

"I do it all. I tell them I need a raise, but the benefits are worth it." He winked at her and patted the table. "Lie down on your stomach."

Karen wasn't sure she should. When she'd come with Wendy, she hadn't seen this room because Wendy had the less expensive package. Karen had assumed a woman would give the rubdowns. She lay on the table and tried not to feel like a blimp.

Hank started rubbing her shoulders. His hands were strong but not hurtful, and she found herself relaxing all the way to her toes.

"You're firm," he said. "Not everyone is."

"I am?"

"You should see some of the women who come in here. They're like mush. You have substance and some muscle tone."

She didn't know how to answer this.

Hank didn't seem to need her input to carry on a conversation. "I've worked here for about a year now and I haven't seen you. Usually a person visits several times before they join, but I hear you bought the full package today."

"I came with Wendy Green once."

"Wendy Green. Nope, it doesn't ring a bell."

"Her instructor is a woman. Naomi, I think."

"Yeah, Naomi is one of the best. Wendy is in good hands."

Karen was willing to bet Wendy had never been in hands as good as the ones now rubbing her back. "That feels wonderful!"

"You were all tense. I don't know why people get so uptight over a rubdown. I love them, personally."

"A lot of people are sensitive about the way they look," Karen said carefully. She had always maintained that if she never told anyone she was overweight, they might not notice.

"I don't know why. People come in all sizes and shapes. There's nothing wrong with that. Personally, I don't like bony women. They aren't soft."

Karen could hardly believe she had heard him correctly.

"You got tense again. Relax." His hands moved lower, brushing the towel aside.

Karen felt herself blushing and couldn't stop. No one but Ryan had ever seen this much of her, and he hadn't seen her lately.

Hank didn't miss a stroke. His hands swept over her as if her body were familiar territory. "I'm not from Dallas originally," he said. "I grew up in Houston. I thought if I came north I'd find cooler summers." He laughed. "Boy, was I wrong!"

"Summers are killers here," she agreed. His hands were moving onto her buttocks. She wanted to tell him to stop but was afraid of seeming too prudish. Besides, it felt good.

"I miss the beach. All that sun's not good for you, though. I see women come in here with skin like leather. You're not like that."

"I've never wanted to get a tan. Not since I was in college, at any rate."

"You went to college? Man, I wish I had. I wanted to be a coach. Maybe even a doctor that specializes in athletic injuries. I'd have been good at that."

"You can still go."

"No, I have to work now. There's not enough time to go to college, too." He sounded as if he really regretted it. "Maybe someday."

"You should go if you really have your heart set on it." She wondered exactly how old he was. "Are you married?"

He laughed again. "No way. I'm not ready to settle down with just one person. Not yet."

She hid her smile. He wasn't married.

He rubbed down the backs of her legs, and Karen was glad she had shaved them that morning. "I think you're going to like it here."

Karen closed her eyes and let him rub the last of the tension from her muscles. If Ryan had done these same things at home, she would have refused to lie still. But Hank wasn't interested in sex, and she was in complete charge. She knew if she said a single word, he would wrap the towel around her again and nothing more would happen. Karen didn't say the word.

At dinner that night, she was still thinking about Hank. Had he been as wonderful as she remembered? Could any man be that perfect?

"Mom, are you in outer space or what?" Ashley asked as she tried to pass her the bowl of peas. "This is hot on the bottom."

"Sorry." Karen was embarrassed that she had been caught daydreaming. She put some peas on her plate but stopped before she added another spoonful. If she was going to see Hank at the gym, she had incentive to lose weight.

"I found a place to live," Chelsea was telling Ryan. "I can't wait to show it to you."

"It's a warehouse, Dad," Ashley said eagerly. "She drove me by there this afternoon. It's cool!"

Bethany put ten peas on her plate and passed the bowl to Chelsea. "I wish I could live there!"

"Both of you are welcome anytime. I'll get some air mattresses for you to use as beds. I'm going to advertise the garage below for rent."

"You're back over a garage?" Ryan asked with amusement.

Karen didn't take any corn bread. "I'm still against it. Who knows who might rent the garage? It's not safe. That's an old neighborhood, and you know how those can go downhill."

"It's safe," Chelsea protested. "The houses are old, but it's in an area where young couples are buying and fixing their places up. I'll probably be safer there than I would be anywhere else. Who would break into the upstairs of a garage?"

"She filed for divorce today," Karen said to Ryan.

"You did?" His eyes sought Chelsea. "I'm glad to hear it. Did you go to the lawyer I recommended?"

Chelsea nodded. "I like him. He's eager to take Lorne to court."

"Good. Hit him in the checkbook. He deserves to be taken to the cleaners."

"I don't know if there's much in the savings account or not. We didn't discuss it."

"You don't know how much money you have?" Ashley asked, her eyes wide. "How can that be?"

"Eat your supper," Karen said warningly.

"Your house is worth a fortune," Ryan said. "You're entitled to half of that, if nothing else."

Karen glanced across at him. "How do you know what her house looks like? We've never been there."

"I described it to him," Chelsea said smoothly.

"I joined the health club today," Karen said. "I think I'm going to enjoy it."

Bethany wrinkled her nose. "I hate to exercise."

"I was hoping you'd go with me sometimes." Karen hadn't been. Not since meeting Hank.

"I'll go," Ashley volunteered. "I'd like to do something like that!"

"We'll see." Karen wasn't at all sure she wanted her daughters to meet Hank and vice versa. He hadn't asked, and he might assume she was unmarried and younger than she really was. During the rest of the meal, she let her mind dwell on every moment of her time at the gym. She could hardly wait for the next afternoon.

After a week, Karen could tell she was starting to lose weight. Hank noticed, too.

"You're starting to tone up nicely," he said as he monitored her work at the machine that strengthened leg muscles. "I don't think I've ever seen anyone respond so quickly."

She smiled. "I'm on a diet, too."

"Don't overdo it. If you lose too fast, you'll just gain it back. Like I always say, I'd rather see a woman that's plump than one that looks like a scarecrow."

"You're too good to be true. You make me feel like a movie star."

He smiled at her. "That's what I hoped you'd feel like."

Karen wished she could ask him if comments like this were meant to be as personal as they seemed, but she couldn't bring herself to do it. If the answer was no, she would be mortified.

After the shower, she hurried to the massage room, and without a qualm, lay down on the table. This had become her favorite part of the workout.

As Hank massaged the knots from her muscles, he said, "You know I was just wondering. Would you like to go out sometime?"

She craned her neck around to see him. "I beg your pardon?"

"I guess not. Forget I asked."

"I suppose I might be able to go out with you. Just as friends, I mean." Her mind was racing. She shouldn't have said that, but she didn't want to take it back. Now was the time to tell him she was married. She kept her mouth firmly closed against the words.

"Yeah? How about next Saturday? But don't say anything to the others that work here. We're not supposed to see the clients after hours, and I could get into a lot of trouble."

"I won't mention it. Next Saturday will be fine."

"Where do I pick you up?"

"I'll meet you." She was wondering what excuse she could give Ryan for leaving the house on a Saturday night. "Say at Nevilles?" That was a medium-priced restaurant she never frequented with Ryan or the girls. It was also nowhere near her house.

"Nevilles is great. I'll meet you there, say, at seven?"

"Seven is perfect." She wondered what she could possibly tell Ryan.

During dinner at Nevilles Karen kept casting sidelong glances at Hank to reassure herself that this wasn't a dream. As it turned out, he was a vegetarian, so she ordered a salad instead of the steak she had intended to eat. He rewarded her with a smile.

"I'm glad you were able to come tonight," he said. "Did you have trouble getting out of the house?"

"Trouble in what way?" she evaded.

"I've seen your chart. You're married, according to line three."

"Oh. No, I didn't have any trouble." She hadn't thought about his seeing the form she had filled out when she'd bought her membership. Had he known that when he asked her out?

"It's an open relationship? I like that. When I get married, that's how I want it to be. That way everybody stays free."

Karen smiled as if that described her relationship with Ryan. She was trying to remember whether she had filled in the blank requesting her age. Usually she didn't.

"Today is important to me because it's my birthday."

"It is? You should have said something."

"I didn't want you to feel you had to get a card or anything."

She wondered how old he was, but didn't want to ask. That might give him the option of asking her age, and she didn't want to admit to being thirty-seven. "What are you doing for Christmas?"

"I don't know. I'm not close to my mother, and I don't know where my father is these days. I have a stepfather who would rather not have me around." Hank frowned down at his salad.

"That's terrible." Karen decided to buy him a Christmas present. Otherwise the holidays would be too lonely. She could give it to him as a friend. Surely he would accept it on that condition.

"It's not so bad, really. Naomi doesn't have any family nearby either. We'll probably do something."

"Naomi? Wendy's instructor?" She remembered Naomi as being young, lithe, and pretty in an empty-headed sort of a way.

"Yeah. We've dated a time or two." He grinned at her. "Jealous?"

"No! I mean, of course not."

"That's the great thing about you. I mean, you have somebody and I sort of have somebody, but we can still have each other."

"I don't understand."

"I'm not ever going to ask you to leave your husband," he said in a voice too low to be heard by the other diners. "I'm safe to be with. No demands. No embarrassing phone calls at home."

"I never thought about that." Karen's mind was in a turmoil. It suddenly occurred to her that she shouldn't be here, eating dinner with Hank, considering having an affair with him. What if Ryan found out? Worse, what if her children heard of it? She knew she should end the meal and the conversation and leave at once.

"I live on Wascomb, about three blocks from the gym."

"Oh?"

"I thought you might like to come over sometime." His eyes met hers, and he smiled again, this time as if they were conspirators.

Karen's conscience lost its voice. "Maybe. Yes, I would like that. Sometime." She hadn't felt this excited even when she was in college and being courted by Ryan. "Yes, I most definitely would."

When they finished their meal, she insisted on paying the waiter. "It was my choice to eat here. Besides, it's your birthday," she said. She knew Hank probably didn't have much money. He let her pay.

They walked out to their cars, and he opened her door for her. "Next time, we should park farther apart. In case anyone is noticing."

"I would never have thought of that."

"Like I said, you can trust me to keep our secret." Before she knew what he was about to do, he leaned over and kissed her on the lips.

The kiss was short and not filled with passion, but Karen found her heart racing. If he had asked her, she would have gone with him to his apartment then and there. Being courted was so much more exciting than being married!

On the drive home, she found herself smiling. She let herself into the house and was glad to see Ryan was working late as usual. Chelsea was in the den, and she could hear the distant sounds of the girls talking in Ashley's room. Karen went into the den.

"Hi. Is the meeting over so soon?"

Karen shook her head. "I lied about having a meeting tonight. Chel, you'll never guess where I've been!"

"You look as if you're about to burst. Where?"

Karen sat on the ottoman beside Chelsea's chair. "I met someone."

Chelsea didn't understand. "What are you talking about?"

Karen glanced at the door to be certain the girls hadn't come down the hall. "I met someone interesting. A man."

Still Chelsea didn't seem to grasp what she was saying. "So?"

"I just had dinner with him. Chel, he's asked me to come to his apartment."

Chelsea's mouth dropped open. "You had a date? You're seeing someone?"

"Hush! I don't want the girls to hear. Tonight was our first meeting. I wanted to tell you, but I was so nervous." She clasped her hands together. "He's so good-looking! And you wouldn't believe how he's built!"

"Karen, I don't believe I'm hearing any of this! Are you telling me you're having an affair?"

"No, not yet. I may. Does a dinner date constitute an affair?" Karen felt as if she were filled with bubbles. "He's so wonderful!"

"What about Ryan? Karen, you're not really seeing this person, are you?"

"I need you to help me. He works at the gym where I exercise. He's my instructor. That's how we met."

"You just started going a week ago!"

"I know! It was like an instant attraction. For both of us! Can you imagine anyone being interested in me at first sight?" She laughed and hugged herself. "He makes me feel thin and pretty."

Chelsea stared at her.

"I need you to cover for me. Not often, of course, just when I can't come up with an excuse Ryan will believe. You'll do that for me, won't you, Chel?"

"I'll do no such thing! You must be out of your mind!"

"Please! I'd do the same for you."

"No, you wouldn't! You'd tell me about fidelity and keeping promises and doing what's right. Tell me you won't see him again!"

"I can't promise that. If you met him, you'd understand." Karen reached out and touched Chelsea's arm. "He's young. Way too young, I guess. But it doesn't seem to matter to him. Nothing does. He likes me just the way I am. It doesn't even bother him that I'm married!"

"Has it dawned on you that Ryan would leave you if he found out? Doesn't that matter to you?"

"Of course it matters, but he's not going to find out. Hank and I discussed it over dinner. That's his name, Hank Farley."

"Don't tell me his name! I don't want to know anything about him." Chelsea leaned over and covered her ears.

Karen laughed. "I have to see him again. I feel alive when I'm with him. I don't feel like a middle-aged mother of two teenagers."

"What about Ryan? He could find out a dozen different ways. Don't you know how this would hurt him?"

Karen made a waving motion with her hand. "Ryan never asks me any questions and never notices what I do. I'm going to be careful." She stood and stretched. "I'm even going to lose weight!"

"What you're going to lose is Ryan!"

Karen frowned and sat down beside Chelsea. She felt as if all her bubbles had burst. "I thought you'd understand. You were married a long time. Didn't you ever get bored?"

"Of course I did. But I never had an affair. Karen, I've been on the other end, and I know how it feels. You know if your spouse is having an affair. I think deep inside everyone knows, whether they admit it or not. Maybe not at first, but eventually. It's not worth the risk. Believe me!"

Karen leaned back on the cushions the way her daughters did when they were hearing something they didn't want to acknowledge. "If you met him, you'd understand." She couldn't help sounding petulant. "I thought you'd be more open-minded."

"I'm giving you good advice and you know it. Don't risk everything for this!"

Karen looked around at the familiar den. She did enjoy her life, even if it was boring at times. Her house was lovely, and her daughters were beautiful. She certainly didn't want a divorce, and much as she wanted to deny it, Ryan wouldn't overlook something as serious as her having an affair. She thought back to the time, years ago, when he had left her for almost an entire night. She had been devastated. "I guess you're right."

"You know damned well I am."

Karen studied Chelsea's angry expression. After a while she said, "You're a good friend. Maybe better than I deserve."

"Nonsense." Chelsea looked away. "I just don't want to see you make a mistake that you'll come to regret."

Karen leaned over and hugged her. "Thanks."

She left Chelsea and went down the hall to her bedroom. She could hear the rise and fall of the girls' voices, the soft sounds of the house that were so familiar as to be unnoticeable. As if she had never seen it before, she took stock of her bedroom.

Like everything else in her house, it was a reflection of herself. The stamp of her personality was on every item from the matching drapes and bedspread to the silver comb and brush set. Even in her wildest dreams she knew Hank Farley wouldn't ask her to move in with him, and even if he did, she would refuse. He would never be able to offer her a place as nice as this one. Nor would he ever earn a fraction as much as Ryan. Not unless he really did become a doctor, and she knew that was more pipe dream than plan.

No, she thought, as she sat on her bed. It wasn't worth the risk. All the same, she let her mind present her with every detail of their evening together, and she dwelt a long time on the spontaneous kiss that had ended it. At least she could see him at the gym and remember that it could have been. She might be middle-aged and overweight, but she could have had an affair with a man young enough to excite her daughters. The thought made her smile.

Chapter Twenty

Bethany walked carefully down the hall between classes. Lately she had become weak, and she didn't want to embarrass herself by falling. Also the pads of her feet were so thin it was as if bones were rubbing against skin every time she took a step. She smiled to think how slender she had become. She was certain to be popular now that she had lost all her fat.

Ashley was cutting school again today. Bethany wondered how her sister managed to get by with it. She was certain that if she missed so much as one class, she would be caught and probably expelled. Ashley didn't seem to care whether anyone found out or not.

Several girls and boys pushed by Bethany, and she almost bumped into a locker. She glared after them. The girls were all fatter than she was and loud into the bargain. She didn't see what the boys found so interesting in them. As she watched, one of the girls took a candy bar from her pocket and offered a bite to one of the boys. Bethany's stomach growled, and she swallowed. Even now her body rebelled sometimes. She congratulated herself on having enough willpower to keep her body free of the additives and chemicals and calories that were packed in that candy bar.

Her last class that day was English. Bethany was particularly good at this subject, especially now that they were in the second semester and studying literature instead of grammar. She intended to make all *A*'s again. Ashley would be lucky if she passed English. Bethany worried a lot about her sister lately.

Her parents didn't seem to notice, but Ashley's crowd of friends had changed. She never brought these kids to the house, Bethany only knew about them because she saw Ashley with them in the parking lot. They were all much older than Ashley, who was still twelve but looked sixteen, and they weren't the sort of kids that attended St. Anne's.

Bethany was looking forward to summer. Then she would be fourteen and Ashley thirteen. They would both be teenagers at last. She thought she wouldn't worry so much about Ashley if her sister were older. Twelve was so young.

She took her seat and looked up to find the teacher motioning for her to come forward. Bethany went to see what the woman wanted. She hated to be singled out by a teacher. It made her feel like her mother did when a phone rang in the middle of the night.

"Are you well?" the teacher asked in a whisper. She looked concerned.

"I'm fine. Thanks."

"When you came in, I noticed you're unusually pale. If you need to go to the nurse's room, just raise your hand. Understand?"

"Yes, ma'am." Bethany went back to her seat, wondering what all that had been about. Surreptitiously she fished her compact from her purse and looked at her reflection. She did look pale, but no more so than usual.

Her health had begun to worry her a bit, though she hadn't told anyone. She hadn't had a period in over two months and lately she had noticed she had more hair on her arms than she normally had. She hid it by wearing long sleeves, but she wondered what she would do in the summer.

As for the periods, she hadn't been having them all that long anyway, and she could usually reassure herself by thinking that her body was merely fluctuating between childhood and adulthood. Though at times she wondered if this was something she should discuss with her mother, she knew Karen was always reluctant to talk about anything pertaining to sex. Bethany decided to ask Chelsea.

The class seemed to speed by. Bethany rarely answered questions, and the teacher seldom embarrassed her by asking her to speak out loud, but she knew the answer to every question the teacher asked about Keats and Shelley. Poetry was one of her favorite subjects, and she sometimes considered being a poet when she was grown. She just wasn't sure how one went about doing that, especially if one were also a top fashion model.

When the bell rang, Bethany stood too quickly and the room spun around her. She paused, palms on her desk, waiting for the sensation to pass. When she looked up, she saw the teacher watching her, that same concerned expression on her face. Bethany smiled at her and pretended to be looking for a pen in her notebook.

She went out of the building with the other students and looked up and down the parking lot for her mother's car and for Ashley. Ashley's usual routine was to come to the first class to answer the roll, then cut out for the rest of the day, returning in time to ride home with Bethany as if she had been there all day. Today she was nowhere to be seen.

Bethany found Karen and got into the front seat of the car. Her mother smiled at her. "Where's Ashley?"

"I don't know. I guess she hasn't come out of the building yet." She squinted her eyes against the sunlight as she searched faces for her sister's. Didn't Ashley know she was going to get caught if she didn't stop doing this?

Karen tapped the steering wheel impatiently. "You might know she'd be late today. I don't have time to wait." She glanced at her diamond watch.

"Why? Do you have an appointment somewhere?"

"No, I made an appointment for you."

"For me?"

"With Dr. Butler. It's just for a checkup."

A sinking sensation struck Bethany. She hated doctor appointments. "There's nothing wrong with me."

"I knew you'd argue. That's why I didn't tell you about it sooner. Your daddy says you need to go in, and he's probably right. You haven't had a proper checkup in well over a year."

"But I'm not sick!"

"Checkups are so you don't get sick."

Bethany frowned and slid lower in the seat. She hated being a child. When she was grown, she would do exactly as she wished and that wouldn't include seeing a doctor for yearly checkups.

"Do you think Ashley rode home with someone else and forgot to tell us?"

"Probably." Let Ashley find her own way home for a change, Bethany thought. Maybe that would remind her to be more careful. Besides, their house was close enough to the school for them to walk. Karen just didn't like them to be on the street unattended. She always feared they would be kidnapped, though why they should be more vulnerable walking home from school than to a friend's house, Bethany had never been able to figure.

Karen started the car and began working her way out of the parking lot. "We're going to be late as it is. I do wish Ashley would be as thoughtful as you are. She never seems to think."

Bethany hid her smile. She liked it when anyone noticed how good she was. She tried very hard to be perfect, and with Ashley's conduct as a measuring stick, it wasn't hard to appear to be.

Dr. Butler's office was located in the commercial district between Bethany's house and her grandparents'. The entire family went to Butler, and Bethany couldn't imagine seeing anyone else. She sat in the familiar waiting room and glanced at a magazine. The models were all rail-thin with gaunt cheeks and radiant smiles. Bethany thought they were beautiful beyond reality. She noticed that some of them were fatter than she was, and this made her proud. Someday she would be one of them.

When her name was called, Bethany obediently followed the nurse. To her embarrassment, her mother went, too. "I'm too old for you to come with me," Bethany whispered when the nurse left them in an examining room. "I can do this alone."

"I know you can, honey. I just want to hear what the doctor says."

Bethany sighed. Her parents were going to treat her like a baby all her life. She was positive of it. She could imagine herself at fifty, still going to the doctor with her mother in attendance.

Dr. Butler came into the room, smiling from ear to ear. "Hello, Mrs. Morgan, Bethany. How are you two doing today?" His eyes swept over Bethany, and a note of concern touched them. "I assume you're the sick one?"

"I'm not sick."

"Ryan wanted you to check her. She hasn't been in lately and you know how careful he is about our daughters' health."

"You've lost a lot of weight since I saw you last," Dr. Butler said as he checked Bethany's eyes and ears. "Why is that?"

"I didn't want to be fat," she said simply.

"I think it's a rebellion against me," Karen said with a laugh. "I have to watch every bite I eat. I told Ryan, if she wants to be thin, let her! I just wish I were!"

The doctor made a noncommittal sound. He put his stethoscope on and listened to Bethany's heartbeat. "Your ticker sounds fine." He gave her another smile. "I'm concerned about this weight loss, though." He unbuttoned her sleeve and pushed it up her arm. Bethany was embarrassed at the silky, dark hair that now grew on her skin. "Are your periods regular?"

Embarrassment flooded her face. "Yes," she lied. She certainly wasn't going to discuss this with a man.

He looked as if he didn't believe her. "When was your last one?"

"At the end of January," she said off the top of her head. She knew there was no way he could verify it.

"What did you have to eat today?"

Karen spoke up. "She had scrambled eggs and toast. No bacon. She doesn't like to eat meat."

"Is that right? You had eggs and toast?" he asked, watching Bethany closely.

"That's right." She had become adept at pretending to eat. She put the food in her napkin and threw it away later.

He made a notation on his chart. Bethany wondered what he had written, but he was holding it in such a way that she couldn't read it. "You were a little on the thin side the last time I saw you," he said as if to himself. "I think we need to do some blood work on you." Again he gave her that fatherly smile. "I just want to rule out some things."

Bethany knew he was talking about AIDS and that he wouldn't find anything wrong. "I hate having my blood taken."

"I know. Everyone does." Dr. Butler looked at Karen. "Are you familiar with the disease anorexia nervosa?"

Karen looked puzzled, but she nodded. "Who hasn't heard about it? But that's not what's wrong with Bethany. She's been dieting and losing weight intentionally. It's not because she's sick."

Dr. Butler smiled at Bethany. "Would you say you're just about the right size now?"

Bethany thought for a minute. "Not really. My arms are still fat, and I have fat here." She touched the inner part of her knee where it joined her thigh. "I bulge out."

"What if I told you that I see you as being extremely underweight? That you no longer have any fat anywhere on your body?"

"I guess everybody has their own opinion," Bethany said carefully. "I just wouldn't agree."

Dr. Butler wrote on his chart again. "I want you to go

into the hospital for a few days. Just so we can run some more extensive tests."

"The hospital!" Karen exclaimed.

"I can't go to the hospital!" Bethany gasped. "I have an English test tomorrow and a paper due in biology on Friday!"

"Is it really necessary?" Karen asked. "I mean, spring vacation will be in a few weeks, and Bethany is trying to have a perfect school record this year—no absences or tardiness. I hate to take her out of class."

The doctor thought for a minute as he regarded Bethany. "I don't know. In my opinion, she needs to be under around-the-clock care until we get some weight back on her. It's not healthy for her to be so thin."

Bethany's eyes widened. They were going to put her in the hospital so they could fatten her up again! Tears sprang to her eyes. She had worked so hard to get to this point! "I don't want to go into the hospital! What about my tests?"

"Maybe the teachers will give you makeup tests if I send them notes."

Karen looked worried and somehow helpless. "You really think she needs to be in the hospital? Is it necessary?"

"I'm afraid so. Anorexia isn't something to be taken lightly. It should have been seen to before this."

"Then I guess that's what we'll do," Karen said in a small voice. "I'll take her home to get her things."

"Good. I'll call the hospital and tell them to be expecting you." He smiled at Bethany again. "I'll see you later," he said to her.

She couldn't believe what had just happened. When the doctor left, she hissed, "I'm not going to the hospital!" She was so close to tears she had to fight crying.

"You heard him. And you have lost a great deal of weight." Karen was looking at her as if she hadn't really seen her in a long time. "I wonder if he wants the nurse to draw the blood here or if you're to wait until you've been checked in?"

"I'm not having it done here." Bethany stomped out. She was so angry she was shaking. The hospital! She would be the size of a blimp by the time she got of there!

In spite of her arguments, Bethany was checked into the hospital within the hour. Her room was stark in spite of its pale green walls and green- and yellow-striped curtains. Bethany hated it immediately. Another girl was in the other bed. Although she was gaunt, Bethany was pleased to see that she was larger. There were definite pockets of fat on her arms.

She smiled when they were alone. "Hi. I'm Stacy Ridge-way. I wondered if they would put anyone else in here. It's lonesome by myself."

"I'm Bethany Morgan. Why are you in here?"

"Same as you, probably. Anorexia." Stacy sighed. "My parents brought me in last week."

"You've been here a week!"

"You will, too, if that's why you're here. They don't let you go until you gain a certain amount of weight. This is my third time in. I'm getting to be an old hand."

"I'm not staying here a week! I have to go to school."

Stacy leaned forward. Her skin seemed to be tautly stretched across her cheekbones and jaw. "There's a trick to getting out," she whispered. "Gain the weight fast."

"I don't want to gain. I have fat arms as it is!"

"They don't care about that. If you gain it fast, you get out quicker. It's easier to lose it again if it's not on you for long." Stacy winked as if she knew this from long experience.

"I guess that makes sense."

"Like I say, I'm practically a pro."

Bethany lay back and stared up at the TV hanging from the ceiling. She wasn't going to like it here.

"I can't see you again," Karen said to Hank that afternoon at the gym. "This time I mean it." In the two months since she had first gone out with him, Hank had talked her into slipping out several times. Each time she was beset by guilt. "My daughter went into the hospital yesterday, and I have too much on my mind."

"I hope it's not anything serious." He sounded genuinely concerned.

"I don't think so. She went on a too strenuous diet. I'm sure that's what the tests will show. Our doctor is very careful." She frowned as she remembered seeing Bethany in the hospital bed. Without sleeves and pants legs to conceal her body, she had been thin to the point of emaciation. How had that happened without her noticing it?

"I'm always saying, 'diet' is just 'die' with a *t* on the end." He laughed as he dropped the correct amount of weights in the tray of the machine she was about to use. "Besides, if everyone went on one, I'd be out of a job."

She smiled. In the past two months she had lost fifteen pounds and felt wonderful. "When Bethany gets out of the hospital, I'd like her to start coming to the gym occasionally."

"Great. I'm sure there's a package that will be perfect for her. They can tell you in the office."

Karen wondered how she would be able to bring Bethany and perhaps Ashley and not have that interfere with her own sessions. She didn't want to share Hank with anyone, least of all her daughters. Even if she wasn't seeing him after hours, she enjoyed the banter and flirting. That would not be possible if her daughters were here. "Wednesdays might be good for them," she said thoughtfully.

"I'm off on Wednesday."

"Are you? I had forgotten. I believe that's the only day both my daughters are free. I guess you'll miss meeting them." She hid her smile. Wednesdays would be perfect.

Bethany stared into her mirror. Her cheeks were filled out, and her arms were rounded. She looked terrible.

"It's good to have you home," Ryan said as he put her

suitcase on the bed. "It seems as if you've been gone forever!"

"Almost a month." She couldn't turn away from the mirror. She was fat!

Ryan came to her and hugged her. "You look great! You're my old Bethany again. Let's keep it this way. Okay?"

"Sure, Dad." She was barely listening to him. Stacy had taught her a lot in the weeks they had shared a room. She had never thought about using laxatives and diuretics in addition to dieting. It made such perfect sense.

"Mom's making your favorite casserole for dinner. She's excited about your being here again. Ashley wanted to stay home from school today so she would be here when you came in, but I told her she would see you soon enough. She's missed you."

"I've missed all of you, too." Bethany wondered if Ashley was still skipping school. They hadn't been alone for her to ask.

"Chelsea will be here for dinner. She's been concerned about you."

"I know. She visited me often."

Ryan looked as if he wanted to say something but was afraid to voice it. She had seen that look on both her parents and on Chelsea since she was hospitalized. She knew they were worrying about her and wondering why she had turned out the way she had. "I'm okay, Daddy. I really am."

"You haven't called me that in years."

She went to him and hugged him. He was so familiar and so safe. She couldn't remember a time when she hadn't felt perfectly secure if he was in the room. "I didn't mean to worry you."

"We just don't want anything to happen to you," he said softly. He kissed the top of her head. "Just take care of yourself. Okay?"

"Okay." She smiled up at him.

He left her alone, and she stared in the mirror again.

Fat! She had known she was gaining, had seen herself in the mirrors at the hospital, but this was different, seeing herself in her own mirror in her own room. She looked huge!

Bethany went down the hall and into her mother's bedroom and through to her bathroom. In the medicine closet she found an assortment of pills. Quickly, before anyone could catch her and ask questions, she read the labels. Because of her constant dieting, Karen had a supply of both laxatives and diuretics. Bethany put some in her pockets and started back to her room. She almost ran into her mother.

"Bethany? Were you looking for me?"

"No, I needed an aspirin. I have a headache. I found what I needed."

"All right." Karen touched her cheek as if she were checking for fever. "It's so good to have you back again."

"It's good to be home. You have no idea!" Bethany smiled and went to her room.

Ashley had found it was a lot more fun to be wild than to be good. Her new friends laughed at her when she tried alcohol for the first time and when she tried to learn to smoke. She didn't see the humor in coughing her lungs out, but she loved the attention. Bethany had always been the good one in the family, had gotten perfect grades without trying, and was constantly being used as a good example for Ashley. Ashley was tired of trying to meet the impossible standards her sister set and was making her own way these days.

Her new boyfriend, a senior named Scott Stark, went to public school. He smoked and drank a great deal, and he drove a red pony Mustang—it had the pony insignia on the glove compartment and on the side of the car. In Scott's circle, pony Mustangs were considered the best possible cars.

Ashley had met him at the skating rink during a birthday party for one of her friends from St. Anne's. He had assumed she was older than twelve, and Ashley hadn't corrected him. Once he'd learned how young she was, he didn't seem to care. Scott had taught her how to skip school so that her absence didn't always show up. He also wrote her absence notes as needed and signed them with her father's name. The school never checked the signature, so these days Ashley only went to school when she felt like it.

It had been more difficult seeing Scott while Bethany was in the hospital. She was used to Bethany covering for her. But she soon found she could still do as she pleased if she thought it out carefully. It was like a game, outwitting the adults in her life. Ashley had always enjoyed living on the edge.

"I saw your sister today," Scott told her as she slid into the car beside him. "She was going into the school. She sure is skinny."

"I know. She's scared she'll be fat like Mom when she grows up." Ashley frowned. "She's lost a lot since she came home from the hospital. I heard Mom and Dad arguing about it last night. Dad says Bethany should go back to the doctor. Mom says she can't afford to miss any more school this year. They were still fighting when I went to bed."

"You know, I'll bet you could figure a way to slip out at night if you put your mind to it." Scott reached out and tickled the hair on the back of her neck. "I'll just bet you could."

She smiled. Lately they had been doing some heavy petting as well as drinking. She liked to kiss Scott, and she liked having him touch her. So far she had stopped at going all the way, however. He wasn't happy about that, and she didn't want to lose him. "Maybe I could. What would we do?"

He gazed across the parking lot. "We would have all night to decide. I could meet you on the corner up from your house and bring you back before daylight. What do you think?"

"I don't know. Let me think about it."

He winked at her and gave her a lazy smile. "Don't think too long. You can't expect me to wait forever."

She frowned at him. "You'll wait as long as I please. You aren't the only boy in Dallas who drives a pony Mustang and likes to fool around."

He laughed. "You're something else, kid! Well, you think about it and let me know."

She leaned over and kissed him. "I will. I have to get back into school before history today. We have a test, and I have to take this one. It's going to affect my report card."

Scott grimaced. "I'm thinking about quitting."

"Now? You're a senior!"

"I don't care. I'm sick of school. Maybe you and me ought to run off together." He poked at her until she laughed.

"I'll think about that, too," she said saucily as she opened his car door. "I have to get in there now. See you tomorrow? We could go to the lake."

"It's a date." He lit a cigarette as she slipped out.

Ashley was smiling as she went back to the school. Life could be so interesting with so little effort.

That night she paid close attention to the routine of her parents and to what time her father checked the locks on the doors. Her mother went to bed when the evening news came on. Ryan sat up later, but she heard him coming down the hall to his room before midnight. As Scott had said, it wouldn't be that difficult to slip out. She would have from around midnight to nearly dawn. That was plenty of time to do anything they might decide on.

As Ashley lay listening, she heard Bethany's door open and the padding of bare feet into the bathroom. In a few minutes the sound of gagging came to her. When it came again, Ashley sat up and frowned into the darkness. Was Bethany forcing herself to vomit again? She considered that gross and disgusting and went to tell her sister so.

Bethany was sitting on the bathroom floor holding onto the toilet. Her face was slick and as white as the tiles. Ashley hesitated. "Are you sick?"

Bethany nodded and retched into the toilet again. After she flushed it she said, "I feel awful funny. My muscles hurt and keep going into spasms. And my heart feels funny."

"Funny how?"

"I think you'd better get Mom."

Ashley turned and hurried down the hall. If Bethany was vomiting on purpose she would never have asked for Karen. Ashley went to the bed and shook her mother's arm. "Mom, wake up. Bethany's sick."

Karen turned over and tried to open her eyes. "Ashley? What time is it?"

"I don't know. After midnight. Bethany's sick."

Karen sat up and rubbed her eyes as if still fighting sleep. "Sick?"

"She's in the bathroom and throwing up."

This sank in and Karen put her legs over the side of the bed. "I'm coming."

Ashley stayed at the bathroom door as Karen felt Bethany's face and asked questions. Bethany was obviously too sick to be of much help. Karen said to Ashley, "Get your father. We have to take Bethany to the hospital."

Ashley ran to do as she was told, then hurried to get dressed. She wasn't going to miss any of this. She rarely got outside at this time of night, especially on a school night.

They put Bethany in the car, not bothering to do more than wrap a robe around her pajamas. Ashley wondered if Bethany would be embarrassed about this when she was herself again. Bethany became embarrassed so easily.

Ryan drove to the hospital, glancing from time to time at Bethany who was huddled against Karen in the front seat. More than once his eyes met Karen's in silent worry. He had been able to tell as soon as he saw Bethany that something was desperately wrong. Now she stared sightlessly ahead, her body barely rising and falling with her breaths.

In the emergency room the doctor took one look at Bethany and started barking out orders to nurses and orderlies. Ryan and Karen tried to stay out of the way but in sight of Bethany. Under the hospital lights, her skin had taken on a blue sheen.

Bethany was admitted and taken to ICU. Ryan heard Dr. Butler being paged over the speakers and wondered what the physician was doing at the hospital so late. He felt reassured as soon as he saw the familiar doctor coming toward them, clipboard in hand.

Dr. Butler didn't smile. He nodded to them and went to Bethany. He lifted her eyelid and took her pulse as the nurse finished putting Bethany on oxygen. If she was conscious she gave no sign. Except for an occasional tremor of her muscles, Bethany was perfectly still. He turned back to Ryan. "I think you'd better go out to the waiting room. I'll be with you in a few minutes."

Karen was about to argue, but Ryan turned her and Ashley toward the doors. "He has to see to her. You can ask questions later."

The waiting room was empty except for one man who sat alone at the far end, apparently dozing until the time scheduled for the next five-minute visit. Ryan, Karen, and Ashley sat close together at the other end. Karen put her hands on his, and he noticed they felt cold and clammy. "She'll be okay."

"She's so sick! Why didn't she call me sooner?"

"Maybe she just woke up," Ashley said. "I didn't hear her moving around until she went into the bathroom. Do you think she has the flu or something?"

"I don't know." Karen shook her head. Her face was wrinkled with worry. "I just don't know."

Ryan kept quiet. He had noticed Bethany was losing weight again. She was at least as thin as she had been when she went into the hospital last February. How had she managed to lose what she had regained so quickly? He glanced at Karen and knew she was remembering the argument they had had the night before about bringing Bethany in for another checkup. Karen had wanted to wait until summer so Bethany wouldn't miss any more school if Dr. Butler wanted to hospitalize her again. Ryan felt angry just thinking about it. He took his hands from Karen's.

It seemed to be forever before Dr. Butler came back out. He looked grave. "I don't have good news, I'm afraid. Bethany is a very sick young lady."

"You'll have to keep her then?" Karen asked. "She'll have to miss more school?"

Dr. Butler sat with them before he answered. "Let me explain what seems to be going on with her. She's lost all the weight she gained, from the looks of her. I suspect she's been taking laxatives and probably diuretics as well. Are you missing any?"

Karen looked at Ryan. "I haven't noticed."

"She's suffering kidney damage. In fact, I'm afraid her kidneys have pretty well shut down."

Karen shook her head, her eyes wide. "How do you get them started again?"

Ryan felt as if he were hearing all this from a great distance away, and it seemed everything was happening in slow motion, as it appears during car wrecks or other highly traumatic events.

"It's not that easy." Dr. Butler avoided her eyes. "I'm afraid she's in critical condition and is highly unstable."

"What are you trying to tell us?" Ryan asked.

"Bethany may be dying." Dr. Butler met his eyes, and Ryan could read a certainty there.

He was unable to say anything. Not a single word.

"You have to be wrong," Karen said in a rising voice. "That's just not possible. She went to school today! She wasn't sick then."

"It's possible she was. I've seen these girls do things that baffle the rest of us. We'll have to wait and see. I could be mistaken."

Ryan knew he wasn't. He was only trying to ease the blow. "How long?" His voice was gravelly.

"If her kidneys are completely shut down, it won't be long, I'm afraid. I'll stay here with you, of course." He patted Karen's hand and left.

Ryan stared after him. Bethany was dying?

"She went to school today," Karen repeated. "He's wrong."

Ashley was crying quietly. Karen automatically put her arms around her. They huddled together. Ryan felt isolated, completely alone. Karen looked up at him. "Call Chelsea."

"Now?" He glanced at his watch. "It's one-thirty in the morning."

"I want Chel. I need her."

Ryan went to find a telephone. He dialed the number by memory. When Chelsea answered he said, "Hi. It's me." He found he didn't want to say any more.

"Ryan? Is something wrong?"

"Yeah." He straightened and looked up at the ceiling to steady himself. "We've had to bring Bethany to the hospital. They have her in ICU. Could you come down?"

"I'll be right there."

He hung up. That was Chelsea. No questions, just "I'll be there." He went back to Karen. "She's coming."

When Chelsea arrived they filled her in on what had happened. Like them, Chelsea was astonished that it had happened so quickly. She hugged Karen and Ashley, and gave Ryan a look that made him feel included. He found himself relaxing now that she was here. Some of his hope returned.

By mid-morning they were allowed to see Bethany for five minutes. She lay like a doll in the bed, tubes and gauges everywhere. Her blond hair, the exact same shade as her mother's, seemed matted with sweat to her head. She didn't open her eyes.

"What's wrong with her skin?" Ashley asked in a whisper.

Ryan had already noticed. A sheen of sweat lay on Bethany's pale skin. It wasn't like anything he had ever seen before.

Dr. Butler was there with them. "It's called an anorexic frost," he said in a low voice. "I'll leave her with you for a while."

Ryan caught his arm. "What does that mean? Anorexic frost?"

Dr. Butler shook his head sadly. "I'm afraid it means that my diagnosis was correct. It's only a matter of hours."

Karen and Ashley were crying but trying to be quiet enough not to disturb Bethany. Ryan wasn't sure that was still possible. She appeared to be already dead. He went over beside her and touched her face. Sweat came off on his fingers.

"We're going to lose her," Karen said, leaning into his embrace. "We're going to lose my baby!"

He wanted to tell her it wasn't so, but couldn't. He held her, hoping he could be strong enough to do all that would have to be done in the next day or so. A part of him refused to believe any of this was true.

"I forgot to call Mother and Daddy!" Karen exclaimed suddenly. "Go call them, Ryan!"

He shook his head. "Let me be with her as long as we can. It's only five minutes." He knew Karen would blame him for this later. He didn't care. Nothing could take him from Bethany's side.

For the next twelve hours they sat with the Bakers and Chelsea in the waiting room of the ICU unit. For five minutes every hour one or two of them were allowed in to be with Bethany. She never seemed to know they were there or to be aware of anything. She only lay motionless, looking more and more waxy as the hours passed.

When it was over, it seemed impossible that the whole thing was real. Karen cried, but Ryan couldn't shake the feeling that this was some huge mistake, that she was only sleeping and soon would wake and be herself again.

Chelsea was also dry-eyed. She was in shock. He could

tell that. She had loved Bethany as much as she would
have loved her own child. The Bakers were stiff in their
grief, not letting any more of it show than was possible.
Ashley looked like a little child lost in a nightmare. Ryan
held her, and she cried as if her heart were breaking.

Decisions had to be made. A funeral home had to be
notified. Chelsea took care of all of it. Karen was unable
to do so, and Ryan had his hands full with her and Ashley.
The Bakers advised Chelsea, but seemed willing to let her
do it all.

Chapter Twenty-One

Ryan did well until he had to pick out Bethany's casket.
Chelsea had gone with him. She knew he was too calm, too
composed, and she was worried. Karen had fallen completely apart and was under sedation, her parents looking
after Ashley and handling all calls. Everyone had agreed it
was a good idea for Chelsea to go with Ryan.

She glanced at him as he quietly told the funeral director
who they were. The man had been expecting them. Chelsea
tried not to let herself remember that Bethany's body was
here in this silent, still place being prepared for burial.

"I was hoping you'd be able to come so quickly," the
man said solicitously. "It's best this way." He led them
toward the back of the building.

At the door to the room the undertaker had entered
Ryan hesitated. Coffins were lined up like cars on a lot,
each one slightly different than the next. Chelsea felt faint,
but she knew she wasn't suffering as much as he was. She
put her hand under his arm so he could feel her there
beside him. They went into the room together.

"This is a lovely model," the man said in his whispery
voice. He rubbed his long, bony hands together. "Over
there is another I think you'd like. What was her favorite
color?"

Ryan looked at him in confusion. "Her favorite color?
Pink, I think."

"It was pink," Chelsea agreed.

"Then I recommend this one." The man put his hand caressingly on a dusty rose and silver coffin beside them. He lifted the lid to show the pink satin lining and small pillow. "It's quite lovely, isn't it? Of course one hates having to choose one. And she was so young. Yes, I think pink would be a good choice, given her age."

"How much is it?" Chelsea asked bluntly. She was more than ready to be through with this, and she could see Ryan was having problems with being in this room. When the man answered, the amount staggered her. "Are you serious?"

He moved away with mincing steps. "Or we have this model. It's also dusty rose, but the fittings are stainless steel, not silver plate."

Chelsea tried not to frown. She had always hated the trappings of funerals and was convinced the majority of expenses were unnecessary. The price on this casket was far more in line with what Chelsea had expected Ryan and Karen to spend.

"We'll take this one," Ryan said, barely glancing at it. His voice broke, and he cleared his throat.

"It's difficult, I know," the man said. "It never comes easy, but when the person is so young . . ." He let the sentence remain unfinished.

They went back to his office, and Chelsea and Ryan sat opposite the undertaker at a large and impressive desk to make the other arrangements. As he listed the rental of cars and hearse, the minister's transportation to and from the burial site, and pall bearers, Chelsea's mind reeled. These matters had not been discussed or even considered. She wished Karen had been here to help in these decisions.

At last the man told Ryan the sum of all their choices, and Ryan stared at him for a moment before reaching for his checkbook. Chelsea found herself wondering how the fee had become so high and what people less able to pay did. Under the circumstances she couldn't challenge the fees, but she was positive the markup was beyond reason.

"I commend you on the choices you've made," the fu-

neral director said. "I couldn't have done better myself.
I'm sure you'll not regret any of them later."

"What happens next?" Ryan asked.

"We'll have your daughter ready for viewing by six
o'clock this evening. I recommend that only family come.
After you've all said your goodbyes, the public will be
welcomed in." His slightly ingratiating voice was beginning to abrade Chelsea's nerves.

"Six o'clock," Ryan said. "That's when we're usually all
eating dinner together." He looked up at the ceiling as he
tried to quell his emotions.

"If another time would be better . . ."

"No, no. Six is fine. I was just thinking aloud." Ryan
stood. "Is there anything else I need do?"

"No, everything is in our hands." The man gave him a
professional smile.

Chelsea was glad to escape to the outside. Ryan got in
her car and looked stonily ahead. "Are you all right?" she
asked.

He shook his head. "I can't believe any of this is happening. Two days ago Bethany . . ." His voice cracked, and
he paused before saying, "Bethany was alive and well. At
least we thought she was well." He looked out the window
as if the passing traffic mattered, or was even noticed, by
him. "Today . . . How do we go on from here? How do I
go back to work and come home in the evenings knowing
that she's not going to be there?"

Chelsea reached out and took his hand in both hers. "I
know. I wish there was something I could do to ease this
for you. You should have taken the medication the doctor
offered you."

"I couldn't do that. One of us had to make the arrangements. Karen wasn't able to come." Anger touched his
voice. "Chelsea, all I can think about is I saw Bethany
losing too much weight and I didn't force Karen to take
her to the doctor. Karen didn't want her to miss any more
school this year. Now . . ." Tears brimmed in his eyes and
overflowed. Ryan seemed not to notice. "I should have

forced her to take Bethany to Butler. Or I should have stayed home and done it myself!"

Chelsea held his hand tightly. "You didn't know. Neither of you did. If you'd thought anything like this might happen, you'd both have walked through fire to prevent it!"

"All I can remember is Karen saying that I was over-reacting. That Bethany could wait until school was out in two months. Two months! She didn't have two days!" His composure cracked and he leaned toward Chelsea. "God! I want to tear Karen apart!"

She held him as if he were a child and let him cry on her shoulder. "There, there," she soothed as she would a child who was crying. "I know it hurts. Karen didn't do this on purpose. You know that."

He held her close. "In my heart I know it, but I have this terrible anger toward her. All the time Bethany was getting thinner, Karen kept saying it could wait. That she didn't have time to run back and forth to the doctor's office every time she turned around. What the hell does she have to do that's so damned important she can't take her daughter to the doctor?"

He sat up and looked away. "I'm sorry. I shouldn't be saying these things to you."

"Yes, you should. You certainly can't say them to anyone else. Especially not to Karen. She's brokenhearted, Ryan, just as you are. As you said, you had no idea it was so serious. If anything, blame the doctor for not impressing on you the importance of watching Bethany closer."

"She had gotten so thin! When did it happen, Chelsea?" His voice was broken. "I knew she was losing weight again, but I hadn't noticed how bad it was."

"Neither did I. She wore clothing to conceal it from us. She knew you'd put her back in the hospital if we realized she was back where she started."

"But we should have known! I guess I was afraid to see it."

Chelsea put her arms around him. "We all were. I'm

also to blame. I should have paid closer attention. I thought since she was hospitalized so recently it would take a while before she got to this stage again. I feel guilty, too." Her own voice was unsteady.

Ryan hugged her. "Don't blame yourself. None of us should. It doesn't change anything." He held her close, letting her hurt for a few unguarded moments. They both knew they would have to be strong for the others when they returned home.

The day passed in misery for Chelsea. Like Ryan, she was finding it difficult to believe that Bethany was really gone. Life had taken on a dreamlike quality, and she had to remind herself occasionally that events were real.

The funeral was held the second day. Ryan's parents and brother, along with his wife and children, had flown down from Colorado. The Bakers surrendered their extra bedrooms to them, though the families had never been close. Chelsea was holding her breath that Cecilia Baker would refrain from offending Mrs. Morgan and that Karen would get through it all without crumbling.

Chelsea had never seen a more moving service. The chapel at the funeral home was packed with Bethany's classmates and friends, as well as distant cousins on her mother's side. The front of the chapel was entirely filled with flowers, and more displays stood in the vestibule. Chelsea saw almost no dry eyes. Bethany's death, coming unexpectedly to one so young, had touched everyone.

Karen was doing better than Chelsea had expected. She was deathly pale and her eyes were haunted, but she wasn't hysterical and was able to sit through the service without breaking down completely. Ryan, who looked as if he had aged ten years in the past two days, was more silent than usual. Karen seemed to agree with all the decisions he and Chelsea had made regarding the funeral. Her only stipulation was that Chelsea sit with the family. No one objected.

It was all Chelsea could do to file past the casket and look down at Bethany lying within it. Later she was glad she had. The undertaker had done a better than average job, and Bethany's sunken cheeks seemed rounded and pink with life. She appeared to be asleep rather than dead. Her blond hair was combed loose on the pillow, and Chelsea could imagine her reaching up to toss it behind her in one of her typical mannerisms.

When Chelsea moved away, she was crying. She put her arm around Karen, and for a minute feared neither of them would be able to control their grief.

She rode to the cemetery with Ryan's parents and stood beside Karen as the minister delivered the final words. A cool March breeze lifted her hair and tugged at her skirt. It was much too beautiful a day for them to be at a burial. This was the sort of day Bethany had loved.

Chelsea put her arm around Ashley and the girl leaned into her. Everyone had more or less been ignoring Ashley what with all that was happening, and she had kept to herself, not being one to cry easily in public. Chelsea hugged her and felt Ashley tremble. The child wasn't doing as well with her grief as they had all assumed, Chelsea realized. She kept her arm around Ashley's shoulders, and the girl didn't pull away.

After what seemed to be forever, the minister finished the service and the mourners started to leave the grave site. No one wanted to linger until the casket was lowered into the grave. That was more reality than those present could handle.

Back at the Morgans' house, Karen went straight to her bedroom. Chelsea followed her.

"I can't talk to anyone else right now," Karen said as she lay down on the bed and covered her eyes. "I can't handle any more."

"Do you want me to leave you alone?"

"No."

Chelsea sat on the edge of the bed. "You did well. I was worried about you."

"It hasn't been easy. Not for any of us."

"No. It hasn't."

Karen sighed. "Mother will be back here in a few minutes, demanding that I get up and come speak to friends and family who brought food over."

"I'll do that for you, if you'd like."

"Would you?" Karen opened her eyes a bit to look at Chelsea. "I just can't pretend any longer that I'm holding up well or that I'm handling this or that life goes on." She rubbed her eyes. "All I want to do is sit on the floor and cry."

"I know."

After a while Karen said, "I've learned one thing, though. Life is too short."

"Yes."

"And too precarious to let it drift by. I'm not going to do that anymore."

Chelsea looked down at her. She knew Karen was hurting deeply and needed to talk, but she didn't know what, if anything, her friend was going to say.

"I'm going to live to the fullest from now on. I owe that to Bethany."

There was a knock at the door, and without waiting for Karen to answer, Cecilia opened it. "You have company arriving, Karen. You can lie down later."

"She needs to rest. I'll come down in her place," Chelsea said.

Karen sat up. Her eyes met Chelsea's. "No, I have to do it. Besides, it will keep me from thinking."

Cecilia held the door until they passed through.

By mid-April Karen felt able to go on with her life. Though at first guilty that she was alive and Bethany was not, she gradually became aware that her grief was no longer a sharp pain but a dull ache, and she started doing things she had once enjoyed. Among the first activities she reinstated were her trips to the health club.

"We've missed you," Hank said. "I was really sorry to hear about your daughter."

"Thank you." Karen swallowed down the too-familiar

sorrow the words invoked. "We're putting our lives back to normal."

"Would you like to meet for dinner at Nevilles? If it's too soon, I understand." His strong hands were massaging away her tension with practiced ease.

Karen hesitated for only an instant. "I'd rather come to your place, if you don't mind." She held her breath as she waited for his answer.

"I thought you weren't going to go there, that you wanted to keep it all on the up and up. I don't want you to think I'm pressuring you at a time when you're vulnerable."

"No. I've made some decisions lately about life. I'm tired of living for everyone else. I'm not going to be young forever, and I don't want to look back and have regrets." In the past few weeks she had regained most of the weight she'd lost, and this had added to her depression and to her resolve to change her life. "I want to come to your apartment."

"How about next Wednesday? I'm off that afternoon."

"During the day?" She hadn't expected this. She and Ryan never made love in the daytime, not even when they'd been newlyweds. Karen had always been too shy.

"Sure. That way you don't have to do so much explaining. Your husband will be at work then. Right?"

"Yes, he will. I suppose I could come over then."

"Great. I'll be expecting you."

Karen was silent as she contemplated the move she had just made. This was unlike anything she had ever thought she would do. But this was living. She had heard enough gossip to know that most affairs were conducted during daylight hours when husbands were safely at work, and she knew from her therapy that an aversion to lovemaking in the daytime wasn't the norm. If everyone else could do it, so could she.

On Wednesday Karen spent an hour putting on makeup and deciding what to wear. Nothing seemed right. She had no idea what was appropriate to wear to a lover's house.

The notion of calling Joyce to ask, made her laugh. This was one time she would have to figure things out for herself.

She finally settled on a simple dress basic enough for almost any daytime occasion. She brushed her hair back from her face. Lately she had started dyeing it, and she thought that made her look younger. The weight was a problem, but it wasn't as if Hank wasn't already familiar with the shape of her body, she reminded herself.

She drove to his apartment and circled the block twice before she got the nerve to park where he had told her to leave the car. It wasn't visible from the street there, and his apartment was entered from an inner patio so she could come and go without being seen. All the same, Karen felt conspicuous as she crossed the patio and knocked on his door.

Hank opened it right away and grinned at seeing her. He wore only jeans. She had never seen him without a shirt, and she was impressed by his array of muscles.

His apartment was small. She had forgotten how tiny some places could be. It had a couch and a chair and a TV, but not much else. Several amateurish sketches and watercolors were hanging on the walls. They seemed to have been done by the same hand. He saw her looking at them and said, "Naomi did those. She's pretty good, isn't she?"

Karen looked at them more closely. They showed some promise, but were a long way from what she would have termed good art. "Nice." She glanced at him, then back at the pictures. "Are you still seeing Naomi?"

He shrugged. "From time to time. We're also friends."

Karen didn't want that statement clarified. It implied there was something in addition to the friendship.

"My bedroom is in here." He took her hand and led her toward the doorway.

She hadn't expected him to be quite this forward about the reason she was here. "Do you have any wine?"

He thought for a minute. "I think so. Would you like a glass now?"

"Please." She was so nervous sweat stood out on her upper lip. It suddenly occurred to her that she didn't know the first thing about having an affair.

Hank went into his tiny kitchen and found a wineglass stamped with the name of a popular restaurant and a bottle of opened wine. It was a cheaper brand than Karen had ever bought, but she didn't care. She would welcome anything that would relax her.

"Hey, there's no need to be so uptight," he said, as he handed her the glass. "We aren't going to do anything you've never done before."

"I hadn't thought of it like that."

"This is your first affair!" He grinned. "That's right, isn't it?"

"Of course." She felt slightly annoyed that he had assumed it might not be. "I told you a long time ago, I don't see other men."

"I know, but I thought you meant you didn't right now. Hey, this is really special!" His infectious grin was working along with the wine.

Karen relaxed somewhat. "I feel foolish being here. I mean, we've never talked about it, but I'm older than you are—and married. I have no right to be here."

"I know you're older. I don't care. And you have a right to be anywhere you choose to be."

"How can you be so perfect?" she asked as the wine warmed her all the way through. "How can you not mind my being older and overweight and married to someone else?"

"It's easy. I just don't have a lot of hangups." His smile was disarming. "How's the wine?"

"Better than I expected." She smiled back at him.

"Let me just show you the bedroom. You can still leave if you'd like. That's one thing I want understood. You can always leave or say no." He gave her a measuring look as if he wanted to be absolutely certain she understood that.

She wondered if something in his past made him particularly careful on this point. "I understand."

His bedroom was even smaller than the living room. The king-sized bed filled it almost wall to wall. "How did you manage to get it in here?" she asked.

"It wasn't so hard." He pressed on the mattress, and waves rippled across the surface. "It's a water bed. I put it in place and just filled it up."

"A water bed?" She pressed the mattress experimentally. "I've never been on a water bed in my life!"

Hank grinned. "You're in for a treat." He took the glass of wine from her and started kissing her neck.

Karen forgot that she wanted to object. His lips were too warm and were already stirring fires in her that she hadn't known existed. She had skipped lunch, and the wine had gone straight to her head. As the room spun lazily around her; she held to Hank to steady herself. Beneath her fingers his hard muscles were hot and firm. Karen quickly forgot that she didn't like to make love during daylight.

Chapter Twenty-Two

For the next two weeks Karen seemed to be floating on soap bubbles. Every time the phone rang, she would jump and then hurry to answer it. She had told Hank not to call her at home, but occasionally he did. The extra element of danger was like an aphrodisiac to her.

After nearly fifteen years of marriage, she had finally discovered that lovemaking could be enjoyable. Hank wasn't a better lover than Ryan—he was more selfish and less attentive to her pleasure—but perversely Karen found him exciting. He was apart from her normal life, the affair could end at any moment, they might be discovered. Intercourse wasn't the thrill for her—it was the secrecy.

At first Hank was all she could wish for. He called daily and they met several times a week. Karen would pretend to go out for milk or bread and would go to his apartment instead for a few fevered minutes on Hank's rippling bed. After a couple of weeks, however, she noticed a cooling in his eagerness.

He told her he no longer had any time for the other things he enjoyed doing. Karen had even started slipping over at night, so he wasn't getting enough sleep either. She couldn't understand his attitude. It was her opinion that men wanted sex every hour of every day, and she saw no reason why Hank shouldn't fit that stereotype.

"I can't see you tonight," he said. "I have to run some errands."

"If I had a key to your apartment, I could be waiting for you when you come back," Karen whispered into the phone. She knew Ryan and Ashley were watching TV in the next room. Her heart was racing at her daring.

"I don't give a key to my apartment to anyone."

"Is someone there with you?" she asked. "I thought I heard someone behind you."

"I'm watching TV."

Karen frowned. She didn't believe him. "Why can't you run your errands later? I can only stay a few minutes."

"Look, I have a life of my own, you know." Hank sounded peevish. It made her want to hug him.

Karen glanced at her watch. "I can be there in ten minutes and be gone in half an hour."

"I have to go. I'll call you tomorrow."

"All right. But I'll miss you." She heard footsteps coming toward the door and hung up. A few more exchanges and she might have convinced him. She glanced over her shoulder at Ryan.

"Were you on the phone? I thought I heard someone talking in here?"

"Then I must have been. I haven't started talking to myself," she said testily. She hated it when he asked questions like that. It was as if he were checking on her. Karen almost laughed at what Ryan would think if he learned she was having an affair.

"Would you like some popcorn? Ashley and I are making some."

"No, thanks." She looked thoughtfully at the phone. "Actually, I was talking to Chelsea. I need to run over there for a minute. I won't be gone long."

"Drive carefully." He went through to the kitchen and left her alone.

Karen got her purse and drove to Hank's apartment. Instead of going to the door, she parked in a space where she could see it clearly and waited. After several minutes his door opened and a dark-haired girl stepped out. Karen recognized Naomi at once, and jealousy surged through her.

Hank stood in the doorway, talking. The pair were laughing, and Naomi reached out several times to touch his chest or arm. He leaned closer and kissed her as passionately as he had ever kissed Karen, patted her on the bottom, and shut the door.

Karen felt heartsick. Naomi had been there when she'd called. Had they discussed her? Was that what they were laughing about?

She started her car and drove away before Naomi could come into the parking lot. She didn't care if she was seen; but she didn't want to face Naomi at that moment. She couldn't guarantee she wouldn't yank the younger woman's hair out.

She couldn't go home too quickly, so she drove to Chelsea's. She rarely went there at night. Even though Chelsea thought it a perfectly safe area, Karen always thought someone might be lurking by the outside stairway or around the corner of the building. Fortunately, Chelsea was home.

"Hi. Can I come in?"

"Sure." Chelsea glanced past her. "You're alone?"

"I need to talk to you." Karen looked around. "You've done a lot with the place." It was true. Chelsea had placed potted plants in corners and had used large ones as room dividers. Some of her bigger canvases also served to divide one section from another. Her furniture was tasteful, and the entire place was spotless, even the end devoted to her painting.

"I needed to keep my mind busy."

"Have you heard anything about the divorce?"

Chelsea nodded. "I'm to go before a judge in two weeks. Will you go with me? I'm already nervous. My lawyer says Lorne probably won't be there, but he could be wrong."

"I'll go." Karen automatically wondered if this would preclude her seeing Hank that day. She hoped not.

Chelsea sat on one of the two couches and curled her feet under her. "So, what's going on?"

"Not much, I guess." Karen sat on the other couch and crossed her legs.

"Are you still missing Bethany as much? Maybe you should go back into therapy for a while. I expected you to."

"It's not that. Of course I still miss her. She was my baby. I'll think about her every day for the rest of my life. But this is something else."

"Should I make coffee? You look as if it's serious."

"No, it keeps me awake if I drink it this late. You know, it's funny, we've told each other everything for most of our lives, but I can't seem to say this."

"Now you're worrying me. Nothing wrong with Ryan or Ashley, is there?"

"No, no. There's no point in your trying to guess. You'll never hit it." She took a deep breath. "I've been seeing another man. There! I've said it!"

Chelsea stared at her. "You're not serious."

Karen found herself smiling. "Yes, I am. He's the man I told you about earlier."

"I thought you decided not to go through with that!"

"I did. But then Bethany died and I realized how fast life can slip away. I don't want to be an old woman and discover I never really lived. What do I have to fill my time? Housework and the social scene. I was living in a vacuum!"

"You're in a happy marriage! Karen, how could you risk your marriage for this coach?"

"Hank's not a coach. He's a gym instructor at my health club."

"Whatever!"

"If you had ever met him, you'd understand." Karen picked up a throw pillow and held it on her lap. "Haven't you noticed how much weight I've lost? It's because I have an incentive now."

"There are other ways of gaining an incentive!"

"We see each other nearly every day, and on the days we can't get together, we talk on the phone. It's so exciting, Chel! I feel younger than I have in years."

"Don't give me any details. I don't want to know."

"I drove to his apartment before I came over here."

"Can't you hear me? If Ryan ever asks me about this, I want to be able to say I know nothing about it. If you're going to throw away everything you have, I don't want to be an accomplice."

"But I need your advice."

Chelsea spread her hands, palms up. "When did I get to be an expert on having an affair? I've never had one."

"You ran around a lot in college. It can't be much different. My problem is this: I think Hank is seeing someone else."

"Karen, use your brain! What does it matter if he is? You're *living* with another man. Your husband!"

"That's entirely different. When I called Hank, he said he was alone, but I thought I heard someone else over there. It didn't sound like the TV to me. So I told Ryan I was coming here, and I drove to his apartment and waited. Not fifteen minutes had passed when a girl came out!"

Chelsea stared at her. "You went to his apartment and spied on him? We didn't do things like that in college!"

"How else could I have known for sure? So what should I do?"

"You should tell this Hank person you'll never see him again and then behave yourself."

Karen frowned. "You're the last person I'd have expected to be so prudish."

"What's that supposed to mean?"

"This is me, Chel. You're forgetting I know all your secrets. You haven't exactly lived in a convent. Especially that last year of college."

Chelsea turned away. "Sometimes that year is a blur to me. It's hard to believe I was ever that young and naive."

"We all were. We were brought up to be. Just the same,

you may have been naive, but you certainly weren't innocent."

Chelsea frowned at her. "I had hoped you'd never bring that up."

"It's not something I'm ever likely to forget." Karen felt a coldness in her middle. At times she didn't like Chelsea very much, and that was especially true when she remembered Chelsea had once been pregnant with Ryan's baby. She shook her head. "I didn't mean to bring that up. Not really. I only meant to illustrate that you would know more about having an affair than I would. I mean, I rarely dated anyone but Ryan."

"Sorry to disappoint you, but I wouldn't help you with this even if I'd had affairs with many different men. You have a good husband who doesn't drink or beat you or run around with other women. You have a daughter who needs you now more than ever. It's hard for me to dredge up much sympathy for you."

"That's easy for you to say. You've never been bored a day in your life."

"Of course I have."

"You were never tempted to have an affair, at any rate. If you had been, you'd be more sympathetic."

Chelsea looked away.

"Why aren't you denying it? Have you ever been tempted by a married man?"

Chelsea got up and went to the area she had designated as a kitchen. "I told you, I don't have affairs. Are you sure you don't want any coffee?"

"I can't stay. Ryan thinks I've been here the entire time. I need to be getting home. Will you do this much for me? If he ever calls, looking for me, will you tell him I just left and that I had an errand to run before coming home? I'm never at Hank's for very long. This will be a good cover for me."

"You're not listening." Chelsea faced Karen across the width of the loft. "I won't help you at all in this. Not at all."

"Fine." Karen drew her lips into a straight line. "All I can say is it's a good thing I didn't take that attitude when you needed me that time in college. What if I had told you I wouldn't drive you to the clinic? It seems to me you might remind yourself of that whenever you're acting selfish."

"You'd better go. I'm afraid we're both about to say things we may regret."

Karen glared at her. "I never say things I regret. You owe me, and I'm only asking to be repaid."

"Friends don't keep score."

"That's very clever. It would make a lovely motto," Karen snapped. "But it's not true. Everyone keeps score. Friends most of all."

"What are you saying? That if I don't help you run around on Ryan, you won't consider me your friend anymore? You can't mean that."

"Why can't I?"

"Because it's crazy! I'm giving you good advice. If you'd just stop to think, you'd realize that."

"You never used to parent me. You used to say everyone should follow their own star and make their own rules."

"These aren't the 'seventies. The world has changed."

"And I've changed, too. I'm tired of being a housewife. I want some excitement in my life. You're about to be divorced and can date anyone you please. Why should I sit at home and let you have all the fun?"

"Because you're married and I'm not! You can't date just because I can! That doesn't make any sense!"

"Fine. I don't make any sense. I'll try to remember that next time you ask me to do you a favor."

"Karen!"

"Goodbye, Chelsea. I've got to go home to my perfect family and be perfectly bored all evening with my perfect life." Karen slammed out the door. As she drove home, she reflected that her friendship with Chelsea wasn't what it used to be.

* * *

"I'm glad you were able to meet me for lunch," Ryan said when the waiter left their table. "I need to talk to someone about Karen, and you know her better than anyone."

Chelsea glanced at him warily. She wouldn't lie to protect Karen's affair, but she would to prevent hurting Ryan. "What about Karen?"

"I'm worried about her. It started just before we lost Bethany." He paused as if the words still hurt too much. "She's acting differently."

"Differently in what way?"

"It's as if she always has something else on her mind, no matter what she's doing. And she's losing weight."

"Karen has been on a diet all her life, practically."

"Yes, but now it's working. I'll bet she's lost fifteen, maybe twenty, pounds since the funeral."

"I've noticed. She's looking good."

Ryan shook his head impatiently. "I don't care if she loses weight or not, as long as she stays healthy. What I can't figure out is why!"

"Grief can do that."

"Yes, but Karen's response to unhappiness has always been to head for the kitchen, not to avoid it. I don't know how to explain this. It's like she has a secret she's always thinking about. Does that make any sense?"

It made too much sense in view of Chelsea's last conversation with her friend. "You must be imagining it. Maybe the three of you should take a vacation. Get away from everything for a while. School will be out in a week or so. You love the Blue Ridge. You might be able to catch the last of the rhododendrons in bloom."

"Karen says she's allergic to everything there."

"She could take a medication for her allergy." Chelsea tried to keep the edge from her voice. She was tired of seeing Karen make her entire family revolve around her.

Ryan sounded tired of that, too. "She says allergy medication makes her too sleepy. Her idea of a perfect vacation is the Bahamas or some other spot that's full of tourists."

Chelsea managed not to voice what she thought about that.

Ryan smiled. "I can hear what you're thinking. Marriage ought to be give and take—both ways. Right?"

Reluctantly Chelsea nodded.

"I'm not sure why I let things get this way. I've always hated conflict. At first it was easier to give in to her because we were newlyweds and she was still so sweet and seemed so terribly vulnerable. I wanted her to have anything she wanted."

"I know. She affected me the same way." Chelsea smiled at the memory. "I can't tell you how many times I've confronted someone who was frightening her or trying to bully her."

"What I didn't realize," Ryan continued, "was that she's about as vulnerable as a pit bull. She may look and sound soft, but once she gets something in her head, that's the way it has to be, no matter what anyone else may say or feel. It's not easy living with someone like that."

Chelsea glanced up as the waiter brought their food. When he was gone, she said, "I know. But for some reason we both chose to live with it. Neither of us will ever abandon her."

Ryan seemed thoughtful as he cut into his steak.

"How's Ashley?"

He shook his head. "We're having problems with her. I'm sure it's a result of losing Bethany, but she's doing all she can to stay in trouble. The school called me at work last week. It seems Ashley has an unusual number of absences."

"Has she been sick?"

"Not a single day. I told them she hadn't missed more than a couple of days all year, but the office has a stack of excused absences, most of them with my name on them."

"I don't understand."

"Ashley's been cutting school and forging my signature."

"Why yours? Why not Karen's?"

"I assume it's because Karen on occasion sends notes to school, so it would be easier for the office to check her signature. I went by to verify that these were not my signatures—or even close. The office says they'll call if another one shows up, but school will be out soon."

"You'll have all summer to let her work through whatever is going on with her."

"I blamed it on Bethany's death, but many of the excuses were dated before March. It's just that the absences have increased since then."

Chelsea was concerned. She had noticed an evasiveness in Ashley. "I'll talk to her, if you'd like."

"Thanks. I'd appreciate it. I don't know how much good it will do. She's become so closed off to Karen and me. It's like she's rebelling against everything." He smiled faintly. "And she's not even a teenager yet. Not until July fifth."

"I always said she was precocious." Chelsea smiled. "It's probably no more than a stage she's going through. After all, Bethany was so good, you were spoiled. I think all kids rebel at some point in their lives. Otherwise, they'd never leave home."

"Maybe. It's just hard to be philosophical about it when you have to live with it. If Karen would come down from the clouds, maybe she could deal with it. After all, she doesn't work. She could watch Ashley more closely than I can."

"She stays busy. I doubt she's home much more than you are. Her calendar looks like a memo pad—something written on every square."

"I know." Ryan pushed the food aside. "How did I get here, Chelsea? When did it happen? I never set out to have a family that's fraying apart and a daughter that makes James Dean look subservient. It's like rolling downhill and gaining momentum. I feel there's not a damned thing I can do to stop it!"

Chelsea put down her fork. "You're all going through a rough time right now. The loss of a child isn't something you can pull out of in two months. It's going to take a while."

"Maybe this isn't connected with Bethany, but you could be right. I don't know."

"Have you given more thought to getting some family counseling?"

"Of course. Karen says she's too busy, and Ashley says it's all bunk, that she won't go, and if I force her to, she won't talk or listen."

"Well, that pretty well sums that up. What about counseling for you?"

"I think I should make an appointment. I can't feel much worse than I do now. Any change would be an improvement."

"I think you should see to it as soon as you go back to work. Before you forget it or find a reason to put it off."

Ryan nodded. "I'll do it. What about you? I know how close you were to Bethany. Are you handling it okay? You've been pretty much overlooked in all this."

"I'm handling it pretty well. I've always thought of Bethany and Ashley as being like my own daughters. It hasn't been easy."

"No. Not for any of us."

Chelsea let the waiter take her plate away. "Do you want me to talk to Karen?"

He thought for a minute. "Have you two had an argument? I mentioned having you over for dinner the other night, and she made it clear she didn't want to cook for company. You haven't been considered company in fifteen years."

"We had a disagreement. It was nothing, really. She's probably still angry with me, but it won't last." Chelsea wondered if this was true. She and Karen had argued before, but they'd always made up in the next day or so.

This time when Chelsea had called, Karen had been cool to the point of rudeness.

"Can you tell me what the argument was about?"

Chelsea shook her head. "No, I can't. And I don't want you to ask Karen about it, either. It's something we have to work out ourselves."

"Okay. If you say so." He was clearly puzzled. "I'll try talking to Ashley."

"You probably won't recognize her. That's another part of her rebellion. She has the worst haircut I've ever seen. She came in with it last night. She's shaved the sides of her head and left the rest of her hair long. When she pulls what's left back in a ponytail, her appearance defies description."

Chelsea smiled. "Now that's rebellion!"

Ryan managed to smile, too. "I always feel better after talking to you. Maybe instead of making appointments with a counselor, I should make them with you."

"You couldn't afford me," she said with a laugh. "I just sold a painting and know my worth."

"You did? Which one?"

"River of Time. The one I had on exhibit at the Franklin Building."

"See? I told you you wouldn't be blackballed forever."

"Signing the canvas with my married name didn't hurt, either. Maybe everyone has forgotten Jason's lies about me, but I'm not taking any chances." She leaned closer and whispered, "I got a bundle!"

He laughed. "Art for art's sake? I can remember when you said you didn't care if anyone ever paid you, as long as you could create."

"I was young and on a scholarship. Now I'm paying bills and trying to build a career."

"Is the court date set?"

She nodded. "It seems strange to think I'll soon be Chelsea Cavin again. It doesn't seem real."

"Do you want me to go with you? I'll take time off if you need me."

She shook her head. "Karen said she'd go, but since she's still so upset, I'm afraid that's out of the question. No, I have to do this alone. Thanks anyway. Can you imagine what a field day Lorne would have if you were there with me? He might implicate you."

"I don't care."

"Karen would. Besides, I want to do this myself. It's important to me."

"Okay. If you change your mind, call me."

She nodded. "You're a good friend, Ryan. I don't know what I'd have done without you and Karen through all this."

He smiled back at her. "We'll always stick together. Thick and thin. The Three Musketeers to the end."

Chelsea thought of the last conversation she'd had with Karen and made her tone sound optimistic. "I hope so."

Chapter Twenty-Three

By June Karen knew Hank was seeing Naomi regularly. More than once she had watched from the parking lot as the young woman came out of his apartment. Karen had always been jealous, and this competition was too blatant for her to ignore. Worse, it made her feel used and middle-aged. So before Hank could tell her it was over, she broke up with him and canceled her membership in the health club.

She was slimmer than she had been since college and knew her parents finally approved of her appearance. Ryan was also complimentary, but she discounted what he said. Ryan had even been complimentary when she'd worn dresses several sizes larger. More than ever before, she viewed her husband as a necessary inconvenience. He paid the bills, made few sexual demands on her, and was loved by Ashley. He had his place in the household and she had hers.

In the days that followed her breakup with Hank, Karen was despondent. Ryan and Chelsea both noticed and expressed concern, but Karen didn't confide in either of them. Since Chelsea had refused to aid her in her affair, Karen had cooled toward her. Unfortunately, Karen found herself reverting to her old method of combating depression and boredom; she was eating more. In order to keep her figure, she started looking around for a replacement for Hank.

She found him at a party given by her parents. The gathering was to celebrate the wedding anniversary of a friend and business acquaintance of her father. At the last minute Ashley had refused to go, and Karen had arrived angry at having to leave her behind. "When I was a girl, I never would have refused to go to a party Mother wanted me to attend," she fumed as Ryan opened the car door and she stepped out onto the street in front of her parents' house.

"You and Ashley aren't much alike," he said. "I hoped she'd come, but neither of us wanted her to come here wearing what she had on."

"She dresses as if she's on her way to a Hell's Angels meeting." Karen glanced up and down the street before crossing. "She isn't leaving the house, is she? Does she have a date?"

"If she did, she didn't admit it. She said she was going to stay there and watch TV."

"Why is it I don't believe her? She's such a disappointment." Karen thought about Bethany, who had dressed correctly and who had always been so gentle and sweet. She couldn't understand why it had to be Bethany they'd lost. At once she felt guilty.

"She's just going through a phase. She'll outgrow it."

They went up the drive and opened the front door. A polite murmur of conversation reached them. A number of people, all expensively attired, were mingling in her parents' living room. Several of them glanced at Karen and Ryan as they entered, then smiled in recognition before resuming their conversations. It was the sort of party Karen loved.

As Cecilia met them at the door, Karen smiled apologetically. "I'm so sorry we're late, Mother, but we had some problems with Ashley just as we were about to leave."

"She's not with you?"

"She had previous plans." Karen knew her mother would never understand Ashley's preferring to watch TV

to coming to one of her parties. Karen couldn't understand it either. "It's a nice crowd."

"Mingle," her mother said. "The Dreyers are over there
by the piano. Their son has come with them. You remember Mark, don't you?"

"Mark? I don't think so."

"Of course you do. Go speak to them." With a cool
smile at Ryan, Cecilia faded back into the crowd.

Karen made her way across the room. She recognized
the Dreyers at once. She had known them casually for
years. A young man who appeared to be in his mid-
twenties stood with them. The resemblance to Mr. Dreyer
was strong enough to tell her this was his son. Karen put
out her hand. "Mr. Dreyer, Mrs. Dreyer, how good to see
you again. Congratulations on your anniversary."

"Thank you, Karen. You remember Mark, I trust?"

Karen glanced around and discovered that Ryan hadn't
followed her. "Mark. Yes, of course," she lied smoothly.
"It's been a long time."

"Yes, it has."

"Is your husband with you?" Mrs. Dreyer asked.

"I seem to have lost him in the crowd. He's here somewhere." She shrugged to indicate that she misplaced Ryan
often. "He's probably talking to Todd and Joyce."

"We were so sorry to hear about the loss of your daughter," Mrs. Dreyer said in a sorrowful voice. "So young!"

"Yes, thank you. She was."

Mark had regarded her steadily all this time. "My wife
is here, too," he said. "I'd like you to meet her."

"It will be my pleasure." Nothing was further from the
truth. Karen found Mark interesting, and she didn't particularly care to meet his wife.

"Do go find her," Mrs. Dreyer said. "She's probably
lost in the crowd and having one of her panic attacks." She
laughed as if she didn't give credence to panic attacks.

Mark took Karen's elbow and steered her away from his
parents. When they were safely out of range, he said,

"Have we met before? I have to confess I don't remember it."

Karen laughed. "Neither do I. I suspect our parents know each other so well they just assume we know each other by osmosis."

He took her to the punch bowl. "I would have remembered it if we had met. You're not the sort I'd forget."

"Why, Mark, are you flirting with me?" She cast a sideways glance at him and smiled. "With your wife in the same room?"

"Are you flirting back? With your husband here somewhere?"

Karen laughed softly. He knew how to play the game. "Do you live in Dallas?"

"I do now. The company I was with in Houston folded unexpectedly. I thought it would be a good idea for me to come here to start over. I've had enough hurricanes to last me for a while."

"I like Houston. It's so near the beach."

"I'll probably end up dividing my time between the two places. My wife grew up in Houston, and her family still lives there."

"What sort of work do you do?"

"I'm an accountant. I was hoping to get on with Data-Comp."

"Daddy's company? I know they have accountants working there. I really don't know much about the firm."

Mark smiled and exuded charm. "Maybe you could put in a good word for me."

"I believe I could." Karen assessed him rapidly. He was slightly older than Hank and infinitely more sophisticated. Mark fit into her world and wouldn't care for a gum-popping fitness instructor in the least.

"I'd be forever grateful." His dark hazel eyes promised gratitude and more.

"Would you?" She let her voice become sultry and seductive. "How grateful?"

"Enough to ask you to show me the town."

"You and your wife?"

"No, just me."

Karen smiled. She hadn't felt this alive since the first days with Hank. "I'll see what I can do."

"Mark, I've looked everywhere for you," a voice said from behind Karen.

She turned to find a small woman gazing pitifully at Mark. She had dark, straight hair cut in an unflattering pageboy, and her dress, though expensive, didn't fit correctly. She looked completely out of her element.

Mark's smile grew strained. "This is my wife, Polly. Polly, this is Karen Baker."

"Karen Morgan," she corrected. "Baker is my maiden name."

"Then your parents are the ones giving the party?" Polly asked. "They're very nice."

"Thank you." Karen looked back at Mark. "It's been nice meeting you. I'll go speak to Daddy about that matter."

He smiled and gave her a promising look. "I'd really appreciate it."

She threaded her way through the guests until she found her father. He was engaged in conversation with several other men. When Karen stepped up to his side, he beamed down at her. "I was hoping you and Ryan had come. He's with you, isn't he?"

"He's here somewhere. May I talk to you a minute?"

Fulton excused himself from his companions. "What is it?"

"I just met the Dreyers' son, Mark. Did you know he's looking for a job? He's in the process of relocating from Houston."

"He is? No, I didn't know."

"He's hoping to join the staff of DataComp. He's an accountant."

Fulton glanced around thoughtfully. "I've known his father for years. I wonder if the boy is anything like him."

"I was impressed with him. His wife is here, too," she

added so it wouldn't sound as if she were inappropriately interested in him. "She's a mousey little thing."

"Yes, I met her when they arrived. The boy looks a great deal like his father, doesn't he? It was like seeing the clock turn back."

"Do you have an opening in the accounting pool?"

"I just might have. We're about to lose a man. Retirement, you know. I'll go talk to the boy."

"I believe he's still over by the punch bowl." Karen felt quite pleased with herself as her father went in search of Mark. She didn't doubt for a minute that Mark would want to demonstrate his appreciation.

Because of the years away from painting, Chelsea had more objectivity and she could see that something was missing from her canvases. She just couldn't tell what it was. When she heard Jean-Paul Armand, a noted French artist, was giving a week-long seminar at SMU, she immediately signed up.

She hadn't expected to be more interested in the artist than in his paintings. Jean-Paul was blond, and his blue eyes seemed to see right into her soul. She told herself it was only because he'd been trained to notice and record every detail in what he saw, but she knew it was more. He was interested in her.

By the third class Chelsea knew it wasn't her imagination. Jean-Paul spent as much time watching her as he allowed for all the others in the class. When the class was over, he came to her and said, "Would you like to have coffee? Perhaps you are not in too great a hurry to go home?" His slightly accented words touched her heart.

"I'd like that. I'm in no rush."

He smiled, and his teeth were white and straight. "You have no jealous husband who will come looking for us?"

"I'm divorced."

"We have something else in common. So am I."

"Something else?" she asked.

"Our art."

"Of course." She closed her notebook and put away her pen. "I've been taking a lot of notes."

"So I have noticed. You seemed to be writing reams." His peculiarly piercing eyes met hers. "Were my words so interesting?"

"Extremely." She glanced around to find the other students had left. "Where would you like to go for coffee?"

He shrugged. "I know so little of the city. You choose."

"I know just the place. We can take my car."

Jean-Paul laughed. "So American. You take charge so easily. I place myself in your hands."

Chelsea drove to a small cafe not far from the campus. It was popular with the college crowd and stayed open almost all night. "I'm learning so much from your class," she said when they had ordered. "I never thought of using the techniques you described. Before I signed up, I was afraid I would have forgotten how to study."

"It can't have been so long since you were in school."

"I'm thirty-seven."

"So blunt! I know of no other woman who admits to being over thirty, no matter how old she may really be."

"I don't believe in age. Besides, I'm not worried about growing older."

He looked as if he were fascinated by her every word. "You're so different from anyone else I've met." He reached out and touched her hair, which she wore braided over one shoulder. "I'd love to paint you."

She studied his face to see if he really meant that. "I'd be flattered! But you won't be here long enough to do a painting. Your class is half over. Are you staying in Dallas afterward?"

"No, sadly I mustn't. I have another seminar scheduled in Nashville. Perhaps I will learn to write country and western songs while I am there? Perhaps I will write one for you. Yes?"

"You do that." The waiter brought their coffee, and Chelsea sipped it carefully. "This is hot!"

"Then we must wait until it cools. You are in no hurry, you said."

She put down the coffee and regarded him. "I never dreamed I'd actually meet you. I've followed your career for several years."

"Now I am the one to be flattered. Tell me, Chelsea, do you paint, or are you merely interested in learning about it?"

"I paint. I have a studio at my house."

"Will you show me some of your work? I would like to see what you can do."

"I'd like that."

"I am free after class tomorrow night." His hypnotic eyes seemed to gaze at her soul.

"Tomorrow night will be perfect," she heard herself saying.

"Tonight is also perfect," he said with Gallic charm. "I have had the opportunity to talk about art all evening, and now I have a lovely woman across the table from me. Who could ask for more?" He reached out and took her hand.

Chelsea was surprised by this development. "You move fast," she said as she withdrew her hand. "I was only offering to show you my paintings. Nothing else."

"You have misunderstood me," Jean-Paul said in a wounded voice. "I meant nothing unpleasant. It is only that I have so little time here. I feel I must press so many days and nights into one." He held out his hand, palm up.

After a moment, Chelsea put her hand in his. "I just wanted to be certain we understood each other."

"I would say we understand each other perfectly. You are a woman, and I am a man. Neither of us have anyone at home waiting for us, and the night is young. What do you do here on a hot summer night, Chelsea?"

"We drink coffee and try to keep our heads out of the clouds, our feet on the ground. You and a summer night could be a dangerous mixture."

"Could I?" He sounded pleased to be described in those terms. "I would like to be dangerous to you."

Chelsea smiled. She knew she would have been vulnerable to Jean-Paul even if she weren't newly divorced and lonely. "You have a way about you, as my grandmother used to say."

"What does that mean? Sometimes my English isn't broad enough."

"I mean that you could charm the birds out of the trees. You have a talent that has nothing to do with art."

"I am flattered again. You find me charming, then?"

She hesitated. "I do."

"Then why do you pull away again?"

She put her hands safely in her lap. "Because you'll be gone by Sunday, and I don't let myself be swept away by men who won't be around a week from now."

"You mean you are not what they call a one-night stand," he said in sudden understanding.

"That's one way to put it."

"Why do you think I will be gone forever after Sunday?" He seemed genuinely interested in her answer.

"Because you've told me you're booked for a seminar in Nashville. That's nowhere near Dallas."

"No, but planes fly back and forth all the time. I could come back."

She thought carefully as she studied him from across the table. "You confuse me," she said at last.

"Because I want to live all of life? What is so remarkable about flying from Nashville to Dallas? Surely if I can go from here to there, I can come back again."

"Yes, but why would you?"

He leaned closer. "Maybe because I have found something in Dallas that I cannot let go yet. Someone who interests me greatly."

She shook her head. "I can't believe that."

"Why not?"

"Because you're Jean-Paul Armand. You're famous."

He laughed. "Do not famous men fall in love in your country? I would not have guessed this to be true!"

"You're not falling in love with me."

"No? How do you see into my heart and know this?" He was watching her closely.

"It doesn't happen like this. People don't fall in love so quickly. We don't even know each other. Not really."

"So prosaic! Have you no French in you at all?"

She found herself smiling. "Actually, I am part French."

"I am so relieved! We must save that part from extinction. The rest of you is trying to smother it!"

She knew it had to be a line, but she found herself not caring. It had been too long since a man had found her desirable and said so.

"How long have you been alone?" he asked, his voice suddenly more gentle.

"It seems like forever. My divorce was final last week. We were married twelve years, but I was lonely during most of that time."

"That is a sin on his part." Jean-Paul sounded offended for her sake. "No man should let you feel lonely. Did you not live together?"

"Yes, but that doesn't preclude loneliness."

"Ah. Spoken like a true Frenchwoman. Perhaps that part of you is not smothered after all. I know what it is like to be lonely but not alone."

"I think that's the worst loneliness of all. To feel that way when someone else is in the house with you." Chelsea tried her coffee again.

"Was he cruel to you?"

Her smile wavered. He knew exactly what to ask to put her off balance. "I would rather not talk about him."

"Then he was. No woman wants to talk about something like that. Have you no brothers to see to it that you are treated right?"

"I'm an only child."

"Another sin. Once your parents saw how beautiful you would be, they should have given you brothers for protection." He smiled as he reclaimed her hand. "I am only partly teasing. I would have taken care of you if I were the one you were living with. I would not have mistreated you."

"How long have you been divorced?"

"Forever. More than a year." He smiled at her until she smiled back. "There now. You need not ever be lonely again. Not when you have such a smile. The very angels would come down to keep you company."

Chelsea laughed. "Angels make poor conversationalists."

Jean-Paul sat back and regarded her thoughtfully. "I think perhaps I will find a plane that flies back to Dallas. I think I cannot get to know you well enough in only three days."

Chelsea told herself not to read too much into his words. Jean-Paul was charming and obviously enjoyed flirting. Still, his command of the English language was faulty at times, so it was possible he didn't mean his to sound as intimate as he did. Nevertheless, she was enjoying the sensation of knowing a man found her appealing enough to fly from Nashville to Dallas just to see her again. She found herself dreading his departure.

The next night he accompanied her home from class. Chelsea was nervous as he strolled around her apartment, studying one canvas in silence, then moving on to the next.

When he had at last seen them all, he nodded, still in silence. He went back to the first ones then, and stood thoughtfully in front of them.

"Are they that bad?" she asked when he still made no comment. "What are you thinking?"

He glanced at her as if he had almost forgotten she was awaiting his verdict. "They are not bad."

Chelsea relaxed visibly. "You had me worried for a minute there."

"They are not great, but they are also not bad."

She frowned. "What's wrong with my work? I know I'm not Michelangelo, but I thought you'd be more enthusiastic than this."

"The world has already had a Michelangelo. It does not

need another one. Today he would have difficulty selling. Tastes have changed."

"I know that." She followed him to the next canvas.

"They lack heart." He stood with his feet apart as if prepared to take on the painting in a contest. "They have no soul."

Chelsea shook her head in disagreement. "How can you say that? I painted *Interlude* during a time of great emotion. I all but wept as I painted it! How can you say it has no soul?"

"You look at the canvas and remember what happened in your life at the time you painted it. I was not there. It does not speak in the same way to me." He stepped nearer. "These colors here—they play together prettily, but they would do so in a necklace or a fabric. They do not make me feel an emotion."

"Excuse me, Jean-Paul, but you're wrong. My friends all see the emotion in it. They told me so."

He smiled and shook his head. "They are your friends. Perhaps they, too, were going through the emotions you were when you did this one. They see what you have done, and they, too, remember the time. That is not art. That is a diary."

Chelsea frowned at the canvas. Until now she had considered it one of her finest. "How do I get soul in my work? How can I put emotion into my canvases so strangers will feel them as keenly as I did?"

With a laugh, Jean-Paul put his arm around her shoulders. "You ask me the riddle of the ages. How can I teach a person this? It comes from the depth of your soul, undiluted, and flows onto the canvas along with the paint."

"You're saying I lack depth because I lack soul? Thanks!"

"Now you are angry! This is good! Anger makes soul. So do love and sorrow and all the other passions. When you have enough experience with creating your soul, it will become a part of your work, so that a person may look on it and say, 'I feel sad from just looking at this!' or 'I look at this and feel as if I am falling in love.' When that happens you'll have true soul."

"If you were anyone else, I'd say you're full of bull." She glared at the canvas. "I haven't exactly led an uneventful life. How much more will I have to experience before I can transmit it to canvas?"

Jean-Paul shrugged. "I cannot answer that. When it happens, you will know." He looked at her. "I did not tell you this to hurt you or to discourage you. I can tell you have a great deal of talent. More talent than I've seen in quite a while."

"But you just said—"

"Talent is technique. Your canvases lack soul. It is not the same thing."

Slowly she nodded. "I think I understand."

He strode quickly to the opposite end of the loft and pointed at the canvas on her easel. "Here I see the beginnings of soul."

"I haven't finished that yet."

"You have not overworked it, you mean. When I see it, I feel a sadness. A sense of something lost."

"I started it the day of my divorce. I worked on it all night and haven't touched it since."

He nodded encouragingly. "And why have you not?"

"Because every time I look at it, I feel sad." Her eyes widened. "That's what you're trying to show me, isn't it? How did I get it into that painting and not into the others?"

"One of the secrets of painting is knowing when to quit," he said with a sage smile. "Of presenting the emotion whether it is pretty or not."

"You've given me a lot to think about."

Jean-Paul came to her and put his arms around her. "I hope so. I believe that you can become quite good, with proper training."

"But where do I go to get that training? You won't be here that long, even if you do fly back from Nashville."

"Let me think on that puzzle for a time." He pulled her

closer and gazed down into her eyes. "I believe I may have a solution for you."

She knew he was going to kiss her, and she didn't pull away. Although she had only known him for four days, it seemed much longer. His kiss was demanding and passionate and carried her along with his emotion. She returned it, matching passion with passion. It was as if her usual rules didn't apply to him.

When he led her to her bed, she didn't object. And by the time he left in the early morning, she no longer felt so lonely.

Chapter Twenty-Four

On his last day in Dallas, Chelsea took Jean-Paul to meet Karen and Ryan. It was no surprise that he charmed both Karen and Ashley. Chelsea watched with a smile as Jean-Paul discussed music with Ashley, who was hanging on his words. She hadn't realized he knew anything at all about rock.

"This is more than I've seen my daughter talk in months," Ryan said as he came into the kitchen where Chelsea was getting another pitcher of tea. "It's nice to know she can still carry on a conversation."

Chelsea smiled. "I didn't know Jean-Paul liked children. Of course Ashley's almost thirteen so I guess she no longer fits into that category."

He studied her profile. "How much do you like him?"

She glanced up in surprise. "I like him a great deal. Don't you?"

"No, I don't."

"How can you say that? You've only known him half an hour!"

"Would you accept my opinion if I said I liked him? If I can form a liking that fast, I can also form a dislike."

Chelsea glanced at the door to be sure they couldn't be overheard. "You're not being fair!"

"I don't trust him!"

Karen came into the room. "What's holding up the tea?

Ryan, stop bothering Chelsea and let her do what she came in here to do."

"How do you like Jean-Paul?" Chelsea whispered.

"I think he's great! He's so handsome and so intelligent! Not at all like some of the men you've dated."

Chelsea ignored the barb. "See?" she said to Ryan. "Karen likes him."

"I'm not Karen, and I still don't trust him."

"Oh, for heaven's sake, Ryan," Karen said impatiently. "Stop being so provincial! I love his accent! And he's so sexy!" Conspiratorially she whispered to Chelsea, "Have you been to bed with him?"

"Karen!" Ryan exclaimed.

Chelsea didn't answer. She dumped the ice cubes into the bucket and put it on the tray with the five tea glasses and the pitcher. "I thought I'd take it all in and save steps."

"You *have* been to bed with him," Karen crowed triumphantly. "Otherwise you'd deny it."

"That's none of your business," her husband snapped.

"Will you carry the tray, Ryan? I seem to have made the load too heavy."

He lifted it easily, glared at Karen, and went back into the den.

"He's so sexy," Karen repeated. "What was it like to make love with him?"

"I'm certainly not going to tell you!" With a passing frown, Chelsea went into the den after Ryan.

Jean-Paul was still talking to Ashley about the merits of various rock groups. "When I am painting, I often listen to music to set the mood. Perhaps you will not like to hear this, but rock music expresses anger and madness for me. So many discordant sounds! So much passion!"

"I've noticed the passion," Ashley said.

"Ashley!" Karen exclaimed as she came into the room. "What a thing to say! You'll have to overlook her, Jean-Paul. Sometimes she says things she doesn't really mean."

"I'm not a baby, Mom!"

Jean-Paul calmed Ashley with a wink and a smile as if they were conspirators. "I would say that Ashley understands music quite well. We find the same elements in it. Passion is not wrong in an art form." He smiled at Chelsea, and she found herself actually blushing.

Ryan frowned at Jean-Paul and then her. "How long did you say you'd be in Dallas?"

"I leave today, regretfully." Jean-Paul made a Gallic gesture that indicated fate was driving him. "I must go to Nashville for another seminar."

"That's too bad!" Karen said as she sat next to him and claimed his attention by pressing her knee against his. "We've hardly gotten to know you." Her smile was full of invitation.

Chelsea found herself staring. Karen was blatantly flirting with Jean-Paul in front of her and Ashley and Ryan. Once she would have said Karen wouldn't have known the first thing about flirting. Karen certainly hadn't in college.

Jean-Paul seemed to enjoy the attention. "I expect to come back soon. The seminar is only for a week; then I will fly back to Dallas. And Chelsea," he added.

"How long will you be in the country?" Ryan asked.

"I do not know yet. Nashville is my last booking. It depends on many things." He smiled at Chelsea.

Chelsea returned his smile and saw Karen's brief frown. Uneasiness stirred in her. Ashley had noticed, too. Ryan gave no hint that he noticed what Karen was doing, but Chelsea knew he had to be aware of it. He wasn't nearly as blind to nuances as he liked to pretend.

"I hope you intend to stay for dinner," Karen was saying. "I know Chelsea rarely cooks, and I'd like you to have at least one good, home-cooked meal while you're here. We haven't hired a cook, though it would be more convenient, so I've taken courses in gourmet cooking. I like to prepare meals."

"Regretfully, I must leave before dinner. My flight is at six o'clock."

"Such a pity! Well, when you come back to Dallas, you must eat with us. I insist." Karen was using the stilted accent she affected at formal parties. "I'll arrange a date with Chelsea."

"That would be wonderful," Jean-Paul said with a smile. "I will look forward with delight to your cooking."

"I just love your accent. Have you been speaking English long?" Karen let her eyelashes drop to half-conceal her eyes, then opened them wide.

Chelsea watched her flirt with Jean-Paul, not knowing how to end this display, until Ashley frowned at her mother and stood abruptly.

"I'm going out," the girl announced and left the room.

"Where are you going?" Karen called. "Will you be back for dinner?"

Ashley didn't bother to answer.

Ryan followed his daughter out and soon Chelsea heard tense whisperings from the direction of the side door. When Ryan returned, he looked angry. The slamming of the door signaled that Ashley was gone. "She says she'll be home for dinner," he told Karen.

Karen laughed as if the scene hadn't been unpleasant in the least. "She's so independent at this age. She has her first boyfriend. I think that's so cute!"

Chelsea didn't see anything appealing in Ashley's actions or in her punk style. And what was this about her having a boyfriend? She was only thirteen! If Ashley were her daughter, Chelsea would worry every time she left the house, but apparently Karen was determined to see only what she wanted to see. Chelsea glanced at her watch and was relieved to find an hour had passed. "I hate to say it, but we should go."

Jean-Paul consulted his own watch. "Yes. I still have to get my things and travel to the airport."

"So soon?" Karen's voice was almost a wail. "You just got here!"

"He'll be back," Ryan said in a tight voice. He stood

and held out his hand to Jean-Paul. "It's been nice getting to know you."

Jean-Paul stood and shook the proffered hand. He looked as if he saw Ryan's jealousy and was amused by it. "I will see you all again soon."

Karen met Chelsea's eyes and gave her a small, secretive smile. With a jolt, Chelsea realized Karen thought they were competing for the same man. She was glad to escape.

Ryan closed the front door behind them. He felt as if Chelsea were rushing into another bad situation, but he knew there was no way to stop her.

"I liked him," Karen said smugly.

"That was obvious." Ryan went into the den and carried the tray of untouched tea back into the kitchen.

"What's that supposed to mean?" she challenged, following him.

"You can figure it out. I'm not blind, Karen. You did everything but crawl into his lap."

"Jealous?" she asked in a taunting voice.

"No, just appalled." He put the pitcher of tea in the refrigerator and poured the ice cubes back into the tray under the automatic icemaker. "You could have saved it for a time when Ashley wasn't in the room."

"What do you mean by that?"

"Stop asking me to explain the obvious. Do you honestly think I haven't seen you flirting at the parties your parents give? If you want to make a fool of yourself, that's your business, but lay off Chelsea's boyfriends, especially in front of Ashley."

Karen's anger flared and she started shouting at him, but Ryan had heard it all before. He went out the side door and drove away. His jealousy hadn't been for his wife, and he had a lot to sort out away from Karen's tirades.

For the next week and a half, Chelsea painted almost feverishly. As Jean-Paul had suggested, she tried painting to music, but she found she did better work when the studio was completely silent. She worked on two canvases at once to prevent herself from overworking either one. The results were pleasing to her.

She didn't know Jean-Paul had returned until he knocked at her door one evening. Her surprise at finding him there rendered her speechless for a moment. "Come in!" she said, finding her voice. "You really did come back!"

"I said I would, did I not?"

"Yes, but after you left, I thought perhaps you said that in order to make our goodbyes less difficult. A lot of people can't stand to say goodbye."

"I'm not one of them." He came farther in and went to where she was working. In silence he studied the two canvases.

"Well?" she asked impatiently.

"You have improved." He grinned at her. "Was it my lovemaking that inspired you?"

"You certainly aren't overwhelmed by humbleness, are you?" Chelsea asked with a laugh.

"Not at all. I find humbleness to be detrimental in my work." He pulled her close. "Tell me how much you missed me."

"A great deal," she said honestly. "I was lonely without you."

"There! You see? I have no reason to be humble. When I leave I am missed, and when I return I get embraces. There is no reason in this to wear sackcloth and ashes."

"How long will you be in town?"

"Long enough to return to Karen's house for the meal she was so eager to cook for me. I leave for Paris on Saturday."

"So soon?" She let down. "I had hoped to see you longer."

"And you will. I want you to return to Paris with me."

"What? Me go to Paris? With you?"

"Why not? It is only a city. Would you not go to Houston or New York with me?"

"Probably, but Paris is halfway around the world!"

"Not completely. Will you go?"

"I have to think about it." His words had caught her by surprise. Paris?

"I have news that will sway you. I have telephoned an old friend of mine, Meneir."

Her mouth dropped open. "You know Meneir? *The* Meneir?"

"Yes. I believe there is only one. We have known each other for years. He was my teacher, you see. We live close together, not five blocks apart. Meneir says he will consider taking you as a pupil."

Chelsea had to sit down. "Meneir would teach me?"

"As a favor to me, yes. Must you still think about it? I have to remind you that Meneir is an old man and cannot wait forever."

"Of course I'll go! I couldn't turn down a chance like this!"

Jean-Paul pretended to be offended. "To think my little Chelsea is persuaded by the promise of an old man rather than by my charms alone."

Chelsea put her head to one side thoughtfully. "What do you want out of this?"

"What do I want?"

"I'm still not sure I want to live with you. That's the arrangement you had in mind, I assume?"

"I have not asked you to live with me," he said in surprise. "What did I say to lead you to think such a thing?"

In confusion she replied, "I assumed . . . That is, I thought that's what you meant. It's how it sounded."

"Ah, Chelsea, you must forgive me! I had no intention of making you think such a thing. Why, to promise you lessons with Meneir in exchange for your living with me would be to prostitute you!"

"I know."

"No wonder you had trouble with your so excellent conscience!"

Chelsea thought he was protesting a bit too emphatically, but she let it pass. "What exactly did you mean then?"

"I will find you a flat near my own and Meneir's. I hope to visit you often, but not to live with you. You forget, I have my own work to consider. I cannot create with anyone talking to me, and I've found that women do love to talk."

"You're forgetting that I'm an artist, too, and can understand that." She couldn't conceal her flare of anger. "You can be such a chauvinist!"

He laughed and shrugged. "Perhaps I am. I live in a different world from yours. In my world, I am not considered to be one, or if I am, it doesn't matter. I want only to turn you into an artist of great quality."

Chelsea didn't think it was likely that French women enjoyed being stereotyped any more than American women did, but she let that slide. "In that case, I'll come with you and have no reservations."

"Good. We will leave on Saturday."

"I'm not sure I can leave so soon." She looked around her apartment. "I have a lot to do if I'm going to move to Paris."

"How difficult can it be? You have no family here, no real ties. You can rent out this place or leave it vacant until you return. If you choose not to come back, Ryan can sell it for you."

"You make it sound so simple."

Jean-Paul smiled. "It is. It is not good to be encumbered by belongings. They begin to own you instead of the other way around." He turned back to her newest paintings. "I can see from your progress that you will be a good student. Even Meneir will be pleased."

"I'm going to study under Meneir," Chelsea said almost to herself. "I can't believe it."

*   *   *

"You're making a big mistake," Ryan said in a tight voice. "Why do you want to move to France?"

"I can study under Meneir," Chelsea repeated. "Don't you see what this could mean to my career?"

"I can see that Jean-Paul has a line of malarkey a yard wide. What if you get over there and find out he's lying?"

"Why would he do that?" she demanded.

Ryan paced to the window of the den and frowned out at his back yard. "I can think of dozens of reasons."

"It's not to get my money. He doesn't know how much I received in the divorce settlement. He hasn't even asked."

"Concern for your money wasn't on the top of my list," Ryan retorted. "You're making a big mistake, Chelsea."

"I don't see how you can say that. He's offering me *Meneir*. This could mean the difference between my remaining mediocre or becoming truly great!"

"This Meneir knows how to teach talent? The only person who ever told you your work is mediocre is Jean-Paul!"

"He's in a position to know!"

"So are a lot of other people who have seen your paintings and say that you're unusually talented."

"Then why am I having so much trouble selling? Jean-Paul says my work lacks soul. If Meneir can teach me how to paint with emotion, it will be worth whatever it takes to attain it!" She turned away from him. "When will Karen be home? I'll bet she's more receptive."

"She'll be home within the hour, I guess. I'm not sure where she went."

Chelsea sighed. "I don't want to argue with you, Ryan. I was hoping you'd be happy for me."

He came to her. "I'm happy that you have the opportunity to study with this Meneir person. I'm just concerned about the part Jean-Paul is playing in this."

"We aren't going to be living together. He has no ulterior motives. Why don't you like him?"

Ryan shook his head. "I don't know. He's just too slick, too polished. I feel as if he lies whenever it suits him."

"That's not fair. You barely know him!"

"That's true." He sat beside her on the couch. "Maybe it's just that I don't want you to move all the way to France, where you won't know anyone but him. How will I know if you're all right?"

She smiled at him. "France has mail service. I hear they even have telephones."

He laughed briefly. "I'm going to miss you, Chelsea."

"I know. I'll miss you, too." She wished she could reach out and touch him. No one else was in the house. No one else would ever know. But she refrained from habit.

"I suppose I shouldn't bring this up, but you don't have a great track record when it comes to choosing men."

"I have to admit Lorne was a loser."

"And Jason Randall, and a few others."

"Okay, so I'm not great at picking men to be in love with. But I don't love Jean-Paul, and he doesn't love me. This is different."

"Is that supposed to make it better? Karen has told me several times that he's your lover." The words seemed to hurt him. "Is he?"

"Do you really want to know?" she asked quietly.

"No. I think you just told me." He drew back and stared at the window across the room.

Chelsea reached out and took his hand. "Ryan, I have to do this. Studying with Meneir is the chance of a lifetime."

His fingers closed over hers, but he said, "Don't expect me to give it my blessing. I still say you're making a mistake. What if you get all the way to Paris and find out Jean-Paul is another Lorne?"

"I'll come home again. I've learned a lot since leaving Lorne. I won't remain in such a situation now."

"That's not what statistics say." He lifted her hand and studied it. "I don't want to lose you, Chelsea."

"You don't have me to lose," she reminded him gently.

His eyes met hers. "These last few months have been hell," he said. "There are things happening around here that you don't know about. I know, for instance, that Karen isn't out shopping."

"Why do you say that?"

"I think she's seeing someone else." He leaned forward and rested his elbows on his knees. "I don't know who it is, and I don't have any proof that I'm right, but it's true."

Chelsea shook her head. "I don't think so, Ryan. She hasn't said anything to me." She knew Karen no longer saw Hank. "She doesn't even go to the health club anymore."

"What does the health club have to do with it?"

"Nothing. I was just pointing that out." She would have to be careful, or she would say too much. She did not want to hurt Ryan. "You know how Karen likes to shop."

"Yes, but lately when she's gone 'shopping' she hasn't returned with anything. That's certainly not like her."

"I'm sure you're imagining things." She rested her hand on his shoulder. It hurt her to see his pain and embarrassment. "Karen would have to be out of her mind to see someone else when she has you!" It was more than she had intended to say. "I should be going. Ashley isn't at home, and Karen might not be too pleased to find us here alone."

Ryan laughed wryly. "Believe me, she couldn't care less. She's made that clear."

"I don't believe that for a minute." Chelsea rose to leave. "Karen will be in soon. Tonight is the big dinner. She's probably out scouring the city for special ingredients."

"Maybe."

"I only wanted to tell you about Meneir and Paris before the dinner. Jean-Paul is almost certain to mention it, and I didn't want it to catch you by surprise."

"Thanks. I'll pass it on to Karen when she comes in."

Chelsea left, but she couldn't get Ryan's words out of her mind. Was Karen seeing another man? She had thought when Karen stopped seeing Hank she would stay at home, that the affair had been an isolated fling and

Karen now had it out of her system. What had she done
to make Ryan so suspicious?

Chelsea worried about that all the way to her apartment. If Ryan's marriage was in trouble, he might need
her. Paris was a long way from Dallas. But, she told herself
firmly, she couldn't live her life on the supposition that
Ryan might someday need her. She focused her mind on
deciding what to pack and what to leave behind.

For the rest of the afternoon Chelsea sorted through her
belongings. She would need to take all of her painting
equipment, but she wasn't at all certain that the airlines
would allow it, since most of it was flammable. That would
mean the expense of purchasing everything anew in Paris,
as well as the inconvenience of learning to use unfamiliar
paints, canvas, and brushes.

She had no idea what sort of clothing to take because
she didn't know how long she would be there. When Meneir agreed to take her on as a pupil, had he envisioned six
weeks? Six years? She finally decided she would have to
ask Jean-Paul many questions.

That night she went to his hotel to pick him up, rather
than have him take a cab. He had a room on the top floor
of one of the most prestigious hotels in Dallas. From his
window Chelsea could see a panorama of skyline. The July
sun was slow in setting, and a shimmer of heat haze hung
in the still air.

"Homesick already?" he teased, coming up behind her
and kissing her on the nape of the neck.

"Does it show? I love Dallas. No true Texan transplants
well."

"Wait until you see Paris. You will forget all about
being homesick."

She laughed. "Naturally you feel that way. Paris is your
home." More seriously she said, "How long will Meneir
teach me?"

He put his arms around her and held her back against
his chest. Chelsea leaned her head back against his cheek.
"It depends. A man like Meneir does not give six-week

courses. He will teach you for as long as you continue to learn."

"We haven't even discussed the cost."

"I had wondered when you would ask about that." When he told her the figure, Chelsea drew in her breath. "Is it too much? One does not ask Meneir for a discount price."

"I can manage that amount." She was mentally calculating, however. In three months she would go through half her divorce settlement, and she needed that money to live on unless she found a regular job. "I didn't expect it to be that expensive."

"You will be learning from the best. Besides, you Americans are all rich." Jean-Paul grinned as he stepped away from her and sat on the bed to put on his shoes. "I am almost ready to go."

Chelsea wondered if he really believed she was independently wealthy. Money had never been mentioned, but he knew she had no job and her clothing, all bought during her marriage, was of excellent quality. It was easy to see how he could think her well off.

When Jean-Paul went into the bathroom to comb his hair, Chelsea crossed to the mirror over the dresser to check her makeup. Should she tell him she had only the divorce settlement and that when it was gone there would be no more? In Texas no alimony was paid after a divorce. As she was wondering how to tell him her situation without it sounding as if she thought he had designs on her money, her eyes fell on a scarf.

It lay beside Jean-Paul's suitcase, half-hidden by a shirt he had discarded. Slowly she pulled it free and stared at it. The colors and designs were distinctive—were why she had bought it for Karen's last birthday.

"You are being very quiet out there," Jean-Paul called out, making her jump. "Have you perhaps run away?"

"No. No, I'm still here." She wadded up the scarf and thrust it into her purse.

He came back into the room. "I am ready if you are. We will advance on Karen's gourmet meal and devour it."

She managed a smile. All the way to the car the scarf seemed to burn holes through her purse. It might not be Karen's. After all, the store must have sold more than one of that design and color. But Karen had been away from the house most of the afternoon, and Ryan had expressed doubt that she was out shopping.

When they arrived at the Morgans' house, Chelsea made an excuse to corner Karen alone. Without a word she pulled out the scarf and handed it to her.

Karen hesitated, then took it. "Thanks. I was wondering how I would get it back."

"Then it *is* yours? What were you doing in Jean-Paul's hotel room?" Chelsea demanded in a low voice that wouldn't carry to the men in the den.

"Hush. Someone might hear you. What difference does it make why I was there? Jean-Paul says you two don't have any sort of agreement. He called me, and I went over."

Chelsea stared at her. "You admit it? You aren't going to offer any excuse?"

"Why should I? After all, you were there, too, or you wouldn't have found it." Karen turned back to the oven. "I had hoped you wouldn't find out, but it doesn't really matter to me that you did. After all, we're grown women now. I don't have to answer to you." She gave Chelsea a cool look over her shoulder.

Chelsea felt she had been slapped. Her friendship with Karen had been tapering off for a long time. Now, she realized with a pang, it was over. That look had told her more than Karen's words. Karen not only didn't care whether Chelsea believed Jean-Paul was seeing her, she hoped Chelsea would be jealous.

Slowly Chelsea backed away, tears rising in her eyes. She fought them back. She wasn't going to let Karen see how hurt she was over the end of a friendship she had assumed would last forever.

Somehow she got through the meal, though she didn't taste a thing. She made the proper responses to questions and even initiated conversation. But inside her heart was breaking. When Jean-Paul asked if she was ready to go, she nodded and stood, ready to make an escape. Karen's eyes shot daggers at her as she left with him.

When they reached his hotel, Chelsea pretended she had a headache and didn't go up to his room. Nothing could have persuaded her to lie in the bed he had shared with Karen that afternoon. Instead, she went home and lay awake all night, wondering if she should still go to Paris, when she knew Jean-Paul had no more scruples than to try to make love to two friends on the same day. But she was going for Meneir, not Jean-Paul. And she couldn't bear to stay in Dallas knowing that Karen was no longer her friend.

By morning her resolve to leave was firm.

Chapter Twenty-Five

Paris was large, confusing and exciting. Chelsea had been there as a child, but the Paris she saw with Jean-Paul was entirely different. She became enamored of the *passages,* streets enclosed by glass and lined with various shops. To walk down them was to find herself in Paris of the 1820's. The modernization served only to point out their archaic beauty.

One of her favorites was the Galerie Vivienne, where Jean-Paul had exhibited in the late 'seventies, when he was yet unknown. At the time, he told her, the *passage* had been owned by an artist named Huguette Spengler and had been a gathering place where artists, both famous and struggling, rubbed elbows and presented their work. Now fashionable shops had replaced some of the galleries, but for Jean-Paul the nostalgia remained.

He found a place for her on a tiny street called the rue Benoît. Number twenty-two was located up some steep stairs and over an antique shop that opened onto the street behind. On one side it overlooked a tiny courtyard she was to share with a newlywed couple. Chelsea loved it at first sight.

Jean-Paul lived a block away on the more fashionable rue Delacroix. He had both the upper and lower floors of one of the narrow buildings decorated with delicate black wrought iron. People seemed to come and go from his abode at all hours of the day and night, but when he chose to work, Jean-Paul locked himself away on the upper floor and refused to answer any summonses.

Chelsea hadn't been in such a relaxed atmosphere since her college days, but she had to struggle to follow the language. Her high school and college French sometimes seemed a different language entirely.

When she was to meet Meneir for the first time, she found herself trembling all over. Jean-Paul laughed at her, but he held her hand as he knocked on the bright red door. Almost at once it was opened by a plump woman who smiled when she recognized Jean-Paul. Chelsea tried to follow the lightning-swift French, especially since her own name was mentioned several times, but it was beyond her. The woman finally gave her a motherly smile and led them into a well-lighted room.

At first Chelsea thought the room was empty. Then, from behind a bank of canvases, an elderly man came into view. Meneir, he was never addressed by any other name, was well into his eighties and bent with age, but his eyes were as young and as clear as any youth's. He sized her up before he spoke, then smiled. "You would be the young woman my friend has so often spoken of."

With relief, Chelsea realized he was speaking almost flawless English. "I'm Chelsea Cavin."

Jean-Paul smiled at his old mentor. "She has promise. Otherwise, I would not have asked you to see her." He put down the package of paintings he carried under his arm. "These are some of her small works, but you can get an idea from them of her capability."

Chelsea clasped her hands as Meneir slowly lifted one canvas after another, placing each on an easel for viewing. He didn't speak until he had studied them all at length. "Yes. You have promise," he said at last. "Jean-Paul has done well to bring you to me." He looked at her closely. "I will expect hard work from you. I am an old man, and I do not have a great many years left to me. I have no time to waste with a lazy student."

"That suits me perfectly. I want to learn, and I'm willing to work as hard as I can."

Meneir nodded as he motioned for Jean-Paul to remove the paintings. "We start tomorrow morning. Be here at seven."

Chelsea thanked him as she helped Jean-Paul replace the packing around the canvases to prevent them from rubbing against one another.

"He's going to take me!" she cried out when they were back on the street. "He's actually going to teach me what he knows!"

"Was there a doubt?"

"Yes, in a way. It's seemed too good to be true. I kept thinking, what if I meet him and he doesn't like my work. He did like it, didn't he? He's not just saying that he does?"

"Meneir never gives idle praise. If he says he likes something, this is higher praise than you may receive from anyone else. He is a perfectionist—as much as an artist may be—and he has no time or interest in pretending to like something he does not care for."

"He's much older than I expected him to be. With his health, will he be up to teaching me? I gathered he expects me to put in long hours."

Jean-Paul shrugged and smiled. "He would not have taken you on if he did not think he was up to it. He has remarkable energy for a man of his years."

"To think! I'm a pupil of Meneir!"

"This calls for a celebration. I will tell all my friends to come to my home, and we will celebrate all the night."

Chelsea didn't see how this would be any different from the other nights at Jean-Paul's house, but she laughed and nodded. She thought she was going to enjoy living in Paris with Jean-Paul as her guide and friend.

Early the next morning she went back to Meneir's and was taken into his studio. His entire house was filled with paintings, some his own, some that Chelsea was positive must be by Soutine, Matisse, and Bonnard, all of whom Meneir must have known. The thought almost took her breath away. It was as if she were treading on holy ground.

By noon she had lost much of her awe in the necessity for concentration. While Memoir spoke English, there were some ideas he insisted were comprehensible only in French. She struggled hard to understand and to remember every word he spoke.

In spite of his age, Meneir seemed impervious to tiring. He kept her at the easel all day, letting her stop only long enough to stretch her muscles and to grab a bite of lunch. He didn't let her leave until the shadows were stretching all the way across the street outside his window.

"Tomorrow," he said as she was leaving. "We will begin again tomorrow at the same time. We have much to accomplish."

Chelsea was exhausted by the time she walked to the rue Benoît and climbed up to her room. She fell across the bed and closed her eyes. Phrases and word pictures inspired by Meneir kept racing through her mind, as did the way he held a brush, the technique he used for laying on a background or blending one color into another so that both layers could be sensed. She hadn't realized how much she had to learn.

She fell asleep and was wakened by a knocking on her door. Knowing it could only be Jean-Paul, she struggled up and responded. He came into the room on a burst of energy. "What were you doing? Sleeping? The night is young!"

"The night was old when I got to bed last night, and Meneir has worked me half to death all day."

"Surely you do not regret coming here already!"

Chelsea smiled. "No, I don't regret it at all." Here in Paris Jean-Paul was in his element. She could almost forget having found Karen's scarf in his hotel room. Since that night she hadn't shared a bed with him, though she knew it was only a matter of time before the subject would come up.

"Come. Get your purse. Everyone is coming to my

house for dinner. Come, come. You do not want to miss seeing them all."

Chelsea grabbed her purse and told herself she could rest later.

As Jean-Paul had said, everyone did come to his house. He seemed to have a huge number of friends, most of whom changed from day to day. Chelsea gave up trying to remember all the names and faces, and just enjoyed, in a blur, the camaraderie that flowed through the rooms.

Jean-Paul's crowd was different from Chelsea's friends in Dallas. While she wouldn't have classified herself as prim, she didn't allow her guests to use marijuana or any other illegal drug. Jean-Paul seemed not to make that distinction. Chelsea was nervous until she considered that the same laws might not apply in France. Several times she told herself this must be the case, as none of the users attempted to hide what was going on.

After hours of frenzied talking and laughing, the guests departed as spontaneously as they had arrived. Jean-Paul grinned at her. "They are great, no?"

"Is marijuana legal in Paris? And I thought I saw someone using cocaine!"

"That would be Françoise. She has the habit badly."

"But isn't that illegal?" Chelsea pursued.

Jean-Paul went through the rooms, collecting glasses and emptying ashtrays. "No one was hurting anyone. Do not worry about it." He caught her around the waist and kissed her. "Come. Help me straighten up and we will go to bed."

Chelsea paused. She didn't want to go to bed with him, but how could she refuse? After all, he had voluntarily introduced her to Meneir, had found her a place to stay in Paris and had included her in his circle of friends so she wouldn't be lonely. Besides, it wasn't as if she hadn't made love with him before. "I'm awfully tired," she hedged.

He set the glasses back onto the end table and propelled her toward the back of the house. "Then we will clean up tomorrow. My protégée must have her rest."

"But I'll rest much better in my own place. I didn't bring a change of clothes—"

"No problem. I am an early riser. I will see to it that you are awake in plenty of time to get to Meneir on schedule."

Chelsea knew she was outmaneuvered. She gave in with a smile and let him undress her.

The next few months seemed to fly by. Summer turned into fall, and the heat slackened with the rains. Chelsea spent every waking moment painting or with Jean-Paul. Gradually she became used to the idea of not sleeping and discovered she was turning out her best work.

She hadn't rented her warehouse loft in Dallas, and from time to time, she mailed canvases to be stored there until her return. Ryan took care of this and wrote her, giving her the news. Karen did not write.

Chelsea still missed the friendship they had had, but she was discovering a freedom in not having to worry about what Karen might think or whether her schedule might conflict with whatever Karen had planned. Until she was away from her, Chelsea hadn't realized how much Karen had controlled the relationship. Over the years she had become so accustomed to deferring to her that she hadn't given it much thought.

Jean-Paul was satisfactory as a lover, but she never thought for a minute that she was falling in love with him. It caught her by surprise when he told her he was in love with her.

"Why do you look as if that never crossed your mind?" he asked, sharing her pillow in the predawn light. "Surely you must have known how I feel?"

"I care for you a great deal, but I don't want to be married."

"Neither do I."

Chelsea propped her head up on her palm. "You love me, but you don't want to marry me?"

"Yes. I would like you to move in here. Why should you keep your own place when you are so seldom there?"

"I thought you needed your space. When you paint you want to be alone."

"Yes, but you need not be bothered by that. You always paint at Meneir's so you would not need room in my studio."

"I also work on some things at home. I don't think you realize how much work I do."

He thought for a minute, trailing her auburn hair through his fingers. "I could give you the small bedroom at the front of the house for your studio. Yes?"

She considered it. Her money was so limited and rent in Paris was exorbitant. "That might be a good idea. I could stay longer that way."

"Then it is settled. You will move in here. Now, get up and hurry over to Meneir's. You know how he is if a person is late."

Chelsea hoped she was making the right choice. Financially it was a good move, and she was at Jean-Paul's most of the time anyway. She was concerned about his statement that he was in love with her, but he had said he didn't expect marriage. In fact, she had assumed he'd been seeing other women. She just didn't understand Jean-Paul and probably never would.

By the time she finished working under Meneir, Jean-Paul had talked to Chelsea's landlady and had arranged for her things to be moved to his house. She tried not to feel perturbed that he was proceeding so quickly and without further consulting her. Since her rent was due the following day, she knew she should be glad that he had taken care of things for her. But, somehow, she wasn't.

She had brought little with her to Paris since she hadn't known how long she would be staying, so her belongings fit easily into Jean-Paul's house. Within days she seemed to have lived there forever. She wondered what his friends thought of the arrangement, but none of them made any comment about it. For some reason this was unsettling.

Did those in his crowd live together so freely that her sharing Jean-Paul's house didn't seem worthy of mentioning?

One week after she had moved in with him, Jean-Paul told her his landlord was increasing his rent.

"I'm sorry to hear that," Chelsea said. "Is it a large increase?"

"I am afraid so. Of course with you paying your portion, it will not be so bad. It will still be less than it was when I lived here alone."

"Excuse me?"

"Naturally you will pay your part of the rent," he said as they had discussed this and agreed prior to her moving in. "Is this not so? You know how I admire your independence."

"Of course," she stammered. "You just caught me by surprise."

"Someday I will own my own place. It is a dream of mine, not to have to pay a vulture of a landlord."

Chelsea was mentally figuring her remaining bank balance. "Exactly how much will my portion be?" When he told her, she couldn't believe her hears. "But that's more than I was paying for my place!"

He shrugged. "This one is bigger, nicer. Is it not?"

Chelsea didn't know what to say. She had traded her privacy for a larger rent. Her gratitude to Jean-Paul didn't stretch quite this far. "Yes, it is. Jean-Paul, maybe I should have told you something before now. I'm not independently wealthy, you know. I only have my divorce settlement and whatever I make on my paintings."

"Yes, but all Americans are rich." He grinned at her as if he knew she was joking.

"No, we aren't."

He put his arm around her and hugged her. "You are not to worry. My friends are coming over tonight, and Françoise is to make dinner for us all. There will be music and laughing."

"I didn't expect anyone tonight." She glanced around.

The house needed straightening if company was coming, and she was already tired from painting all day. "And Françoise takes drugs every time she's here. I'm not comfortable with that."

"Then you should not stay in the room when she does it. There are plenty of other people to talk with."

"This is my house, too, now. I don't want anyone doing something illegal in here." Since she was expected to pay half the rent, she was determined to have some say in the activities.

"That is why I do not want to marry. Not even you." He kissed her on the nose. "I do not mind if my friends bring drugs into my house. I, too, have tried them and see nothing wrong with taking them. You should try some, too."

"No way," Chelsea said firmly. "I don't do drugs."

He smiled indulgently. "Until you have tried them, how can you judge them? Besides, Françoise is an old friend, and I cannot tell her what she should or should not do. Friends do not do such things."

Chelsea didn't agree, but she knew there was no point in arguing with Jean-Paul. He always did exactly as he pleased. She regretted agreeing to move in with him. Since the move he hadn't mentioned loving her. Had he said that only because he knew his rent was about to go up and he wanted her to help finance him? She didn't like thinking this.

People began arriving within the hour. Chelsea told herself the house was as orderly as she could get it with no more warning than she'd had. Anyway these were people who were over so often it didn't really matter if the living room needed dusting or the bed hadn't been made. There was no reason for anyone to go into their bedroom anyway. She closed the door to that room and went to greet her guests.

Françoise arrived with her current boyfriend, Édouard. With them was a dark-haired young woman who stared openly at Chelsea. Françoise introduced her as Mariette

Armand. When Jean-Paul saw her, he embraced her enthusiastically.

Chelsea nudged Françoise. "Who is she?" she whispered. "Is she a cousin of Jean-Paul's?"

Françoise giggled. She had arrived high this time. "No, no. She is his wife."

"Say that again? My French is still shaky."

"Mariette was Jean-Paul's wife until a few months ago."

"I thought he'd been divorced over a year." Chelsea watched Jean-Paul laugh down into Mariette's face. "They certainly get along well for a divorced couple."

"It is their way. She left him for a man named Didier, but it did not last. I could have told her it would not. Didier has never been faithful to anyone, and he was not to her." She shrugged her thin shoulders as if she couldn't understand why Mariette had thought he would be. "I told Jean-Paul not to divorce her, but he did it anyway."

Chelsea crossed to where Jean-Paul and Mariette were talking, their heads together, and laughing. She smiled politely at them as she covertly studied the other woman. Mariette appeared to be in her twenties, and she was beautiful. Chelsea was uncomfortable with her in the house. Jean-Paul looked altogether too glad to see the woman.

"Look who is here, Chelsea," Jean-Paul said. "Mariette has come back to Paris!"

"We met at the door." She watched as Mariette and Jean-Paul had a rapid exchange in French. Mariette glared at her and crossed her arms over her breasts.

"She speaks no English," Jean-Paul said. "I've told her you live here now."

Chelsea nodded thoughtfully. It was possible that Mariette was another reason for Jean-Paul's wanting to move her into his house so hastily. What would make a woman more jealous? "Could I speak with you for a moment, Jean-Paul?"

She led him away from the others. Mariette stared after them, her lower lip protruding in a childish pout. "Did you know she would be here tonight?"

"I had heard she was in town. Françoise had seen her."

"She looks as if she would like to tear me limb from limb!"

"Mariette is a jealous woman. She was surprised to learn you live here. That is all." He grinned at her. "Perhaps you are jealous, too?"

"No, I'm not." This wasn't entirely true. She was living with Jean-Paul as his lover, and to her that implied some degree of commitment.

"I think perhaps you are," he repeated. "But you need not pout. You are the one I love." His eyes traveled back to Mariette, and they held a great deal of interest.

"I'm not pouting!" She frowned up at him. "I'm just saying that you should have told me she would be here. Can't you see how awkward this is?"

"No, no, Chelsea," he said in his most charming way. "Nothing is awkward here. You and I are independent, intelligent people. Now," he turned her toward the kitchen, "our guests need glasses for the wine."

Chelsea didn't see how independence and intelligence figured into this, and she thoroughly disliked being sent to fetch glasses as if he thought she wouldn't know how to be a hostess on her own.

People kept arriving until the house was packed. This wasn't an unusual state at Jean-Paul's. Chelsea sometimes wondered if he knew everyone who gathered at his place. She had been to the market on the way home from Meneir's, but the crowd had quickly eaten their way through the bread and cheeses she had expected to last for the rest of the week.

By midnight, some of the crowd began to drift away. Chelsea wasn't sorry to see them go. She moved through the rooms in search of Jean-Paul, but could find him nowhere. Françoise was in the kitchen eating the last of the fruit when Chelsea asked her if she had seen him.

"Jean-Paul? He left with Mariette over two hours ago."

"He did? Where were they going?"

"I do not know." She called to Édouard in French,

"Where are Jean-Paul and Mariette?" When he answered, she said, "He thinks they went to Mariette's flat."

"Why?" Chelsea knew it was a foolish question before she voiced it, but she could see no other way to ask. There could be a reason other than the one that seemed obvious.

"I have no idea. You may ask him when he comes home." Françoise tossed the apple core onto the cabinet and went to Édouard. "I want to go now."

He draped his arm over her shoulders, and they sauntered out.

Chelsea tried to keep her anger and embarrassment from showing as she waited for the last of the guests to leave. They seemed to take forever. Still there was no sign of Jean-Paul.

When she closed the door on the last of them, Chelsea went to the bedroom and sat on the bed to think. There was only one reason he could be at Mariette's apartment so late. She lay down fully clothed to wait for him, found a wineglass in the covers and groaned. Someone had been in their bedroom. Tired as she was, she stripped the bed and put on clean linens. Whether Jean-Paul liked it or not, she wasn't going to continue to live like this.

He finally returned. His clothing was rumpled and misbuttoned. He needed a shave and was still drunk enough to weave in the doorway. *"Bonjour,"* he called out unnecessarily loudly.

"Where have you been?" She knew she sounded like a jealous wife, but in the last few hours, she had begun to fear that something had happened to him. Now that she could see he was safe, her anger flared.

"With Mariette." He looked over his shoulder. "Has everyone gone?"

"I should hope so! It's almost dawn!" Her angry glance took in his bedraggled appearance. "You must have dressed too fast."

He gazed down as if surprised to find his shirt buttoned wrong and half-out of his trousers. "I must have," he agreed.

"You went to bed with Mariette?"

He shrugged. "I have not seen her in a long time. She was lonely. Poor Mariette! She is so young and innocent. Not like you independent Americans."

"She's about as innocent as Diamond Lil!"

"I do not know anyone named Lil," he said in drunken confusion. "Come to bed. We will talk of Lil later."

Chelsea backed away from the bed. "We'll talk about it now. How could you go to bed with her, if you love me?"

"We Frenchmen are romantics," he said as if it were obvious. "I do not love Mariette."

Chelsea glanced at her watch. "I have to go. Meneir will be waiting for me. Go to bed and sleep it off. We'll talk later." Not waiting to see if he obeyed, she hurried out of the house.

As she walked to Meneir's, she was thinking frantically. She had assumed that Jean-Paul no longer wanted to see other women since he had asked her to live with him and had said he loved her. She would mean that if she had said the same to him. She couldn't understand his going to bed with Mariette. And drunk as he was, had he used protection? AIDS was nothing to take chances with, and Chelsea certainly didn't see Mariette as being choosy. Not if the woman went to bed with her ex-husband when he was openly living with another woman. What was she going to do?

By the time she returned that evening, she was tired enough not to care that Jean-Paul didn't want to discuss Mariette. She made them dinner, and when he said he was going out afterward, she didn't question him. She wanted nothing so much as to be alone with her thoughts and to wrestle with the decisions she had to make.

Chapter Twenty-six

Ryan knew something was wrong, but he couldn't quite put his finger on it. Karen was gone too often, and frequently her excuses were flimsy at best. Ashley was usually out, too. She, however, flatly refused to tell him where she was going or with whom. He had grounded her more times than he had thought possible, but Karen always released her from any restrictions before two hours had passed.

Arguing with his wife did no good. She lost her temper more easily than ever these days and did as she pleased anyway. She couldn't, or wouldn't, see that Ashley was behaving in a way that was unacceptable and that the child was heading for trouble.

"She's only thirteen!" Ryan said, his temper boiling over. "She has no reason to stay out until midnight, let alone on school nights!"

"She'll only be young once," Karen retorted as she powdered her face. "Let her enjoy it. Maybe if we had treated Bethany more leniently she would still be here."

That hurt, as Karen had planned it should. Ryan stared at her in the mirror. "I don't know you anymore. We can't talk about anything these days."

She sighed as if he were boring her to distraction. "All you ever want to do is complain. I'm tired of listening to you."

"It's not complaining to want to maintain some control

over our daughter! You've undermined my authority with her so, she won't even set the table if I tell her to!"

"If you can't make her mind, that's not my fault. Ashley minds me." Karen smiled smugly and tipped her head back to apply more mascara.

"No, she doesn't. She just waits until you aren't paying attention and does as she pleases. Do you know she went out tonight?"

Karen's blue eyes flicked in his direction. "Of course." He could see she was lying.

"Where did she go? Who's she going to be with? No one came to pick her up—she left on foot. There's nothing for her to do around here within walking distance. Who's she meeting?"

"How on earth should I know? I don't spend my time spying on my daughter."

"Maybe you should. Or at least you should spend some time with her. Where are you going?"

"There's a meeting of the Ladies Auxiliary tonight."

"On a Tuesday? Isn't that a bit unusual?" He couldn't keep the sarcasm from his voice. "You told me they only meet on Wednesdays."

"It's a called meeting." She slammed her mascara wand down onto the vanity top and glared at him in the mirror. "You have no right to insinuate that I would be going somewhere else."

"Don't I?" He leaned forward and whirled her around to face him. "Something is going on, Karen. I'm not too blind or too stupid to know that."

She shoved his hands away from her shoulders. "I'm not going to stay here and be talked to like this. Get out of my way." She pushed past him and pulled a dress from a hanger.

He watched as she slipped it over her head and fastened it. "What happened to us?" he asked dully. "How did it ever get to be this way?"

"I have no idea what you mean." She buckled the fabric belt and stepped into her heels.

"How long will the Ladies Auxiliary be meeting this time?" he asked in a tired voice.

"I have no idea. Don't wait up for me."

"Why not? I'll still be waiting up for Ashley anyway. I assume no group will meet until midnight on a Tuesday. Right, Karen?"

"Whatever you say." She sounded as if she could hardly wait to get away from him.

Ryan watched her take her purse from the bed and walk briskly down the hall. She neither said goodbye nor looked back. The slamming door told him she was gone.

Depression settled over him. This wasn't the way he had expected his life to go. True, he had married Karen too hastily, but he had been willing to make the marriage work. He had tried as hard as any man could. It just seemed that whatever it was Karen wanted, he couldn't supply. And Ashley! He had adored her when she was a little child and she had loved him selflessly. Where had that baby gone?

He went into Bethany's old bedroom and turned on the light. Most of her things had been cleared away. Karen had given Ashley first choice, then had sent the rest to some charity organization. But he could still feel the essence of Bethany.

He sat on her bed and remembered the many nights he had tucked her in and kissed her good night. She had been so sweet, so gentle. Of the two, she had always been the most obedient, the most loving. Ashley had been independent and a bit of a rebel most of her life. Not Bethany.

Ryan pulled her pillow from the bed and buried his face in it. In spite of the clean pillowcase, he could smell Bethany in the linen. His eyes burned and he hugged the pillow, glad that Karen wasn't here to see his pain. At times he missed his eldest daughter so much it hurt.

Karen's grief had apparently healed. She never talked about Bethany and became impatient if he spoke her name. Ashley mentioned her sister occasionally, but it happened less and less often. Ryan's grief had dulled, but at times like this, when he was alone at night and had no idea where the rest of his family was, his misery was almost more than he could bear.

He replaced the pillow and smoothed the bedspread over it. In time, he supposed, Bethany's scent would be gone. Until then, he didn't want to do anything that would cause Karen to replace the pillow and do away with what little was left of his daughter.

Ryan went into the den and found pen and paper. Usually he refrained from writing Chelsea when he was so depressed, but tonight he needed to feel someone was near. He didn't want to go out and find companionship—he wasn't unfaithful by nature. Chelsea was different. He had loved her for so long he didn't feel he was being untrue to Karen in writing to her.

Karen had steadfastly refused to correspond with Chelsea or to call her. She'd said they were no longer friends and that Chelsea wouldn't want to hear from her anyway. Ryan knew this wasn't true, but there was no dissuading Karen. Once his wife got a thought into her head, it stayed there. She no longer wanted to be friends with Chelsea, so the friendship was over. Karen assumed he had also broken off all relations with her, but she was wrong there. Ryan chose his own friends.

The letter was hard to compose. He hadn't told Chelsea just how worried he was about Ashley. She loved the girl, and he'd feared she would be too concerned. But he had to tell someone. Keeping his emotions bottled up was starting to wear too heavily on him. Perhaps, he thought, he was too close to the situation, and Chelsea would put it into perspective by telling him all thirteen-year-old girls acted this way, felt this way. He just had to talk to someone, even if it was on paper.

* * *

Chelsea spent her spare time over the next few days walking along the rue Jacob and peering sightlessly into shop windows. She didn't want to go home.

Since the party, Jean-Paul had started going out frequently. She had made the mistake once of asking where he was heading, and he had told her truthfully that he was going to Mariette's apartment. After that, she had never asked.

Her old apartment had been rented. She had asked about it the morning after the party. If it hadn't already been taken, she would have moved out that day. When she had time, she halfheartedly looked for other lodgings, but found nothing she could afford that was within walking distance of Meneir's house. The amount of money she had set aside for her stint in Paris was almost gone, and she had to make a decision.

Should she stay here longer, depleting the rest of her funds, or go back to the States? She was dreadfully homesick and had been since her first days here. She had never liked moving and didn't transplant well. Also she knew there was a limit to how much Meneir could teach her.

The man was a brilliant artist, but she was becoming aware that he was far less inspired as a teacher. He wanted to talk endlessly about techniques, mediums, exhibitions of his works, but he was spending less and less time actually showing her how to paint. Part of the problem was his failing health. It was causing his mind to wander. Most of what Chelsea was learning now came from studying his canvases and trying to duplicate what she had seen.

Meneir was reluctant, and rightly so, to let her copy his canvases. This meant she had to find her own inspiration, use his techniques, and see if that worked. In the last few weeks, Meneir hadn't touched a brush, so she hadn't been able to watch how he laid on paint or mixed the colors. She wasn't sure she was getting her money's worth.

Matters with Jean-Paul were strained, to say the least. She had tried to move into the spare bedroom, but he had refused to allow that and they had had a thundering argument. Afterward he had accused her of destroying his ability to paint and had sulked for days. This left Chelsea sleeping in the same bed with him and feeling as if she were prostituting herself, especially since she had to pay to live there and be treated so badly.

She gazed at the antiques in the shop windows and wondered what she was going to do. All her life she had wanted to study with a truly great artist, and she had, from time to time, even considered living in Paris. She hadn't envisioned that it would be like this.

One of the store proprietors stood at his door and nodded pleasantly at her as she passed. Lately Chelsea had wandered on this, her favorite street, so often that she was a familiar figure.

She walked until the shops closed for the night, then headed up the rue de Seine and down the boulevard Saint-Germain. This branched off into several streets that led to the rue Delacroix. Number Sixteen was dark as she approached it, so her steps quickened. Jean-Paul was gone. She wouldn't have to talk to him. It was her relief on thinking this that decided her course of action. She was ready to go home to Dallas.

The next day she told Meneir of her decision. At first he looked confused, as if he had forgotten that she wasn't a permanent resident of Paris. "Home?" he asked. "To America?"

"I had hoped to stay longer, but everything is more expensive than I had expected." She clasped her hands in her lap. This wasn't as easy as she had thought it would be. "I'm running out of money."

"You'd let money stand between studying with me?" Meneir frowned at her and drew himself taller. "Men have starved in order to work in my studio!"

"I appreciate all you've taught me. You've helped me immensely. But I only have a hundred dollars left in the account I set aside to study here. I haven't been able to get a job because my French isn't that good and because I'm studying here during the hours I would have to be working. I can't paint all day and work all night."

"You're young! When I was studying under my master, I never slept!"

Chelsea didn't point out the impossibility of that. "Thank you for all the help you've given me. I'll never forget the time I've been here."

Meneir made a sputtering noise. "You've only studied with me three months! You haven't learned a portion of what I have to offer a student!"

"I know I haven't been here long, but we've worked every day from dawn to dusk. I have learned much!" She could see he wasn't going to listen to her reasons for leaving so she gathered up her things. As he followed her around the studio, shouting at her that she was selfish and American and lazy, Chelsea realized that his agreement to teach her had been based on money. He hadn't chosen her for her talent as he had said in the beginning. His tirade left her no doubt of that.

She struggled to carry all the painting paraphernalia back to Jean-Paul's house and was exhausted by the effort. At this hour of the day she expected him to be working, locked away in his studio on the second floor. Instead he was standing in the kitchen reading a piece of mail. When he saw her, he glared at her and waved it at her.

"A man is writing to you!"

Chelsea took the letter from him and read the signature. "It's from Ryan. Why are you reading my mail?"

"You are living with me, sleeping in my bed, eating my food, and receiving mail from another man?" He looked as outraged as if they were married and she was having a flagrant affair.

Tired and upset from the exchange with Meneir, Chelsea was in no mood for Jean-Paul's unreasonableness. "You have no right to open my mail and read it!"

"It came to my house. Mail that comes to my house belongs to me!" He made a grab at the paper.

Chelsea jerked it away and read it hastily. Ryan was

having trouble with Ashley. The letter was short, but nowhere did it mention Karen. She knew Ryan well enough to know something was very wrong by the way he had phrased the sentences.

Jean-Paul snatched the letter from her, wadded it up, and threw it across the room. "You will not receive mail from another man while you live under my roof!"

"What gives you the right to say that to me?" she retorted, her anger flaring to match his. "You went to bed with this man's wife! You stay all night with Mariette, and I've heard that you take her to parties to which I'm never invited! You're having an affair with your ex-wife, yet I'm not supposed to get mail? Are you out of your mind?"

Jean-Paul lashed out at her. It happened so fast that Chelsea had no time to react. The blow caught her on the cheek, and she fell to the floor.

It was as if time had rolled backward and Lorne were standing over her. For a moment she couldn't feel or think. Then the pain hit, and she pressed her hand to her cheek.

At once Jean-Paul was apologetic. "Forgive me, Chelsea! I should never have done that!" He reached down and helped her up.

She held to the table to steady herself against the emotions bursting inside her. It was clear now. She had once again chosen a man who would mistreat her! What frightened her most was that until he had actually struck her, she hadn't noticed that he was being abusive! He was having an affair, making her pay half his rent, using her as if she were his property at night, but she hadn't known he was being abusive? The admission sickened her.

She turned from him and went to the closet where she kept her suitcases.

"What are you doing? You are not leaving me, are you? Because I made one tiny slip? A Parisian woman would understand and forgive!"

"I doubt that. Any woman knows when she's being hit,

whatever country she comes from, and I've never heard of one that likes it. Get out of my way."

"No! I will not let you leave! Besides, where will you go? It's starting to rain, and you have no one else."

"I'm going to the airport. I don't know when the next flight leaves for America, but I intend to be on it."

He stared at her. "All because I hit you? Because I made one tiny slip? This is not reasonable, Chelsea."

She ignored him, her loathing for him surpassed only by her disgust with herself. She had found another Lorne and hadn't even realized it!

As quickly as possible, she packed, cramming everything into the suitcases and forcing the zippers shut. She was glad now that she hadn't brought all her belongings or had the money to buy many things here.

"I forbid you to go!" Jean-Paul said, standing in the hall, his arms crossed resolutely.

"Jean-Paul, I'm leaving. You can hit me again or you can block my way, whatever. But eventually you have to sleep or go to your studio, and when you do, I'm out of here. Now we can do it the easy way or the hard way, but I'm definitely going!"

For a long time he glared at her without speaking. She was beginning to think he would call her bluff. Then he stepped aside and let her pass. Chelsea deposited her bags by the front door, found heavy paper to wrap around her canvases, then tied them together with a string. Oil paint wouldn't be affected by a little rain, still, if the canvases were damaged in some way, there was no help for it.

"How are you going to get to the airport carrying all that?" he demanded sullenly.

"I'll call a cab. I'll manage." She wasn't going to ask him for help.

He went to the phone and dialed a number. "Send a taxi to sixteen rue Delacroix," he said brusquely in French.

"Thank you."

"I do not want you to go." He faced her across the room, not coming near her.

"It's time, Jean-Paul. It's not only that you hit me, though that would have been enough. It's that I don't know how to have a completely open sexual relationship, and I don't want to learn. I'm monogamous, and I expected you to be."

"I never told you that I would be," he said defensively.

"I know. One of these days I'll learn not to assume so much about the things that are important." She felt alone and small, but she didn't want him to come near her. She was too vulnerable at that moment. A kind word might melt her resolve. "I need to get some counseling," she said as much to herself as to him. "I seem to make the stupidest choices."

"I will miss you," he said.

She managed a smile. "I'll miss who you used to be."

The taxi arrived with a blare of its horn, and she bent to pick up her suitcases. Without another word, she loaded everything into the back seat. Jean-Paul didn't make a move to help her, and she was glad. At the moment she didn't want any pleasant or considerate gestures to remember him by.

As the taxi took her to the airport, Chelsea wondered why she had not seen sooner the sort of relationship she had been in. She hadn't realized the battered-wife syndrome was so far reaching, so insidious. Until today, she really hadn't seen a parallel between Lorne and Jean-Paul. A pounding headache was throbbing in her temples, and she was too close to tears to speak. She paid the driver, then let him help her carry her belongings into the terminal.

No flights were leaving for the States that night. Chelsea sat in the upright chairs in the lobby and was thankful that her passport was still good and that she had been able to get a ticket on a flight leaving the following day. Every time the outside doors opened, she was afraid Jean-Paul had come to take her back by force or by charm, but he didn't appear.

By morning she was exhausted. She boarded her plane and settled down in the padded seat, too tired to dread the flight. At least she would have hours to sleep before she had to talk to anyone or explain why she had come home with a bruised cheek. Tears brimmed in her eyes as the plane started to taxi. A light rain was still falling, and that seemed appropriate. Lately it had rained almost every day. The sky seemed to be crying along with her. As the plane took off and lifted high above Paris, Chelsea relaxed for the first time in days.

Long hours later, she landed in New York and boarded another plane for the final leg of the flight. By the time she landed at Love Field in Dallas she was so tired she could barely move. She waited with the other passengers to clear customs, and for her baggage to be unloaded. She was numb from exhaustion, jet lag, and emotional stress. Now and then someone would glance at her curiously, and she wondered if the bruise on her cheek was that obvious. All she wanted was to be home.

A taxi took her to her apartment, and she lugged her things upstairs. The place was dark and cold. She touched the switch and realized the electricity had been turned off. She had forgotten such small details.

She felt around in the dark until she located candles and matches. Her apartment looked like paradise to her. The candlelight didn't illumine the far corners, but she knew them all. She was home!

The water was flowing because the upper floor shared the meter with the garage downstairs. She showered and washed her hair. As the water sluiced over her, she imagined it was rinsing away Jean-Paul and Paris, leaving her clean and untouched.

She dried herself off and wrapped a towel around her long hair. As tired as she was, she wasn't sleepy. She was a bit hungry, but there was no food. Her refrigerator stood open and empty. Chelsea decided she wasn't hungry enough to call out for pizza, then remembered the phone wouldn't have worked anyway.

She began unpacking by candlelight. By morning she wanted no reminders of the past few months.

Chapter Twenty-seven

In the next couple of weeks, Chelsea settled back into her life as easily as if she had never been away. Her tenants in the garage below left, but she was able to rent it at a higher price to a man who restored antique cars. She was glad she had bought the building while she'd had some money, for the rent the garage was bringing in gave her enough to live on and even some to put in her depleted savings account.

Karen didn't call, so Chelsea called her. She was polite, but cool, and Chelsea felt lonely after having talked to her. The following day Ryan phoned to invite Chelsea for dinner. After some hesitation, she accepted. She wanted to repair her friendship with Karen.

Chelsea was greeted warmly by Ryan, and even Ashley, behind her facade of bored sullenness, seemed glad to see her. Karen was as coolly polite as if she and Chelsea were the most casual of acquaintances.

"What's going on in your life?" Chelsea asked Ashley. "I feel I've been gone for years instead of just months."

"Not much."

"If you can get anything out of her you're better than we are," Karen said, glancing with distaste at her daughter. "I can't even get her to dress properly for dinner."

Ashley rolled her eyes and let her head fall back onto the chair as she stared at the ceiling. She wore jeans that were more holes than fabric and a boy's camouflage shirt with a canvas vest studded with plastic gemstones. Her hair was still shaved on the sides, making her look as if she were bald and wearing a bad toupee. Enormous earrings hung from her lobes. They did not match.

"How do you like the eighth grade?"

"I hate it." Ashley closed her eyes and pretended she couldn't hear her mother.

"Her grades are disgraceful," Karen said. "She's been cutting classes again, according to the school."

Ryan had been in the kitchen, but he came back in time to hear Karen's last statement. "She has promised not to do that anymore."

"And you believe her, I suppose?" Karen snapped.

Chelsea tried desperately to find grounds for a neutral conversation. "I wish you could have seen Paris, Ashley. It's the most fascinating place."

"Mom said you were living with that French guy who came here that time. Is that true?"

"Ashley!" Ryan exclaimed.

"Yes," Chelsea said calmly. "It's true. It didn't work out."

"Is that why you came home?"

"Not entirely. It was the deciding factor."

"Why didn't it work out?"

Karen frowned at her daughter. "That's enough out of you! Apologize at once!"

Ashley regarded her mother as if she couldn't see any reason to do as she had been told. "I was just asking a question."

"It's okay," Chelsea put in hastily. "I don't mind talking about it. I studied under Meneir, and at first I thought I had found the pot of gold at the end of the rainbow. Then I realized his mind was wandering and he really had little to teach me. He soon stopped demonstrating his techniques and only wanted to lecture me. I wasn't learning anything, and I was running out of money fast. It's very expensive in Paris."

"Maybe I'll go there someday." Ashley draped her leg

over the arm of the couch. "I'll find me a rich Frenchman and be kept."

"Go to your room!" Karen said. Her voice was trembling with anger.

"I don't know what you're trying to accomplish by being rude," Ryan said to his daughter, "but you've said more than enough."

Ashley made no move to leave the couch. By the look on her face, Chelsea could tell she was hoping her mother would be pushed into creating an even more unpleasant scene.

Chelsea went to sit by the girl. "You know what we could do with these jeans? We could sew printed fabric behind the holes and it would look as if you were wearing pants made out of the peek-a-boo book I used to read you. Remember? You had to open the windows and doors to see the pictures?"

Ashley smiled before she remembered to be sullen.

Chelsea touched her topknot of hair. "Won't this be cold in the winter?"

"I knew you wouldn't like it." Ashley was sullen again.

"I didn't say that. I was just wondering if your ears wouldn't get cold." She smiled. "I could get you some of those Mickey Mouse earmuffs."

"Or maybe the ones that look like an arrow is sticking through your head," Ashley suggested.

"That sounds charming," Karen said dryly.

Ryan was watching the exchange. His wife had lost all control over Ashley, and he was afraid to test his own authority these days. He hadn't seen Ashley act like herself for a long time, but Chelsea was drawing it out of her. Maybe he would ask Chelsea to spend some time with her.

Chelsea looked different since her return. She had lost weight, and her face was thinner—a sure sign that things weren't going well with her. He had seen her the day after she'd come home and had noticed the pale bruise on her cheek that her makeup didn't completely hide. He hadn't asked about it, and she hadn't volunteered any information. Thinking about the bruise made protective anger rise in him.

Why did she put herself into such damaging relationships? It certainly wasn't because she was foolish or had no sense of self-worth. Chelsea had more going for her than the average person. She was beautiful, talented, and intelligent. So why was she attracted to losers?

Aware that he was watching her, Chelsea looked at him. Ryan let his eyes meet hers for as long as he could without arousing Karen's suspicions. Seeing the deep sadness in Chelsea's gaze, he wondered if she was hiding a life as miserable as his own.

Inviting Chelsea to dinner had been his idea. Karen had found a dozen excuses for not doing so. Two weeks had passed before he'd realized his wife had no intention of asking Chelsea over. Then he had insisted on an invitation for tonight. He was as worried about Karen as he was about Ashley.

He was almost positive that Karen was seeing someone. The idea had seemed preposterous when it had first occurred to him. Karen hated kissing, let alone sex. That she would seek out someone for the purpose of going to bed with him had seemed impossible. But he had considered every other possibility, and nothing else fit the pattern of her unexplained absences and elusiveness. Who could it be? He hadn't a clue.

Karen had lost weight again and looked younger and prettier than she had in a long time. Her slimness had prompted a rash of shopping for clothes, but he didn't begrudge her that. He knew how difficult it was for her to diet. Unfortunately, Karen had no brakes when it came to shopping, and her closet was beginning to bulge. He dreaded getting the bills every month, but it would do no good to tell her to be more prudent. When he had tried that in the past, she had simply headed for the stores.

He frequently wondered why he stayed with her. His home life wasn't pleasant. He had buried himself in work to compensate for it. Fortunately he still liked working for

DataComp. He even liked the idea of eventually inheriting half the business, but not enough for that to sway him about leaving Karen. There were many other companies he could work for, probably for a higher salary than he was making with his father-in-law.

Chelsea had drawn another smile from Ashley, and Ryan found he was smiling, too. Then he saw the unguarded expression on Karen's face and his mouth tensed. Karen looked jealous of the smiles Ashley was giving Chelsea, as if she felt her daughter were being stolen away from her. Not for the first time, Ryan wondered if Karen was mentally on shaky ground. She had an overwhelming need to control everyone and to be the undisputed center of attention—even to overshadow her own daughter.

Yes, he thought, it would be a good idea to ask Chelsea if she would try to help Ashley. Karen couldn't or wouldn't and the child was heading for trouble. He made a mental note to ask Chelsea in private. Karen didn't need to know he had done it.

Over dinner Karen kept up the conversation, talking nonstop about nothing in particular. Chelsea observed her with the objectivity of an outsider. She was too brittle, too glossy. Chelsea had known many women like this during her marriage to Lorne. How had Karen managed to become like her mother? Chelsea would have said that could never happen. Not to Karen. The shy, sweet girl she had known all her life seemed to have vanished entirely.

After the meal, Ashley escaped from the house and Karen frowned after her. The girl hadn't said where she was going or who she'd be with, nor had Karen asked her. Chelsea was mystified. In spite of how old she looked, Ashley was only thirteen. "Is a friend picking her up?" she asked.

Karen gave one of her new, plastic laughs. "She probably has a date."

"A date? Ashley is dating someone old enough to have a driver's license?"

"She's always been more adventurous than Bethany was. She became boy crazy last year, you'll remember."

"I knew she had a boyfriend, but I assumed they were being driven on dates by his parents." Chelsea looked at Ryan. "You said once you weren't going to let either of the girls date until they were thirty and you were going along with them, even then."

"It didn't work out quite that way," he said. "Ashley has a mind of her own." He avoided her eyes.

"It's not like when we were in school," Karen said as if she considered Chelsea's attitude to be puritanical. "Then we didn't date until we were half through our teens! Girls now date much earlier."

"At thirteen? What's this boy like?"

"We haven't seen him," Ryan said. A worried frown puckered his forehead. "She seems to think it's asking too much for us to meet him."

Karen shot him a glare. "You make her sound awful. She's just out on a date. I imagine Scott lives in the neighborhood and they walk to the shopping center and see a movie."

"You 'imagine' that's what she does?" Chelsea was so concerned she forgot to be tactful. "Why on earth would you let a child of that age have so much freedom? Why don't you insist that she tell you where she'll be?"

Karen said sharply, "It's easy for you to give advice; you can't possibly know how it is. I trust my daughter. I'm not going to interrogate her as if she's a criminal!"

"It's not an interrogation to ask a thirteen-year-old where she goes at night." Chelsea stared at Karen. "How long has she been doing this?"

"You're not a mother, and at your age, I frankly doubt that you ever will be." Karen locked her cold smile back into place. "You are not the best person to be giving advice on child-raising. More coffee?"

"Karen!" Ryan exclaimed in a shocked voice.

Chelsea stood. "No. I have to be going."

"So soon?" Karen rose and walked to the door. She was making it clear that she considered the visit over.

"It's early yet, but I understand." Ryan looked both angry and embarrassed over Karen's rudeness.

Chelsea shook her head. Something was very wrong in this house, and she felt like an interloper for realizing it. "Thank you for having me over."

Karen opened the door. "We were glad you could come," she said formally, as if Chelsea were little more than a stranger.

Chelsea was glad to step out into the night. As soon as the door clicked shut she walked briskly to her car. Looking up and down the street, she saw Ashley going around the far corner, her shoulders hunched against the chill wind.

She drove in the direction Ashley had taken, intending to offer her a ride. By the time she reached the corner, Ashley was halfway down the street, where two boys awaited her. As Chelsea stopped at the intersection, one of the boys tossed his cigarette into the street, put his arm around Ashley, and hugged her possessively. Ashley returned the embrace, and the pair exchanged a passionate kiss while the other boy looked on. Then Ashley slid into the car, and both boys got in with her. Seconds later, the car peeled away from the curb and roared down the street.

Chelsea's first impulse was to go back and tell Ryan and Karen what she had seen. The two boys were obviously older than Ashley, and had looked tough. Certainly they hadn't seemed to be the sort Chelsea's thirteen-year-old godchild should be dating. The inappropriateness of the kiss had been enough to show her that. But she knew Karen wouldn't welcome the intrusion. She could call Ryan tomorrow at DataComp and tell him.

As she drove home, Chelsea couldn't shake her feeling of uneasiness about Ashley or the sting of Karen's coldness.

* * *

"Did Mom put you up to asking me over?" Ashley asked as she wandered around Chelsea's studio.

"No. As far as I know, she doesn't know you're here."

"I can't stay long. I've got plans for this afternoon."

"Ashley, what's wrong?"

The girl glanced at her, then looked away. "I don't know what you're talking about. Nothing's wrong with me."

"Don't give me that. I've known you since you were born."

Ashley flopped onto the couch and lay across the cushions. "I hate school, I hate my parents, Saint Anne's is full of the dumbest kids in Dallas, my grades suck, Mom hates all my friends, and she treats me like I was five years old. Other than that, nothing's wrong."

"Most of that sounds pretty much like I felt at thirteen." Chelsea went to the refrigerator and took out two colas. She handed one to Ashley and sat on the floor opposite the couch. "Just how bad are your grades?"

Ashley sat up enough to drink. "Real bad. Like I may flunk half the stuff I'm taking." She frowned at Chelsea. "Don't tell Dad, though, or he'll be on my case!"

"Have you been cutting classes?"

"School is dumb. I don't care about all that crap." She glanced at Chelsea to see if her language had been sufficiently shocking.

Chelsea had heard worse. "That may be true, but you still have to go. It's illegal to drop out at thirteen."

Ashley showed more interest. "It is? When can you drop out?"

"Seventeen, I think. I'm not sure about that. I dropped out of college, you know."

"Yeah. Mom told me. Over and over."

Chelsea decided she didn't want to know exactly what Karen had said, since she had obviously been used as a bad example. "I've always regretted it."

"Then why did you do it?"

"Because at the time I thought it was a good idea.

Because I thought most of the stuff I was learning was crap." She grinned at Ashley. "Turns out I was wrong."

"You can save the lecture. I'm not dropping out. Dad would kill me."

Chelsea leaned back against the chair and propped her arm on the cushion. "I saw you with your boyfriend night before last."

Ashley shot her a quick look. "Oh?"

"He looks older than you."

"Scott's nineteen."

"Where did you meet him?"

"At the skating rink."

"Where were you going?"

"We just went riding around. You're starting to sound like Dad."

"Would you like to bring Scott over here sometime? I'd like to get to know him."

"Why?" Ashley was instantly on her guard.

"You're almost like a daughter to me. I'd like to know your friends. I'll make that chocolate cake you like if you give me enough warning."

Ashley thought for a minute. "I don't think he'd come. He's real funny about meeting people. Especially people who are like parents to me."

"Then I gather you don't intend for them to meet him?"

Ashley gave a short laugh. "Do you think they'd let me go out with him if they did? Mom wants me to date Ivy League types, and Dad thinks I'm about three years old. Scott would be too much of a shock."

"Is that why you're dating him?"

"What are you, a shrink all of a sudden?"

"No, I'm an expert on picking the wrong men, but even I can tell when some people are trouble. I want to meet Scott so I can stop worrying about you."

Ashley drank her cola and thought for a while. "I wonder if you could do something for me."

"I'll try."

"I want to get birth-control pills."

Chelsea nearly choked. "Excuse me?"

"You heard me. I want some birth-control pills. I sure can't ask Mom! She'd kill me for knowing such a thing exists. Dad would probably nail me into my room."

"Do you have a reason to need them?"

Ashley looked at her in exasperation. "I'm not a baby, Aunt Chel! I don't want to take a chance on getting pregnant."

Chelsea hadn't expected anything of this magnitude. "I really think you should ask your parents about this."

"I should have known you didn't really want to help." Ashley looked away, and the sullen look settled back on her face.

"That's not it. You're *thirteen.* I know that seems grown-up to you, but you shouldn't be having sex at your age."

"Okay. Whatever you say." The bored note was back in her voice.

"Let me think for a minute. You caught me by surprise." Chelsea was remembering her own school years. Girls could get pregnant much more easily than most of them thought possible, and pregnancy would be far more traumatic to Ashley than taking birth-control pills. If she was determined enough to ask for the pills, telling her not to have sex probably was doing no good. "I don't know if it's possible for me to get them for you. You're not my daughter."

"That's okay. I talked to a girl at school, and she said all I have to do is go to one of the clinics and get them. I don't need permission, just a way to get over there."

"Do you have any idea what you're asking me to do?" Chelsea got up off the floor and paced to the window. "Give me permission to talk to your father about this."

Ashley seemed surprised. "Not Mom?"

"I have a feeling your Dad would be the most understanding in this case."

"Yeah, he probably would. But I don't want him to know." She paused. "It's not like I just want to sleep with

Scott. We're in love, and we're going to get married some day. After I'm out of school," she added.

Chelsea nodded. That was always the story. It hadn't changed since her own school days. "Are you sleeping with him now?"

"I don't want to talk about it. I've already said way more than I should have." Ashley went to put her can of cola on the cabinet. "I have to go."

"Give me time to think," Chelsea repeated. "And, Ashley, please don't make any mistakes. There's AIDS and—"

"I know. We have films in school all the time." She didn't look in Chelsea's direction as she shouldered her book pack and started for the door.

"Come back anytime."

Ashley hesitated, then nodded. As she left, Chelsea had the distinct impression that there was something she had wanted to say or ask, but she had thought better of it at the last minute. Chelsea couldn't imagine anything that would be more serious than her request for birth-control pills.

She sat where Ashley had been and buried her face in her hands. The girl was desperately unhappy. What could she do to help her?

The phone rang, and she answered it to find Ryan on the other end. "You just missed her. She was on her bicycle and should be home before long."

"Did she say anything? Were you able to find out what's bothering her?"

Chelsea paused. "I think so, but she doesn't want you to know."

"Is it something I need to hear?"

"In my opinion, yes. But I'm not sure she wasn't exaggerating. I think she was hoping to shock me. Let me talk to her again and see if I can convince her to talk to you about it. Like I say, I'm not entirely sure I was getting a straight story from her."

"I appreciate this."

"Ryan, can I ask a question that's none of my business?"

"Of course."

"Are you okay? I've only been away a few months, but I can see so many differences in you all."

"Losing Bethany was a shock. We still aren't over it."

"I can understand that."

"Grief pulls some families together and blows others apart. We seem to fit into the latter category."

"I'm sorry. Is there anything I can do?"

"Help me with Ashley. She's the important one." He hesitated. "I'm sorry Karen was so brash the other night. I think she's just worried about Ashley and you hit a nerve."

"It's okay. She's been upset with me before. Time will probably heal it." Chelsea didn't believe this, but had to pretend.

"Maybe. I don't know what's going on with her. She's changed so much lately."

Chelsea thought wryly that he didn't know the half of it. At least Karen hadn't confessed her affair. "I'll spend more time with Ashley. She seems to trust me. That's why I don't want to tell you all she said. I don't want to destroy her confidence in me."

"I understand. Thanks. She won't talk to Karen or to me."

"How about you? Are you okay?"

There was a long pause. "I'm fine."

"Right."

He laughed. "I guess I need somebody to talk to as well."

"I'm here if you need me." She knew this was setting up a huge temptation, but she couldn't stand by with him suffering and not offer him a willing ear if he needed to talk. "Or I can give you the name of the counselor I used when I left Lorne."

"Thanks. I may take you up on both counts." There was another pause. "How about you? I think more went on in

Paris than you've admitted. Do you need a shoulder your-self?"

"No. I was glad to leave Paris and come home. I miss Jean-Paul surprisingly little." She laughed shortly. "I seem to have a real talent for picking the wrong men, don't I?"

"I wasn't going to point that out."

"At any rate, I don't have a broken heart and I left before I damaged my bank account too severely. I'm painting. My life will soon be back in order." She was surprised by how believable that sounded.

"Either you're becoming a more accomplished liar or you're doing better than I thought. Will you call me if you need me? I'm available day or night."

"That should endear Karen to me. Especially if I were to call you at three in the morning. That's when I tend to hit bottom."

"Don't worry about that. Just call if you need me."

"Thanks, Ryan." Her throat tightened. She knew he meant the words.

After she hung up, she sat down on the floor and looked at the couch where Ashley had been. Her real worry was over the girl. Was this child foolish enough to be going to bed with that boy, or had it all been an attempt to shock her? Chelsea didn't know.

Chapter Twenty-eight

Ashley answered the roll in gym, told the teacher she felt sick, and ostensibly went to the nurse's office. Between the gym and the office, she slipped out the door and ran across the parking lot. Scott was waiting for her where the buses parked, just as she had expected.

Leaning against his front fender and smoking, he looked as if he had nothing at all to do. He was dressed in black, and his dark hair was slicked back like James Dean's in posters. Scott never dressed like the other boys. He had style.

She hurried up to him, and he gave her his sexiest smile. She went on tiptoe to kiss him. He prolonged the kiss until her head whirled. "I almost wasn't able to get out. I think Dad's talked to my gym teacher and told her to keep me in sight."

"Parents suck." He offered her a cigarette.

Ashley started to take it, then stopped. "There's something I have to tell you. I think you're going to be real excited."

"Yeah? What's up?" He lit another cigarette from the butt and then arced the old one onto the pavement.

"I'm pregnant."

For a minute Scott just stared at her. "You're what?"

"I'm going to have a baby. Isn't it great? Now my parents can't tell us not to get married. They have to give their approval." She hoped she didn't sound as scared as she felt.

"Have you told anybody about this?"

"No, I wanted you to know first. I thought about telling my Aunt Chel the other day, but I wasn't positive then."

"And you are now?"

"I bought one of those pregnancy tests. It was positive."

Scott gazed off into the distance. "I'll get somebody to drive you to the clinic. Hell, I'll even give you the money."

"Money? What are you talking about?"

"You're going to have to get an abortion."

Ashley took a step back. "An abortion! No way!"

"You can't have this baby. Your parents would kill me!" He looked younger and more frightened than she had ever seen him. "You're only thirteen! That's statutory rape. They could have me put in prison!"

"They wouldn't do that," she said uncertainly. "Especially not if we get married."

"I'm not getting married. I'm nineteen. I don't want to be saddled with a wife and baby!" He frowned down at her.

Ashley shook her head as she backed away. "Tell me you're kidding. You can't mean that. You're just teasing me, right?"

"Pregnant!" He said the word as if it were new to him and he was considering its exact meaning. "Shit!" He shoved his hands in his tight black jeans and shifted his weight. "Damn, Ashley!"

"Maybe we could slip off and get married without telling my parents. I look older than I really am. I've got that fake ID."

"You don't look *that* old. Anybody who really looked at that ID could tell it's not a real one. Besides, I already told you I don't want to get married."

Ashley hesitated for a minute, then walked away.

"Hey! Where're you going?"

"Away from you! You don't love me! I don't think you

ever did!" She brushed at her tears angrily. This was something she hadn't expected.

"Fine! Just be that way!" he shouted after her. "I've got better things to do than hang out in a parking lot!"

"Good!" she yelled back and kept walking.

She had no place to go. At this hour her mother would be at home, and Ashley certainly didn't want to see her. Could pregnancy tests be wrong? She tried to recall everything she had ever heard about them. The girls talked about the kits a lot, but she had never heard anybody admit to having used one. Maybe they weren't as accurate as TV shows claimed.

She went to a vacant lot where she'd spent other absentee afternoons and sat under the tree at the back corner. What was she going to do? When she'd first missed her period, she hadn't thought much about it, but now she was nearly a month late and had realized she could be in trouble. At thirteen she had thought it practically impossible to become pregnant. Scott had seemed so sure, and they had used the rhythm method. Wasn't that supposed to work? Her health and science book had confirmed that it would. When she had asked Chelsea to get the birth-control pills, she had thought of them simply as an extra precaution.

She drew her knees up against her chest and let herself cry. She was too young to be a mother! But she didn't want an abortion. Even if she did, she didn't think there was any way to get one without her parents being notified.

Chelsea came to mind. Chel had always kept Ashley's secrets. Could she be trusted with this? It was too big a secret to take the chance.

When Ashley was tired of sitting under the tree, she walked aimlessly through the strip shopping center between the school and her house. The time to go home from school came and passed, but Ashley didn't care. Her mother coming to pick her up at school was the least of her worries. Karen would assume she had ridden home with someone else and be angry, but not worried. That was one thing about her mother, she never seemed to worry about her.

Tears stung her eyes. Ashley had always had to fight for Karen's attention. Bethany had been everything to her. She'd seemed to forget her other daughter existed unless Ashley needed to be scolded for something. So Ashley had seen to it that there were plenty of opportunities for scoldings. Now, with Bethany gone, she wasn't paid any more attention. Karen had simply directed her interests elsewhere.

Dinner time came and went and Ashley used her lunch money to get a hamburger. It tasted like cardboard, and she ended up throwing it away. Food was unappetizing these days.

When she was too tired to walk anymore, she went home. The house was dark. Ashley got the key from the hiding place behind the mailbox and let herself in. The silent house told her neither parent was at home. She could hardly believe her good luck. A note on the hall table told her Karen was "out" and Ryan was working late again.

She went down the hall to her room and lay on the bed. For a long time she stared up at the ceiling she had seen every day of her life. Then she got up and went into her mother's bathroom and opened the well-stocked medicine cabinet.

Karen was with Mark Dreyer in an exclusive restaurant on top of one of Dallas's tallest buildings. The city was spread out below in a panorama of lights, and the dance floor was crowded enough so that no one would notice she was there with Mark. This was one of their favorite spots.

"Polly wanted me to bring her up here last week," Mark said as he spun her to the music.

Jealousy sprang into Karen's voice. "What did you tell her?"

"I told her no. This is our place."

She relaxed a bit. "What on earth would she want to come here for? I can't imagine her dancing."

"She's heard the shrimp is good." They laughed together as if his wife were ridiculous. He twirled her again, and her chiffon skirt swirled against both their legs.

"Didn't she ask why you didn't want to come?"

"Not really. Polly doesn't have much curiosity. Where does Ryan think you are?"

"At home. He's working late again. As usual. I could be in China and he wouldn't know for days."

"He's been preoccupied at work. I had to speak to him several times this afternoon before he heard me."

"That's Ryan, all right," she said wryly. "I don't know where his mind is half the time."

"It's a good thing he's like that. Otherwise we'd be taking too big a chance."

"Would it be the end of the world if he found out? He'd never leave me."

"You're sure of that?"

"He's too comfortable. Besides, his boss is my father, remember. No, Ryan would pretend it never happened."

"It could cost me my job, though," Mark said thoughtfully. "I forget who you are at times. I don't think Mr. Baker would look kindly on the fact that I'm having an affair with his daughter."

"Daddy will never know," she said airily. "We have nothing at all to worry about."

Several hours later Karen drove herself home from the hotel where Mark had taken a room for the evening. He was on his way home to dull little Polly while she was returning to Ryan. Assuming that he was at the house. Sometimes he stayed at the office until nearly midnight.

Their home seemed dark when she arrived, just as she had expected. Ashley would have been back for hours and was probably asleep by now. When Karen went upstairs she was startled to see a light on in Ashley's room. She glanced down at her dress. It was her best black chiffon with a sequined top and low neckline. If Ashley was still awake, how would she explain it? As she formulated her story, she went down the hall.

Ashley lay curled on her bed, seemingly fast asleep. Karen almost turned out the light and left her there undisturbed. Something, however, made her look closer.

Ashley's face had the same look Bethany's had had the night they'd rushed her to the hospital. Her eyelids were partially open and a thread of saliva beaded from her parted lips. Karen frowned and went over to shake Ashley, whose body rolled limply.

Karen heard her own scream as if it came from far away. She shook Ashley until her arms ached. She then ran to the nearest phone, which was in her bedroom, and dialed 911, her fingers shaking so she could barely hit the numbers. As she told the woman on the other end to send an ambulance, she noticed the light on in her bathroom. When she hung up, she ran in there and saw the empty bottle of sleeping pills. Hurriedly she grabbed it and thrust it into the small purse she still carried. The doctor would need to know what Ashley had taken.

She ran back to Ashley and tried to give her CPR. Karen had never taken the class and didn't know if she was doing it right or not, but she had to try something. In a few minutes she heard the wail of the ambulance and ran to open the door to the paramedics.

They took one look at Ashley and the man in charge started issuing orders. Karen gave him the empty pill bottle and stood back as they worked to make Ashley breathe. She could hear someone in the next room calling poison control for the correct procedure for an overdose of the drug Ashley had taken. Karen clasped her hands and cried silently. No one seemed to notice she was there.

One of the men found a heartbeat and clapped an oxygen mask against Ashley's face. Karen thought she saw a faint rise and fall of the girl's chest. She followed them into the ambulance. She couldn't drive to the hospital in her state of panic. As the paramedics worked constantly on Ashley, the driver threaded in and out of traffic. All Karen could think of was that if she had danced to one more number or spent a few more minutes in the hotel room with Mark, Ashley would have been dead.

At Parkland Hospital Ashley was put on a gurney and whisked away. Alone in the hall, Karen walked over to a phone and dialed Ryan's work number. After the tenth ring she slammed down the receiver. He was probably in some other office. After hesitating, Karen called Chelsea.

Chelsea was watching a movie on one of the all-night channels when the call came. After hearing what had happened, she grabbed her purse and hurried to the hospital.

"Is she all right?" she asked when she found Karen.

"I don't know. The doctor is still with her." Karen buried her face in her hands. "She looks so awful!"

"Where's Ryan?"

"That's a good question," Karen said testily. "I tried to call him, but got no answer on his work phone."

"He's still at DataComp?"

"Of course. Isn't he always?" Karen sounded bitter and frightened.

"I'll go try him again."

Karen didn't seem to notice that Chelsea didn't ask for Ryan's work number. What Chelsea did was dial every number Ryan had ever given her in case of emergency. Finally she located him.

Half an hour later he was in the waiting room. "What happened?" he demanded as he sat down by Karen.

"Ashley tried to commit suicide," Karen said in a dull voice. "She wanted to kill herself."

"Why? What happened?"

"How should I know? I'm not a psychic," his wife snapped. "I only found her. I didn't see her do it."

Ryan glanced at the dress she was wearing, and a muscle tightened in his jaw. "You're dressed rather well to have been watching TV. Were you at home when it happened?"

"No." She didn't offer an explanation.

He didn't need one. Her appearance said it all. He looked at Chelsea. "Thanks for coming."

Chelsea nodded, then sat on Karen's other side. "Do you want me to go see if I can learn anything at the nurse's desk?"

Karen nodded.

When Chelsea was gone, Ryan said, "What did she use?"

"She got into my sleeping pills." She said it as if Ashley were a toddler. "The bottle was empty, and I had refilled the prescription only last week."

Ryan frowned and looked away. He wanted to shout at her that she should never have had the pills in the first place, that she should have been home, but there was no point in it. Karen wouldn't have harmed Ashley on purpose. The real fault lay in Ashley's trying to commit suicide, not in the fact that Karen had sleeping pills or even that she had been out.

He moved his leg so it wasn't touching her chiffon skirt. Any contact with her was too much at the moment. Who was she seeing? Apparently someone who could afford to take her to an expensive place. Bile rose in his throat. Even though he had thought for several months that his wife was seeing someone, he felt sickened by this evidence of it. She wasn't even being particularly careful not to get caught.

Enveloped in her worry and grief, Karen never thought that Ryan could comfort her or that he might need her, and he felt entirely alone with his wife sitting beside him. He wished desperately that he could see Ashley, see that she was still alive. Every time someone walked by, he looked up expectantly.

Chelsea returned and drew up a chair so she could sit facing them. "She's coming around, I think. The nurse wasn't supposed to give me information, but I know her and she realizes how frightened we are. It may be a while before the doctor can leave Ashley and talk to us. She isn't out of danger yet, but it looks as if she has a chance."

"God! Why would she do such a thing?" Ryan lowered

his face to his hands as if he felt frustrated and helpless. He looked at Karen. "Did you two have an argument?"

"No. She never came home after school. I had to leave so I put a note where she would find it."

Chelsea suddenly noticed the dress Karen was wearing. It was an odd choice to put on in a hurry. Had Karen been out with someone?

"She didn't come home? Did you call the school?"

"At first I assumed she had ridden home with someone and hadn't told me. She's done that before. By the time I realized she was late, there was no one at the school."

"Damn!" Ryan didn't elaborate on whether he was damning Karen's lack of attention to Ashley or the situation in general.

"She was probably with her boyfriend," Chelsea said. "What's his name? Scott Stark?"

"That seems likely," Karen said. "Maybe they had an argument."

Ryan looked at Chelsea and said, "What has she told you about him?"

"Nothing, really. He's several years older than she is and drives a black car with heavily tinted windows. I saw them together once, from a distance." She had been paying more attention to Ashley that night and hadn't noticed what make or year the car was, only the color.

"He might be able to tell us why this happened. I'll see if I can find him. It's possible his father has the same name and is listed in the phone book." Ryan stood and went to the pay phone down the hall.

Chelsea sat in silence with Karen. There was so much she wanted to say, but none of it could be expressed.

After a long time, Ryan returned. "I found him. He says they broke up this afternoon. He sounded upset that she overdosed."

"Who wouldn't be?" Karen said angrily. "You say the most foolish things!"

Ryan gave her a cold glare, and Chelsea saw the muscles tighten in his jaw. He wouldn't put up with Karen's arrogance for long. Not on a night like tonight. Hastily Chelsea said, "Do you want me to get us some coffee? This could take a while."

"Yes," Karen said. "Ryan can go with you." She didn't ask Chelsea to take him out of her sight, but she might as well have.

They went to the elevator, and Chelsea was glad to see the doors slide shut, cutting them off from Karen. "She's pushing me too far," Ryan said without preamble. "I don't know how much longer I can put us with this."

Chelsea put her hand on his arm in a comforting manner. "She's just upset. You know she always acts angry when she's frightened."

He was visibly trying to get himself under control. "I know. It no longer helps. Lately she always talks to me as if I were a fool or dirt under her feet. A man can only stand so much!"

"I know. It will be better when this is over."

"Did the nurse say anything else about Ashley?"

"No. She told me more than she should have as it was."

Ryan struck his palm against the side of the elevator. "Where the hell do you think Karen went tonight, for her to be dressed like that?"

Chelsea had hoped he wouldn't mention that. "I have no idea." She wouldn't insult Ryan's intelligence by saying Karen might have a reasonable explanation. It had gone too far for that.

"I told you she's seeing someone. That's all it could be," he said as the elevator slowed to a stop. The doors glided open. He sounded exhausted. "I don't suppose she's told you who it is."

Chelsea shook her head. "She doesn't confide in me anymore. I'm amazed she called me."

They went to the row of vending machines, and Ryan put change into the one containing coffee. "I wasn't positive until tonight. She looks as if she's been out dancing."

"Could she have gone somewhere with her parents or Joyce? You know how they dress up for every occasion."

"Fulton Baker was with me, and Todd doesn't strike me as someone who'd be out this late on a work night. Besides, if she had been with her family, she would have told me that."

"What are you going to do?" she asked as he handed her two cups of coffee.

Ryan was quiet while the machine filled the third cup. "I don't know. I guess a lot depends on Ashley."

Chelsea had already guessed that would be his answer.

Ashley didn't die. When she awoke two days later, she was in a hospital room. The doctor informed her that she was on the ward reserved for suicide attempts and would be there for several weeks. Ashley felt too bad to care.

Later she discovered that part of her treatment, as with the other patients on this floor, included extensive counseling. She also discovered that her period had started. Whether the overdose had caused her to spontaneously abort or whether the pregnancy kit had been wrong, she never knew. She didn't ask the doctor, and nothing showed on her record.

When she was finally released, it was with the stipulation that she go to weekly sessions with either the man who had counseled her in the hospital or someone else approved by him. Ashley didn't care. She had finally found an adult who would listen to her and who wasn't friendly with either of her parents.

To her surprise, Scott called her the day after she came home. By the end of the week, they were going together again. By mutual consent, they never discussed what had led up to her going to the hospital.

As mid-November came, Karen grew tired of driving her daughter to the psychiatric appointments. "She's perfectly fine," she told Ryan. "It's just throwing money away for her to go over there every week!"

"No, it's not. I can see a big difference in Ashley. Can't you?"

"No. She still talks to me as if I were an idiot. I would never have talked to Mother that way!" Karen frowned at Ryan across the den. "I don't know what's wrong with her anyway! She has everything she could possibly want."

"I don't think money is the issue," he said with fading patience. "You just admitted you don't know what's wrong with her. She should continue seeing Dr. Fleishner."

"That's easy for you to say. You don't have to drive her over there, then sit for an hour until she comes out. And that man won't tell me anything she says. With all we're paying him!"

"Good. I'm glad to see he's keeping her confidences. It's what he's supposed to do, unless she's showing signs of hurting herself or someone else."

"Then *you* take off work and drive her over."

"You know that's impossible. Maybe Chelsea could take her occasionally."

"I'm not going to ask Chelsea. She's not as friendly toward me as she used to be."

"Probably because of the way you treat her," he retorted. "Not everyone will put up with your barbed comments the way I do."

Karen glared at him. "I have no idea what you're talking about."

"You just did it again. Do you hate me as much as it sounds?"

She gave an exaggerated sigh. "I don't hate you, Ryan. Don't start on that."

He looked at her thoughtfully for a long time. "You never told me where you were that night."

"I don't remember." She got up and left the room.

Ryan stared at the chair she had occupied. How long could he bear to live like this? If it wasn't for Ashley, he'd be gone now. He had talked to a lawyer, and the man had assured him that, given Ashley's age and sex, he stood virtually no chance of getting custody of her, so a divorce was out. He couldn't leave her behind with Karen. Without him around, Karen might ignore her entirely.

He closed his eyes and leaned his head against the back of the chair. In five years Ashley would be eighteen and away at college. Somehow he would wait.

Chapter Twenty-nine

"Don't be ridiculous, Ryan. Of course we're having Thanksgiving dinner at Mother's house." Karen went back to reading her magazine.

"Put that down. We're going to discuss this for once."

Karen dropped the magazine onto her lap and glared at him. "There's nothing to discuss. We always go to Mother's."

"I know. This year I want to spend Thanksgiving with my parents. Brady and his wife will be there. We've never seen their new baby."

"One baby looks pretty much like another to me. At their age, they shouldn't have had another child anyway. Besides, I don't like your brother or his wife."

"How would you know? I doubt you've ever said more than a dozen words to them."

"Ryan, I don't want to go to Boulder and be bored to death for a long weekend."

"Then we'll go Christmas." He wasn't willing to let it drop this time.

"No, we won't. Mother would be crushed if we didn't spend Christmas in town."

"I'm tired of living to please your mother!"

Karen gave him a look filled with disgust. "Why must you be so unpleasant every year at this time?"

"Because I never have a say in where we spend the

holidays. We've been married almost sixteen years, and we haven't been to my parents' house twice!"

"They come here often enough."

Ryan stood and went to look out at the back yard. The grass would soon be browning for winter, but one lone flower was struggling valiantly to survive. "Karen, it's more than where we spend Thanksgiving, and you know it. What's going to happen with us?"

"What on earth are you talking about? Nothing is happening. You're just on one of your tangents. That's all."

"I never thought you'd speak to me this way. That it would reach the point where we couldn't discuss something as trivial as where to spend a weekend without an argument."

"Thanksgiving is hardly trivial! Mother has already ordered the turkey, and Daddy is buying the wines today or tomorrow. I suppose if you're so dead set on going to Boulder, we could go the week after Thanksgiving."

"Brady and Susan won't be there then. Maybe you don't care for them, but I miss seeing him. In spite of our age differences, he and I were close as boys. And I like Susan."

"It's beyond me how you could like anyone who can't talk about anything but how wonderful her children are."

"They started their family late in life. It's still new to them."

"Ashley would simply die if we left town over Thanksgiving. I'm sure she has a date."

"There's nothing new about that." Ryan pulled the blinds, shutting out the view of the yard. "She has a date every night. I worry about her."

"There you go again. You worry more than anyone I've ever seen." Karen jerked up the magazine and turned the pages angrily. "She's popular."

"I don't like the looks of him. It's no wonder she didn't want us to meet him! Did she say when she would be in or where she was going?" Following her stay in the hospital, Ashley had relented and let her parents meet Scott Stark.

He had been to the house only twice, but all the alarms in Ryan's head had gone off. The boy looked like a gang member or worse.

"You're always the first to say looks aren't important, and I didn't give her the third degree. You're home. You could have asked her yourself." Karen's voice sounded studiedly bored.

"Damn it, Karen! Show some interest in the girl! She's the only one we have left!"

Karen threw the magazine away from her. "I should have known you'd bring that up again!" She stormed from the room.

"Where are you going?"

"Out!" she called back over her shoulder.

Ryan sat tiredly in his chair. It was the same sort of answer he would have expected from Ashley. He heard Karen leave, and the house seemed peaceful at last. Ryan closed his eyes, then put the chair in a reclining position. How had it come to this, and how long was he going to put up with it?

Although he had decided to stay until Ashley graduated from high school, that was beginning to seem awfully far into the future. Besides, he seldom saw her these days. Since her return from the hospital, she and Scott had been together more than ever. He tried to remember back to when he had been her age. Had he been interested in girls yet? He couldn't remember.

For that matter, how old was Scott? Ashley had said he was sixteen, but if that was so, frogs could fly. No sixteen-year-old boy had ever looked that worldly wise. During both short visits, Ryan had been certain the boy was all but openly mocking him. He had tried to convince Ashley not to see him, but Karen had given her permission behind his back. It hurt to admit he had lost all control over his daughter.

So why was he staying?

Ryan pulled out his wallet and opened it to the place where he kept his driver's license and company ID. He fished in the plastic pocket between them and pulled out a photo of Chelsea.

No one knew he had it. It was one he had taken before she had left for Paris. The wind was blowing her bright auburn hair over her shoulder, and she was laughing at something Ashley had said, her eyes sparkling and her skin glowing. Ryan's face softened as he gazed at the picture. How long had he loved her? He couldn't remember a time when he hadn't.

Chelsea seemed happy now. She was dating occasionally, but no one in particular. She seemed to prefer it that way. If the truth were known, he preferred it, too. Chelsea had a bad track record when it came to men, and he didn't want her to be hurt again.

The phone rang, and he slipped the photo back into his wallet before answering it. Ashley was on the other end.

"Daddy? Can you come get me?"

"Ashley? Are you crying? Where are you?" His blood nearly froze, and he gripped the phone. She was crying!

"I'm in Mesquite. At the police station."

For a moment Ryan couldn't think what to say. "Did you say you're at the Mesquite police station? What are you doing there?"

"Will you come get me? And don't tell Mom. Please, Daddy?"

She hadn't called him that in years. "Of course I'll come. Are you hurt?"

"No, I'm all right. And, Daddy, will you bring Chelsea?"

"What the hell's going on, Ashley? Are you under arrest?"

"I don't think so. Just come get me!"

"I'm on my way." He hung up and called Chelsea. In minutes he was in the car.

The Mesquite police station wasn't difficult to find. He and Chelsea had barely talked on the way there. Neither knew what to say or how to offer comfort to the other. When an officer took them to the back room, Ashley ran to them and held on to Ryan and Chelsea as if she were frightened half to death.

"What's happened?" Ryan demanded of the man still seated at a scarred desk.

"We arrested the boy she was with for driving while intoxicated. He's a minor and had no one to go bail for him. We have him in the holding tank, along with the other intoxicated minors who were in the car. Your daughter passed the test, so she's free to go if you can give me proof that you're her parent or guardian."

"I'm her father." Ryan pulled identification from his pocket and handed it to the officer. He untangled Ashley's arms from his waist. "You were drinking?"

"Not me, Daddy. It was the others. I only had a taste. I swear it!"

Chelsea stroked the girl's hair. "Calm down, honey. Tell us what happened."

"Scott met me at the corner like always. Mike and C.J. were in the car, too, but I didn't think anything about it. They go riding with us sometimes. We went to this place where there's music, and they picked up a couple of girls." Her voice broke.

"Go on," Ryan said.

"Well, we were riding around, me and Scott in the front seat the others in the back. Somebody said something about going out to the lake. Scott stopped and bought some beer, and we were going there when we were stopped by the police."

The officer said, "The driver was legally drunk and then some. So were the others. The car was swerving all over the road. That's why the arresting officer stopped them. The driver had consumed more than a couple of beers."

Ashley looked down at the floor and sniffled. Chelsea fished in her purse for a tissue.

Ryan felt older than his years. "How do I go about paying her fine or whatever? I've never had to do this before."

"She's not fined. Like I said, she's not intoxicated. We

just couldn't release her to anyone but a parent or guardian. She's free to go.''

They went to the car, and Ryan sat behind the wheel instead of starting it. There was too much to be said. He wanted to proceed carefully. "Why weren't you drinking?" he finally asked.

"I'm under age," Ashley said in a small voice.

"Don't give me that crap. I've suspected you of drinking before." It had been one of his worries recently. He suspected Ashley was hitting his bourbon and watering it to hide the fact.

She let out a quivering sigh. "I was scared. Those girls they picked up looked wild to me. You know, like they were on drugs or something. And they were making out like crazy in the back seat. I mean, *really* making out. I was scared of what was going to happen when we got to the lake.''

"I'm going to kill that punk!"

"Daddy, you'll just make it worse! I'm not going to see him anymore." Ashley addressed all this to her lap. Her hair fell forward, obscuring most of her face.

"Why should I believe you?" Ryan was so angry he was shaking. He was thankful Scott was safely locked away or he might have done him harm. "Just give me one reason why the hell I should believe you this time?"

Ashley didn't answer. She cried quietly.

Chelsea put a gentling hand on Ryan's shoulder along the back of the seat. "Your dad has a point. I remember your telling him you weren't going to see Scott anymore when you were in the hospital."

"That was different. Now I can see what kind of a jerk he really is." Ashley looked tearfully at Chelsea. "Can I talk to you alone?"

Chelsea looked around. The police station parking lot was anything but private. "Ryan, give us a few minutes. Okay?"

Ryan slammed out of the car and paced to the corner of

the building. Chelsea knew he was fighting against his own emotions. "Well?"

"Scott was telling Mike and C.J. that we could switch around after we got to the lake. You know, him take their girls and let them have me."

Chelsea felt sick inside. "He said that?"

Ashley nodded. "And there's something else. Scott took me to the clinic and got me birth-control pills. That's why I never mentioned it to you again."

"Your dad ought to know all this!"

"No! If I tell him, he'll half kill Scott! I just won't see him again. I promise! I'm telling you all this so you'll know I won't go back on my word. Scott couldn't love me and want to trade me to Mike and C.J.!"

"You're right about that," Chelsea said grimly. "What makes you think I won't half kill him myself?"

Ashley gazed out the window at her father. "I don't know what to do about all this. Everything blew up so big, so fast! It's just all out of hand, and I'm scared. I can't let Mom know. That's why I asked him to bring you."

"How can you keep this from her? She's bound to find out."

"Not unless you or Dad tell her. I figure you can convince him not to tell."

Chelsea frowned. "I don't like this. Not at all."

"What should I do, Aunt Chel?"

"Tell your father about the birth-control pills, at least. If you don't tell him, I'll have to do it."

After a long pause Ashley nodded. "I'll tell him. What about the swapping? Do I have to tell him that, too?"

"No. It didn't happen so there's no reason for him to know as long as you never see Scott again. You have to keep this promise, Ashley. You could have been badly hurt in all this."

"That's what scared me."

Chelsea went to where Ryan stood. "Are you okay? I can drive."

"I'll do it. I need something to keep me from thinking.

What the hell am I going to do with her? I can't watch her twenty-four hours a day, and Karen lets her run wild. When I think what could have happened today, I . . ." He couldn't finish the sentence.

"I know. I'm shaken, too. She wants to talk to you."

"I'm not sure I want to hear it. If you ask me, this Scott was the reason she tried to commit suicide, even if she didn't ever admit it. I could tear him apart with my bare hands!"

"I know. So could I. Will you talk to Ashley?"

After a while Ryan nodded. "I have to deal with it. Whatever it is."

They went back to the car, and Ryan sat waiting for Ashley to speak. He couldn't look at her. He wanted to take her in his arms as he had when she was two and had a scraped knee. But she wasn't two. Her problems were far more serious now.

"I've been taking birth-control pills," she said in a whispery voice.

This was so far from what he had expected her to say, he thought he must have misunderstood. "Birth-control pills?"

"I asked Aunt Chel to get them for me, but she wouldn't. She said I would have to ask you or Mom. I couldn't do that, so Scott helped me get them."

Ryan frowned at Chelsea. "You never told me this!"

"She told me in confidence. It never occurred to me that she got them anyway." Chelsea frowned at Ashley. "Or that she would break her promise to me about needing them."

Ashley sniffed again, and a tear dropped onto her jeans. "I didn't promise. Not actually."

"You're playing with words," Chelsea said. "You knew I assumed you weren't doing anything to cause you to need birth-control pills."

"I'm sorry. I'm so sorry for all of it!"

Ryan was trying to digest the fact that his thirteen-year-old daughter needed birth-control pills. That had to mean

. . . "I'm going to press charges on that son of a bitch!" He jerked on the door handle.

"No, no!" Ashley cried, grabbing his arm. "That's why I didn't want to tell you!"

"You're under age! That's statutory rape!"

"He didn't force me, Daddy."

Ryan stared at his daughter. Emotions were pounding through him. He wanted to hug her and yell at her at the same time. And more than anything, he wanted to smash his fist into Scott's smug face. Now he understood the half-smirk the boy had given him from time to time. Anger made him hot all over.

"Ryan," Chelsea said, touching his shoulder again, "I'm upset, too. But this is why she didn't tell you before. She knew how angry you'd be."

"I have a right to be mad! Damn it, Chelsea! Look what that son of a bitch has done!"

"I know. Just listen to her."

Ryan turned his frown back at Ashley. "There's more?"

"Not really. Not anything that matters. I'm not going to see Scott again. I promise!"

"Why the hell should I believe you this time? I've caught you in too many lies. Maybe you can talk your way around your mother, but I've had it! I'm sick of the way you talk to me, of your leaving the house when I've told you not to, and of your skipping school and dating that street scum! Don't deny it! I knew Scott was no good the first time I saw him! He's every parent's nightmare! I don't care if Karen did give you permission to date him! Your disobedience to me has to stop, along with your insolence!"

She ducked her head back down, but he could tell she was still crying.

"I don't want you to see Scott, Mike, C.J., or anyone else like them. Is that understood? If you do, I'm going to press charges against him!"

"I understand."

"And you're going to straighten your life out. No more

skipping school. No more dressing as if you're a member
of the Hell's Angels!"

"Okay," she said meekly.

Ryan drew her into his embrace and rested his cheek
against the top of her head. Ashley clung to him, letting
her sobs go unchecked. "I couldn't stand it if I lost you,"
Ryan said in a muffled voice.

Chelsea's eyes met his and she smiled at him sadly but
encouragingly.

"Will you have to tell Mom?" Ashley asked finally.

"I don't know. No, I guess not." He was too strung out
to deal with Karen over this.

After a while Ashley's sobs slackened and she pulled
away. "I'm so sorry," she repeated. "I never thought anything like this would ever happen. If Mom found out
about it, she'd never forgive me. Not ever."

Ryan backed the car out of the parking place. He didn't
agree with Ashley's assessment. It was more likely that
Karen would simply leave for one of her trysts and not
deal with it at all. He didn't trust himself to speak. He still
wanted to beat Scott to a pulp.

The next week was uneventful. If Karen had any suspi-
cion that something out of the ordinary had happened the
day Ashley called from the police station, she didn't say so.
Karen's entire world was centered around herself, more
than ever these days. Ryan felt increasingly trapped in the
marriage, but Ashley was keeping her promises and that
gave him some incentive to stay.

At night Ryan found his situation difficult to justify,
however. He was lonely, and he was tired of celibacy. He
no longer wanted Karen sexually, even if intimacy had
been offered, though it wasn't. These days he found it
impossible to remember why he had wanted to marry her
in the first place. During almost every argument, she
taunted him with the fact that she had maneuvered him
into marrying her while Chelsea was out of the picture,

simply so Chelsea couldn't have him. She enjoyed the pain that gave him. Did she suspect he was still in love with Chelsea? Impossible. Karen would never be silent about something like that.

More and more often he called Chelsea and asked her to meet him for lunch. At times their meeting was all that got him through the day. With Chelsea he felt alive, himself, instead of the husk he had become at home.

"We've got to stop meeting like this," Chelsea teased as she took the chair opposite him.

He smiled. "You're late. I was beginning to think you weren't going to make it."

"I had a phone call just as I was leaving. Guess what? I'm being booked for a one-woman show at the Meadowlane Gallery!"

"You are? Isn't that the one near the Galleria? The one where you've been wanting to exhibit?"

"That's it! I'm so excited! This is my first really important show. Ryan, just think what this could mean!"

"I'm proud of you," he said sincerely. "I've always known that someday you'd be famous."

She laughed. "It's rare for artists' names to become household words." She tilted her head in the way he found so intriguing. "Tell me I'm not dreaming! That this really is as big a break as I think it is, that I'm not building castles on a cloud!"

"I'm sure of it."

She ordered a chef's salad. "I'm too excited to eat anything else. They called me! Not the other way around!" She could barely sit still for her excitement. "I have to decide which canvases to take. Should I include any I did before I went to Paris?"

"*River of Time* has always been one of my favorites."

"Can you come over this afternoon and help me choose? I'm so excited I can't think."

"I will if you think I'd be of any help."

"Thanks!" She seemed relieved. "I know I shouldn't place too much hope in this, but I can't help it."

"Go with it. If you don't enjoy the highs, the lows are too deep. Trust me. I've been there."

"How's Ashley?"

"She's doing remarkably well. Even Karen noticed that she's home at night and actually studying."

"Is Karen okay?" Chelsea looked away, and he knew it still hurt her that Karen no longer wanted to be her friend.

"I guess. Who can tell? She only talks to me if we're having an argument."

"I still don't know what happened between us. I've thought it over, and I can't see what caused such a break."

"One thing I've learned about Karen is that no one can really understand her. She doesn't seem to experience the same emotions as the rest of us, at least not to the same degree."

"She's turned into her mother," Chelsea said thoughtfully. "That's what has happened."

"Unfortunately, I agree." The waiter brought their food, and Ryan cut into his steak. "I never wanted to be married to Cecilia Baker."

"They say all daughters have something of their mother in them."

"You don't. You're as different from your mother as a person could be."

"I guess I skipped a generation and took after my grandmother. You'd have liked her, I think."

"If you're like her, I know I would."

They finished their meal, making companionable small talk. It was this kind of togetherness that seemed to revive Ryan and make him able to face the rest of the day. And there was the afternoon visit to Chelsea's studio to look forward to. He wasn't all that anxious to go home these days.

After work he drove to Chelsea's loft and went up the outside stairs. Before he could knock, she opened the door.

"I thought I heard you. Come in." She was dressed in jeans that fit like a second skin and a garnet-colored sweater that was several sizes too large. Her hair was held back from her face with a gold clip. As always, Ryan was taken aback by her glowing beauty. "I put the canvases against the wall back here."

He followed her the length of the spacious room. The canvases were like familiar friends to him. He came here more often than Karen realized, though nothing happened that she couldn't have known about. "I like the red one with the crystal ball."

"That's *Mystic's Dream*. I just finished it last week. You don't think it's too far out?"

"I like the way you did the glass. It looks real." In her newer canvases, she had started using recognizable forms but in a surrealistic way. He liked the ones with objects he could identify. Some of the earlier works had only looked like blobs of paint to him. He bent closer. "I can see someone in the reflection."

Chelsea laughed. "It's me. Sort of a private joke, I guess you'd say."

"I think this is my new favorite."

"What about this one? It's an old canvas I've reworked. *Might Have Been* is the title."

"I remember it from before. I like it better now. But it makes me sad to look at it." She had added a tiny figure that seemed to be lost in the swirls of blue and smoky gray. "She looks lost and lonely."

"That's exactly what you're supposed to feel! Maybe Meneir taught me more than I thought." She studied the painting as if it were new to her.

Ryan turned in a circle, studying the works that now surrounded him. "I like them all. I can see you in them. That's why the sad ones bother me, I guess." He looked at her. "Are you that sad?"

"Not anymore. Lonely, yes, but not sad." She thought for a minute. "No, I'm not unhappy."

"You don't sound all that convincing to me."

She went to a canvas almost as large as she was. "I did this one last month. It's *Autumn*. I had been walking in the park, and the leaves fascinated me. No two are exactly alike, you know."

"Yes, I know. They're like snowflakes. Or people." He was watching her, not the canvases.

Their eyes met, and Ryan had the curious sensation that their souls merged. "Our radar is active today," he said, knowing she was feeling the same thing.

"After all these years, and it's never needed repairs," she said in an attempt to pass it off lightly.

He went to her. "Chelsea, why did you really ask me over?"

"I told you. To help me choose which canvases to take to the gallery."

"You know more about paintings than I ever will. You didn't need my help."

"I got a letter from Jean-Paul today." She avoided his eyes. "He's asking me to come back to Paris."

Ryan felt he'd received a blow to his middle. "Are you going?"

She lifted her head to look up at him. "I don't want to."

"That's not the same as a simple 'no.' "

"I don't know what to do. He says Mariette has found someone else and that he's sorry for having treated me so badly."

"Exactly how badly did he treat you? You never told me."

"He wasn't so bad—in retrospect."

"Why don't I believe you?"

Chelsea's eyes met his. "I'm lonely, Ryan. When I get this way, I make stupid decisions. I know that, but I can't seem to help it. Going back to Paris and Jean-Paul is the wrong move, but I'm considering it."

"Why?"

"Have you ever been lonely?"

"Frequently. But I've never wanted to go live with Jean-Paul."

She smiled slightly. "That's just it. I don't either. Not

really. He hit me. Did I ever tell you that? Just once, but that was enough to send me to the airport."

"No, you omitted that detail. But I saw the bruise on your cheek and wondered. Why on earth would you ever consider going back to a man who would mistreat you? I can't understand that, Chelsea. I'll never understand that!"

"I'm not considering returning to him because he mistreated me. I'm not a masochist. There were good times, too. Maybe I pushed him into hitting me."

"You know better than that. Karen has pushed me past my limits many times, but I've never hit her."

Chelsea nodded. "I know." She started to go around him, but he stopped her.

"Don't go back to him, Chelsea." He was aware of her slender arms beneath the sweater. She felt warm and soft. "You deserve so much more than some creep who mistreats you."

She didn't answer.

Ryan gently drew her closer to him, and she stepped into his embrace as if it were the most natural thing to do. He bent to her and kissed her. He hadn't touched her in a long time. It had been even longer since he had kissed her. Dreams didn't count.

Her lips melted beneath his and opened as the kiss became more passionate. Her arms encircled him, and he laced his fingers in her long hair. Her body was small in his arms, but it fit to his exactly.

The kiss seemed to last an eternity. He was never sure afterward which of them had the strength to end it. For a long time he held her in an embrace that needed no words. Holding Chelsea was like a glimpse of paradise, and he wasn't sure he could ever let her go.

"What are we going to do?" he asked at last.

"I'm not going to Paris," she replied. She sounded as shaken as he was by what had just happened between them.

"I have no right to ask you to stay."

"I know." After several seconds, she repeated his question. "What are we going to do?"

"I don't know. But one thing is clear to me. It may be wrong for me to be holding you like this, but it's a greater sin for me to stay in a loveless marriage simply because I made a mistake when I was little more than a boy."

"I'm not asking you to leave Karen. I'd never do that."

"I'm not there because of Karen. That hasn't been true for a long time. I'm there for Ashley."

"Then you have to stay." She pulled away, but he could tell how difficult it was for her.

He couldn't let her go just yet. "Ashley won't need me forever. She's almost grown."

Chelsea smiled softly. "We don't have to make any decisions now. Maybe after today we won't feel quite as lonely."

"I don't feel at all lonely now."

She stepped back into his arms and he held her, breathing in the scent that was a mixture of Chelsea, shampoo, and faint perfume. "We don't have to decide today," he repeated. At the moment it was enough just to have his arms about her.

Chapter Thirty

It was a point of honor with Karen that her house be as clean when her housekeeper arrived as it would be when the woman left. Although she would never have admitted it, Karen enjoyed housework and only hired the woman to save face with her mother and Joyce.

Ashley's room was always a challenge. The girl seemed able to create chaos out of thin air. Karen sorted through the strewn clothes, put a load in the washer, then returned to make the bed. This was a point of contention with Ryan. He was of the opinion that Ashley should keep her own room clean. Karen saw that as another way to lose control over her daughter. Besides, she was bringing Ashley up to leave such chores to a housekeeper, not to be a slave to housework. Karen had Ashley's life all mapped out.

First she would go to college. Karen had already sent in an application to SMU. Everyone in the family had gone there and Ashley was not to be an exception. She would live in Karen's old dorm. Perhaps even in the same room. Karen had written the number down on the dorm application. By the time Ashley graduated from high school her name would be on the top of the list for a room. That was another family tradition. Everyone who attended college lived on campus. This was a safe way to try out independence.

She smoothed the bedspread over Ashley's pillow and

propped a stuffed bear in a ballerina costume upon it. Ashley was getting too old for the bear, but Karen liked the little-girl look of it on the bed. She dreaded having Ashley grow up, no matter what Ryan might think.

One of the dresser drawers was shut on the arm of a sweater and Karen went to tidy it. Keeping Ashley's drawers in order was practically impossible, but it gave Karen something to do. She took out the pile of sweaters and refolded them neatly.

As she was about to return them to the drawer, she happened to see the corner of a pink plastic container. Curious, she picked it up, and was stunned to discover it contained birth control pills.

Karen's first thoughts were incoherent. The box belonged to someone else and had somehow gotten in the drawer. It belonged to Joyce, or even to Chelsea, and Ashley had taken it by mistake. Karen found a dozen reasons why the box might not mean what she already knew it did.

The truth was not to be denied forever. Ashley was taking birth-control pills.

She went to the phone and called Ryan at work. "Come home," she said. "Now. Come home at once!" Then she hung up.

Minutes later Ryan hurried into the house. "What's wrong? Is it Ashley? She's not hurt, is she? Why didn't you tell me . . . ?" He stopped when he saw the look on her face. "What's going on, Karen?"

Wordlessly she held out the pink container.

Slowly Ryan came closer and took it from her. She glared up at him, not rising from the couch. "Do you know where I found these?" She didn't wait for him to answer. "In Ashley's dresser!"

He sat on the chair nearest the couch. He didn't seem as stunned as she had been.

"I was straightening her sweaters, and when I started to put them back in the drawer, there it was. Ashley's on birth-control pills!"

"I assumed she had thrown them away." He sounded tired as he handed them back.

For a minute Karen was speechless. "You knew about this?"

Ryan nodded. "Ashley didn't want you to know."

"You got birth-control pills for our thirteen-year-old daughter?" Her voice was icy cold. Her fury was building.

"No, I didn't. She got them herself. When she was dating Scott Stark. He drove her to the clinic, and she got them there."

"How do you know about all this?"

Ryan leaned forward and put his elbows on his knees. He spoke slowly as if he were thinking everything through carefully. "Ashley called me one night from the police station in Mesquite. Scott had been picked up for drunken driving, and she couldn't leave the station until I went to get her."

"Police station?" Karen asked in disbelief. "When was this?"

"I don't remember exactly."

"Why didn't I know about it?"

"You were out." He gave her a level look. "When I went after her, Chelsea convinced her to tell me everything—that she was on birth-control pills and that Scott had gotten them for her. At least I think I know everything."

"Wait a minute. What's Chelsea got to do with this?"

"Ashley asked me to bring Chelsea with me when I went to pick her up."

Karen stared at him. Ashley had requested that Chelsea be there and that her mother not be told?

"Ashley asked Chelsea to get them for her, but Chelsea told her she would have to ask you or me. Ashley knew we wouldn't do this for her, so she and Scott took matters into their own hands."

"I can't believe you knew something of this magnitude and didn't tell me about it." Karen stared at him.

"If you had been home, I would have." He looked at her as if she were a stranger. "Didn't you think something was up? Ashley stopped skipping school and being a problem for the teachers. We haven't had a call in weeks. And she's dressing more like a thirteen-year-old and less like a member of an outlaw motorcycle gang."

"I hardly think that describes my daughter," Karen said coldly.

"Think what you please. She's stopped shaving her hair off and is wearing decent clothes and makeup. More important, she's doing her homework. Her grades are coming up. Haven't you noticed any of this?"

Karen never asked to see Ashley's grades these days. She had assumed that a girl of Ashley's age would know enough to do her schoolwork. "I'm not her keeper, Ryan. I don't notice every single thing she does and write out a report on it." She looked with distaste at the pink box of pills. "I'm going to give that clinic a piece of my mind! They have no right giving birth-control pills to a child that age."

"Use your head for a minute," he said in a tone as cold as hers. "If she needs birth control, it's good that she was smart enough to get it. What would you prefer? That she have a baby at thirteen? It happens, you know."

"Not to girls like Ashley!"

"Yes, it does. Every day!" He took the box from her and stared at it. "Ever since I learned about her wanting these, I've thought about her suicide attempt. I think it's possible she may have believed she was pregnant. That might drive her to such an extreme."

"My Ashley? Pregnant?" Karen seemed to be choking.

"I could be wrong. But if she was, she either lost the baby from taking all those pills or was wrong in the first place. I've been paying close attention to her, and I see no reason to panic over it now." He looked at Karen. "She needs more supervision. From both of us. I can't be here during the day because I have a job. And that job also requires that I work late—frequently. When I'm gone, you should be here."

Karen gave a short laugh. "I can't watch her twenty-four hours a day. I have a life of my own, too. She's a teenager, for goodness' sake!"

He tossed the box into her lap. "Even finding these doesn't change your mind about her needing supervision? She's behaving now, but there's no guarantee that will continue. I think she's after attention, and if she can't get it from us, she'll find it somewhere else."

"Chelsea knew all about this!" Karen's anger rose. "She knew and she didn't call me."

"How could she? You're barely civil to her these days. We never have her over anymore. This isn't the sort of thing she could call and tell you out of the blue. Don't blame Chelsea for this. If you'd been home, you would have known all about it."

Karen took the box and went to the kitchen. She put the pills down the garbage disposal and threw the box into the trash. Her anger was growing steadily. "What else does Chelsea know that I don't? Are you keeping anything else from me?"

"No. I've told you all we talked about. If there's more, Ashley didn't tell me." He glanced at his watch. "I have to get back to work. I have an appointment in half an hour."

"Right! Go back to your precious office!" Karen wheeled to glare at him. "Leave me to have a nervous breakdown all alone. That's no more than I could expect from you."

"You're not having a nervous breakdown," he said with studied calm. "You're just upset. If I were you, I wouldn't mention it to Ashley when she comes in. If you want to talk to her, wait until I'm here so I can mediate. We don't want to blow this sky high again."

"Yes, dear," she said with heavy sarcasm. "Are there any other instructions?"

After giving her a cold look, he turned and left.

Karen was glad to see him go. She could hardly bear to talk to him these days. He was becoming harder to manage. She knew she was pushing him too far, but she didn't care. She had seen her mother and sister control their husbands this way all her life.

As soon as she heard the front door slam, she went to the phone and dialed the number at his office. When there was an answer she said, "Let me speak to Lee Brent, please." She tapped her fingers impatiently on the countertop until Brent responded.

"Lee? This is Karen Morgan. Fine, thanks." She found herself smiling. This would show Ryan he couldn't order her about. Lee not only worked in the same company, but in Ryan's office. "I was wondering if that offer for dinner is still open." She made her voice soft and velvety.

Brent paused for a split second. "Sure it is. I thought you weren't interested." She could tell from his tone that he was being careful because of co-workers.

"It's my prerogative to change my mind. Would tonight be convenient?"

"Tonight's perfect!" His surprise was evident. He hadn't expected her to take him up on his offer.

"I'll meet you at Nevilles." After she hung up, Karen threw a triumphant smile in the direction Ryan had taken. She loved the danger of having affairs, and the one with Mark Dreyer was cooling. Seeing two men at the same time, both of whom worked with Ryan, one in his own office, filled her with excitement. If Ryan found out, so much the better. He would never dare leave her.

Karen was humming as she finished cleaning the house.

When Chelsea answered the phone, she was surprised to find Jean-Paul on the other end. "Chelsea," he said, his accent as sexy as ever. "I have missed you!"

"Jean-Paul? Where are you?" She put her brush aside and wiped her fingers on the paint cloth.

"In Paris, of course. It is so good to hear your voice! How are you doing?"

"I'm fine. How are you?" It was odd, exchanging small talk with him as if there had been nothing between them.

"I am perfect as always. I want you to come back to me. Come home to Paris."

"I'm already at home. I don't want to move back."

"Chelsea! You will break my heart!"

"How's Mariette?"

"She is a bitch! A whore! She has left me for another man again. This time it is Édouard!"

"Françoise's Édouard? I thought they were practically married."

"She became too expensive. Her drug habit, you know. It was so hard on poor Édouard. Mariette tried to comfort him, and you know how it goes. Now they are together in Avignon. So foolish. Neither of them will ever be happy outside of Paris! In her letters she is already homesick."

"She ran away with Édouard, but she still writes you?" Chelsea knew she would never understand Jean-Paul's lifestyle. "How's Meneir?"

"Failing, I am afraid. His mind wanders so, it is difficult to talk with him. You were fortunate to meet him when you did. Now he would be of no help to you."

How like Jean-Paul, she thought, to put everything in terms of whether or not personal gain was possible. "I'm sorry to hear that. I was fond of him."

"So you will come back? My heart is broken without you. Did you not get my letter?"

"I got it. Thank you for caring enough to want me back, but I'm staying here."

"I do not merely want you. I love you! I would marry you if you were to come back to me."

Chelsea found herself smiling. "You never change, do you? You can propose to me after the way we parted and with me knowing that Mariette still writes you? I want more from a relationship than that."

"No man loves exclusively, Chelsea."

"Some do. One of those is what I want. I was never that good at sharing."

"You search for rainbows. Come back to me. We are

perfectly suited." He sounded petulant, as if he hadn't expected any opposition.

"Jean-Paul, I'm not rich," she said bluntly. "I know you somehow got that impression, but it's not so."

"All Americans—"

"Bull. I'm not rich and probably never will be. I have enough to live on comfortably, but not nearly enough to support you and all your friends." She hesitated. "The last time I saw you, you hit me. Even if I loved you, I wouldn't come back to you. I may be a slow learner when it comes to relationships, but I'm not *that* slow."

"But Chelsea—"

"No, Jean-Paul. I won't be back. Give my regards to Meneir and the others."

He hung up abruptly, and she replaced the receiver in the cradle. She was glad he would never know she had been tempted to run back to him.

At noon she met Ryan in one of the cafes they frequented. "Sorry I'm late," she said. "I always seem to be running behind these days."

"That's okay. I was late, too." They ordered and he reached across to touch her face where a dot of vermillion had missed her washcloth. "I see you're still painting more than your canvases." He showed her the small smear on his finger.

She rubbed the spot on her cheek with her napkin. "Sorry. I was in such a hurry I only glanced in the mirror."

"How's the show going?"

"It's wonderful! Remember what a crowd there was at the opening? The owner said it's been almost that busy every day since! I think I'm finally discovered. Three of the canvases sold, and two other galleries have contacted me for shows."

"Hey, that's great!"

"And Jean-Paul called me," she added. "I thought I should tell you."

"Are you leaving for Paris?" His eyes were wary as if he feared her answer.

"No, I told him I won't go back to him." She smiled as Ryan relaxed. "While I was talking to him, I discovered something about myself that I don't particularly like. I'm always settling for second best."

"I don't understand."

"With Jason Randall it was his wife and family. Lorne was married to his work. Jean-Paul still had a sleep-in relationship with his ex-wife. I always chose men who put me behind something or someone else. Why do you suppose I did that?"

"You left me out." He was watching her closely.

"You're married. Our relationship is no different from the others." She hated to admit that.

Ryan was quiet for a long time. She couldn't tell what he was thinking. The waiter came for their order and went away again. Finally she said, "Ryan?"

"I don't put you in second place. I haven't for a long time now," he said quietly.

Her eyes met his.

"Our last year in college. You've never told me why you left for Germany without telling me goodbye."

Chelsea hadn't expected him to ever ask that, and she was unprepared. "I . . . I went to see my parents."

"With graduation so close? You passed up graduating from college just to visit your parents?"

She looked away. "I can't remember. It was so long ago." She avoided his eyes.

In a low voice Ryan said, "I know why you went, Chelsea."

Her head snapped toward him. "What?"

"Karen told me. Years ago."

Chelsea felt she had been struck. "She told you? And neither of you let me know?"

"I couldn't. You had your life, and I had mine. There was nothing I could do about it at the time. I was still trying to hold my marriage together—and I was hurt that you had aborted my baby. As for Karen not telling you, then she wouldn't have wanted you to know that she broke your confidence."

The waiter returned with their sandwiches. Chelsea waited for him to leave before she said, "I can't believe you knew! That Karen would tell you. Why did she do it?"

"We were having an argument. Karen has always used whatever weapons she's had at hand. That one was particularly effective. She's used it several times since. It's one of her favorites."

"That's terrible!" Chelsea felt sick. Karen had not only told Ryan, but had used it against him? "I trusted her!"

"So did I at one time. Maybe she changed, or maybe we just never really knew her. At any rate, I wanted you to know."

"Why?" she whispered.

"So I can tell you that I no longer hold it against you. I now understand why you did it. You've always been independent to a fault, as well as impulsive. You would never have come to me with a demand to marry you, and it was harder then for a woman to have a baby out of wedlock and raise it herself." He reached out and took her hand across the table. "Most of all, I'm telling you so you won't think I put you in second place."

"You were engaged to Karen when I came back."

"I didn't know what had happened, and I had no way of knowing you would ever come back. Since you never told Karen what your plans were, what was I to think? We both thought you would stay in Germany permanently."

Chelsea shook her head. "No, Karen knew I was only there for a visit. I wrote her nearly every day. She knew . . ." Her eyes widened as the truth sunk in.

"You did? Karen knew? But she told me you were planning to live there in order to be with your parents. That you might never come back. She said you wrote the college and dropped out!"

"I was dropped for lack of attendance. I never wrote the college. She told you that? She did that deliberately?" She pushed her plate away. No food would pass the lump in her throat. "She was my best friend!" Tears rose, and she blinked hard to keep them back.

"Let's get out of here." Ryan put money on the table, and they left their untouched food on their plates.

When they reached his car, he drove them to a nearby park. No children were on the playground, and a cold wind shook the bare trees above them. As they sat in the shelter of the car, Ryan took her hand. "I guess we both learned quite a bit today. I knew Karen was underhanded, but this surprises even me."

"Not as much as it does me." She held to him as if he were an anchor. "How could she have done that to me? I shouldn't have done what I did, I shouldn't have acted so impulsively, but at the time I couldn't see that I had a choice. It would have been next to impossible for me to have the baby and for you not to realize it was yours. I didn't want to force you into marriage." She smiled mirthlessly. "I was afraid of pressuring you into a decision and of us being trapped in a relationship. Maybe I would do the same thing again. I don't know."

She was quiet for a long time. "When I was watching Bethany and Ashley grow up, I would have given anything to have had that baby back. I wanted children so badly. I used to hold your babies and wonder if mine would have looked like them."

"I've thought the same thing." He stroked her hand gently.

"And Karen used that to hurt you! God, she's a monster!"

"She had us both fooled. She started changing as soon as the wedding ceremony was over. It was like watching a snake shed its skin. I was determined to make the marriage work, but one person can't do that."

"No one could fault you for not trying. I've heard the way she talks to you. It hurts me."

"She doesn't have any respect for me." It seemed painful for him to admit that.

Chelsea took his hand in both hers. "I respect you,

Ryan. I can see you much more clearly than Karen does."
She could tell by the look in his eyes that she had said the
right thing. After years of being ground down, Ryan didn't
have a lot of self-confidence and self-esteem.

"You don't think I'm a fool for staying? That I'm simply too weak to leave? Karen seems to hold that opinion."

"No. It takes a strong man to put up with all you have
to cope with every day. I know you're staying for Ashley,
and I admire you for it."

He put his arms around her and pulled her close. He
didn't kiss her, just held to her as if she were a lifeline. As
Chelsea embraced him, she wished she would never have
to pull away. So much was clear now. She understood
Karen too well. Her knack for getting into warped relationships had extended to her friendship as well.

At last he said simply, "I love you, Chelsea."

"I know," she whispered. "I love you, too." But as long
as Ryan lived with Karen, both reflected that their physical contact would go no further than embraces and an
occasional kiss. Chelsea feared this wouldn't be enough
for either of them for long.

Chapter Thirty-one

Karen's affair with Lee Brent proved to be more than she had expected. "I've never felt like this," she said as she lay in his arms, the sheet, over her breasts, tucked snugly under her arms. "I find myself waiting for your phone calls and thinking about you all the time."

"I know. I feel the same." He kissed her temple, but didn't try to touch her again. He knew she disliked being touched once the lovemaking was over. Karen had been amazed to find that he had the same preference. "I still don't see why you don't leave Ryan and live with me."

Karen sighed and looked away. "It's not that simple. What on earth would I tell Daddy? I don't care if Ryan loses his job, but what about you? Who knows how Daddy might take this? I've heard him say a thousand times that DataComp is a family-oriented business."

"I could find another job. DataComp isn't the only computer company in Dallas."

"No, but it's the best," she said with automatic loyalty. "And Daddy has been grooming Ryan to take over the company when he retires."

"I could take it over in his place." Lee propped his head on his bent arm and gazed at the ceiling. "I could do it. I know I could."

"Of course you could. If Ryan can do it anyone can."

He looked at her. "You don't care for him at all do you?" It was more of a statement than a question.

"Not any longer. I suppose I did at first." She paused thoughtfully. "It's funny, but I really can't remember."

"He's not a bad sort. He's easy to work for, doesn't mind carrying the bulk of the work himself."

"Of course he doesn't. That way he can stay away from home more of the time."

Lee laughed. "I hadn't thought of it that way. If I were your husband, I'd want to spend every minute I could with you."

"I don't know what Ashley would say if I were to divorce Ryan. She loves him." Karen said this last with a touch of sarcasm. It still hurt her that her daughter had talked to Ryan and to Chelsea about those birth-control pills, not to her.

"She's how old? Ten?"

"Thirteen." Karen had shaved several years off her age and therefore off Ashley's as well at the beginning of the affair. She glanced at him. She wasn't too sure of his age, either. He was certainly younger than she was, but not nearly as young as Hank Farley had been, or even Mark Dreyer. Being with him made her believe in her own youth.

"It would be odd having a teenage daughter. My boys are nine and six."

"I got an early start," she lied smoothly. "Do you miss the boys?"

"Of course I do. Especially at Christmas time. As soon as the dust settled from the divorce, their mother took them to Galveston. That's about as far from Dallas as you can get."

"She just did it to be hateful." Karen vaguely remembered meeting his ex-wife at a party soon after Lee joined the company. Soon after that, the Brents had separated.

"At least I can see them every second and fourth weekend."

She didn't want to talk about children. She rolled onto her stomach and looked at him with a smile. "What if I were to leave Ryan? What would we do?" The question had begun as a fantasy, but these days she was seriously considering following through.

"I'd give you the name of my lawyer, and you'd file for divorce," he said as if he were telling a story to a child. "Then you and I would be married, and you would move in with me or I'd move in with you."

"My house would be the best place for us. Ashley is used to living there."

Lee hesitated. He had seen the house from the street. "It's awfully big. I'll bet the payments on it are high!"

She shrugged. "They aren't that bad. We have no problems with the running costs." She didn't consider that they could make the payments so easily because Ryan worked many extra hours and had a larger salary than Lee. These were details she preferred to leave to the men in her life. If she were married to Lee, she would expect him to take care of her just as Ryan did and just as her father had before him.

"Maybe it would be better to get a place all our own."

Karen shook her head. "I'd hate to move. Clutter and packing boxes depress me. No, I want to stay exactly where I am."

Lee smiled. "It sounds to me as if you're really considering this."

"I am." She tilted her head back so the tiny wrinkles on her neck didn't show. "I just don't know how to go about it."

"The first move would be to tell Ryan you want a divorce." Lee thought for a minute. "That could get me fired if he hears I'm involved. He's my supervisor, after all."

"I'll tell Daddy that I don't want you to leave the company. Maybe he can put you into another division or something."

"Maybe," Lee said doubtfully.

"I could tell Ryan tonight." She tilted her head to one side as she considered. "I really could. I could tell him he has to move out and then file for divorce next week."

"Or tomorrow," Lee suggested.

"Maybe." Karen was trying to remember what was on her calendar for the rest of the week. She kept as busy as possible with clubs and social groups so she wouldn't get bored. "I may do that. Tell him, I mean."

Lee kissed her, and she made up her mind. There was no reason to stay with Ryan when she could have Lee. It would be so much more convenient if he were living with her. She wouldn't have to get up, dress, and drive home after making love with him.

An hour later she let herself into her house. It was quiet, and she thought for a minute that Ryan was already asleep. The lights were turned off on the Christmas tree. That usually meant he had gone to his room for the night. As she passed the den she saw the lamp on. He put down the book he was reading and looked at her silently. Karen was on the defensive immediately. She tried to remember whether her dress looked rumpled from lying on Lee's floor all evening, whether her makeup was messed up. "I thought you'd be asleep by now."

"You're late. As usual," he finally said. "We need to talk."

"Yes," she replied in the tone she always used when she spoke to him these days. "We do."

"I'm not happy. I doubt that you are either."

"That's an understatement." She came into the room and tossed her bag onto the couch before sitting on the arm.

"I think we should get a divorce."

Karen stared at him. *"You* want a divorce? What on earth do you have to complain about? I cook your meals and clean your house. I raised your children. Now you want a divorce?" She thought for a minute. He had caught her by surprise. "So do I. I was about to say the same thing to you."

Ryan regarded her silently. "I never thought it would turn out this way. Did you?"

"I knew from the beginning that there was a possibility it would. After all, look at the divorce statistics."

"I was thinking along other lines in the beginning. I was determined to beat the odds and have an ideal marriage and a perfect family."

"I certainly did my part," she said defensively.

"We won't get anywhere if we start blaming each other. I think the best thing to do is just separate, divorce, and try to keep it as peaceful as possible—for Ashley."

She looked at him curiously. "I'm amazed that you'd leave her, frankly."

Ryan was quiet for a moment. "I drove over to the cinema so Ashley could meet the Robbins girl. I saw your car parked on Redbud."

Karen paled. "I was there to talk to someone about the charity horse show that's coming up in the spring." She had tried not to stammer.

"Your car was still there when I went to pick Ashley up. She didn't see it," he added. "Who really lives there, Karen?"

Her chin came up suddenly. "Lee Brent."

"That's what I thought." He felt tired to the bone. He had expected her to deny it.

"I've been seeing him for several weeks."

He stared at her and wondered why he wasn't hurt by what she was saying. "I knew it was somebody. I didn't guess it was Lee."

Karen glared at him, angry that he wasn't more upset. "I've seen other men as well. I've been seeing Mark Dreyer for months!"

He felt an absurd urge to laugh. "Mark Dreyer? You've got to be kidding. How old is he? Twenty-four?"

"Twenty-five," she shot back.

"Whatever." He stood and started for the door.

"Come back here! Aren't you even man enough to care that I'm dating your co-workers?" She was on her feet, harrying him as he tried to leave the room. "Don't you have any spine at all?"

Ryan whirled, grabbed Karen's arm, and shoved her against the wall. She gasped and her eyes widened with fear. In carefully controlled tones, he said, his nose bare inches from hers, "If I was less of a man, I'd have left you years ago. I tried to last it out. I was even faithful to you. I'm damned if I know why!" He released her and she dodged away.

He gave her a contemptuous glare and then went down the hall to his room, took his suitcases from the closet, and started packing.

"You're leaving tonight?" she asked from the doorway. She looked vulnerable and frightened, as if things had gotten out of hand and she didn't know how to regain control.

"Yes."

"What will I tell Ashley?"

"Tell her you're screwing Lee Brent and Mark Dreyer and that I'm tired of pretending not to know about it." He had packed so often in his imagination he had no trouble deciding what to take. "I'll be back for the rest of my things tomorrow—after I see the lawyer."

"*You're* filing?" she exclaimed.

"Of course. I'm the one leaving." He threw her a wry smile. "What's wrong, Karen? Am I not following the script you had worked out? What did you expect? That I'd be crushed and beg you not to leave me? That I'd make all sorts of promises to convince you to stay?" The look on her face confirmed it. "No way. You've pushed me too far, too long."

"I'll see to it that Daddy fires you!" she shouted at him, almost choking on the words.

"I'm sure you will."

"I'll see that no one else hires you, either!"

"Fortunately, you can't do that. And keep your voice down unless you want to explain all this to Ashley tonight." He snapped the bags shut and then picked them up. He still felt numb and dead inside.

"Where are you going! You're not walking out of here until I know where to find you."

He smiled mirthlessly. "I'm going to a meeting—one of

the ones you're always going to. A charity benefit planning committee, a group to raise the city's awareness of butterflies, a club to promote flower arranging. You fill in the blanks."

She stared at him. "Are you out of your mind? Nothing meets at this time of night!"

"I know. I've been aware of that for years. I'm not as stupid as you prefer to think. As for where I'm really going, it doesn't matter. All that matters is I'm leaving here and I'm leaving you." He went down the hall with her at his heels.

"You can't do this! You can't just walk out on me in the middle of the night!"

"Remember to pay the bills at the end of the month. The house payment is due on the fifteenth."

Karen tried to hold the front door shut so he couldn't leave. "Ryan! Let's talk this over!"

He paused to look into her eyes. "No. You've gone too far this time. Until you told me about Lee and Mark, I could pretend it was all in my imagination. Now I know. How could I possibly stay under the same roof with you, knowing that you're sleeping with men I work with every day? I had hoped to stay until Ashley graduates, but that's no longer possible. Move out of my way."

"No! I'm not letting you go like this."

"Everything can't always go your way, Karen. Maybe that was the mistake I made. I was too ready to keep the peace at any price—it turns out the price was higher than I realized." He put down a suitcase long enough to pull her out of the way.

Karen stood in the doorway and stared at him as he walked to the car and put his bags in the trunk. He looked back at her and the house as he opened the driver's door. "I sure as hell hope Lee is able to wangle a raise. I wouldn't be in his shoes for anything!" He smiled bitterly as he drove away.

For the next hour he simply drove around. In spite of his words to Karen, he had no idea of where to go. Checking into a motel didn't appeal to him. The last thing he wanted was to be alone.

When he found himself driving down Chelsea's street, he parked beside her car and went up the stairs. She answered the door and he went inside.

She had been in bed and had pulled on a garnet coverup to answer the door. It had slipped off one shoulder, and he found himself wondering if she was wearing anything underneath. When she closed the door behind him, he said, "I've left Karen."

"No! What happened?" She motioned for him to sit down beside her on the couch. "What time is it?"

"Late. I'm sorry I woke you. I didn't plan on it happening quite this way." He hesitated. His thoughts seemed to be skittering off in all directions. "She came in about an hour ago. I guess it was around midnight. I told her I wanted a divorce. She told me she's having two affairs. They're with co-workers of mine."

"Men you work with every day?" Chelsea sounded more shocked than he had been.

"One of them even works in my department. Lee Brent is his name."

Chelsea shook her head to show she had never heard of him. "Karen never confides in me anymore. I had no idea this was going on. Not with *two* men. That's not like Karen."

"You're telling me. I've been married to her for sixteen years, and every time we had sex it was like I was forcing her into some unnatural act." He avoided her eyes. "Now I find out she's sleeping with not one, but two men. It's enough to deflate anyone's ego, I can tell you." He had meant the words to be light, but there was too much pain behind them.

Chelsea slid closer and put her hands over his. "It's not you. Don't blame yourself."

He met her eyes. "Who else can I blame? If I had been able to please her, maybe the marriage would have worked. But damn it, I tried everything I knew!"

"I know Karen well enough to realize she's not having an affair because of sex. It's something else. Don't ask me what it could be, but I'm certain I'm right."

"Maybe." He wanted to think so. For sixteen years he had suffered from worrying that he simply wasn't any good in bed. Tonight he desperately needed to believe that wasn't the reason Karen had sought other men. "I wonder what we'll talk about around the coffee pot tomorrow at the office," he said wryly.

"Don't do that to yourself. Do you want me to go over and talk to her?"

He shook his head. "I told her I want a divorce, and I do. I'm going to see a lawyer tomorrow. I tried to stay for Ashley, but I just can't handle knowing that she's using me for a baby sitter while she carries on. I've suspected she was seeing someone for a long time, but now I have names. That makes it entirely different."

"Yes. It would."

"Maybe I shouldn't have come here, but I didn't know where else to go." He looked at her. "Do you want me to leave?"

"I would have been upset with you if you'd gone anywhere else." She ran her fingers through her hair to shove it out of her face, and it tumbled over her shoulders and down to her waist. "Would you like some coffee? Maybe some wine?"

"Wine. My nerves are already on edge."

She went to the kitchen and poured two glasses of chablis. Coming back, she handed one to Ryan. "Where are you going to stay?"

"I don't know."

She paused. "You could stay here."

He met her eyes for a long moment before speaking. "I don't know if that's such a good idea."

"It's probably not a good idea at all, but do you want to stay?"

He glanced around at the familiar surroundings. "You only have one bed. Are you offering me the couch?"

She shrugged the shoulder that was bared. "I'm offering you whatever you want. As much or as little."

He shook his head. "I can't drag you into this. Karen is certain to find out where I am, and I don't want your name brought up in court."

"You're divorcing her. What does it matter if she knows you're staying here?"

"And Ashley?"

Chelsea caught her breath. "Oh. That's right. I hadn't thought about that. Okay, so we'll find you an apartment. I'll help you look tomorrow if you'd like."

"I'd like that." He tasted the wine. It was cold and smooth in his mouth. He leaned his head back against the couch and closed his eyes. "Tonight was a nightmare. I couldn't feel anything. Nothing at all. It was as if I was watching all of it happen to someone I didn't even know."

"How did Karen take it?"

"At first she was cold and sarcastic. Then I told her I wanted a divorce and she became really angry. She said she was about to tell me the same thing and started in about seeing Lee Brent and Mark Dreyer. She said I was," he hesitated, "spineless and no man at all."

"She said that?" Chelsea whispered.

"She was about to elaborate on it when something snapped inside me. For years she's been grinding at me, like water on a rock. This was the last straw. I didn't hurt her. I wouldn't do that no matter how hard she pushed me, but I couldn't let that roll off my back."

"Sure. That's more than anyone could ignore."

"I pushed her up against the wall and told her she'd gone too far. When I released her, it was as if she were the old Karen again. She looked scared and like a little girl— you know the look."

Chelsea nodded.

"I went to my room to pack, and she followed me. She was still shouting at me, but the coldness was gone. I don't think she ever believed I would actually leave her. She has no idea how close I've come so many times. She tried to prevent me from going. After I left, I drove around for a long time. At least it seemed like a long time. Then I came here."

"It sounds as if she might be willing to try to work it out," Chelsea said as if trying to convince them both.

Ryan shook his head. "It no longer matters. I'm not going back. Too much has happened." He finished the wine and finally was numb and relaxed. He doubted he could sleep, but he might be able to get past the pain that was threatening to overwhelm him.

Chelsea put her half-empty glass on the coffee table. "I'll call Ashley tomorrow morning. I won't tell her where you spent the night, but she needs to know you're safe."

"I'm worried about her. She's just getting her life straightened out. What's this going to do to her?"

"We'll have to face that when we see what her reaction is. It might make her behave more responsibly. It's hard to tell."

Ryan leaned forward and buried his face in his hands. "Have I screwed up royally?"

"You mean in leaving?" she asked.

"No, in all of it." He was suddenly so tired he could hardly talk. "I'm afraid I haven't made a good decision in my entire life."

She touched his arm gently. "Things will look better by morning. You've been through a lot tonight."

As she started to move away, Ryan caught her hand. "Chelsea, I've got to know. Do you see me as some spineless creature?"

She shook her head and her eyes were bright with tears. "When I look at you, I see the man I most admire in all the world. I couldn't have put up with what you have. I see you as warm and gentle and sexy and intelligent. No, I don't see you the way Karen does."

He suddenly knew a vast relief, not because Chelsea wouldn't have lied to salve his wounded pride, but because he would have known instantly if she weren't telling the truth. "Thank you. And thanks for the place to sleep."

She nodded. "I'll get you some bedding."

He leaned back on the couch and watched her get sheets and two quilts from an antique wardrobe near her bed. She was as unself-conscious as if she were fully clothed. Ryan felt a stirring in him that was all too familiar where Chelsea was concerned.

Together they made him a bed on the couch. Chelsea hesitated as if reluctant to tell him good night, and he turned off the lamp, leaving the apartment in near darkness. He reached out and touched her cheek. She leaned her face into his palm caressingly.

"Tomorrow," she whispered. "Everything will be better then."

"Right. Tomorrow." He watched her cross to the bed. She paused and glanced back, then turned off the last lamp.

He was all too aware of her in the darkness. He hadn't expected to find his body so eager to respond to hers. Not tonight when his life had been turned upside down. He heard the whisper of sheets as she lay down and the rustling of covers that meant she was settling in to sleep.

Slowly he pulled off his sweater and jeans, tossing them onto the nearest chair, then lay down. The couch wasn't long enough to accommodate his height, and he knew it was going to be a long night.

As his eyes adjusted to the dark, he made out the shape of Chelsea's bed, her body reclining under the covers. Yes, it was going to be a long night indeed. Two things kept him on the couch: fear that Chelsea might regret any intimacy in the morning if he went to her and his concern that Karen was right about his lovemaking ability. What if he joined Chelsea in the bed as he wanted so much to do, only to discover that he couldn't satisfy her any more than he had satisfied Karen? He couldn't handle that tonight.

He pretended to sleep.

Chapter Thirty-two

When Ryan went to work the next day, he was aware of several people watching him covertly. How many, he wondered, knew about Karen's affairs? Gossip spread like wildfire at DataComp. Had everyone known all along? Had they been discussing her for years behind his back? He wasn't sure how long her indiscretions had been going on, and he hoped he never found out.

He went to his desk exactly as he always did. His secretary brought him a cup of coffee as she had for sixteen years. Today she glanced at him with interest and seemed to have something she wanted to say. "Thank you, Mrs. Dobbs," he said in dismissal. She went back to her own desk.

Ryan's area was separated from the general office by glass. Usually he liked this arrangement, for he felt it obviated barriers between him and his workers. Today he might as well have been in a fishbowl. A movement caught his eye, and he noticed Lee Brent shifting the papers on his desk and glancing worriedly at him.

Ryan turned his back and pressed the button on his intercom. "Mrs. Dobbs, call Mr. Baker and tell him I'm coming up to talk to him, please."

He gave her time to complete the call, then walked briskly through the office to the elevators. Behind him he heard whispers and an usual amount of paper shuffling. He ignored both.

Once in the elevator, Ryan slumped against the padded wall. This was more difficult than he had expected.

The doors slid open silently on Fulton Baker's outer office, discreetly decorated for Christmas with expensive ornaments on a small tree. Fulton's secretary looked up with a smile and motioned for him to go into the inner office. Ryan decided she hadn't heard the news yet.

Fulton smiled when he saw Ryan and said, "Coffee?"

"No, thanks."

"So . . . what's up?" Fulton was perfectly relaxed, and his smile was friendly. "I don't seem to have a meeting scheduled with you for this morning. Is there a problem with the Xavier order?"

"No, it will go out on time." Ryan took his father-in-law's measure. "I'm giving my notice. I'm going to leave DataComp."

Fulton stared at him. "I beg your pardon? I can't have heard you correctly."

"You haven't talked to Karen today, have you?"

"No. I came in early. Is something wrong?" His forehead puckered in concern.

"We've separated. I'm filing for divorce. I thought it would alleviate some unpleasantness if I give my notice."

"Divorce!" Fulton sat down as if stunned. "You and Karen? What's the reason behind it?" He wasn't one to bandy words.

"I'd rather not say."

For a long time Fulton simply stared at him. "It's none of my business, of course, but I'm not just your boss, you know. This is my daughter we're discussing."

"That's why I'm not going to tell you the reason I left."

"Are you staying in the Dallas area?"

"Yes. Will you give me a reference?"

"Certainly. I've never had a complaint about your work."

"I appreciate that. And, Fulton, I'm sorry it worked out like this. I tried to hold it together, but my attempts just didn't work."

"How's Ashley taking it?"

"I haven't talked to her yet. I left after she had gone to bed. I'm worried about her, frankly. We've had some problems with her."

"I know." Fulton sounded as if his mind was on the divorce, not his granddaughter. "A divorce! Well, you certainly caught me off guard!"

"I know. I apologize for that. I have a recommendation for my replacement."

They had a short discussion, and after he left Fulton's office, Ryan went back downstairs. In view of the fact that he was divorcing Fulton's daughter, the two men had agreed that he would take his yearly vacation, effective immediately. Ryan was relieved not to have to spend the next two weeks rubbing elbows with Lee Brent and Mark Dreyer. There was only so much civilization he could muster under these circumstances.

When he reached his office, he began to empty his desk drawers. He realized someone was in the doorway and looked up to see Lee standing there.

"I think we should talk," Lee said.

"I can't think why I would want to do that." Ryan went back to removing his personal items from the drawers.

Lee stepped in and shut the door. "I want to ask you whether I should give notice or whether you're firing me on the spot." His tone was guarded, and he was evidently ready for unpleasantness.

"Neither. I just recommended to Fulton that he move you into my position. I'm leaving."

"You did that?" Lee asked in surprise. "I'm not fired?"

Ryan saw no reason to reply. He went to the filing cabinet and pulled open the drawer that contained his personal files and phone numbers.

"Why would you do this for me?" Lee asked suspiciously. "What's going on here?"

"I'm not doing it for you. I did it for Ashley. I want this to have as little negative impact on her life as possible." Ryan finally smiled. "You're going to need the raise. I know. I've been there." He was still smiling when he dumped the files into the box with his possessions, put it under his arm, and walked out of the office for the last time.

Ryan felt oddly free as he drove toward the law office he had chosen to handle the divorce. What could have been a thoroughly disagreeable scene with Fulton had gone more smoothly than he could have anticipated. During sleepless hours the night before, he had compiled mentally a list of firms to which he could apply for a job. At thirty-eight he wasn't eager to start anew, but he was far from discouraged.

Filing for divorce turned out to be relatively easy. Ryan found it hard to believe that a long-term commitment could be dissolved with so little effort. Because he didn't expect Karen to contest the action, his lawyer had assured him it was just a matter of paperwork, deciding who would be awarded what items, and waiting for the court date to arrive.

The import of what he was doing hit Ryan as he drove back to Chelsea's apartment. He was divorcing Karen and had quit his job! His world was atilt. Until now, he hadn't let himself think too clearly. At this moment it seemed reality had gone awry. At the beginning of the marriage, he had never considered that it might not work out. Even during the bad times he had thought that somehow, in some way, he and Karen would make it through as a couple. Now he had to get used to the idea that he was single, not part of a couple; "we" could no longer be used instead of "I."

"Are you okay?" Chelsea asked as he came in. "I didn't expect you back until after work."

"This is after work. I'm on a vacation—permanently. I'll start interviewing for jobs tomorrow."

"He fired you?"

"No, I quit. Fulton hadn't talked to Karen yet, so I had to break the news to him. We decided it would be best if I left now, under the circumstances. He says he'll give me a recommendation. I hope he stands by that after he talks to Karen. Lord knows what reason she'll give him for my leaving."

"You didn't tell him why?"

"How could I tell Fulton Baker his daughter is screwing around with his employees? He's not *that* understanding." He put the box containing his belongings on the table. "I also went to the lawyer and got the divorce started."

"Come sit down. You look exhausted."

When Ryan plopped onto the nearest chair, Chelsea went behind him and began massaging his shoulders and neck. "You're so tense! This must be difficult for you."

"You know, it's really odd. At times it's as if I'm running on automatic; then it hits me and I'm jolted into realizing this is for real. It's as if some of the cogs in my brain have teeth missing."

"I felt the same way when I left Lorne. I guess everyone experiences that."

"I'll start looking for an apartment today. I won't be under your feet much longer."

"You're not in the way."

"I'll have to set up job interviews. And call the credit card companies and places where I have charge accounts—have my name taken off the list." He rubbed his eyes. "Damn! There's so much to think about!"

Chelsea drew up another chair and sat facing him, their knees touching. "These next few days will be the worst part. At least that's the way it was for me."

He gazed into her eyes. "From here, it seems as if this is only going to get worse."

She reached out and put her hand on his cheek. "I know," she said gently. "I wish I could go through this for you. I've become an expert at ending relationships. Endings are always difficult. Even when you know it's time."

He put his arms around her and leaned forward so their foreheads touched. "What would I do without you, Chelsea? You've always been there when I needed you. Every single time."

"I always will be." Close to tears, she had to struggle to control her voice. "It hurts me to see you unhappy." With him so near she was having trouble thinking straight. She could smell the faint odor of aftershave and the more subtle scent of his skin.

Ryan brought his hands up to cup her face. For a long time he gazed into her eyes. Then he kissed her.

For Chelsea it was as if fireworks were exploding inside her. His lips were firm but soft against hers, and her leashed passion began to break free. With a soft moan, she returned his kiss, matching his ardor with her own.

He stopped kissing her to hold her close, his breath warm in her hair. She held to him as the world whirled around them.

After a few moments Ryan stood and drew her to her feet. Silently he led her to the bed. Neither of them needed to speak. Chelsea loosened his tie before she started unbuttoning his shirt. Her fingers trembled as she did the things she had dreamed of doing for so long. His chest was walled with hard muscles and was hot and smooth against her hands. As she loosened the buttons, she kissed the skin she exposed.

Ryan asked her no questions, and for this she was grateful. She didn't want to stop, perhaps couldn't at this point. She pulled his shirttail from his slacks and slipped the garment off his shoulders. He was beautifully made, his chest broad, his waist lean.

Slowly Ryan pulled her sweater over her head and tossed it aside. His hungry eyes devoured her breasts, barely concealed by the sheer lace of her bra. Chelsea reached behind her and loosened the fastenings and tossed the scrap of lace aside. "You're beautiful," he whispered. He cupped her breasts, rubbing his thumbs over her nipples until they beaded, hard against his hand.

Chelsea unfastened her jeans and stepped out of her shoes before kicking free of them. Her hands were no steadier than Ryan's as she worked the button free at the waist of his slacks, while he stroked her sides and hips, removing her panties meanwhile.

Naked, they lay on the bed and held each other. Chelsea felt she had finally come home as her skin pressed against his from head to toe. Ryan rolled onto his back, bringing her with him so she lay on his chest. He reached behind her to loosen the clip that held her hair, and her tresses formed a curtain about Chelsea's face.

He touched them almost reverently. "I've always loved your hair. You've never cut it."

"You told me once that you like it long."

His eyes met hers. "That's why you've kept it this way?"

"It's one of the reasons."

He threaded his fingers through her hair and drew her face to his. The kiss started gently, all the wonder of their newfound happiness in it. Chelsea deepened it to passion as she opened her lips to his tongue. "I love the way you taste," she whispered between kisses. "And the way you smell and especially the way you feel." She ran her hands over him, hungry to touch every inch of his body.

They rolled over again and she was beneath him, her breasts flattened against his chest. Ryan's eyes had darkened with desire for her, and his breath came as quickly as hers. She could feel the faint trembling in his muscles as he held himself back from taking her at once. Chelsea smiled up at him and ran her hands over the swell of his back to the dip at his waist, then lower to stroke his buttocks. There wasn't a spare inch of flesh on him. He had filled out since college, but it had all gone to muscle.

"There have been times when it was all I could do to keep my hands off you," he said, his voice husky with emotion. "Times when the sound of your voice haunted my dreams for weeks."

"I know. I've felt the same."

"We've wasted so damned much time."

She shook her head. "It wasn't wasted. We're together now."

"I'm never going to let you go again, Chelsea. If you run away to Germany again, I'm going to follow you."

"I'm through running away."

He smiled down at her as if she were too infinitely precious to touch. "I love you. I always have."

"I know. I've loved you, too."

This time when he kissed her, his passion mounted, too fierce to be quelled. Chelsea rolled onto her side, and his hand found her breast. He lowered his head to take the nipple into his mouth and suckled it gently, then with more demand. Chelsea arched her back as desire hammered her. The moan of sheer pleasure she heard was her own. She could focus only on the way his lips and hands were lifting her into ecstasy.

Ryan didn't rush their loving. He was fiercely determined to enjoy every moment, every sensation with her, and though Chelsea was trembling for completion, she was equally reluctant to rush the conclusion. She tasted the skin on his shoulders and arms and licked his chest. Her tonguing of his skin drove them both on.

At last she could stand it no longer and drew him between her legs. Ryan didn't hesitate. He entered her, and Chelsea held to him as passion roared in her veins. She began moving and he matched her rhythm with long, sure strokes.

Almost at once her passion leaped to completion, and she held to him as she cried out in a mingling of ecstasy and regret.

Ryan lay still for a moment, still deep inside her, then began to move again.

Chelsea was surprised to find he still hadn't reached his own peak. She was even more surprised to find her body respond as hungrily as it had before. He carried her expertly to another climax, and this time as she whirled into pure pleasure, he went with her.

They lay entwined, neither wanting to pull away from the other. "I've never known anything so wonderful!" she whispered when she could speak.

"You're crying?" He was instantly concerned.

"I'm so happy," she said brokenly. "I love you so much!"

He drew her closer, and she lay her head on his shoulder. Beneath her cheek she could hear the steady pounding of his heart. It seemed to be beating in perfect rhythm with her own.

"I love you, Chelsea. I'm never going to leave you again."

"You'll stay here? With me?" She looked up at him eagerly.

"I want to stay here. I feel as if I belong here."

"You do," she whispered. She smiled as she held him. "By the way, Ryan, Karen's a fool. You're a perfect lover."

He made no comment, but he held her closer.

They lay in each other's arms until the light from the window dulled to the hazy pink of sunset. There seemed to be too much to say, too much to explore, for them to part for even an instant. As night flowed into the apartment, they made love again. Chelsea gave herself to him over and over again throughout the night, and by dawn, though happily exhausted, they were more in love than ever.

Ryan told his family that he had left Karen, but he did not speak of his involvement with Chelsea. She was glad, for they would never have understood that his love for her hadn't influenced his decision to leave his wife and child. He was to fly to his parents' home on Christmas Eve and return on Christmas Day. After that, he told Chelsea, he would never leave her again. She agreed it was best for him to go to Boulder without her. There was plenty of time to break the news of their love to his family. She and Ryan would celebrate Christmas when he returned.

Two days before the twenty-fifth, Chelsea went shopping. Usually she dreaded the chore. It was no fun to cook for one person, so holidays had depressed her. This year it was entirely different. She had shopped all afternoon for just the right gift for Ryan and was determined to enjoy turkey and all the trimmings on Christmas Day.

On the aisle with the cranberries, Chelsea almost ran into Karen. For a long moment, they stared at each other. Then Karen pushed her cart on past as if she didn't recognize Chelsea. A hurt pierced Chelsea, but she didn't call after her former friend. As painful as it was, it was best this way. Karen looked tired and sullen, and Chelsea wondered if she was as glad to be rid of Ryan as she had claimed in the past that she would be.

Chelsea continued to feel guilty until she saw a younger man go up to Karen and put a box of cereal in her cart. Karen smiled briefly at him, then glanced covertly back at Chelsea. Chelsea pretended not to notice. So this was the man Karen wanted more than Ryan. She studied him critically. He was young, but his face showed little character or strength. Yes, Chelsea thought, Karen was a fool.

As she finished her shopping, she no longer felt guilty.

Chapter Thirty-three

In the next two months Chelsea saw Ryan try hard to rebuild a life for himself. He found employment with a new company that was swiftly rising and was in competition with DataComp. His salary was higher than it had been under Fulton Baker, and there was an opportunity to buy into the company's ownership after five years.

He missed Ashley deeply, and even though he didn't admit it, Chelsea knew he also missed Karen. He had lived with her for many years, and he was monogamous by nature. At times Chelsea wondered if he regretted his decision to get a divorce, although he never hinted that he did.

Chelsea and Ryan's love grew stronger the longer they were together. When she had known she couldn't have him, she had been strong enough to accept the fact that he was married to Karen. Now that he was living with her, she sometimes worried that she loved him too much to let him go. She was having to face her old fear of loving Ryan too much to survive without him.

He talked to Ashley on the phone daily. His daughter believed he was living alone, and Ryan didn't correct her assumption. He made an excuse when she asked for his phone number, saying that he hadn't had one installed and he was using a friend's when he called. Ashley didn't question this story, but Karen did. When she demanded that Ryan give her a number where he could be reached, he simply refused.

February blew in with a blast of cold, wet air that left ice on every surface. Dallas was no stranger to ice storms, but this one left traffic snarled and many businesses closed until the freeways could be safely navigated.

Ryan and Chelsea enjoyed the unexpected vacation by spending the day making love and eating by the fireplace she had installed in a corner opposite her work area. The wind rattled the windows and sent puffs of smoke back down the chimney from time to time, but they didn't care. Their love was stronger than a storm.

In a few days the ice was gone and businesses were back to normal. Chelsea was becoming used to having Ryan come home. Whether the change was due to the new company or the new home, he no longer worked late. If there was work to do, he brought it home and did it with her sitting beside him, curled against his side. Chelsea had never been so happy or felt so secure in all her life.

One night as they were finishing dinner, there was a knock at the door. They were engrossed in a TV movie, and as Chelsea responded her mind was still on the plot. Without looking through the peephole, she opened the door wide. Ashley stood on the small porch.

"Aunt Chel, can I come in and talk? Mom is—" She broke off as she saw Ryan across the room, his shoes off, his shirttail out, obviously at home. For moments she stared at him, then at Chelsea. Finally, without another word, she turned and ran down the steps and out into the darkness.

"Ashley? Ashley!" Chelsea called after her. "Come back!" She turned to Ryan.

He was pulling his shoes on and stuffing his shirttail into his jeans. "Where did she go?"

"I don't know." Chelsea went out onto the porch and leaned over the rail to look in all directions. Although the street was well lit, she didn't see Ashley anywhere. "She must have run into the alley."

"Damn!" Ryan grabbed his coat from the rack as he hurried out.

Chelsea wrapped her arms around her against the cold. Why hadn't she looked out first? They would have had some warning that way. They might not have looked quite so intimate. As it was, Ashley had to realize that he was living here.

Ryan came back, his hands shoved into his coat pockets. "I can't find her. Was she in a car?"

"I don't know. It happened so fast I didn't notice whether one was parked below or not."

"Surely she's not on her bike on a night like this! What would Karen be thinking of to let her ride her bike on such a cold night?" He went to the phone and dialed Karen's number. After a while he hung up. "Karen's not there. Naturally."

"Ashley's no fool, Ryan. She must have had a ride over. Give her some credit."

He frowned at her. "Now she knows where I'm living."

"She had to know sooner or later."

"Not like this, she didn't."

Chelsea was more worried than she let him see. His divorce from Karen wasn't final, and if Ashley told her mother, the proceedings might be delayed and the settlement made more difficult. Karen was vindictive about lesser things. His living with Chelsea might be just the weapon she was seeking to use against him. However often she might be seeing Lee Brent, the man wasn't living in her house. Ryan's living with Chelsea might be enough for Karen to convince the judge that he shouldn't have visitation rights with his daughter.

"I'm going to drive around and look for Ashley."

Chelsea nodded. "I'll stay here in case she comes back."

She watched him leave and locked the door behind him. She had a terrible feeling that her house of cards was about to come crashing down.

Ryan was back in an hour. "I couldn't find her anywhere. I even drove by the house several times. No lights were on, and no one answered the doorbell."

"Then she must be in a car," Chelsea reasoned. "She's

had ample time to go home, and she certainly wouldn't ride a bike all over town on a night like this."

"You saw how upset she was." Ryan paced to the fire and warmed his hands against the blaze. The TV threw colors over his face, but neither of them noticed it was still on. "I even drove by the Bakers. I didn't stop, though. The light was on, the one they leave burning when they're out. Ashley doesn't have a key so she couldn't have let herself in."

Chelsea went to him and put her arms around him. "Ryan, she had to know eventually," she repeated. "I'm only surprised she hasn't been over before now."

He held her tightly. "I must be a fool not to have realized this could happen. For some reason I thought I could stay here and no one would ever know. This was a sanctuary to me. I forgot it's one for Ashley, too."

"Try calling the house again. Maybe she's home and just not answering the door."

Ryan dialed the number in quick pokes. "Hello? Karen, is Ashley there?" He waited for her to look, his fingers tapping impatiently on the phone. "She's not? Do you know if she's with someone? If she's in a car or on her bike? No, I'm not trying to frighten you. No, I'm not saying she's in danger. I'm just trying to find her." He frowned and Chelsea knew Karen was launching into a tirade. That was her pattern in any communication between them these days. "When she comes in, have her call me." He hung up. To Chelsea he said, "She's not home."

"Call her friends' houses. She has to be somewhere. Call the Bakers."

For the next half hour, Ryan searched by phone for Ashley. Although Chelsea didn't admit it to him, she was becoming more and more worried. Ashley had looked crushed to find him at her place, and the girl was given to dramatic and impulsive acts.

Until midnight Ryan alternated between pacing and calling numbers where Ashley might be. They both jumped when the phone jangled loudly. Chelsea grabbed it before it could ring twice. "Hello?"

"Chelsea, this is Karen."

"Hello, Karen." Her eyes met Ryan's, and she took his hand to calm him.

"If you know where to find Ryan, you'd better contact him. He called earlier looking for Ashley. She still isn't home. Do you know where to find him?"

"Yes. I can find him."

"That figures," Karen said with heavy sarcasm. "Tell him to call home." She hung up.

"She says you're to call home," she said as she hung up the receiver.

"Shit! That's not my home any longer." He took the phone and stabbed out the number. "Karen, this is Ryan."

"That didn't take long," Karen said coldly. "She must have your number memorized."

"What about Ashley?"

"She's not here. I've looked everywhere, and she didn't leave a note saying where she would be. It's been a long time since she stayed out this late. Do you think I should call the police?"

"I doubt they can do anything, but try anyway. I'll call the hospitals."

"Where can I call you back?"

"I'll call you." He hung up and his eyes met Chelsea's. "She's not home."

"I gathered that."

He leafed through the phone book and started calling hospitals, beginning with Parkland where emergencies were usually taken. When he had no luck, he called Karen back. "I guess it's good news, but I didn't find her at any of the hospitals."

"The police were no help at all. You'd think they get calls about missing thirteen-year-old girls all the time. What should I do?" The little girl sound was back in her voice.

Ryan hesitated and looked at Chelsea. "I think I'd better come over. Maybe we can find a phone number for some friend of hers if we both look." He hung up and said numbly, "I have to go."

"I know. I think it's for the best. Karen will need you. She's never been good in a crisis."

He stood and held her in silence for a long time. Then he went to the door and was gone without a backward look.

A ball of fear was growing in Chelsea. What if they didn't find Ashley?

She couldn't sit there doing nothing but worrying, so she pulled on her coat and hurried down to her car. Ryan was out of sight before she reached it, and she felt desperately lonely. Karen had told him to phone "home." Did this mean she was going to try for a reconciliation? She knew how keenly Ryan missed Ashley. This might be enough to send him back to Karen. Trying not to think about that, she started her car and drove down the lighted street.

She drove aimlessly, not having any idea where to search for Ashley. If Ryan's daughter didn't go to her grandparents', where would she go? An idea occurred to Chelsea, but she dismissed it at first. Ashley wouldn't go there. The idea returned and seemed more likely than before. Chelsea drove to the bus depot.

An inquiry sent her to the section where a bus would be leaving for Boulder, Colorado, in an hour. She spotted Ashley sitting a bit apart from several street people who looked as if they lived in the chairs they were occupying. She ran to her.

"Ashley! We've looked everywhere for you!" Chelsea was so relieved she was about to cry. "What are you doing here? Are you running away?"

"No. I'm going to see Grandma and Grandpa." Ashley frowned at Chelsea. It was easy to see she had been crying. "I don't want to live in Dallas anymore."

"Your Mom and Dad are worried sick about you! Call them and tell them I'm bringing you home."

"No. I'm not going back." She glared at Chelsea. "I saw Dad watching TV at your house. He looked to me as if he was living there!"

Chelsea was aware of the attention they were drawing, but this had to be hashed out. "He is."

Ashley jerked away and tried to leave. Chelsea caught her. "No, Ashley! You asked me, and I think you deserve to know the truth. I'm not going to lie to you!"

Ashley whirled to face her. "Does Mom know about this?"

"I doubt it. He may have told her. I don't know."

"He's with Mom?" Surprise replaced the anger in the girl's face. "That's where he is?"

"Yes. I told you they're both worried sick over you. What did you think he was going to do? Finish watching the movie on TV?"

"If he cared anything about me he wouldn't have left us in the first place!"

"You're old enough to know that's not so. Don't give me that line of bull. You know their marriage hasn't been sound for years."

"So why did he leave now? To be with you?" Scorn dripped from the words.

"No, I wasn't the reason he left. If you want to know what was, you'll have to ask them."

"I have! Mom says he left because he doesn't love us anymore. Dad says he left because it was 'for the best'! What the hell does that mean? It wasn't best for me!"

Chelsea felt helpless. She certainly wasn't the one to tell Ashley about Karen's affairs. "I don't know, honey. I just don't know. If that's the reason he gave you, I suppose it will have to do. He still loves you, though. He's divorcing your mother, not you."

"It's the same thing." Ashley dropped back on the scarred seat, crossed her arms, and stared glumly ahead. "That's why I'm going to live with Grandma and Grandpa. They won't run out on me or be gone nearly every night. Mom's never home anymore. It's not fair!"

"Was she staying home at night before he left?" Chelsea asked gently as she sat beside her. "She's not leaving to avoid you. I know her better than that."

Ashley frowned at her. "I hate my life these days. Scott Stark is trying to get me to go out with him again, and when I said I wouldn't, he spread all kinds of awful stories about me. Everybody at school hates me!"

"There are other schools."

"I hate Saint Anne's! They have a terrible football team, and we never win any games. All the kids run with their own bunch. They don't want to include me. It's like I'm a freak or something!"

"Tell your Dad. Maybe you could transfer to the public school."

"Mom won't even talk about it. She says it's not as nice as Saint Anne's, that they let just anybody go there and I wouldn't learn nearly as much." Her voice was filled with sarcasm.

"You won't learn anything at all if you start cutting class again to see Scott. You know he's bad news."

"I do, and I told you, I'm not going out with him. That's why he's talking trash about me."

"Running away to your grandparents is no answer either. We can't flee from trouble every time it crops up. You need to work through this problem at school."

Ashley faced her squarely. "I don't want my Dad living with you."

Chelsea hadn't expected her to be so direct. "We're adults. We have to make that decision ourselves."

"He would come home if you told him to. You're just selfish and want him for yourself. Mom sure doesn't know where he's been all this time. She's going to have a fit when she finds out."

"Our decision to be together wasn't one we made lightly. We love each other, Ashley."

"I don't believe it! Dad really loves Mom! You're just taking him away because you know you can do it!"

Chelsea wondered if Ashley really believed this, when

only minutes before she had said Ryan didn't love her or her mother. This was no time to argue logic. "That's not true."

Ashley thought for a minute. "I'll go home on one condition."

"What's that?" Chelsea already knew what was coming.

"You have to send Dad home, too. You have to give him back!"

"I can't make him go back if he doesn't want to. He's a grown man and makes his own decisions."

"If he didn't have you, he would have been back already."

Chelsea thought this was probably true. Ryan missed Ashley enough to have tried to work things out with Karen if he hadn't had Chelsea. "I'm not going to bargain with you. What Ryan does is up to him."

Ashley thought about it. "He's with Mom now?"

"Yes."

"All right. I'll go home. I'll bet they've made up already." Ashley stood and walked briskly in the direction of the entrance. "Where are you parked?"

"In front. How did you get here?"

"My friend Brittany gave me a ride. She got her driver's license last week."

"So you do have friends at Saint Anne's." Chelsea had to hurry to keep up. Now that Ashley was determined to go home, she was all but running.

"No way. Brittany lives down the street. She's in public school."

Chelsea wondered if public school would be a better atmosphere if Ashley's best friend was in it and was willing to help her run away.

They reached the car and got in. Chelsea started the motor, but before she pulled away she said, "Ashley, if they really are making up, it will be better if you don't tell your mother about seeing Ryan at my place."

Ashley looked as if she was about to disagree, but she thought about it and nodded.

Chelsea felt more lonely than ever as she drove away. Whether she lost Ryan or not, she had almost certainly lost Ashley. Would it have been better to tell her the truth at the beginning? No, she decided, that wouldn't have helped in the long run. Ashley was rebellious, always had been. She probably would have found some other reason to run away.

All the lights were on in Karen's house. Chelsea parked and waited for Ashley to get out. The girl sat where she was. "Well?" Chelsea asked.

"I'm sort of scared to go in alone. What if they're mad at me?"

"I can almost guarantee that they are. What you did was terrible."

"Will you go in with me?"

"Ashley, make up your mind. Am I the enemy or not?" It seemed to Chelsea she was on an emotional roller coaster. She didn't want to see Ryan with Karen, to know he might not be leaving. After the two months she'd had with him, she was no longer able to be philosophic about it.

"Come in with me?" Ashley repeated in a small voice.

With a sigh, Chelsea got out of the car. They walked to the front door and Ashley opened it and went in, pulling Chelsea along behind her. Karen and Ryan were sitting in the den, as Chelsea had seen them do for years. When they saw Ashley they both jumped to their feet. Karen grabbed her daughter and hugged her. Ryan put his arms around her.

"I found her at the bus station," Chelsea said awkwardly when they released their daughter. "She was on her way to Boulder."

"Boulder!" Karen exclaimed.

"Also, Ashley would like to change schools. She wants to go to public school."

"You never told me that!" Karen said, staring at the girl.

"Yes, I did, Mom. You just never listen."

"I think that would be a good idea," Ryan said. "I've never been convinced that Saint Anne's was the best place for you."

Ashley hugged him, and Karen reached out to smooth her hair in a maternal gesture. Chelsea backed away. Her eyes met Ryan's over Ashley's head, and for a long moment they gazed at each other. Then Chelsea turned and left.

She cried all the way home. He wasn't coming back. He had been too glad to be with Ashley, too relieved to have her home safely. If he left again, there was no guarantee his daughter wouldn't run away the next day or the day after that. And to Chelsea's tortured mind, he had seemed engrossed in conversation with Karen when they had arrived. It had looked as if they were working out their differences. Chelsea wanted Ryan to be happy, but her heart was breaking.

When she let herself into her house, the TV was still going but the fire had burned low behind its screen. She turned off the TV and added another log to the fire. After putting on his robe, she sat on the floor in front of the flames and hugged her knees to her chest. What would she do without Ryan?

It didn't help to tell herself that she had survived without him for so many years. That had changed. Now she knew what it was like to live with a man who loved her and who never hurt her in any way. It was an experience she had never known before, one she wasn't sure she could find again. She loved Ryan, and she knew no other love would ever fill the emptiness he left.

But she also knew she wouldn't try to win him back. She loved him too much to cause him to be pulled in two directions. And she was no home wrecker. She would abide by Ryan's decision, somehow.

Dawn was paling the sky when she heard a key turn in the lock. She turned to the door as it opened and Ryan stepped in. She had thought all her tears were gone, but she found her eyes filling again. "Have you come after your things?"

He came to her and sat beside her. "Have you been sitting here all night? I expected to find you asleep."

"How could I sleep on a night like this? I've been thinking." She was going to make this as easy for Ryan as possible. "I'm going to Paris."

"Excuse me?"

"Jean-Paul called before Christmas and asked me to come back to him. I'm going to go."

"To Paris," he said as if it were a statement. "To Jean-Paul Armand."

"Yes. I'll leave early next week. That gives me the weekend to be certain my passport is in order. I guess I'll have the canvases sent over this time. I probably won't be coming back." She was surprised at how easily the lies came out of her mouth. She didn't know where she would actually be going, only that she couldn't stay here. Perhaps she would move to Houston.

"I wish you had told me before. I have to give two weeks' notice at work, and I don't have a passport. How large a house does Jean-Paul have? Will we be crowded?"

"What are you talking about?"

"I'm not letting you go over there alone. I told you, if you run I'll follow you. I don't especially want to live in Jean-Paul's house, and I'll bet he doesn't expect me to arrive with you, but that's the way it's going to be."

"You can't come with me! You're staying here with Karen and Ashley!"

"No, I'm divorcing Karen. That means I won't be living with her or with Ashley."

Chelsea stared at him. "You've been with her all night! It's morning!"

"Yes, it took that long to argue Karen into letting Ashley transfer to public school. You know how she feels about Saint Anne's. In her opinion there's no other school worth mentioning in all of Dallas."

"That's what you've been doing? Arguing with Karen?"

He pulled her closer. "Chelsea, you've got to get over this assumption that everyone you love is going to mistreat you. I love you, I'm not deserting you, and I certainly wouldn't desert you for Karen!"

"You wouldn't?" she asked in a small voice.

"As soon as the divorce is final, I want to marry you. Incidentally, I'd prefer to stay here in Dallas and not live with Jean-Paul. How determined are you to go to him?"

She swatted at him. "Quit teasing me! You want to marry me? What about Ashley? She's really upset that you're living here."

"I know. She told me. Karen is upset about it, too, by the way."

"Ashley told her? She all but promised that she wouldn't!"

"No, I told Karen long before you brought Ashley home. We were fighting over it when you walked in. If Ashley hadn't been with you, Karen would have said the same things to you that she was saying to me."

"But you looked so intense. You didn't seem to be arguing."

"We've become very good at it over the years. We can argue in public and not draw attention at all. Karen doesn't always throw a tantrum when she's angry."

"I don't know what to say. I was so sure you were reconciling. You didn't come home and . . ."

"I'm home now."

"But Ashley—"

"Knows where I am and she's okay with it now."

"I'm never going to understand that child! Not if I live to be a hundred."

"I probably won't either. So how about it? Will you marry me, or do I have to learn to speak French?"

Chelsea found herself smiling. "I'm never going to understand you, either. Yes, I'll marry you."

He kissed her gently, the teasing gone from his eyes. "I love you, Chelsea. I'm not going to lose you again."

"Good," she whispered. "Don't let me go. Not even if I say stupid things about Jean-Paul."

"We're going to be happy together. I'd say it's about time for both of us." He kissed her forehead and temple, then her lips again.

"Yes," she murmured, and she held him close. "It's about time for us both." She felt safe and at home in his arms. Ryan held her close as if he would never let her go.

Epilogue

Chelsea looked over the table one more time. Was everything there? What had she forgotten?

Ryan came up behind her and drew her away from the table and into his arms. "Stop being so nervous. Everything is going to be just fine."

"How can you be so calm? It's not every day Ashley graduates from college. And you know she and Hunter are announcing their engagement tonight. I want everything to be perfect for her." She looked past his shoulder and pointed at a young boy. "I see you, Cody! Don't you eat another strawberry!"

Their son smiled up at her mischievously and reached for a pineapple wedge instead. At five years, Cody was the image of his father, and Chelsea could never be very firm with him.

"If he eats all the fruit, we'll buy more," Ryan said with a laugh. "There's more food here than we could work our way through in a week!"

"That's not the point. You know he gets a rash if he eats too many strawberries." But she smiled and didn't pull away.

Cody had apparently been sneaking fruit to tease his mother, and with her attention elsewhere, he wandered away from the table.

"I'm not so sure I'm ready for Ashley to be married,"

Ryan said as he helped her rearrange the plates of food. "She's just a baby."

"Your baby is graduating from college. She and Hunter are in love. He's perfect for her."

Ryan frowned. "Do you think she'll be happy with him? He's likely to move her to some other city. Maybe some other state. What if she doesn't want to move?"

"Are we talking about the same girl?" Chelsea laughed and shook her head. "If she's unhappy, she'll be the first to tell him. Ashley doesn't have a co-dependent bone in her body. She's much smarter than I was."

Ryan reached out and touched Chelsea's cheek. "At times I still have nightmares about what Lorne put you through."

"That was a lifetime ago," she said softly. She caught his hand and kissed it. "Hunter would never treat Ashley like that, nor would she put up with it."

Ryan felt a tug on his pants leg and he looked down at their small daughter.

"Daddy, Cody's feeding my kitten a piece of pickle," Miranda said, her mouth drawn down in concern.

He swept her into his arms. "Kittens don't eat pickles. She won't take it. Your new dress looks pretty. It's blue like your eyes."

Miranda giggled. "My eyes aren't blue. They're brown! You're silly, Daddy."

"Not blue? Wait a minute! Whose kid is this anyway?" He ticked her tummy, and she dissolved in giggles.

Chelsea became almost teary as she watched them play with each other. She'd been afraid to get pregnant so late in life, but she'd wanted to have children with Ryan.

Cody came trotting back into the room. "Mom? Dad? Ashley and Hunter are here. And there's some other people parking out front."

Chelsea smoothed her dress and tried to quell her nervousness. They rarely gave formal parties—they were too reminiscent of Lorne for her.

Ashley came hurrying into the room and hugged first

Ryan and then Chelsea. She took Miranda from her father. "Everything looks so nice! You've even managed to clean up Piglet." She grinned at Miranda.

"I'm not Piglet," Miranda piped up, giggling. "I'm 'Randa!"

Hunter was behind Ashley. He grinned self-consciously at her parents. "I guess you know what we're going to announce tonight," he said, looking from one to the other.

"I heard something about a wedding," Ryan said, forcing himself not to smile.

"Oh, Dad, don't look at him like that. Hunter will think you mean it." Ashley put Miranda on the floor and took Hunter's hand. "Don't listen to him. He's only joking."

Hunter grinned and ducked his head.

Chelsea liked Hunter even if he was somewhat shy. Ashley was his exact opposite, and she thought they made a good pair. She took Ryan's arm. "I hear the doorbell. Come with me and stop picking on Hunter." She winked at Ashley. "Sometimes you're worse than Cody!"

As they went to the front door, Ryan said, "He never asked me if it was okay to marry her. He never said a word to me about it at all."

"I know, honey, but the Victorian era has ended. I meant to tell you sooner, but it slipped my mind." She laughed up at him. "You scare him, you know."

"Good," Ryan said grimly.

The guests arrived quickly, friends of Ashley and Hunter, friends of Ryan and Chelsea. Chelsea moved from group to group, making sure everyone was taken care of and that contacts were congenial.

As she was making her way back to Ryan, she found herself face to face with someone she had never expected to see in her living room.

"Karen?" she said in amazement.

Karen was watching her with a guarded expression. "Ashley invited me."

"I know. I just didn't expect you to come." Chelsea found herself clasping her hands tightly, and she made an effort to relax. "Ashley and Hunter are over by the punch bowl."

"I saw them a moment ago. I wanted to talk to you."

"Oh?" Chelsea didn't know what to expect. Neither she nor Ryan had spoken with Karen in several years. When they had, it hadn't gone peacefully. Ashley kept them more or less up to date on where her mother was, but Chelsea had never inquired. At times she'd worried about Karen, but had been unable to help her.

In the past six years Karen and Lee Brent had married and divorced, and Karen had taken to drinking. She was also eating to excess the way she always had when bored or unhappy, and it showed. Chelsea almost hadn't recognized her.

"I've moved back to Dallas," Karen said. "I have a place a couple of blocks from Mother and Daddy. It's small, but there's only me, you know."

"I know. I'm sorry it didn't work out with Lee."

Karen shrugged. "I'm over him already." Her gray eyes searched the crowd and found Ryan.

Chelsea saw the longing in Karen's look, and she found herself feeling pity for her. Once Ryan had left, Karen had discovered she didn't really want to let him go. This, in Chelsea's opinion, had been the real reason her marriage with Lee hadn't succeeded. He wasn't Ryan.

"He looks happy," Karen said grudgingly. "So do you."

"We are." Chelsea automatically put her hand on Miranda's head as the child grabbed her about the knees.

"This must be Miranda," Karen said. "Ashley told me about her."

Chelsea picked up her daughter. "This is Miranda, all right. Cody is over there on the couch."

Karen looked in the boy's direction. "They're good-looking children" She frowned slightly and Chelsea thought she must be remembering the days when Bethany and Ashley were little. "I guess I ought to go."

As Karen turned away, Chelsea caught her arm. "Don't leave, Karen. Ashley was afraid you wouldn't come."

"I told her I wouldn't. She talked me into coming."

"I'm glad she did."

Karen looked at Chelsea in disbelief. "You can't mean that."

Miranda struggled to get down, and Chelsea put her on the floor. "Yes, I do. We've known each other a long time. We've been through a lot together. You belong here today."

"What about Ryan?" Karen asked.

"He'll agree. I don't hate you, Karen. Neither does he."

"I'm not so sure of that. Those last years were so unpleasant. I'm sure he's told you all about it."

"No," Chelsea said gently. "He hasn't. And I've never asked."

Karen wavered. "I guess I could stay for a while."

Chelsea studied the other woman's face. She could see the old vulnerability lurking in Karen's eyes. "We were best friends for so many years," she said softly. "I've missed you."

Karen gave her a long look. After a while the corners of her mouth tilted up in the hint of a smile. "I'd like to say the same, but I can't. Too much has happened between us." She turned and headed in Ashley's direction. "Goodbye, Chelsea."

Chelsea watched the woman who was once her best friend walk away. She sensed Ryan step up beside her, and she turned to him.

"Who was that? Was that Karen?" he asked, incredulous.

"Yes, it was."

"What did she say to you?" He seemed ready to jump to Chelsea's defense.

"Only that she's happy for Ashley." Chelsea glanced at Karen. "She was proving to me something I've known for a long time."

"What's that?"

"That you're the best friend I've ever had."

Ryan smiled down at her and put his arm around her shoulders. "Well, come on, buddy. Ashley and Hunter are about to make the big announcement."

Chelsea looped an arm about his waist and got on tiptoe to whisper in his ear. "I love you."

"I love you, too. Are you sure Karen didn't say anything to upset you?"

"You worry too much." Chelsea smiled up at him, and they made their way through the crowd.

CATCH A RISING STAR!

ROBIN ST. THOMAS

FORTUNE'S SISTERS (2616, $3.95)
It was Pia's destiny to be a Hollywood star. She had complete self-confidence, breathtaking beauty, and the help of her domineering mother. But her younger sister Jeanne began to steal the spotlight meant for Pia, diverting attention away from the ruthlessly ambitious star. When her mother Mathilde started to return the advances of dashing director Wes Guest, Pia's jealousy surfaced. Her passion for Guest and desire to be the brightest star in Hollywood pitted Pia against her own family—sister against sister, mother against daughter. Pia was determined to be the only survivor in the arenas of love and fame. But neither Mathilde nor Jeanne would surrender without a fight. . . .

LOVER'S MASQUERADE (2886, $4.50)
New Orleans. A city of secrets, shrouded in mystery and magic. A city where dreams become obsessions and memories once again become reality. A city where even one trip, like a stop on Claudia Gage's book promotion tour, can lead to a perilous fall. For New Orleans is also the home of Armand Dantine, who knows the secrets that Claudia would conceal and the past she cannot remember. And he will stop at nothing to make her love him, and will not let her go again . . .

SENSATION (3228, $4.95)
They'd dreamed of stardom, and their dreams came true. Now they had fame and the power that comes with it. In Hollywood, in New York, and around the world, the names of Aurora Styles, Rachel Allenby, and Pia Decameron commanded immediate attention—and lust and envy as well. They were stars, idols on pedestals. And there was always someone waiting in the wings to bring them crashing down . . .

NOWHERE TO RUN . . . NOWHERE TO HIDE . . .
ZEBRA'S SUSPENSE WILL *GET* YOU —
AND WILL MAKE YOU BEG FOR MORE!

NOWHERE TO HIDE (4035, $4.50)
by Joan Hall Hovey

After Ellen Morgan's younger sister has been brutally murdered, the highly respected psychologist appears on the evening news and dares the killer to come after her. After a flood of leads that go nowhere, it happens. A note slipped under her windshield states, "YOU'RE IT." Ellen has woken the hunter from its lair . . . and she is his prey!

SHADOW VENGEANCE (4097, $4.50)
by Wendy Haley

Recently widowed Maris learns that she was adopted. Desperate to find her birth parents, she places "personals" in all the Texas newspapers. She receives a horrible response: "You weren't wanted then, and you aren't wanted now." Not to be daunted, her search for her birth mother — and her only chance to save her dangerously ill child — brings her closer and closer to the truth . . . and to death!

RUN FOR YOUR LIFE (4193, $4.50)
by Ann Brahms

Annik Miller is being stalked by Gibson Spencer, a man she once loved. When Annik inherits a wilderness cabin in Maine, she finally feels free from his constant threats. But then, a note under her windshield wiper, and shadowy form, and a horrific nighttime attack tell Annik that she is still the object of this lovesick madman's obsession . . .

EDGE OF TERROR (4224, $4.50)
by Michael Hammonds

Jessie thought that moving to the peaceful Blue Ridge Mountains would help her recover from her bitter divorce. But instead of providing the tranquility she desires, they cast a shadow of terror. There is a madman out there — and he knows where Jessie lives — and what she has seen . . .

NOWHERE TO RUN (4132, $4.50)
by Pat Warren

Socialite Carly Weston leads a charmed life. Then her father, a celebrated prosecutor, is murdered at the hands of a vengeance-seeking killer. Now he is after Carly . . . watching and waiting and planning. And Carly is running for her life from a crazed murderer who's become judge, jury — and executioner!

Available wherever paperbacks are sold, or order direct from the Publisher. Send cover price plus 50¢ per copy for mailing and handling to Penguin USA, P.O. Box 999, c/o Dept. 17109, Bergenfield, NJ 07621. Residents of New York and Tennessee must include sales tax. DO NOT SEND CASH.